BEATRICE OF BAYOU TÊCHE

BEATRICE OF BAYOU TÊCHE

Alice Ilgenfritz Jones

Introduction by
Thomas H. Fick and
Eva Gold

Bowling Green State University Popular Press
Bowling Green, OH 43403

Copyright 2001 © Bowling Green State University Popular
Press

Library of Congress Cataloging-in-Publication Data

Jones, Alice Ilgenfritz, 1846-1905.
    Beatrice of Bayou Têche/Alice Ilgenfritz Jones; introduc-
tion by Thomas Fick and Eva Gold.
        p.   cm.
    ISBN 0-87972-832-9 (pbk.)
    1. Racially mixed people--Fiction. 2. New Orleans (La.)--
Fiction. 3. Women artists--Fiction. 4. Women singers--Fiction.
5. Mulattoes--Fiction. 6. Freedmen--Fiction. I. Title.

PS2150.J2 B43 2000
813'.4--dc21

                                          00-052901

Cover design by Dumm Art

BEATRICE OF BAYOU TÊCHE

———◆———

INTRODUCTION.

WHEN Alice Ilgenfritz Jones published *Beatrice of Bayou Têche* in 1895 with the respected Chicago publisher A. C. McClurg, she was not entirely unknown. Under the pseudonym Ferris Jerome she had published the sentimental novel *High-Water-Mark* with J. B. Lippincott in 1879 and had contributed stories and travel essays to various journals in the intervening years. And in 1893 she co-authored with Ella Merchant the feminist utopian novel for which she is best known today. *Unveiling a Parallel* satirizes nineteenth-century gender constructions during the course of a tour by its naive male protagonist of progressive Martian societies; it is, as Carol Kolmerten writes in her introduction to the Syracuse University Press edition (1991), "one of the most clever and humorous of novels" (x) of the period.

Little biographical information exists for Jones; indeed, until Carol Kolmerten's research for *Unveiling a Parallel*, Jones was identified as a Louisiana writer in the few reference works in which she appeared.[1] She was, in fact, born in Ohio in 1846, the daughter of a furniture dealer who became mayor of Cedar Rapids, Iowa, where she moved in 1863 and lived for most of her life, and her interest in Louisiana culture and history can be attributed to the summers spent with her sister in Jennings, Louisiana. Educated at Evansville Seminary in Wisconsin, she married Herman Jones in 1884 at the age of thirty-eight. Before her marriage she had published, in addition to *High-Water-Mark,* several works of short fiction and travel essays. However, her husband was a widower with a young daughter, and the responsibilities of wife and mother may explain why she did not publish again until *Unveiling a Parallel* appeared in 1893. In addition to *Beatrice of Bayou Têche* Jones published one further novel, a historical romance titled *The Chevalier of St. Denis* in 1900. She published further essays about her travels in California and the West before dying of a cerebral hemorrhage on March 5, 1905, in Havana, Cuba.

Although today Jones's reputation rests on *Unveiling a Parallel, Beatrice of Bayou Têche* is in many ways an even more daring work, and one of great historical and artistic interest. As a white-authored novel about a black woman artist-protagonist, *Beatrice* is (as far as we are aware) unique for its period. Surveying the field of the woman's *Künstlerroman* in 1984, Linda Huf concluded that "the black woman artist is a missing character in fiction" (14). Although this assertion has since yielded to the recovery of neglected black-authored texts and to redefinitions of both what constitutes an "artist" and what defines the *Künstlerroman,* Jones remains the first white woman to take the intersection of race, gender, and creativity as her primary subject. Modifying the utopian framework of her previous novel, in *Beatrice* Jones seeks to unveil the relationships between white and African Americans at a particular historical moment—the United States in the twenty years before the Civil War—rather than between the men and women of an imagined Martian civilization. As one of Beatrice's suitors wonders—in language that echoes the main concerns of *Unveiling a Parallel*—"Who had drawn the lines [of race],—and were they parallel lines which might never converge?" (285).

In following her mixed-race protagonist, who is born a slave in New Orleans but after being freed goes on to become an inspired painter and opera singer, Jones appears to make Beatrice an example of triumphant possibility in both art and racial politics; as one of Beatrice's white mentors tells the young artist, "[Y]ou were created, with all of your rich gifts, on purpose to show that the time for race conflict and race prejudice has gone by!" (299). This comment suggests Jones's distinctive approach: while most authors of the period focused on either the "tragic mulatto" (a staple character in both ante- and postbellum fiction), or on the artist, Jones fuses the two characters, thereby creating an uneasy mix of generic frames and conventions. *Beatrice* renders the white author's effort to find a place for the black woman artist in relation to paradigms of creativity that are not only gendered but racialized. In the process, it exposes the fault lines of ideology and literary convention that underlay attempts to negotiate issues of race, gender, and creativity in late-nineteenth-century America.

Few novels of the period have attempted so much and with such fervor. *Beatrice* brings its protagonist from the New Orleans French Quarter courtyard of her white aunt to the Indonesian island of Java and explores not only the slave society of antebellum south Louisiana, but the racism of Northern culture. Beatrice is the daughter of Ralph La Scalla, a wealthy white resident of New Orleans, and Réné, a slave belonging to his sister Rosamond La

Scalla. When the novel opens, Beatrice is orphaned and living in the French Quarter with Mauma Salome, her quadroon grandmother, and Rosamond, her white aunt and owner. When Rosamond dies Beatrice learns that she is a slave, and is taken with her grandmother to the Bayou Têche plantation of white relatives headed by Maurice La Scalla. Under the tutelage of Maurice's daughter Evalina and her governess, Beatrice moves from ignorance and dialect to enlightenment and proper English, develops her "liking for picture-making . . . into a passion" (144), and charms Burgoyne La Scalla, Evalina's brother and a paragon of Southern manhood. During a vacation on the aptly named "L'Ile Dernière," Maurice dies of apoplexy after agreeing to duel a Yankee who, seeing the physical similarities between Beatrice and the La Scallas, has made insulting comments about Southern plantation owners' sexual practices with their slaves. La Scalla's will sets Beatrice free and bequeaths her what remains of her white aunt's and father's estate. Here, midway through the novel, legally free and financially independent, Beatrice accompanies Madame La Scalla and Evalina to Europe, where her artistic talents blossom: her painting is praised by the French romantic painter Delacroix but, inspired by the famous soprano Marietta Alboni, she takes up opera instead.

Upon returning to the United States she is taken for white and enters an exclusive girls' school in New York, is befriended by Mrs. Thompson (wife of the man whose insult triggered Mr. La Scalla's death), and with her encouragement begins a operatic career that ends when her race is revealed during her first public performance at a charity benefit. In the last few chapters she accompanies Mrs. Thompson to Java, accepts the exiled Italian patriot Madame Rabino as her new mentor, and dedicates herself to her painting and to the improvement of the "gentle natives" (386).

Although, as our synopsis suggests, and as one might expect from the co-author of a feminist utopian novel, *Beatrice* is in many ways an unconventional novel, its protagonist also clearly owes a great deal to the tragic mulatto (often mulatta) of white-authored abolitionist writing, whose purpose was to arouse white sympathy for the white-appearing, black-defined character (Christian 26). The continued fascination after the Civil War with the mulatto in both fiction and nonfiction attests to the power of this character—"neither white nor black" as Judith Berzon puts it—to raise questions about race and identity in the United States. Hazel Carby sees the mulatto/a as a "narrative device of mediation," "a vehicle for exploration of relations between the races and an expression of the relationships between the races" (89). The range of portrayals of the mulatto—from racist fiction like Thomas Dixon's *The Clansman* (1905), to liberal white-authored texts like George Washington Cable's *The Grandissimes* (1880), to black-authored texts like Charles Chesnutt's *Paul Marchand, F.M.C.* (1921; 1998) and Frances E. W. Harper's *Iola Leroy* (1892) that suggest a black-defined identity for the mulatto—indicates that the mulatto in fiction was a crucial means of conceptualizing and understanding race and identity in the years after the Civil War.[2]

In taking as her heroine a tragic mulatto who is an artist, Jones fuses two characters linked with the search for identity: as the mulatto searches for a "place" in a culture structured by the opposition between black and white (and slave and free), so the woman's *Künstlerroman* traces the woman artist's search for a place as artist—"the birth of the artist as heroine" (the title of Susan Gubar's influential essay on the white woman artist). While Beatrice is a multiply talented artist—a painter as well as singer—there proves no place for her in nineteenth-century America because she is not simply "woman," but a black woman: she not only never marries (foreclosing the typical novelistic ending), but abandons the public practice of her arts and leaves the United States for voluntary exile in colonial Indonesia, where she paints for her own pleasure. Neither the mulatto nor the artist plot leads to any resolution of identity for Beatrice; both plots lead to exile, near isolation (except for her nurturing mentors), and relinquishing the full practice of her arts. Although Jones's presentation of the "absurdity of racial classifications" (Karcher 72) gestures toward the challenging if not the dismantling of racial categories within the generic framework of the woman's *Kunstlerroman,* in the end Beatrice is in exile while the United States is fractured by Civil War.

Jones's presentation of the tragic mulatto in *Beatrice* looks back to the abolitionist tradition, in which the character who looks white and is defined by the culture as black reveals the absurdity of racial classifications. The centrality of the tragic mulatto theme is apparent from the outset: like the tragic mulatta of convention Beatrice is a character of great intelligence and refined sensibility who is for a time ignorant of her racial heritage.[3] Beatrice, raised in isolation from the world outside and ignorant of social mores and cultural classification, is asked by Kitty Pembroke, a Northern child visiting her New Orleans relatives, if she is white: "Auntie says you can't always tell whether folks are white or colored down here" (17). Beatrice solves the problem to her satisfaction by examining herself in the mirror: "I reckon I's white" (19). Later, when she is inherited by the La Scallas and is told she is to be the young Evalina's slave/companion, Beatrice objects, "But I'm not a colo'ed person," and, with some confusion, Evalina concurs: "People are queerly mixed up somehow," she responds. As evidence of the complexity of racial classification (and that the subject is too complex to do anything about), Evalina points to the white-skinned and blue-eyed slave Calisty (42). Jones also presents a corollary example of scopic ambiguity in a person defined as white: Madame Derouen, a Frenchwoman who is headmistress of the exclusive Northern girls' school that Beatrice attends after she is freed, is described as having "kinky hair" (233) and "swarthy skin" (293).

Like much liberal racialist fiction, Jones's novel seems to undercut its own apparent message, an effect that, as Carolyn Karcher notes, is typical of the antebellum abolitionist fiction to which Beatrice can trace its origins: "in the long run [the presentation of the tragic mulatto] reinforced the very prejudices antislavery fiction sought to counteract" (72). Maurice La Scalla asserts that she is "an exceptional child," and that "[n]othing is plainer than that she ought not to be a slave. Nature has marked her fo' a higher place" (110), sentiments that are echoed by the many sympathetic white people (Southern and Northern) that Beatrice encounters in the course of the novel. La Scalla says, "we have a good many men and women on this plantation who ought to be free, by right of their unquestionable ability to take their place in the world and fight their own battles. And then, there are othe's too old, or too stupid, or too dependent to shift fo' themselves" (111). The fact remains, however, that Beatrice is the only African-American character who is shown to be capable of fighting her own battles.

In spite of all the sympathetic comments voiced by Beatrice's supporters, the novel's mulatto plot ends up replicating what Joel Williamson has called the Southern mythology of the mulatto promulgated in the 1850s: "Along with an intensified pressure against miscegenation and mulattoes, there burgeoned in the white mind a mythology about mulattoes. . . . Most important, Southern whites insisted, as before the war, that the mulatto was an effete being both biologically and ultimately culturally. Mulattoes . . . could not procreate among themselves beyond the third generation. . . . Mulattoes, then, in the popular white mind were doomed to isolation and demise" (94-95). This statement could be a gloss on the mulatto plot of Beatrice: there is no place in the United States for Beatrice, and she finds no way to express her erotic—and hence bodily—identity: the novel ends with Beatrice's exile to Indonesia and with Burgoyne La Scalla's death at Shiloh. As Beatrice laments, "I have no country, no kindred, no field of action" (369).

It is noteworthy that Jones's resolution of the mulatto plot in exile stands in contrast to the resolution achieved in postbellum fiction by black authors whose mulatto characters also seek identity and a place in the culture. Contemporary works by black writers show African-American characters white enough to pass choosing instead to embrace black identity and black community. Frances Harper and Pauline Hopkins, for example, implicitly concur with W. E. B. Du Bois that "it is the duty of the Americans of Negro descent, as a body, to maintain their race identity until this mission of the Negro people [to make distinctive contributions to civilization and humanity] is accomplished, and the ideal of human brotherhood has become a practical possibility" (46). For characters in black-authored fiction the strength of race identity is imagined as so powerful that it can override biological origins, as we see in Charles Chesnutt's *Paul Marchand, F.M.C.*, written in 1921 but first published seventy-seven years later. Marchand is reared as a free man of color (the title's "F.M.C.") in France and New Orleans, marries a free woman of color,

and fathers two children before discovering that
he is white and heir to the fortune of a leading
white New Orleans citizen. But he is unwilling
to become a white man (which would mean,
among other things, invalidating his marriage
and making his children illegitimate). "It may
be said with equal truth," Marchand explains to
his newly acknowledged cousins, "that the race
consciousness which is the strongest of the
Creole characteristics, is not a matter of blood
alone, but in large part the product of education
and environment; it is social rather than personal" (177). But Beatrice is explicitly barred from
the kind of race consciousness to which
Marchand refers because she has no connection
with black people. Her quadroon grandmother
raises her in isolation from the New Orleans
Afro-Creole community and intentionally sup-
presses any awareness of racial identity. And
once she becomes part of the La Scalla household, she is barred from associating with slaves
other than her grandmother. In claiming her as
her maid, Evalina asserts, "I do not intend to
have her associate with the other servants; for,
really, Papa, she is too nice" (84). Yet when
Beatrice refuses to follow an order given by
Helen Vincent, Beatrice's white rival for
Burgoyne's affection, Helen calls her "slave"
and slaps her. Later Burgoyne confirms her status even as he defends Beatrice against abuse:

"[N]o slave is ever chastized on this plantation," he tells Helen (174-78). Thus Beatrice is
kept from identification with African Americans
even as she is defined as black (and as a slave)
by her family/owners.

The mulatto plot frames and conditions the
artist plot. Since Beatrice cannot find a place in
the United States because of her mixed-race
identity, she cannot find her place as an artist.[4]
Although the narrator's comments suggest that
the novel was intended as the triumphant history of a woman of color who overcomes the limitations imposed by race in mid-nineteenth-cen-
tury America, the cumulative effect, as our discussion of the "tragic mulatto" indicates, is
something both more complex and more
ambiguous. In her portrayal of Beatrice as
artist, Jones was able to draw on the conventions of men's and women's *Künstlerromane,* but many of these conventions operated only within the parameters of an assumed
white racial purity. Elaine Apthorp, for example, has argued that two models of creativity
were available to writers in the late nineteenth
and early twentieth centuries. The first and
dominant model centered on "transformation
and transcendence"; the second and alternative
model was based on "receptivity and interaction
with other (rather than action upon other)" (4).
For Apthorp the alternative model involves "a

creativity which is intersubjective, which dissolves boundaries in erotic fusion between self and other" (3) and, though this model is difficult to articulate explicitly, some women's *Künstlerromane,* like Kate Chopin's *The Awakening* (1899) and Willa Cather's *Lucy Gayheart* (1935), did manage to evoke "the fitful sympathy of the implied author [who] recommends to the reader that posture of sympathetic discernment which is so disastrously absent" (4) from the woman artist's world. One might expect that, as a woman's *Künstlerroman, Beatrice* would engage one or the other of these paradigms. And indeed it engages both, but because Beatrice is black, neither paradigm is acceptable as a way of defining her creativity. On the one hand, a conception of creativity founded on an erotic dissolution of boundaries raised the possibility of racial admixture (an issue provoking considerable anxiety among whites both before and after the Civil War). On the other hand, a model of creativity as transcendence went against contemporary conceptions of the African American as body rather than soul.

The structure of the novel neatly schematizes the problem presented by the competing paradigms of creativity Apthorp describes. The first part explores creativity as erotic fusion, which is commendable while Beatrice is a slave and limited in her choices of association and action but raises unsettling possibilities of sexual and cultural admixture when Beatrice is freed after the death of her owner. In the second half Jones attempts to forestall these possibilities by turning to the paradigm of creativity as transcendence, which (in keeping with the novel's overt social message) is presented as a way of effacing racial and class divisions but in fact becomes a way of confirming them. The model of creativity as transcendence is useful because it substitutes the soul for the body, and if creativity is imagined as the body transcended through art, then the threat of interracial union implicit in a vision of creativity as fusion is much diminished. But embracing the paradigm of creativity as transcendence poses another problem. While the black body may be purged of sexuality, contemporary racial ideology could not imagine a black woman as "soul." Thus in the end Beatrice ends up in a limbo between two competing paradigms of creativity, just as she is neither black nor white. In terms of the plot, this means that at the end of the novel Beatrice is neither a triumphant public artist nor the "fond mother" (12) and erotic companion that she was as a slave but a voluntary exile in colonial Indonesia, ministering to the "gentle natives" (386) under the aegis of her mentor and determined never again to sing in public or to exhibit her paintings. Beatrice is left a woman without a creative paradigm, one whose inter-subjectivity is reduced to colonial ministration and whose public voice is silenced.

Until Beatrice is freed after the death of Maurice La Scalla about a third of the way through the novel, Jones offers a portrait of the artist as a young slave girl, one whose relationship to the natural world is nurturing and fundamentally erotic. She is an almost textbook example of the creativity that Apthorp characterizes as an intersubjective alternative to the primarily masculine paradigm of creativity as "action upon other." In New Orleans, for example, Beatrice spends her days in a French Quarter courtyard playing the "fond mother" (12) to her animal children: she is an eroticized version of Sylvia in Sara Orne Jewett's "A White Heron" (1886). Her pet chameleon, we are told, "would lie upon her arm and blink its bright eyes in an ecstasy of content while she stroked its gently palpitating sides with her tiny forefinger" (12). When her mistress dies and she is taken to the La Scalla plantation on Bayou Têche, her relations with nature remain the same; she enters nature's "private life," for example, by learning "to steal quietly into [the wild animals'] haunts, and sit so still that shy creatures might mistake her for a bit of the dim wilderness" (94). She befriends the birds,

adores her pet fawn Doudouce, and takes the
ferocious but aptly named bloodhound Prospero
as her special companion. At the same time her
intellectual and aesthetic capacities are developing apace. Madame La Scalla recognizes in
Beatrice a "genius, a perception and judgment
amounting almost to divination" (143) that
shows itself in sketches of the natural world that
are "oddly original in substance, and aflame
with a quaint humor" (145).

It is important, however, to note that at this
point Beatrice's activities as well as her art can
be celebrated without conflict because they are
compatible with racist discourse which saw
slaves as little more than beasts. Thus the narrator introduces her as "not [yet] much more
than a finely endowed small animal" (5) and her
young mistress, Evalina La Scalla, treats her
like "a pretty pet animal that could not understand" (36). Whatever danger the latent sensu-
ality of her body—"like a sculptor's dream of
form" (7)—might possess is deferred by her
youth and the transference of eroticism to the
animal world, a world to which, in racist ideology, the African American was inevitably
referred.

Once she is a free and sexually mature
woman, however, the paradigm of creativity as
fusion assumes implications menacing to white
culture obsessed with racial purity, a culture

many of whose assumptions Jones did not question despite (or perhaps because of) her utopian and feminist commitments.[5] It is for this reason the novel quite explicitly abandons the paradigm of creativity as fusion for that of the period's dominant paradigm of creativity as transcendence: by subordinating the literal and physical to the abstract and figurative, this paradigm diminishes—indeed tries to eliminate—the black body's presence. Art loses its corporeal location, becomes disembodied in the process of being spiritualized. Toward the end of the novel Mrs. Thompson, Beatrice's patron and the author's spokesperson, suggests the racial use of transcendence in the guise of a paean to equality: "Treat with men as if they had no bodies at all, black or white," she says, "as if they had no earthly environment: treat with them as *souls,* classified only by Almighty God" (327).

The novel is quite explicit about the nature and racial origins of the paradigm shift from erotic fusion to transcendence. While as a slave child Beatrice expressed her passion for the "great glories of the physical universe" (5), as a free woman she determines to recognize "nothing but God, the Infinite, the Omnipotent"—which is characterized as "a triumph of the spirit over physical consciousness" (199). In the terms established by years of racist conflations of non-white with the body and white with the mind, to triumph over physical consciousness as Beatrice has done is to triumph over her African-American heritage. It is not surprising, then, that one of her first acts is to eschew the literal and physical realm of the black mother for the symbolic and abstract one of the white father: "Oh, you are stupid creatures, that look out at me with your scared eyes" (205), she lectures her animal friends. It is hardly a coincidence, therefore, that shortly after Beatrice inherits her white father's estate through Maurice La Scalla, Mauma Salome—her grandmother and last living black relative—dies.

At first it seems Beatrice will succeed within the paradigm of creativity as transcendence. When she accompanies Mrs. La Scalla and Evalina on a European tour she is taken as white. In Paris her painting is praised by Delacroix, but she falls under the spell of Marietta Alboni, one of the period's best-known divas, and decides to sing opera. Writing about Thea Kronborg (in Willa Cather's *The Song of the Lark*), among others Susan J. Leonardi notes the power of the diva "to change the lives of those who hear her, but especially to change the lives of other women, to give them a voice in all senses" (71), and at first it seems Beatrice will fulfill this promise: the memory of Alboni's voice helps her to find "new powers"

(226), and back in the exclusive New York boarding school where she and Evalina are students Beatrice prepares to perform for a public charity entertainment. In language that anticipates other women's *Künstlerromane* like Chopin's *The Awakening* and Cather's *The Song of the Lark*, the narrator can tell us that Beatrice "felt herself circling toward one of [those] rare culminant moments, as an eagle circles toward the commanding crag" (275). That the commanding crag of art is accessible to her gender, if not race, is shown by the accomplishments of one alumna "of quite unknown pedigree" who had become "a famous sculptress" (231).

But Beatrice's subsequent experiences suggest that (in this white-authored text at least) no amount of rhapsodizing about soul can free the black body to spiral toward that transcendent summit of art. Mrs. Thompson's dictum to "treat with men as if they had no bodies at all, black or white" (327) works on the level of assertion but not of plot. At the grand charity recital one of the women who knew Beatrice as a child in New Orleans refers to her voice as "the gift of her race" (280), and the society singer who is to be her partner in the duet refuses to appear with her on stage. Although an enterprising entrepreneur attempts to exploit the notoriety created by the next day's sensational newspaper revelations, Beatrice refuses to capitalize on her race. And from that moment on her public career as artist is over. She gives no further performances for the same reason that she will later refuse to exhibit her paintings in public: because, as Mrs. La Scalla explains, "her [racial] history would of course go with [them]" (338).

In the final pages of the novel Beatrice has traveled to Java and found a new mentor in Madame Rabino, veteran of the siege of Rome and friend of Margaret Fuller. Madame Rabino paraphrases the fervent optimism of Mrs. Thompson: "[Race] does not matter; the circumstances hedged about a great soul are nothing but straw" (367). "If there is a revolution in your country, which has for its secret meaning the liberation of your people," she tells Beatrice, "you should be in the midst of it; you should lend your spirit to the cause. Women can do so much, so much!" (368-69). Yet Beatrice is clearly peripheral. Perhaps the most extraordinary aspect of the novel is this effort to both evoke and contain black women's creativity: in the aesthetic realm Jones can present no "birth of the artist as heroine."

The difficulty Jones encounters in finding a place for her protagonist is partly due to the way race disables many conventions of the white-authored woman's *Künstlerroman*. Most striking is the curiously weightless and perfunctory treatment given to a central conflict in the nineteenth-century woman's *Künstleroman*: the conflict between one's identity as an artist on the one hand and as a woman and mother on the other—what Rachel Blau DuPlessis terms quest and love (3). The underlying reason seems unmistakable: Beatrice can marry neither a white man nor a black man and the novel must therefore ride roughshod over the conventions of a genre. On the La Scalla plantation Beatrice falls in love with Burgoyne, and he with her. But Burgoyne is too honorable to break his pre-existing pledge to Helen Vincent and Jones is careful to make Beatrice's passion "more of the spirit than of the body" (357). When the white, wealthy, and single Jack Vandever overcomes his class and race prejudice to propose marriage, Beatrice simply answers, "I do not love you" (332), and she meets not a single African-American man after she is freed. In short, the central conflict for the white protagonist of the woman's *Künstlerroman* is here moot because love and marriage are unrepresentable.[6]

The introduction of race into the woman's *Künstlerroman* also demands the revision of another significant literary convention. While the protagonist of virtually every other woman's *Künstlerroman* of the period is confronted by a male domestic dictator, we find no such thing in *Beatrice*. Men are sometimes as nurturing as women, always gentlemen, and never threatening; a few (like Maurice and Burgoyne La Scalla) are muses rather than monsters. This taming of the patriarchy may level the playing field of gender, but it also serves to reinforce the barriers of race. The accommodating male serves racial purity rather than (black or white) women's freedom: he is exempt from the predatory white male sexuality that is the source of miscegenation and to which abolitionists pointed as one of the curses of the slave system.

The specter of miscegenation disables not only many conventions of the white-authored women's *Künstlerroman*, but also those drawn from kindred genres that might serve to provide the novel with a way of recognizing the special demands of race. For example, during the first part of the novel two extraordinary incidents evoke abolitionist and slave narratives. In the first Beatrice refuses to procure adult mockingbirds for her nemesis Helen Vincent (Burgoyne's betrothed) because they have young in their nest, and when Helen tries to capture them herself Beatrice commands her bloodhound Prospero to drive the interloper off. In the second she shoots her pet fawn Doudouce rather than turn it over to Helen as a pet as Burgoyne demands. It is tempting to see the first of these incidents as affirming the novel's kinship with such nineteenth-century women's *Bildungs-* and

Künstlerromane as Emily Brontë's *Wuthering Heights* (1847), Elizabeth Stuart Phelps's *The Story of Avis* (1877), or Harriet Beecher Stowe's *The Pearl of Orr's Island* (1862), in each of which a central incident concerns a woman who attempts to save a bird from male appropriation. But Beatrice differs from her white sister-artists in one important way: she confronts not andro-centric law per se (her antagonist is a woman) but an institutional evil based in racial subjuga-tion. When Helen asks for the parent mocking-birds, she is recapitulating scenes of familial disruption that were staples of slave narratives and abolitionist literature, and Beatrice's mur-der of a loved one aligns her with slaves in both black- and white-authored texts; Cassy in Harriet Beecher Stowe's *Uncle Tom's Cabin* (1852) and Sethe's child in Toni Morrison's *Beloved* (1987) come immediately to mind. Beatrice's ethos is based in violent opposition and resistance because, like Linda Brent in Harriet Jacobs's *Incidents in the Life of a Slave Girl* (1862), she is excluded from the empower-ing realm of white women's spiritual authority.[7]

But while Jones seems to establish a field of action based on abolitionist texts and slave nar-ratives rather than the white woman's *Künstle-rroman*, this field of action is compromised while Beatrice is still a slave, and then eliminat-ed once she becomes "white" and must conduct herself according the conventions of white womanhood. First of all, her relationship with the historical condition of slavery is presented figuratively, as fables: there is no getting around the fact that Beatrice deals with fawns and mockingbirds, not parents and children. Presenting the central issues of the African American slave experience in such consistently symbolic terms suggests a discomfort with the black physical presence; figuration leads away from the body, providing the satisfactions of intersubjectivity without the literal presence of the racial other.[8] It is entirely in keeping with this prophylactic figuration that Beatrice has no contact with her fellow slaves—indeed both shuns and is shunned by them. When she is freed and becomes "white," of course, the possibility of physical opposition—of acting within definitions of black womanhood—is irrevocably withdrawn. Like her artistic career, her moral or political life is as thwarted because physical and spiritual responses are equally out of bounds. Thus when Beatrice laments, just before she is freed, that "[s]he could have no fellowship with her intellectual and moral equals ever again,—not even in books!" and remembers "that there were no delightful stories written about people in her condition, that history itself took no account of slaves" (181), Jones is not so much trying to have her heroine char-

acterize literary history as to anticipate and
account for the erasure of the novel's own previous intertextual foundations.

Beatrice's marginal status is in revealing contrast with the confident social engagement of
black women artists in black-authored texts of
the same period, which embrace the complex
African-American presence that Jones seeks to
distance in the interest of racial transcendence.
Madelyn Jablon has recently argued that tradi-
tional definitions of the *Künstlerroman* do not
accommodate the African-American social and
literary experience, and specifically that
African-American artists are not depicted in
conflict with society but as using art as the
means of strengthening already strong links to
the community: "[T]he African-American
kunstlerroman is a celebration of self and a celebration of community" (27). Jablon is concerned with twentieth-century literature, but her
comment applies equally to the late-nineteenth-
century precursors to the African-American
Künstlerroman tradition. In Harper's *Iola
Leroy*, for example, though raised white the
mixed-race title character has no difficulty
becoming (that is, Harper has no difficulty presenting her as) an active part of the black community, using her art in its service, and marry-
ing an African-American doctor. At the end of
the novel she considers writing a book because

it might be "something of lasting service for the race" (262). Similarly Dianthe Lusk, the protagonist of Pauline Hopkins's magazine novel *Of One Blood* (1902-3), clearly has a field of social action; she makes her first appearance as a Fisk University Jubilee Singer with a powerful rendition of "Go Down Moses," a spiritual which Eric Sundquist says evokes the "Africanist plot" (572) of the novel. Beatrice, however, has minimal contact with African Americans while a slave, and, as we have noted, meets not a single black man or woman after she is freed.

One cannot say that that *Beatrice* is insufficiently didactic about racial concerns—indeed, it is quite vociferous in its insistence that race *doesn't* matter. Yet by so thoroughly effacing African-American culture the novel does not create the stage on which a coherent vision of the African-American woman artist might be enacted. And ultimately, the difficulty of developing the issues of creativity according to familiar literary conventions means that reflections on creativity and art tend to become reflections about social organization that suggest deep-seated anxiety over the presence of the racialized body. Despite the emphasis on "the universal brotherhood of man" (326), the novel underwrites a vision of nature on the evolutionary warpath against racial difference:

"For surely there must be an end of the curse somewhere; and when Nature had wiped out all signs and traces of it, and man's law affixed its potent seal, why should not the world accept the redeemed being?" (18). Beatrice is the sign and the promise of that redemptive obliteration, a "new idea from Nature's infinite brain" (347), but Nature is a way of evoking the trope of America as the land of perennial rebirth in order to eliminate the African-American presence: to be "new" means not to be black. Jones's vision of a raceless society is based not on the acceptance of difference but on its subordination to and final absorption by ruling-class culture and racial ideology. And what is good for the collective solidarity of race and class is bad for the (black) woman artist in a white literary economy, though the novel tries heroically to have it otherwise.

Is it possible to read *Beatrice* as a novel about how the black woman artist is thwarted by racist American culture or, on a more sophisticated level, as a metanarrative, a comment on the impossibility of writing about a successful black woman artist? After all, Beatrice does not transcend race to become a famous singer (precisely the conclusion one would expect if the purpose of the novel were to capture a close historical reality) and as Beatrice herself recognizes, there are "no delightful stories written about people in her condition" (181). What makes such readings highly problematic is the consonance between omniscient narrative commentary and the pronouncements of Beatrice's mentors. Since narrator and mentors alike tirelessly assert that genius transcends race—that "the circumstances hedged about a great soul are nothing but straw!" (337)—there is no ground for an ironic or oppositional construction of narrative voice, no way to see Beatrice's failure as a literary recognition of the complex ways that race matters. The value of the novel—and it is considerable—lies precisely in how it registers, with unflagging intensity, the concerned white author's effort to find a place for the black woman artist in relation to paradigms of creativity that are both gendered and racialized. In so doing, it reveals, with its complementary and conflicting generic frames, the problematics of race, gender, and artistic identity in the United States. It reveals as well how its author both contests and is conditioned by her culture's conceptions of race, gender, and artistic identity. In both its energy and its ambivalence *Beatrice of Bayou Têche* therefore urges us to reconsider how race informs paradigms of creativity and histories of the woman's *Künstlerroman* tradition.

NOTES.

Portions of this introduction originally appeared in Thomas H. Fick's "'No country, no kindred, no field of action': Race and the Women's *Künstlerroman* Tradition," *Genre* 31 (Fall/Winter 1998): 245-68.

1. Our brief biographical sketch relies on Kolmerten's research; for a fuller presentation we refer readers to the introduction to her edition of *Unveiling a Parallel* (xi-xvi). Jones is mentioned as a Louisiana author in: Alderman and Harris 228; McVoy and Campbell; and Brown and Ewell 237. The only critical work on the novel of which we are aware is Williams 139-45.

2. Susan Gillman calls for looking at the "racially oriented fiction of the turn of the century" "as a coherent body of work" (Gillman 221).

3. For these and other conventions of the portrayal of the tragic mulatto in antebellum literature, see Zanger.

4. Beatrice's exile and isolation link her with the male mulattoes in the fiction of white male writers (Cable, Twain, Faulkner) examined by Ladd.

5. Many critics have discussed the problematic relationship between feminism and race, most notably bell hooks in *Ain't I a Woman*.

6. *Beatrice* does not, however, entirely ignore the main conflict of women's *Künstlerromane*.

Jones's ambivalence about race forces her to spin
the conflict between marriage and art off into sub-
plots, switching the quester's gender and race in the
process. Hugh Connelly, for example, is the first
self-conscious artist figure in the novel, the youthful author of "A Tiara of Dewdrops," a collection of
sentimental verse bankrolled by Burgoyne, who is
also much influenced by its romantic visions.
("The twinkling of fairies' star-shod feet" (128) is a
line Burgoyne particularly admires.) But Hugh
soon learns the limitations of his art, begins looking
out for his fortune, becomes a titled lord in
Scotland, and marries the plain but good Evalina.
In Jones's comic rescripting of the conflict between
quest and love it is the man who happily gives up
his inferior art and acquires in its stead wealth, title,
happiness, and a loving spouse. When Evalina
sighs, "poor [Beatrice]! she had such a wide ambition, and now the theatre of her life is so small!"
Hugh can respond, "It is better not to have a wide
ambition, is it not? . . . Then whatever good comes
to us has the flavor of unexpectedness." Evalina,
the narrator comments ambiguously, "took the force
of this logic home to her own heart, and thrilled
with happiness. She had been so timid in her
demands upon life, and so much had come to her!"
(337-38). In this fine example of literary transference the callow male artist gives up his adolescent
infatuation to embrace the generous limitations of
grown-up domesticity, and from this manly example

his bride learns, safely and at second hand, to value her own timidity.

Hugh's marital felicity is offset by Burgoyne's marital disaster. Following a legion of American writers from Tabitha Tenney (*Female Quixotism*, 1801) on, Jones imagines lovers whose intimacy is shaped and misshaped by romantic texts. In his courtship of Helen Vincent, Burgoyne takes his friend's hackneyed lines as the template of his love, convinced that she "might be such a girl as Hugh Connelly had raved about in his lines to The Cruel One" (160). In turn, Helen Vincent fashions Burgoyne in the image of her readings in romance: "She had played Lady to many an imaginary Knight, and was an adept in her role. But here, now, was an actual knight with a part of his own to perform, and to which she must fit hers" (160-61). The result is easily predicted: disillusionment, discord, finally Helen's convenient suicide and, perhaps just as predictably, Burgoyne's death in defense of that other (for him) romantic construction, the Confederacy. Thus in Jones's neat literary subcontracting, Hugh sacrifices his quest in marriage while Burgoyne's *Bildung* is first stalled by marriage and then terminated by death.

7. The way race and gender intersect is powerfully reaffirmed a short while later. Beatrice angers Burgoyne by refusing to give a public demonstration of her power over the dogs: "He took hold of her arm,—not very gently, for a rebellious slave

was a new thing in his experience" (133). Yet a few hours later she "not only willingly, but joyfully" (135) complies with his request for a private demonstration. It is not his masculinity but the racial patriarchy of the master/slave relationship that pains her.

8. A central incident from Willa Cather's *The Song of the Lark* suggests that Jones's stratagem may tap into a deep and continuing anxiety about the relationship between non-whites and the white woman artist. Thea Kronborg, searching for spiritual restoration, immerses herself in the feminine landscape of Panther Canyon and in her imaginative re-creation of vanished Native American women. Sharon O'Brien argues that this experience (re)connects Thea with a "feminine creativity outside the patriarchal artistic tradition" (284), a view affirmed by Josephine Donovan (89) and others. The Native Americans with whom Thea communes, however, are long gone, and while Thea feels "the weight of an Indian baby hanging to her back" (550) as she climbs an ancient water trail, what she salutes, standing "rigid on the edge of the stone shelf," is the "strong, tawny flight" of an eagle—"Endeavour, achievement, desire, glorious striving of human art!" (567)—and she returns to pursue the lonely life of a professional (and commodified) artist. The ability to see the Native American not directly but at one remove—distanced in time or by figurative language—is presented as a sort of rite of passage

for the artist as transcendent creator. The Native American women stand for a universal and trans-racial idea of the feminine. Like Cather, Jones prepares for her protagonist's aristic flight by evoking the Other while keeping her at arm's length. Beatrice too will come to feel as if she is, in the narrator's words, "circling toward one of these rare culminant moments, as an eagle circles toward the commanding crag" (275). But since race is a property of her body and not easy to leave behind it is no surprise that Beatrice never makes it to the commanding crag.

WORKS CITED.

Alderman, E. A., and Joel Chandler Harris. *Library of Southern Literature*. Vol. 15. Atlanta: Martin & Hoyt, 1909.

Apthorp, Elaine Sargent. "Re-Visioning Creativity: Cather, Chopin, Jewett." *Legacy: A Journal of American Women Writers* 9.1 (1992): 1-22.

Berzon, Judith R. *Neither White Nor Black: The Mulatto Character in American Fiction*. New York: New York UP, 1978.

Brown, Dorothy H., and Barbara C. Ewell. *Louisiana Women Writers: New Essays and a Comprehensive Bibliography*. Baton Rouge: Louisiana State UP, 1992.

Carby, Hazel. *Reconstructing Womanhood: The Emergence of the Afro-American Woman Novelist.* New York: Oxford UP, 1987.

Cather, Willa. *The Song of the Lark.* 1915. *Willa Cather: Early Novels and Stories.* Ed. Sharon O'Brien. New York: Library of America, 1987.

Chesnutt, Charles. *Paul Marchand, F.M.C.* Ed. Dean McWilliams. Princeton: Princeton UP, 1999.

Christian, Barbara. *Black Women Novelists: The Development of a Tradition 1892-1976.* Westport: Greenwood, 1980.

Donovan, Josephine. "The Pattern of Birds and Beasts: Willa Cather and Women's Art." *Writing the Woman Artist: Essays on Poetics, Politics, and Portraiture.* Ed. Suzanne W. Jones. Philadelphia: U of Pennsylvania P, 1991. 81-95.

Du Bois, W. E. B. "The Conservation of Races." *The Oxford W. E. B. Du Bois Reader.* Ed. Eric J. Sundquist. New York: Oxford UP, 1996. 37-55.

DuPlessis, Rachel Blau. *Writing Beyond the Ending: Narrative Strategies of Twentieth-Century Women Writers.* Bloomington: Indiana UP, 1985.

Gillman, Susan. "The Mulatto, Tragic or Triumphant? The Nineteenth-Century American Race Melodrama." Samuels 221-43.

Gubar, Susan. "The Birth of the Artist as Heroine: (Re)production, the Kunstlerroman Tradition, and the Fiction of Katherine Mansfield." *The Representation of Women in Fiction.* Ed.

Carolyn G. Heilbrun and Margaret R. Higonnet. Baltimore: Johns Hopkins UP, 1981. 19-59.

Harper, Frances E. W. *Iola Leroy, or Shadows Uplifted.* 1892. New York: Oxford UP, 1988.

hooks, bell. *Ain't I a Woman: Black Women and Feminism.* Boston: South End, 1981.

Hopkins, Pauline E. *Of One Blood. Or, the Hidden Self.* 1902-3. *The Magazine Novels of Pauline Hopkins.* New York: Oxford UP, 1988.

Huf, Linda. *A Portrait of the Artist as Young Woman: The Writer as Heroine in American Literature.* New York: Ungar, 1983.

Jablon, Madelyn. "The African American *Kunstle-rroman.*" *Diversity: A Journal of Multicultural Issues* 2.2 (1994): 21-28.

Jones, Alice Ilgenfritz. *Beatrice of Bayou Têche.* Chicago: A. C. McClurg, 1895.

—, and Ella Merchant. *Unveiling a Parallel: A Romance.* 1893. Ed. Carol A. Kolmerten. Syracuse, New York: Syracuse UP, 1991.

Karcher, Carolyn L. "Rape, Murder, and Revenge in 'Slavery's Pleasant Homes': Lydia Maria Child's Antislavery Fiction and the Limits of Genre." Samuels 58-72.

Kolmerten, Carol A. "Introduction." *Unveiling a Parallel: A Romance.* By Alice Ilgenfritz Jones and Ella Merchant. Ed. Carol A. Kolmerten. Syracuse, NY: Syracuse UP, 1991. ix-xlv.

Ladd, Barbara. *Nationalism and the Color Line in George W. Cable, Mark Twain, and William*

Faulkner. Baton Rouge: Louisiana State UP, 1996.

Leonardi, Susan J. "To Have a Voice: The Politics of the Diva." *Perspectives on Contemporary Literature* 3 (1987): 65-72.

McVoy, Lizzie Carter, and Ruth Bates Campbell. *Bibliography of Fiction by Louisianians and on Louisiana Subjects.* Baton Rouge: Louisiana State UP, 1935.

O'Brien, Sharon. "Mothers, Daughters, and the 'Art Necessity': Willa Cather and the Creative Process." *American Novelists Revisited: Essays in Feminist Criticism.* Ed. Fritz Fleischmann. Boston: Hall, 1982.

Samuels, Shirley, ed. *The Culture of Sentiment: Race, Gender, and Sentimentality in Nineteenth-Century America.* New York: Oxford UP, 1992.

Sundquist, Eric J. *To Wake the Nations: Race in the Making of American Literature.* Cambridge: Harvard UP, 1993.

Williams, Susan Miller. "Love and Rebellion: Louisiana Women Novelists, 1865-1919." Ph.D. diss. Louisiana State U, 1984.

Williamson, Joel. *New People: Miscegenation and Mulattoes in the United States.* New York: Free P, 1980.

Zanger, Jules. "The Tragic Octoroon in Pre-Civil War Fiction." *American Quarterly* 18 (1966): 63-70.

BEATRICE OF BAYOU TÊCHE.

———◆———

CHAPTER I.

THE little creature who bore — and with sufficient dignity — the royal name of Beatrice, sat on a doorstep and looked out upon the world, or as much of the world as she had "correspondences" with, — a large, irregular court surrounded by high buildings in the crowded old French Quarter of New Orleans.

But she had a vague, supersubtle consciousness — gleaned from many sources and compounded of many impressions — of vast, illimitable regions outlying her narrow confines, teeming with life and abounding in undreamable delights.

As yet she was not much more than a finely endowed small animal, with a keen relish for pleasant sensations and an equally keen aversion to unpleasant ones.

She had three absorbing passions, centring upon the three great glories of the physical universe, — color, sound, and odor.

All these passions had been stimulated, and to some extent gratified, within her narrow precinct.

Here all the year round multitudes of flowers blossomed and diffused their fragrance; and the trees and shrubs and vines, crowding upon one another in luxuriance of growth, displayed every shade and tint of green, of red, of yellow, as the seasons changed; while overhead was a patch of sky wonderful in its chromatic effects, its blues and its grays, its crimsons and scarlets and purples, and sometimes — most magnificent of all to her opulent fancy — its deep rich *coquelicot,* as Mauma Salome called the gorgeous copper-color of dense billowy masses that rolled up from the west and flung their flaming banners across the zenith.

For sounds she had the matin and the vesper bells ringing out over the city far and near; and the mysterious roll of an organ in a gray old church whose windowless rear wall formed a portion of the boundary of her world; and the carols of the birds; and the æolian of the winds in certain quarters; and now and then the strange throbbing of drums keeping time to the soul-thrilling strains of marching bands; and the songs of the negro women in the court, now rollicking and now pathetic, touching her sense of the ludicrous at times, and again filling her little soul with a passionate sadness not to be accounted for by any personal experience of her own, for her life had been singularly free from the small but tragic sorrows of childhood.

It may have been an echo from the past consciousness of her race, — she was the granddaughter of old Mauma Salome, a pale saffron-dyed octoroon; though a stranger would never have suspected the relationship. The child's skin was like the white petals of the magnolia flower, and her rippling brown hair showed golden high-lights in the sun. Her eyes, large and dark, were exquisitely set, and their gaze was as steady as a star. They had both the soft brilliancy and the unexplained faint shadow of sadness that lurk in Oriental eyes. Her little body was like a sculptor's dream of form.

But all this was as nothing to the power of fascination her beauty gave promise of, — that subtle and dangerous quality which goes to a man's heart like the thrust of a blade.

All her movements were light and springing and delicately graceful. But she was never frivolous. Even the pretty dances which Mauma Salome taught her — dances which Salome had seen practiced in Parisian ball-rooms whither she had been wont to attend her beautiful mistress in her young days — she executed with grave conscientiousness, and with a kindling of eye and flushing of cheek that betokened profound delight rather than mere lightsome pleasure.

She was charged with an intense vitality, and she was filled with a deep longing to know what the future would bring to her. But she had patience withal, — the infinite patience of a child, to whom a lifetime is an eternity long enough for the attain·ment of everything.

She had not yet begun to take account of time, or to grudge the golden hours as they sped by. Life lay all before her, a magnificent whole out of which she had bitten but a morsel.

Old Salome had a way of shaking her head wisely and responding mysteriously to her eager questionings, " Jus' you wait, honey ! "

The words held a promise which made the child's soul leap with indefinable hopes and anticipations. She felt a tingling in her fingers and in her toes as if wings were sprouting in them to bear her up and away. She often gave herself up to extravagant reveries about the outer world ; and her whole little being thrilled with rapture, with a ravishing, delicious spiritual exaltation.

The court was partitioned off into little kitchen dooryards by rough unpainted picket-fences which the weather had bleached to a silvery gray, thus adding another tone to the color scheme of the place which was not lost on the impressionable soul of the child. She liked it not only for its own beautiful glister when the sun shone upon it, but as a background for the leaves and flowers.

She appropriated all the divisions of the court to her own study and entertainment, by observing through the crevices between the pickets the life that went on therein, — which was chiefly the life of colored servants, a jolly, sociable, demonstrative set ; and of children, black and white, who had no better playground.

But it was varied enough in its way to sweep the whole range of the emotions. Joy and sorrow, pride, anger, friendship, hate, love, betrayed confidence, and all the long list of humanity's virtues and frailties appeared here as elsewhere and on other social levels.

Though Beatrice took no part in this life, — being strictly prohibited by her grandmother, — her personal feelings were often strongly enlisted. She had conceived a deadly hatred for some brutal boys in

one of the more distant yards on account of their
fiendish abuse of any small and helpless creatures
that happened to fall into their power. She could
have torn them to pieces as ruthlessly as they pulled
off the legs of the centipedes they captured. She
made no discrimination in species; a boy's members
— his legs and his arms — had no greater value
than an insect's in her impartial economy.

The yards all looked very much alike. They were
flagged with stone, and each had its little domestic
canal for carrying off waste water to — goodness
knows where ! Beatrice often speculated about that,
and hypothetized a prodigious pool somewhere
beyond.

There were always an ash-barrel, and a coal-barrel,
and a little heap of pine kindlings; and brooms, and
market-baskets, and long-handled gourds ; and the
great wooden water-tank with the cool little room
underneath for storing eatables in ; and a refuse bar-
rel stuffed with potato peelings, and banana skins, and
bones, and feathers, and the scrapings of pots and
pans, and hulls and husks of all sorts.

Of course there were culinary smells, at regular
intervals, of all kinds and grades, upon whose unmistakable testimony she could predicate the sort of
dinner to be served up each day to each particular
household. And here was a key to character and
general standing; for the different families took
rank and distinction from the quality of the odors
emanating from their several kitchens. Some kitchens
exhaled only the commonest smells, as of boiled cab-
bage and turnips and odious pork ; and others of
burnt grease and things spoiled in cooking; while

still others sent out such a ravishing bouquet of fruity and winy things, such an unspeakably delicious aroma of coffee just boiled, and of broiled meats and daintily cooked vegetables, and all commingling with a delicate suggestion of French garlic !

She knew perfectly the value of all these smells, for Mauma Salome had a genius for fine cooking. Though, alas ! there was not much cooking to be done in these days; for that branch of the great La Scalla family to which she belonged had dwindled to one solitary member, old Miss Rosamond, who was an invalid and a victim of melancholia.

Miss Rosamond lived in two rooms of this old gray mansion, haunted from kitchen to garret with memories of a gay and glorious past. It was years since she had tasted the outside air; and she received no visitors except now and then a relative from some distant parish. Her reception of these self-invited guests did not encourage frequent or prolonged visitations.

Salome prepared savory little dishes in the kitchen, morning, noon, and night, — or at such periods as passed for those conventional meal-times, — and sent them up on a dumb-waiter, following quickly herself to serve them steaming hot and enveloped in their own exhilarating vapors.

For Miss Rosamond had an appetite which had been cultivated in the best French schools, and she had never ceased to be fastidious about her *cuisine*. Her great somber eyes would wander over the little board as critically as in former times they had been wont to inspect the grand dining-room table set for distinguished guests. And her fine nostrils dilated with satisfaction, or her black brows contracted with a frown, according as she was affected by the arrangement and fumes of the table.

After she had eaten and the table was cleared, the waiter came down again, and Beatrice was treated to the remainder of the feast, which usually included some little *bonne-bouche* for which she had an especial fondness.

Salome spent the greater part of the time upstairs, for her mistress required almost constant attendance.

Beatrice stood in profound awe of Miss Rosamond, with her colorless but still handsome face, her unearthly dark eyes, and her Pompadour roll of snow-white hair. Sometimes — perhaps merely for the sake of the shuddering sensation it gave her — she would steal upstairs and crouch behind a partially closed door to peep into the great room with its rich red hangings, its grand gloomy furniture, and dim light. In this room Mauma moved about softly, waiting upon her invalid mistress with the tenderest care and devotion. If by chance Miss Rosamond's wandering glance was directed toward the door, Beatrice recoiled with throbbing heart, and hastened back to her own blessed kitchen and sunny court.

The life she led there was far from lonely. She had the silent but entertaining company of those wonderful little weavers, the spiders; and of the busy, burrowing ants; and of the beetles and toads and cockroaches that hid under the honeysuckle vine; and of the saucy bluejays, and the red-headed woodpeckers that tapped the bark of her mulberry-tree.

But the cunning little chameleons were her especial delight. They were such perfect, such elegant little creatures; and swift and alert as they were, she could tame them in an incredibly short space of time. One of them would lie upon her arm and blink its bright eyes in an ecstasy of content while she stroked its gently palpitating sides with her tiny forefinger.

Or, if she tired of these breathing things, — though she never really did tire of them, any more than a fond mother tires of her children, — she had always, save on the darkest nights, her patch of sky overhead, so deep, so mysterious, and so far away, — the emblem and evidence of infinitude.

And she had her singular consciousness of the busy, stirring life outside. She was like a little far-off inland bay, echoing, though it knows not why, the pulse-throbs of the sea.

Once Mauma had taken her upstairs and through a long, gloomy corridor, and, opening a mouldy old shutter, had set her upon the window-sill and bade her look out. A wonderful spectacle greeted her eyes! — a sea, or rather a mighty river, of people, stretching up and down as far as eye could go, dressed in colors and fabrics more magnificent than she had ever imagined. The sun shone splendidly upon prancing horses gayly caparisoned, and on soldiers in glittering uniform; on mighty ships and pinnacled castles so dazzling that she could scarcely bear the sight. A king, sceptre in hand, sat upon a golden throne, with courtiers and ladies grouped about him; and the hundred tales her grandmother had told her about nymphs and fairies, gods, goddesses, and sleeping beauties, came true before her eyes! The whole pageant was moving slowly and majestically onward.

Flags and banners waved, and shining instruments blew those transcendent airs she knew so well.

To Beatrice it was a never-ending pageant, for Mauma took her away before it was over. Afterward, when she begged to be taken back to the window again, Mauma replied enigmatically, "Sakes alive, honey, there's no Mardi-Gras now!"

There were long galleries belting the buildings, one above another. Here much of the seamy business of the stores and shops was carried on, and much of the private life of families cropped out. Here children were disciplined. Here was sometimes paid the shabby price of hospitality; when the family life was repressed or crowded out, and guests were allowed to appropriate all the moral oxygen at the front of the house, there was generated a kind of poison in the domestic atmosphere which resulted in unhappy little explosions on the rear galleries between husbands and wives or between parents and children. If it was not always the reverse side of life which Beatrice saw, it was at least the private and intimate side.

There was one building whose upper story contained a handsomely appointed hall or assembly room, in which there was an occasional ball, or some other form of gay entertainment. At these times the windows were thrown open and the chandeliers were lighted, and she could look in upon the brilliant scene, and observe the beautiful ladies and gallant gentlemen who constituted the class which the humble folk, leaning upon the fences in the dark court below, and gazing up into this bright unattainable world, described as "de quality."

But was it unattainable? Not to Beatrice, if she might trust the prophecy of her inner soul!

Sometimes the ladies and gentlemen stepped out upon the gallery in pairs, after a prolonged spin to waltz-music, to enjoy the moonlight, the cool air, and a *tête-à-tête*.

There was to the child a mystery about these handsome young couples. Why did he bend over her so tenderly and touch her so reverently? And why did she raise her eyes to his, and then let them fall with a blush? They seemed to be conscious only of themselves and of each other! There was an ecstasy in their slightest contact. And yet they were chary of themselves, these discreet young people! There was a delicate poise in their mutual attitude which an innate dignity and modesty warned them not to disturb.

The upper galleries were used exclusively by white people, whose faces and occupations were as familiar to her as were all her other surroundings.

One particularly interesting person with whom she was on very friendly terms, though she had never spoken to him, was an old wig-maker. He was quite destitute of hair himself; but that was an advantage to him in a business way, for he was wont to use his bald head as a dummy to drape his wares upon. He was forever washing and weaving and dyeing and drying and curling out there in the sun. And as a finishing touch to his artistic creations he tried them on, one after another, and patted and arranged them before a greasy little mirror that hung on the doorpost. The grotesque effect of a lady's blond tresses or raven ringlets dangling about his little fat face was

irresistibly amusing; and one day Beatrice unconsciously laughed aloud. He jerked his head around
and glanced sharply down into the court with a
dubious expression of countenance which soon resolved itself into a sort of quizzical complacency.
Evidently he felt complimented by her interest in
his operations; for after that he made a habit of
posing for her benefit, and of calling down to ask in
broken English if he was not a belle, a beauty, a
charmante!

Near by was a man who cleaned gloves; and next
to him a woman who repaired men's clothing, — a
genteel sort of person whose humble calling was a
secret probably, well guarded from her friends.

Still farther along was a small druggist who kept a
lot of little pots simmering over an oil-stove.

From all these people she received from time to
time signs of friendly recognition and occasionally a
trifling gift, — a little bag of nuts, a bit of candy,
a picture card torn carefully from a package of
goods.

But up to the day on which this story opens she
had held very little converse with any human being
save old Mauma Salome. Her reticence was in part
natural, but more in obedience to her grandmother's
orders.

Salome commanded the respect even of those above
her; throughout her life her moral level had been far
superior to her social rank. She possessed the true
spirit of independence, which has reference, not to
physical conditions, but to moral integrity. Slave
though she was, many a proud lady had blushed for
her own weaknesses under Salome's uncompromising

eye.   She had never cringed or purchased a favor at the cost of her self-respect.

In no sense was she a common wench, this pale old octoroon.   She had been all her life long the constant companion of her beautiful and distinguished mistress, Rosamond La Scalla.   She had been taught reading and music and other accomplishments in order that she might be able to entertain Miss Rosamond whenever and in whatever manner that imperious lady desired.

As Beatrice sat upon the old stone step, surveying her world, she was suddenly startled by the sound of children's voices.   Looking up, she saw three little girls climbing out of a window on to the nearest gallery.   Two of them leaned over the railing; and their bright eyes, flashing down into the court, fell upon her.

"Oh, what a darling!" one of them cried.   "Tell us your name, won't you, little girl?"

Forgetting alike her reserve and her grandmother's injunctions, she promptly answered, "Beatrice."

"Beatrice," repeated her interlocutor; "what a funny name!   Beatrice what?"

"Just Beatrice," she replied.

"Oh, you don't mean it; everybody has another name, don't you know?"

"Hush, Kitty, don't tease her," interposed the eldest of the three children.

"Our other name is Pembroke," Kitty went on. "Mabel, — that's this one, — she's my older sister; and Kitty, that's me; and Nell, she's the youngest, — she isn't much more than a baby, you see."

"I'm not a baby!" protested Nell, trying to stretch

up so that she, too, might look over the railing and
see the stranger. Failing in this, she stooped down
and peeped between the spindles.

" You 're white, ain't you, Beatrice ? " Kitty asked
presently.

Mabel gave her a reproving poke with her elbow.

" Well," retorted Kitty, in a shrill whisper, " Auntie
says you can't always tell whether folks are white or
colored down here."

Beatrice knew, from much incidental talk in the
neighborhood, that there was a mighty difference
between " white " and " colored," with the advantages all on the side of the former. But she had
never thought of classifying herself; there had never
been a question in her mind about her own social
position.

She did not reply to Kitty's question, but disappeared inside the kitchen door, and, going up to her
grandmother, — who sat with a wooden piggin between
her knees, shelling peas, — she demanded, " Mauma,
am I white ? "

The old woman started so violently that the piggin
was near falling to the ground.

" Lawd, honey ! whateveh put that idee in yo' little
head ? " she exclaimed.

Salome had read a little, thought much, and acquired
much knowledge of the world. She cherished a deep
and burning sense of the wrongs done to her race.
But she was intensely loyal, and during her younger
days she had let slip many an opportunity to escape
from her bondage. As the years wore on, she came
to think that for herself it mattered little — especially
as Miss Rosamond was entirely dependent upon her

2

care. But no such apathy dulled her feeling with respect to her children. At the death of Beatrice's mother — her pretty, graceful Réné, fair of face and sweet of voice — Salome had gone down upon her knees to young Master Ralph La Scalla, then the head of the family, and prayed for the child's freedom. And he had given his careless promise that her prayer should be granted; and not only that, but, seeing that the little one was white and beautiful, he declared that she should be sent abroad and educated like a lady!

His promise filled the old grandmother with transports of delight. Freedom for Beatrice meant — it seemed to her — a kind of absolution from the taint even of slave blood. For surely there must be an end of the curse somewhere; and when Nature had wiped out all signs and traces of it, and man's law affixed its potent seal, why should not the world accept the redeemed being?

But, alas! news came one day of the young man's sudden and violent death, — and the promise was not fulfilled.

The poor old soul's disappointment was terrible. She had no expectation that Miss Rosamond would carry out her brother's intentions, even if they were known to her, for there had been little sympathy between the two. Moreover, Miss Rosamond had taken a hypochondriac's unreasoning dislike to the child. It was in compliance with her strict commands that Beatrice had been kept always an unsuspecting prisoner. Perhaps it was because she expressed all too plainly in her form and features, and even in certain tricks of speech and in carriage and gesture, the

striking beauty and the fascinating eccentricities of
the La Scallas.

But in face of all these discouragements, old Salome
in course of time resurrected her hope. She began a
cautious but persistent siege at the cold heart of her
mistress, and a strenuous one at the Throne of Grace.
Patiently she labored, and long and faithfully she
prayed.   Her service and her devotions at least
brought their reward in beneficent reaction upon her
own soul. She forced herself to believe that it would
all come right in the end, and read the Scriptures with
a view to fortifying her conviction. It was as if she had
made a compact with Fate, and would not allow a
doubt to encroach upon her belief, lest it should be
construed by that inexorable power as an act of bad
faith.

It had been a sweet conceit of hers, ever since the
child was born, that she was "white" even in the
race sense ; and now Beatrice herself seemed to
challenge the assumption, and she resented it.

"Go look in the glass, yonder," she said sharply,
"and see fo' you'self."

Beatrice climbed upon a chair and examined her
face in an old French mirror which had long ago lost
caste and been relegated to the kitchen.

Salome rested her bare arms on the rim of the
piggin and regarded her triumphantly.

"Well, honey?" she demanded at last.

Beatrice drew a long sigh. "I reckon I's
white," she said, "but my cheeks ain't pink like
Kitty's."

"Who you talkin' 'bout, chile?" the old woman
asked with a frown. "Yo' father had pink cheeks

an' blue eyes." She resumed her work, and went on talking as if to herself. "But Marse Ralph was the on'y La Scalla fair complexioned. The rest was all dark like old Mis' Rose."

"Am I a La Scalla?" asked Beatrice, bent upon knowing something about her own pedigree.

"Well, I reckon you ain' nothin' else, honey!" Salome returned with a kind of defiance. "The Lawd Himself knows that my Mis' Rose up yonder is yo' own flesh-an'-blood aunt."

She got up and set the pan of shelled peas on the table with a bang, and began to kindle the fire.

Beatrice went out into the court again, but, finding that the Pembroke children had vanished, she decided to look after a big brown grasshopper which she had temporarily imprisoned in a stockade made of toothpicks and covered with a banana skin, — with a view to correcting his frivolous habits and making him amenable to the laws of polite society.

Mr. Grasshopper had liberated himself by beating down the walls of his stronghold, and had either left the country or gone into ambush. So Beatrice betook herself to a tiny green bower underneath the honeysuckle vine, where she had constructed a little seat for herself and cushioned it with some tree moss and a scrap of old carpet. This was her favorite retreat. The leaves clustered thickly overhead, and when there was the slightest breeze they seemed to whisper among themselves. Sometimes she went to sleep here, and they kept on whispering through her dreams.

To-day she did not go to sleep. She was too busy

digesting the bits of family history that Mauma had dropped.

Presently she got up and ran into the kitchen again with a question that died upon her lips; for at that moment Salome came stumbling down the stairs with her apron to her face, choking with sobs.

It was so new and terrible a thing that the child was paralyzed with fright.

"Oh, my po' mis', my po' old mis'!" wailed Mauma, dropping into a chair and rocking her body to and fro. "She's done called this time fo' sho'. O Lawd! O Lawd, have mercy!"

"Where is she called to, Mauma?" ventured Beatrice.

Salome took her apron from her eyes, and answered solemnly, "Why, to heaven, of co'se, honey!" and resumed her lamentations.

Beatrice experienced a great sense of relief. So long as the trouble, whatever it was, affected only Miss Rose, it mattered little to her. And if Miss Rose was only going to heaven —

All at once Mauma dropped upon her knees, clasped her wrinkled hands, and uplifted her voice in an agony of supplication. "O Lawd! dear Lawd Jesus! cyan't you wait a little longer, jus' a little longer, 'till her hard heart is done softened an' she's persuaded — sho', she's *almos'* persuaded, Lawd —"

Here the prayer suddenly ceased. Salome became conscious that she was trying to trick herself — and not only herself, but the All-Knowing! — into the belief that Miss Rosamond was "almost persuaded." She knew better, and the words stuck in her throat.

A tiny bell above the stair door began to quiver on its slender wire and then to tinkle a little.

Salome sprang to her feet and hurried up the stairs, drying her eyes and settling her features as she went.

Beatrice returned to the court. Nothing had changed there; the sun was shining, and the sky was a beautiful turquoise blue. The negro women were busy in their several dooryards, laughing and chatting as was their wont. A mocking-bird was trilling in a treetop, and a cricket kept up a monotonous scraping on its one tireless string. A newly caught chameleon which she had tethered to a tree, as a first step toward his civilization, basked contentedly in a sunny spot.

These familiar sights and sounds were reassuring, though the recollection of her grandmother's terrible grief oppressed her in spite of her conviction that it was no great matter if Miss Rose did die. Of course dying and going to heaven meant the same thing. She knew all about that; she had had some very dear pets die, and she believed they were now enjoying the glories of a celestial abode made especially for their kind, and inaccessible to boys.

In the course of half an hour she heard Mauma's lumbering step again, — Mauma had a touch of rheumatism, and her old legs were stiff from much trotting up and down the stairs.

Beatrice ran back into the kitchen, and was immeasurably relieved to find that her grandmother's face wore a lively and business-like expression, and that she had resumed her customary voice and demeanor. She was bustling about, rekindling the fire in the cook-stove.

" Run, quick, and fetch me some wata', honey," she commanded.

Beatrice took the kettle and ran out to the cistern, glad of such little commonplace duties, because they seemed to indicate that things were coming back to their normal balance. She wanted very much to know if Miss Rose was dead, but shrank from touching upon so explosive a subject.

Salome blew the pine knots into a blaze, and set the kettle over, and stood watching it.

" Dr. Chevanne thinks mebbe he can pull Mis' Rose through this time," she volunteered. " But I 've observ' that every one o' these hyer spells is mo' stringent than the last, and she 'll sho'ly have to go befo' long."

Mauma shook her head dolefully ; the corners of her mouth began to droop, and her chin quivered. Beatrice feared she was about to go off again, and hastened to avert the catastrophe.

" Ain't heaven a nice place, Mauma, " she in-quired, " an' won't Mis' Rose like to be there?"

" Bless yo' little heart, honey ! it ain't Mis' Rose yo' selfish old Mauma 's worrying about mostly. The Lawd 'll take care o' her, sho', fo' she 's done been a faithful church-member all her born days. It 's you'-self, Betty darling, and this worthless old cyarcass o' mine I 'm speculating 'bout. What 'll eveh become o' you and me is mo' than I can tell, — mo' than I can tell."

Here was a greater puzzle than ever to the child. She recognized no personal dependence upon Miss

Rose herself, and, respecting the relation between that ghostly lady and her grandmother, she supposed the obligation was on the other side, since Miss Rose's very existence hung upon Mauma's care of her.

"Why, sha'n't we stay hyer?" she asked.

Mauma shook her head dismally.

"But where shall we go, then?"

"Some o' the family kin 'll come and claim us, I reckon, — unless Mis' Rose contrawises them in her will."

Before Beatrice could formulate a question with which to probe this dense mystery, the kettle began to boil, and Salome whipped it off the stove and started upstairs.

The next few days might have been very lonely ones to Beatrice, had she not been so well accustomed to her solitary life. Salome had no time at all to give to her; she could only bestow a kiss, or a pat, or a pet word upon her now and then, in the hurry of preparing something for Miss Rose.

Besides all her old interests, — the insects and the birds and flowers and so forth, — Beatrice now had a new one, the Pembroke children, for whom she watched shyly but anxiously. They appeared again very soon, and immediately accosted her. Kitty begged her pardon for having so rudely questioned her the other day.

This led to an explanation which Beatrice was eager to make. She grew quite interested in establishing her position. She was "white," her other name was "La Scalla;" she too had an aunt, who was an invalid, and stayed always in her room upstairs; her papa and mamma were dead, and Mauma took care of her.

On these recommendations she was invited to climb up on to the roof of her shed, which was on a level with their gallery, — or balcony, as they called it, — to listen to the reading of some wonderful stories in a large thin book.

Mabel did the reading, and Kitty made the comments and explanations when any were necessary. Nell sat by her with her doll, and never took her big round eyes off Beatrice's face.

Beatrice was surprised and delighted to find that none of the stories were new. They were the same that Mauma had told her over and over again, and in which her interest never waned.

She knew them so well, moreover, and was so sure of every word, that she was sometimes obliged to stop the reading and explain that the book was wrong in this or that particular. Whereupon a lively discussion ensued. Kitty would point out to her that the book must be right, for books could not be mistaken. There the words were right before your eyes, just the same as the leaves on the trees; you could n't be mistaken about those, could you?

But Beatrice was not convinced even by such positive evidence. Mauma knew, of course, and there was no going back of that. Her temper rose a little whenever Kitty implied a doubt of her grandmother's infallibility; and Kitty was obliged to apologize profusely in order to keep her from taking a precipitate leave.

It turned out that the Pembrokes were only making a few days' visit in the city; and one morning the children called down their regretful " good-byes," and kissed their hands to Beatrice, and threw her a pretty coral necklace as a parting gift.

When they were gone, the little prisoner experienced for the first time a sense of loss and loneliness.

CHAPTER II.

THE day following the departure of the Pembrokes was Monday, and on Mondays there was always a great deal of life and bustle in the court.

Attached to each dwelling was a rude shed, above which clothes-lines were stretched. Here miscellaneous family washings frankly advertised the respective families' private concerns, — their wealth or their poverty, their extravagance, shiftlessness, thrift, or whatever.

The roofs of these sheds, which slanted a little, were reached by means of rickety outside stairs, up which the women laboriously climbed with their heavy baskets on their heads, vying with one another as to who should be the first to flaunt a snowy banner, — always some big thing, — a sheet, a table-cloth, a bed-spread.

The court rang with their sociable talk and laughter as they shook out the twisted wet garments and hung them on the lines. They were up above the picket-fences here, and felt a kind of large liberty, — a sensation they liked to prolong.

Beatrice, who had betaken herself to the honey-suckle bower and sat disconsolately examining her necklace, lent but a half-attentive ear to their idle gossip, which consisted of the same old commonplaces she had heard a hundred times before.

"You betta' hu'y up dar, M'rye," one lusty wench called across to another; "I's gwine t' get de start o' you dis mawn'n."

M'rye's basket, heaped with a drift of snowy linen, was just looming in sight as she slowly mounted her stairs.

When she reached the top, she lowered the basket to the floor, and stood for a moment, arms akimbo, to get her breath, and leisurely surveyed her neighbor's line.

"'Spec' you is, honey," she returned with a jocose twinkle in her eye; "you's pow'ful sma't! But look a' dem streaks in yo' shirt-sleeves; 'f I done wash that-a-way, my ole mis' pull my wool, sho'!"

"Lucky you's oveh dar out'n my reach!" retorted Chloe, with a playful menace of her fist. "'Case, 'f I got my han's on you, I jes' pitch you in de co'te bodaceously."

"Gor-amighty! I'd neveh hang out no clo'es like dem Pardees', 'f I's Kezi' Jane," M'rye exclaimed, taking pains, however, to guard her voice. But the treacherous breeze caught up the words, and carried them straight to the sensitive ears of Kezi' Jane, whose loyalty was instantly up in arms. The shabbiness of the Pardees' wardrobe was a sore enough trial to her pride without these taunts.

"You jes' ten' t' yo' own business, you M'rye Chevanne!" she called out angrily; "you don't have de handlin' o' dese hyeh clo'es, I reckon."

M'rye shrugged her shoulders, and clapped a broad hand over her mouth. She would have blushed for herself, if her black skin had been capable of this delicate confession of shame.

" Lawdy, I did n't 'low fo' huh to hyeah me ! " she exclaimed repentantly, under her breath.

" She weh heark'nin', " returned Chloe with a wink.

M'rye nodded, but she was too honorable to make Kezi's offence an excuse for her own. " It weh mighty mean o' me, jes' de same," she said.

" Well, I espec' it weh, un' de suckamstances," agreed Chloe. " Kezi' Jane, she 's pow'ful proud."

" Yass, leas'wise it weh tryin' to huh w'en de rich Hèberts done fail up, an' she weh sold t' dem triflin' Pardees. Dey ain' nuffin but po' white trash ! "

" Of co'se dey ain't," assented Chloe.

Chloe and M'rye were confidential friends. Confidential gossip was, in fact, the basis of their congenial relations. They could trust each other with the most deadly secrets, and there is no greater luxury of friendship than that.

When M'rye had emptied her basket she came over as near to her neighbor as the proximity of the two sheds would allow, and folded her bare arms upon the railing.

It was a promising attitude, and Chloe advanced expectantly.

" Docta' Chevanne, he repo't Salome's ole mis' mighty po'ly, dis mawn'n," said M'rye, in the low, level tones which in the negro voice are so musical and mellow, and which in any voice seem to draw a line of privacy round the conversers.

The words were quite distinct to the ears of the child down below, and the mention of her grandmother's name fixed her attention.

" Gwine die? " queried Chloe in the same key.

" I espec' likely," nodded M'rye.

"An' how it gwine be wid Salome an' de chile?"

"Sho' 'nuff! I know w'at dis niggeh do!" M'rye dropped her voice a note or two lower. "I'd jus' cl'ar out an' run away."

"Sho'!" said Chloe.

"Yass, I would, sho 's yo' bo'n! De ole mis' ain' gwine git up out'n de baid an' hunt 'm back, I reckon! Salome she got learnin', 'n' can write huh own pass papers, an' co'se she got little money laid by somewhar' fo' rainy day. But, Lawdy! she neveh gwine do it. Salome jus' stick by dat woman till she die, an' then some o' de kin-folks come 'n' cyarry 'm off to wuk on a suga' plantation, or in de cotton field."

"Salome ought take 'count de chile," said Chloe reflectively.

"She do," returned M'rye. "Salome jus' natch'ly wuship dat chile. But she done have cur'us notions about huh dooty. *Va!*"

M'rye had a profound respect for Salome, but she could not conceal the poor opinion she had of Salome's exalted "notions." It crept into the tones of her voice and wrote itself upon her features.

Chloe gave her shoulders a contemptuous shrug to show that she understood and sympathized with the feeling.

"I 'lowed Mis' Rose did n't have no mo' kin-folks lef' when young Marse Ralph done got killed in de hunt," she remarked.

Chloe's ignorance was easily accounted for; she belonged to a family of inferior social grade, and was but a common creature herself and quite beneath Salome's consideration except in the casual, condescending way people of quality take with their inferiors.

With M'rye the case was different. The Chevannes had always moved in the same circles with the La Scallas, and Dr. Chevanne had long been the La Scallas' family physician. And, besides, M'rye had some sterling virtues, — intelligence, discretion, and a sympathetic refinement of feeling, — which recommended her to Beatrice's discriminating grandmother. She was the only woman in the neighborhood to whom Salome had ever imparted any portion of her private history or sentiments.

M'rye cherished these confidences with a good deal of pride. Usually after a visit to Salome she kept aloof from Chloe for a day or two and nursed her self-importance. But, after all, she had more in common with Chloe than with Salome. The former was as comfortable as an old shoe; the latter she might have compared to her Sunday gown, which had stays and kept her compressed and upright.

Although she was extremely guarded in all she said, M'rye was not above the weakness of seeming to know more about Salome's affairs than the facts would warrant sometimes.

"Oh, yes," she replied airily, "dar's a heap o' La Scallas oveh on Bayou Lafourche, an' on de Têche. Dey live on de big suga' plantations, an' dey's all rich, I hyeah."

"Oh, Lawdy, Lawdy!" cried Chloe, clasping her hands and rolling her eyes, "if Salome an' de little Betty have to go 'n' wuk on a suga' plantation!"

Down under the honeysuckle vine the child's own horror-stricken soul re-echoed the thought. It was all the more terrible because she did not know what it meant.

There were only a few phases of slave-life which she understood. For Salome, always harboring the thought that Beatrice might some day be free, had not only withheld from her the knowledge of the heritage to which she was born, but as much as possible of all that pertained to it.

Beatrice wondered to herself where those dreadful places were, the " Bayou Lafourche " and the " Têche," and what it was to work on a plantation.

A chill seized her little body, and for a time she sat cold and motionless on her moss-covered bench. But this did not last long ; the blood began to course through her veins and burn in her cheeks, and her eyes kindled with the glow of fervent purpose. She would act upon old M'rye's daring suggestion, she would run away ! the world was big and wide, and must have many a hiding-place for a little creature like her ! And Mauma must go too, — oh, she could never leave Mauma !

At this juncture she heard her grandmother moving about in the kitchen, and she got up quickly and ran in.

" Mauma ! Mauma ! " she cried, clutching the old woman's garments and clinging to her hysterically, " let 's run away, let 's go now, quick, 'fo' they come 'n' take us to wuk on a suga' plantation ! "

Salome staggered back against the wall as if she had received a blow. The child had voiced a thought which had lain guiltily at the bottom of her heart for days past, but which she had not dared to breathe even in her prayers. Now she had an awful suspicion that the jealous Fate with whom she had covenanted for Beatrice' freedom had the power not only to seize upon her innermost thought, but to drag it forth and hurl it upon her from the very lips of the child herself! She had known all along that Miss Rose must die, and — though she kept up the semblance and even the effort of hope — she was convinced in her own secret soul that the obdurate old heart would not melt. Well, then, she would remain with her dying mistress and care for her faithfully until the end, and then! — the rest was her secret.

But, alas! something had just happened which put to flight all present plans and schemes; Madame Maurice La Scalla and her little daughter Evalina had arrived from La Scalla Place on the Têche. And of course they would remain until the end, and take charge of Miss Rosamond's effects.

Salome presently staggered to a chair, and her hands fell limply beside her. Beatrice could not bear the stare of her frightened eyes.

"Don't look at me so, Mauma, don't," she cried, and bursting into tears she buried her face in her grandmother's lap.

Salome laid a trembling hand caressingly upon her head, and when she could move her dry lips she whispered, "Who said anything to you 'bout running 'way, honey?"

Beatrice sobbed out the conversation she had overheard in the court.

In an instant Salome's countenance changed. So, then, it was not supernatural powers she had to deal with! It stung her pride and aroused her bitter indignation that M'rye and Chloe had presumed to discuss her affairs.

"Betty," she said, with a severity not intended for

the child, " don't you pay any 'tention to what those
ol' gossips say ; they don't know anything 'bout what
concerns you an' me, nothing at all. Wuk on a plantation, indeed ! It 's no such thing, honey, don't you
be 'fraid o' that ; there 's no La Scalla that 's eveh
go'n' to make any such blunder. They 're a great
family, the La Scallas are, and they know what 's
right and what 's becoming, you can trust 'em fo'
that, Betty."

She lifted the child's face and wiped away her
tears, and forcing a cheerful smile, she said, "I came
down hyeh this minute to tell you a piece o' news,
honey ; two o' the Têche La Scallas are yonder
now, up in Mis' Rose's room, an' you need n't be
afraid o' them, Betty ! You neveh saw so beautiful a
lady as Mis' Corinne, an' sweet a little girl as Mis'
Evalina. They want to see you, honey, an' you mus'
go upstairs, by an' by."

" Oh, no, no, no ! " cried Beatrice. " I want to
run away, I want to run away ! "

It was days before Salome succeeded in allaying
her fears, and before her praises of the visitors
aroused a curiosity in the child strong enough to
overcome her dread of meeting them.

One morning she consented, but with much re-
luctance, to be dressed in her prettiest frock and to
have her hair braided down her back, preparatory
to making the dreaded visit upstairs.

But her heart beat wildly, and she clung desperately
to her grandmother's hand, as they entered the long-
unused drawing-room at the front of the house, which
Salome had hastily thrown open and dusted a little
upon the arrival of the guests.

Exposed to the strong light, the room confessed its age like an old face.

The carpets and the tapestry were motheaten and faded, the furniture was dingy, and the silver ornaments on the mantel were dulled and blackened through neglect and disuse.

But at one of the windows stood a lady whose gracious presence dispelled this whole somber effect.

As the two figures approached she slowly turned her head, — which was poised like a stately flower on her slim round stem of a neck, — and looked at them over her shoulder with a smile which some amusing spectacle on the street below had brought to her lips.

Gradually the smile transferred itself to them, and overspread and illumined her face, but without disturbing a single feature.

She turned from the window and stood regarding the child, whose fascinated gaze was riveted upon hers; and then, giving her shoulders a little Frenchy shrug, said with a light laugh, which had the effect of irony, "It is easy to trace the La Scalla blood there !"

She was still more beautiful when she laughed, her lips parted so exquisitely over her fine teeth. But the child before her was chilled, not warmed, by her loveliness.

Madame moved to an easy-chair and sank into it with a grace and languor indescribable. The languor did not suggest indolence, but ennui. Madame had seen much of life and was no longer easily interested to the depths of her being. But to a certain extent she could still be amused, and she was rather attentive to what was going on around her.

"Has your mammy never taught you to courtesy, child?" she asked carelessly.

Beatrice shrank as if from a touch that stung, and Salome took it upon herself to answer. "Lawdy, Mis' Corinne, Beatrice neveh had ain'body to cou't'sy to, 'cept huh old mammy! she done been brought up in the kitchen an' the co'te."

"Indeed! Now I should have thought Miss Rose would have had her up here to wait upon her."

Salome made no answer.

"You may call Miss Evalina, Salome," said Madame. "No — leave the child here!"

Evalina was in the library. She presently appeared, with a book in her hand, between the heavy portières which separated the library from the drawing-room.

"What is it, Mama?" she asked, in the sweetest voice imaginable, and then her eyes fell upon Beatrice.

"Oh!" she cried, dropping the book and running forward.

"Salome's grandchild," said her mother.

"Oh!" she cried again.

It seemed to Beatrice that something had happened, some strange change had taken place which suddenly put a wide gulf between this other child and herself. She did not know what it was, but something within her rebelled as at an insult, and she resented it, when Evalina came up and took her hand and said, "What a perfectly lovely little creature you are!" — as she might have spoken to a pretty pet animal that could not understand, or about whose feelings it did not matter.

But Evalina's manner was so kind and her words

so sincere that Beatrice's resentment was speedily disarmed, and she reflected, " You are not so pretty as yo' Mama, but I like you better."

Evalina was in fact rather plain. Her complexion was colorless, and her eyes were of a light lustreless blue. But she had a profusion of long golden curls, and her expression was sweet and true.

Madame La Scalla arose presently, and leaving the two children together passed into the library.

She had come over to New Orleans to do her semi-yearly shopping ; and, as was her wont, had called upon Miss Rose, — with no expectation of anything more intimate and friendly, or more disagreeable, than taking a luncheon or a cup of French coffee with her forbidding relative. But at the door she had met Dr. Chevanne who informed her of Miss Rose's serious illness. It was distressing news, chiefly because it imposed an irksome duty which she saw no way of evading. She really dismissed on the instant all thought of evading it. She had a philosophical way of adjusting herself to the inevitable which passed for amiability, and her mental processes were swift. During the few moments that she stood in the hall discussing the matter with the Doctor — in a becomingly serious manner — she revolved the whole situation in her mind and decided what she should do.

After seeing Miss Rose, whose changed appearance gave her a shock, and consulting with old Salome, she went back to the hotel to gather up her belongings, and the following day, with her daughter and her maid, established herself in Miss Rosamond's dingy old mansion.

When she entered the library she closed the

portières and sat down and wrote a letter to her husband : —

"MY DEAR MAURICE, — There has been no change since I wrote you yesterday. I mean no change of any sort, either in Cousin Rose or in our surroundings. It is a dead, unbroken monotony, — save for the dainty little meals Salome serves up to us. What a treasure this old creature has been to Rose all her days! My memory goes back to the time when I first saw her — in Paris — following after Rose like her shadow, armed with shawls, fan, bouquet, vinaigrette, *et cetera!*

"If you were not so busy with your crops I should insist upon your coming on here and giving us the support of your genial company, — for of course I shall remain until the end, now that I am here, unluckily! It would be heathenish of me not to stay, — particularly as you are the heir! I congratulate you on your prospective fortune, my dear, which I believe consists principally of this ghostly old house (which I would recommend you to pitch into the canal) and the two slaves, Salome and her grandchild, — a remarkably pretty little creature who will do nicely as a maid and playmate for Evalina, just what we have been looking for in fact. If I had not dropped in here so opportunely (?), I think Cousin Rose would have freed these people. She says Salome has been pestering the life out of her about it, and she was more than half persuaded that it was her Christian duty to comply with the old creature's wishes. I told her I doubted the kindness of turning a superannuated old woman and a helpless child out into the world to shift for themselves! I am very glad I did, now that I have seen the child. She, of course, will be growing into usefulness; though old Salome's best days are over."

This letter was not yet finished when Madame was summoned by loud shrieks to the sick chamber to find that the breath had just left Miss Rose's body. Salome was in hysterics, and the maid, Calisty, was trying to get her away from the bedside. But she clung with all her mad strength to the rigid form of her dead mistress, fiercely calling, " Come back ; come back an' sign the papers, or God will neveh fo'give you, *God will neveh fo'give you !* "

Madame laid a white hand firmly upon the old creature's shoulder and bade her be silent.

The commanding touch and tone instantly hushed Salome's wild cries, and shaking with sobs, — which surely indicated the last convulsive struggles of a broken heart, of a life-long purpose thwarted in the end, — she staggered from the room and hobbled blindly down the kitchen stairs, feeling all the weight and infirmity of her seventy-odd years.

The two children had gone out upon the front gallery and were not aware of the tragedy indoors.

Beatrice, looking down the broad avenue, — deserted save for a carriage or two vanishing in the distance, — wondered what had become of the splendid procession with its waving banners, its shining musical instruments and vibrant drums. She had never imagined such a quiet world ! And yet it was beautiful. There was not an unsightly thing anywhere. She cast her eyes delightedly up and down the long street, with the strip of greensward and double line of trees running through the center, — in whose lofty tops she fancied some of her own familiar birds were singing. She knew their peculiar notes.

The air was fresh and sweet with the scent of flowers. In the deep blue sky hung motionless white clouds, — soft, flocculent drifts like new-fallen snow.

Evalina was presently called into the drawing-room. When she returned, a few minutes later, two emotions were struggling for the mastery in her face, — awe and gladness.

"Oh, Beatrice!" she exclaimed, but softly, "Cousin Rose is dead, and you are to belong to me!"

"Is Mis' Rose dead? Then Mauma will cry again!" said Beatrice, with dreadful apprehensions.

"Oh, yes, poor old thing! I expect she will," answered Evalina. "She seemed so fond of Cousin Rose." After a moment or two she added, "Did you hear what I said, Beatrice, that you are to be my little maid?"

"I do' know how to be a maid," returned Beatrice unpromisingly.

"You don't know how to be a maid? Oh, dear! how funny! You know what a maid is, don't you? Just somebody to wait on one. You will have to brush my hair — "

"I cyan't!" interrupted Beatrice, incredulously regarding the shower of yellow curls Evalina shook about her face.

"Oh, well, of course you are too small now, but when you are older you can," Evalina assured her; "Calisty will show you how."

"Am I to wuk on a suga' plantation?" asked Beatrice with very wide-open eyes.

"Work on a sugar plantation!" laughed Evalina. "Why you silly little thing! I should think not! Look at your hands, — they are ever so much prettier than mine. No, you queer child! I will tell you what your very serious duties will be; you must fetch my things and run little errands for me, and go walking and driving and boating with me. And when I go off on long journeys, to the coast or the islands, for the hot weather, you will go along with me."

Beatrice's eyes softened as Evalina thus briefly outlined the attractions which the immediate future offered.

"And I'll tell you what," Evalina went on; "I shall teach you to read; it is lovely to read, there are the most beautiful stories in books!"

"Yes, I know," said Beatrice, "I've heard them."

"You've heard them? Well, not all of them, I reckon! Why, it would take a million years to read *all* the stories in *all* the books! I am going to teach you to sew, too, it is such fun to make doll-clothes. Have you any dolls?"

"No," answered Beatrice, "I don't like dolls, they have n't any real eyes an' mouths. I 've got a lot o' things down in the co'te that can hop an' jump an' fly. They can eat, too, an' they know what you say to 'em."

She revolved in her mind the propriety of inviting her companion down into the court to make the acquaintance of these little people. And presently she began, —

"Evalina, would you like — "

"Stop, Beatrice," interrupted Evalina, "we may as well begin right at once, — it will be easier and pleasanter for you; you must call me *Miss* Evalina."

"Why, you 're only a little girl!" said Beatrice.

"Yes, I know; but it is the proper way, you see," returned Evalina, who never dreamed of questioning the conventionalisms by which her life was bounded.

"*I* should n't care, myself, but Mama is very parti-cular about the servants' manners."

"Am I a servant?" asked Beatrice.

"To be sure!"

"But I 'm not a colo'ed person."

"N–o," answered Evalina, doubtingly, "you 're not exactly colored, Beatrice; I don't know how it is, I don't understand those things very well. There 's Calisty, Mama's maid, that 's just as white as I am and has blue eyes. People are queerly mixed up somehow. Papa says it is all wrong, but I don't know what he means. They often talk about these matters at home, and Mama says we ought to take things just as we find them and not bother. And I suppose that 's the best way; don't you think so?"

Beatrice did not know what she thought, and was silent.

"It 's an awful large question, Papa says, so I reckon you and I had b∍tter not meddle with it, Beatrice. I know one thing, I mean to be good to you, so don't you worry!"

Calisty came and called them both into the house. As they stepped through the open window the little mistress cautioned the little maid, "Don't you forget now, Beatrice, to call me 'Miss Evalina'."

Miss Rose's funeral took place toward evening of the following day. The services were held in the old cathedral fronting on Jackson Park, where she had been wont to worship in days gone by.

A large concourse of people — the very best people, as was said afterwards — had assembled to pay re-spect to the memory of this, the last representative of a once proud and notable family. All the other

La Scallas, as Salome had repeatedly stated to old M'rye, belonged merely to " collateral branches, and not to the main trunk."

As the procession moved slowly churchward many interesting and even amusing stories, creditable and otherwise, pertaining to Miss Rose's family, especially the unfortunate young man Ralph, who had been exceedingly wild and popular, were recalled by the occupants of the carriages which followed in the wake of the hearse, and related in undertones, often with subdued laughter decorously smothered in a bunch of white flowers or a black-bordered hand-kerchief. No one of course could more than pre-tend solemnity. An old woman who had practically died years ago was to be buried to-day, that was all.

But the most interesting topic of conversation was Madame Maurice La Scalla, who was well known in New Orleans social circles, and whose devotion to the deceased lady — who was only her husband's distant relative — had been much commented upon by the press during the past week.

Every head had been craned out of the carriage windows as she descended the broad stone steps of the old mansion, leaning upon the arm of Dr. Chevanne.

She was dressed in deep mourning, which however did not eclipse the graceful outlines of her figure, or altogether conceal the beauty of her face, since she must needs put by the veil a little to get her breath, as she apologetically remarked to the Doctor.

Men quickly raised their hats when she appeared, and women whispered, " *Mon Dieu !* It must have gone hard with Madame Maurice to shut herself up in that gloom for a whole week ! "

Calisty, armed with smelling salts and a fan, was put into the carriage with her mistress, and Evalina, at her own request, followed in the next carriage with Salome and Beatrice.

Every incident and circumstance and detail of this strange occasion was followed by the little maid with eyes that widened more and more with wonder and awe.

The careful way in which the casket was removed from the hearse and borne slowly down the long dim aisle, the pictured windows, the figures of saints and angels, the draped altar with its curious emblems, the priest and the acolytes, — everything was noted by her with the profoundest interest, and made an impression which could never fade away.

No slightest touch of levity marred the august solemnity inside the church.

The priest, who was a man of peculiar power, dominated the whole congregation, and drove from their hearts, for the time being, every thought but the thought of death. It was not a mere perfunctory burial service which he conducted, but an intense, realistic bringing-home to each one present of the final lot of all.

A profusion of white wreaths and crosses, and loose handfuls of flowers, were strewn upon the casket and about the altar, but their sweetness was overborne by the thick fumes of incense from the swinging censers.

Beatrice lost all sense of physical feeling, and sat spell-bound, benumbed and chilled by a nameless terror.

The intoned service and the chanting of an unseen choir were the most weird and agonizing sounds she had ever heard. It seemed as if invisible spirits were contending with each other for the soul of the departed, and she felt such a commiseration for Miss Rose — not knowing how the struggle was going to end — as that poor lady's conduct toward herself hardly justified.

But self was out of the question ; it was long before Beatrice gave a thought to herself, and when she finally did remember who and what and where she was, she was filled with an appalling sense of loneliness. Her fascinated eyes followed every motion of the priest, but she had nothing in common with him or the vast crowd of people, who all seemed to be one with him, as was shown in their responses and changes of attitude, and other and more subtle signs. She was outside of it all, cut off from human sympathy and fellowship.

Even Mauma, sitting in stony silence in the awful dignity of bombazine and crêpe, was strange to her here.

She grew frightened at her sense of isolation, and looked about furtively, half wondering if there might not be some way of escape from this horrible oppression. And presently her eyes fell upon an individual, sitting just across the aisle, the familiarity of whose face and figure gave her a start of delight.

It was the old wig-maker, dressed in a rusty but respectable suit of black, of some by-gone fashion. His head was adorned with a glossy black wig. Had it been a wedding instead of a funeral he would have arrayed himself in a blond one ; for a wig was to him simply an article of dress, and should be in keeping with the occasion.

He chanced to meet the child's eyes when he was in the midst of a sepulchral response; but to her surprise and dismay his look, instead of being friendly and reassuring, was stern and forbidding.

As a matter of fact, he assorted his manners and facial expressions the same as his wigs, and selected them in accordance with the rules of propriety.

More frightened than ever, Beatrice shrank back into her place. But presently, noting a slight movement on the part of her young mistress, she timidly raised her eyes.

Evalina met her glance with a kind little smile, and slipped her hand down, and laid it upon Beatrice's little hand, and she no longer felt afraid or alone. Evalina was her mistress, but she was also her friend.

It was a long way out to the cemetery. As the carriage rolled slowly along, the wide freedom of the outside world grew upon the child. There was so much of blue sky through the trees, such a long vista not only ahead but to right and to left, at street intersections!

A current of cool, delicious air was flowing — one could hardly call it blowing — through the streets, which had been freshened by a recent shower.

Once, Beatrice, with the sense of oppression experienced in the church entirely gone, essayed to speak; but Evalina shook her head, and said, "It is n't polite to talk at funerals."

Beatrice was abashed and silent. She looked up at her grandmother, but Salome paid no heed. Ever since the death of Miss Rose she had ignored the child.

Finally the procession entered the beautiful city of the dead, with its marble palaces, its white glistening streets, its wealth of flowers and luxuriant shrubbery, its pure statuary, and its deep silence, broken only by the wheels crunching on the shell drive, and the fluting of the wind among the magnolia boughs.

The casket was again removed from the hearse, and stripped of its wreaths and crosses, and shoved into its appointed niche in the costly La Scalla tomb.

At the other side of the tomb, low tremulous voices chanted a requiem solemnly sweet. Tears sprang to Beatrice's eyes, and hung glistening upon her lashes.

She crept close to Evalina, and whispered, "Is this heaven?"

"Oh, dear, no, child!" Evalina whispered back. "It is the cemetery; heaven is up above the sky."

Beatrice looked up. Nothing there but a vast, transparent sea of ether! The blue had gone from the sky, and left pale tints of pink and lilac and milky white, overlapping and melting together.

On the homeward drive, which was brisk and exhilarating, Beatrice — to whom this, too, was a new and thrilling experience, this swift smooth motion — ventured another question.

"Mis' Evalina, how do people get up to heaven?"

"Their bodies, you know, do not go there," explained Evalina, taking pains to make the explanation very lucid and final, "only their spirits. The angels come down and carry them up."

Beatrice did not doubt her young mistress's statement, but presently she inquired, " Did you eveh see them cyarry anybody up ? "

" Oh, dear, no ! they are perfectly invisible ; you cannot see them any more than you can the air."

There was nothing now to detain Madame La Scalla longer. The old house was put in order, the windows and doors securely fastened, and with Calisty, old Salome, and the two children, she immediately set out on the long homeward journey.

CHAPTER III.

THE journey from New Orleans to La Scalla Place was through those enchanting water-ways which our legend-loving poet, without ever having looked upon them, has described with so much feeling and fervor, and with such instinctive accuracy.

To Madame La Scalla, who accredited herself with the possession of rare poetic feeling, and who certainly had fine moods, every bend and sweep of the current, every islet and silvery lagoon, and every dim, leafy corridor in the weird, colonnaded forests, expressed some sweet or sad thought from " Evangeline."

She had a blue-and-gold copy of the poem in her lap as she sat upon the steamer's deck, and occasionally she read a line, here or there, — some passage fitted to the passing scene. She loved to follow in fancy, as she was repeating in reality, the voyage of the hapless Acadian maiden.

At a certain point where the waters grew dark and sluggish and seemed uncertain of their course, dividing and winding hither and thither among the islands, the steamer was forced to enter a narrow passage where the forest, coming close to the banks, encompassed it as in a dim green vault.

4

Here she partially closed her eyes and, leaning back in her chair with hands folded upon the open book, murmured half inaudibly : —

" Over their heads the towering and tenebrous boughs of the
    cypress
  Met in a dusky arch, and trailing mosses in mid-air
  Waved like banners that hang on the walls of ancient
    cathedrals.
  Death-like the silence reigned, and unbroken."

And farther on, emerging from this somber and mystic silence, she quoted again, applying the words to the marvellous picture her eyes rested upon : —

                " Before them
Lay, in the golden sun, the lakes of the Atchafalaya.
Water-lilies in myriads rocked on the slight undulations
Made by the passing oars, and, resplendent in beauty, the
    lotus
Lifted her golden crown above the heads of the boatmen.
Faint was the air with the odorous breath of magnolia
    blossoms,
And with the heat of noon ; and numberless sylvan islands,
Fragrant and thickly embowered with blossoming hedges of
    roses,
Near to whose shores they glided along, invited to slumber."

Just here in the islanded Atchafalaya — where the weary Acadian wanderers of nearly a century before had moored their bark at noontide under the drooping Wachita willows, and fallen heavily asleep on the greensward — Madame's sensations were most acute.

" Ah," she soliloquized dreamily, " if only Evangeline had remained awake that day ! She might have heard the dip of Gabriel's oar and recognized the sound of his voice as his boat glided ' close under the lee of the island,' behind the ' screen of palmettos.'

And then the story would not have had so sad an ending."

She smiled, half-conscious that she was coquetting with her own emotions. The journey would have been unspeakably dull if she could not have entertained herself with this poetic drama, — in its own sweet and actual setting, or in some other equally fanciful manner.

As for the children, Evalina and Beatrice, they had to be satisfied with their own thoughts about the things they saw and felt. Art had not opened her beautiful palaces to them yet, nor taught them how to understand Nature. To them the course over which they glided was like an unfamiliar but delightful book, full of surprises, though not inconsequent.

Evalina, who knew something of geography, informed her companion — companionship was the only recognizable relation between them — that the river had a purpose, which was to find the least obstructed course to the sea. And forthwith they began to study its purpose, and became deeply interested in divining its intentions and noting its little stratagems, which they thought were quite humanly intelligent.

Sometimes it went straight on, with a swift and noiseless rush as if resolved to overwhelm and bear down every opposing force. Then, suddenly, it changed its tactics, and turned and twisted and doubled like a hound on the scent; shifting the scenes along the banks as rapidly and adroitly as stage scenes are shifted in a play. It knew, of course, just where to cut through the lush green meadows, where it must skirt the oak-crowned *chênière*, and where it might spread out over the reedy morass, or feel its subtle way among the thick ranks of pines and cypresses.

The children pleased themselves with pretending that the river took pains to find out and flow past the most picturesque groves of holly and dogwood and magnolia; and thickets of wild plum and May-haw and pink azalea, and the beautiful flowering crêpe myrtle; and past tangles of sweet-scented jasmine and grape, and the gaudy trumpet-vine; and a thousand other lovely wild clinging, creeping, wreathing things, — which surely could not exist anywhere else in the forest!

Evalina had travelled over the route so many times before that the journey of itself had become tiresomely familiar, — like the poems one cons by heart in childhood but does not understand. In her later voyages she had been well content to ensconce herself in a snug corner of the boat with a book, and let the beautiful scenes which no longer offered novelty to her eye pass unnoticed, — except when her brother Burgoyne, an alert and intelligent lad a few years her senior, had accompanied her. Burgoyne had acquired a kind of lore connected with this romantic chain of waters, far more exciting than the story of Evangeline. The tales he told to Evalina aroused her intense interest and took her mind off her " silly stories," as he called the sort of things she read.

Now, for the first time, she seemed to see the river and the landscape. The presence of the child beside her, who was so acutely alive to it all, awakened in her a new sense, and put her for the first time in her life in touch with Nature.

In all respects the voyage was to Beatrice a thrillingly new experience; though the knowledge she had gained through her close acquaintance with the tiny creatures of the court, and the few trees and shrubs and flowers that grew there, and the little patch of sky, enabled her to understand these larger mysteries which offered themselves at every turn, far better than Evalina understood them. This little being, whom Nature had found ways and means of educating, was so used to giving significance and personality to every living thing, that all life interested her in a peculiar way. Her thoughts about the bees that went buzzing by, the mullet that jumped up in the water, the birds that sang unseen in the thickets or flashed their bright wings through the forest glades, and even about the lazy turtles sunning themselves ecstatically upon drift-logs near the banks, and dropping tardily into the water when the vibrations from the steamer rocked the log, — were intimate and friendly, as are the thoughts of the wise humanitarian concerning the people about him, whether he knows them personally or not.

She was acquainted with the habits and modes of thought of many of these small creatures, and knew that each one of them was dear and important to itself at least, if not to a circle of relatives and friends. And even when she did not know the kind of life they led she sympathized with them, and made up little histories for them in her mind.

But little of this came to the surface. She sat near her young mistress upon a low stool; her exquisite face, the golden high-lights on her rich abundant hair, the perfect modelling of her small body, and the pretty picturesqueness of her attitudes, affording constant delight to Evalina.

Now and then she raised her wonder-bright eyes to Evalina's face, with a " Hark ! " or " Oh, look ! " as some unusually sweet bird-note fell upon her ear, or an exceptionally beautiful vista opened before her eyes.

Nothing escaped her keen sight. From time to time she silently pointed out a tall, feathered creature posing upon one leg on the sunk margin of the stream, scarcely distinguishable from the gray-green moss and underbrush ; or the spectral figure of a man skilfully poling his unsteady dugout through the interminable swamp.

There was such a wealth of things to take note of, — the flight of wild-ducks and wild-geese ; the clouds of blackbirds alighting upon a leafless tree to give a joyous matinee ; the watchful buzzards, perched upon barren limbs and waiting, — as others of their kind wait at the Towers of Silence in the land of the Parsees ; swift sea-birds hurtling by on slender, scythe-shaped wings ; myriads of delicate white spider-lilies, and purple *fleurs-de-lis ;* and whole lagoons given up to great snowy water-lilies, with their broad, green leaves lying flat upon the glassy surface.

Often, as evening approached and they sat wrapped in warm shawls, — for even in midsummer it is cool here when the sun goes down, and a penetrating dampness steals up from the salt marshes below, — Evalina repeated in her own simple language the tales Burgoyne had told her, about the pirates and freebooters who formerly infested these labyrinthine waters. She pointed out to Beatrice the very bayous

up which the notorious Jean Lafitte, chief of a band
of desperadoes gathered from all nations, had sailed
to hide his contraband goods or sell them to the rich
planters.   And Beatrice, listening with eyes full of
wonder and excitement, demanded, —

"Is it true?"

"Why, of course it is true," returned Evalina.   "I
know people who have things that were presented to
them by Captain Lafitte, — rings and pistols and
knives, real murdering knives, you know, with actual
blood-stains upon them.   An old friend of ours at
St. Martinsville, M. Condé, when he was a boy knew
Lafitte quite well, and he has one of the knives.   Of
course, where the blood was there are just rusty spots
now.   M. Condé says he would not have them scoured
off for the world."

"Why would n't he?" asked Beatrice.

"Oh, they make the knife more interesting, I presume.   It has a history; all of M. Condé's relics —
and he has a lot of them — have histories.   He says
it is the history of such things that makes them valuable.   This knife was picked up off the deck of an
English man-of-war, which Lafitte captured after a
dreadful battle.   It has the name of an English
nobleman engraved upon the handle."

"Did you eveh see it?" asked Beatrice.

"The knife?   Oh, yes," said Evalina.   "I 've had
it in my hands; but it makes one feel rather queer."

"I would n't touch it fo' anything!" declared
Beatrice, with a shudder.

"Would n't you?   How funny!   It could n't hurt
you; it is quite dull."

After a moment Evalina added, "Papa never liked

to have Burgoyne hear these stories about the pirates ; he thought they were unwholesome for boys. But M. Condé always poohed, and said it would just make a man of him. I used to ask Papa if they were not unwholesome for girls, too ; but he laughed, and said he reckoned there was not much danger of a girl-pirate, especially a girl like me, afraid even of a field-mouse.''

The stories might not have been unwholesome for Burgoyne if they had been set before him in their true light. But M. Condé, unfortunately, invested them with the seductive glamour of romance, and threw a halo round the head of the famous character, whose ambitious spirit and commanding eye — he had but one — and powerful personal magnetism had made him the despotic but idolized sovereign of men as daring as himself, and more lawless.

M. Condé was a man of leisure, who both visited and entertained his friends with great frequency. His mind was as full of traditions as his cabinet was of curios, and he liked to exhibit both.

He was fond of declaiming, in the old oratorical way, and loved nothing so much as an audience, even though it consisted only of a bright-cheeked lad in knickerbockers, standing before him with feet well apart and firmly planted, his hands behind his back, his eyes admiringly uplifted, and his lips half-open, ready to cry, " Bravo ! " in the right places.

He took pains to assure Burgoyne that he depre- cated Lafitte's career, but was convinced the man possessed some noble virtues as an offset to his colossal crimes.

In M. Condé's opinion, the laurels at the battle

of New Orleans should have been divided between
General Jackson and the patriot corsair. He always
raised his voice at this point and demanded in sten-
torian tones, with an interrogative pause at the end
of the sentence which greatly embarrassed his small
auditor, who feared that something might be expected
of him by way of reply, "For was he not a true and
loyal patriot?"

After an impressive moment, during which Burgoyne wriggled a little under his stern eye, he
would continue in the same dramatic strain, "Jean
Lafitte, smuggler and free-lance though he was,
proudly turned his back upon the tempting bribes
of the English commandant, and, despite General
Jackson's haughty refusal to 'consort with rogues
and pirates,' and Governor Claiborne's hunting him
out of his island stronghold with an army of men,
eventually co-operated with the defenders of the
city, and kept the British ships out of the Pass of
Barataria! Was not that a magnificent act, the act
of a magnanimous man?"

M. Condé loved to dwell upon the contrast afforded
by the fate of the *two* heroes of the famous battle;
the one, with his crimes finally cancelled by the
government through General Jackson's own recom-
mendation, vanishing into oblivion and leaving no
trace that history may take account of; the other,
with his name linked forever with the dazzling victory
for which a general thanksgiving was immediately
offered in the cathedral, with all the imposing ceremonies of the Roman Catholic Church.

But the narrator of these things drew no lesson
from them, and pointed no moral. Burgoyne was left

to his own conclusions.   He admired General Jackson
very much, and loved to hear M. Condé describe,
from vivid personal recollection, the pomp of that
great occasion, when the stern warrior was crowned
with laurel, and his pathway strewn with flowers by
lovely Creole girls.   But his youthful sympathies went
out to the picturesque hero of Barataria.

Evalina imparted to her listener the dreadful fact
that Burgoyne had been so impressed by M. Condé's
stories that he had at one time organized a band of
little negroes on the plantation, and played at smug-
gling and pirating until her Papa was obliged to put
a stop to it.

"And even after that," Evalina added, "Burgoyne
used to regret that the world had become so civilized
— that was what M. Condé said — as to make the
business of pirating not only dangerous, — of course
a pirate would expect that, — but impossible."

"Does he think that way now?" asked Beatrice,
who was getting some curious impressions of the
youth from the side-lights thrown upon his character.

"Oh, dear, no!" answered Evalina, "he has outgrown all that, of course.   He is sixteen now, and
nearly as tall as Papa, — I should n't wonder if he was
quite as tall, I have not seen him for a long time; he
is away at school."

Madame La Scalla spent the evenings pacing back
and forth, erect and graceful, or reclining upon a
couch, or in an easy chair.   Sometimes she called
Evalina to her, and stroked her soft hair and chatted
with her pleasantly; or she made Beatrice come and
stand before her, and examined her beautiful face as
though it were a picture.

Once she remarked, " Evalina, do you observe that the child's eyelashes are exactly like your brother's?"

Evalina deprecated the comparison, fond as she was of her little maid, — it was unconventional. But she was used to her mother's frankness.

Calisty, who was an industrious lass, had her knitting and needle-work, and busied herself from morning till night.

Poor old Salome sat apart, the picture of despair. Often Beatrice went up to her, and wound her soft little arms about her neck. Salome returned the caresses, but never spoke. Evalina advised Beatrice not to trouble her. " Mauma is mourning for Cousin Rose, you know," she explained. " She will get over it by and by."

There was one evening when all on board were impressed by the peculiar splendor of the sunset.

The boat had swung clear of the woods, and was ploughing its way through Grand Lake. There was nothing to hide the sky ; it stretched above them, a vast luminous transparency, touched with every conceivable tint and brilliancy.

Near the horizon line in the west lay a deep red core of fire, with billows of topaz and crimson rolling in upon it, and absorbing and reflecting its splendor. Above them hung banners of purple, edged with flame. Here and there, as through a rent in a curtain, were shown soft undertones of blue, of tender green, the sweetest dream of color !

Across the smooth surface of the water lay a broad track of gold ; and it seemed as if the steamer, like an enchanted boat, might glide over this shining pathway straight into the setting sun! Beatrice was entranced.

Evalina enjoyed the scene calmly, as one enjoys the drama after the hundredth time or so, comparing it in her mind with other sunsets she had witnessed, — as the *blasé* theatre-goer compares actors and plays.

There is value in accumulated experiences, a pleasure in being able to contrast one thing with another, and to bring recollections of the past to add to the interest and delight of the present; but no pleasure of this sort can compare with the first fine rapture, the first intense, passionate consciousness of an undreamt-of glory, — whether of Nature or of Art.

As the river narrowed again, there came suddenly from the near wooded bank a wonderful burst of song. Could Beatrice have defined the impression it made upon her, she would have said that it expressed not only the beauty, the splendor, the ineffable charm of the closing day, but all that she thought and felt. It was the vocalization of emotion, of sensation. So searching were the strains, so charged with a kind of sweet torture, that they left no chord untouched, no fountain sealed.

Madame La Scalla, leaning forward in her chair to listen, recalled the lines describing this same scene and this same occurrence, and wondered with a smile whether the little warbler was always there to make the picture tally with the poem!

" From a neighboring thicket the mocking-bird, wildest of
       singers,
  Swinging aloft on a willow spray that hung o 'er the water,
  Shook from his little throat such floods of delirious music,

That the whole air and the woods and the waves seemed
  silent to listen.
Plaintive at first were the tones and sad; then soaring to
  madness
They seemed to follow or guide the revels of frenzied
  Bacchantes.
Single notes were then heard, in sorrowful, low lamentation;
Till, having gathered them all, he flung them forth in derision,
As when, after a shower, a gust of wind through the tree-tops
Shakes down the rattling rain in a crystal shower on the
  branches.
With such a prelude as this, and hearts that throbbed with
  emotion,
Slowly they entered the Têche, where it flows through the
  green Opelousas."

"Now we are almost home!" exclaimed Evalina,
breaking the spell which the bird's wonderful song
had wrought. "This river we are on now is the
Têche. Oh, I am so glad! I can hardly wait!"

The way through the Têche was the most beautiful
of all the journey. The richest plantations lay along
its banks; and the roofs of noble mansions, and the
smokestacks of sugar houses were visible wherever
there was an opening through the trees.

Sometimes a whole plantation might be seen, en-
closed by an emerald hedge and checked off with
deep draining ditches.

Negroes were at work hoeing cane and pulling
weeds in the cotton-fields, singing as they toiled.

In the midst of each plantation, upon a carefully
chosen spot, stood the mansion, or Great House,
with its wide corridors and peristyle of Grecian columns, — sheltered by mammoth live-oaks, or surrounded by a row of China-berry trees that spread
their symmetrical tops like great umbrellas, and made

a green awning impervious to sun and rain. The purple bloom, covering like a delicate moss the broad, flat surface of these curious canopies, filled the air with perfume.

Not far from the mansion was always the cluster of white-washed negro cabins, with their outside chimneys of mud and sticks, and their frail porticos screened with vines and trailing roses.

Life abounded upon all sides. Immense droves of cattle watched over by mounted herdsmen grazed in the meadows and marshes, where the

> " Grass grows
> More in a single night than a whole
> Canadian summer."

Now and then they met, or passed, a slow-sailing lugger. Dozens of canoes were upon the water; hunters with their trained dogs were moving through the wood or wading in the marshes. Here and there a negro who had been granted an "indulgence" was seated in a shady nook upon the bank with his line dropped in the water, steeping his soul in the highest bliss he knew. For fishing is the colored idler's ideal way of spending a holiday. Christmas, Good Friday, St. Patrick's Day, the Anniversary of the Battle of New Orleans, and the Birthday of Washington, have no other significance to his mind than that they are fishing days.

La Scalla Place was a full quarter of a mile from the river; but the boat's whistle — sounded in a peculiar way to announce the arrival of members of the family, or of guests — summoned the carriage to the landing.

A wagon for the baggage followed close behind the carriage. It had a seat, covered with an old sheep-skin, for the accommodation of Calisty and Salome.

Uncle Smiley, a little old black man with a kindly face, was the driver of this vehicle. Evalina greeted him with great friendliness, and he responded with a vast smile, and took both lines in one hand in order to lift his old white wool hat with the other.

Evalina begged that Beatrice might be permitted to ride in the carriage, and her mother assented with a sarcastic little shrug.

The carriage drove off; but the steamer had some freight to unload, and Uncle Smiley was obliged to wait until Madame's trunks and the old wooden chest containing Salome's belongings appeared.

He secured the lines to a sapling, — though there was not much danger of his scrubby little mules moving out of their tracks, — and after acknowledging the introduction to Salome which Calisty, the haughtiest of maids, condescendingly volunteered, he hurried down to the landing. When the trunks were put off he assumed his blandest air, and tried to wheedle the roustabouts into helping him to drag them up and load them into the wagon.

" Oh, we-all 's up to yo' tricks, Unc' Smiley ! " was the derisive answer as they hauled up the gang-plank.

The boat steamed slowly away, and Uncle Smiley scratched his head and looked up and down the river.

" I espec' C'listy mought he'p me," he soliloquized, " she 's pow'ful strong an' handy ; but I ain' gwine put dis hyeh big lifts on a lady."

His eye finally alighted upon a familiar figure, with

rod and line, seated upon an old upturned dugout a few yards below; and he started off with great alacrity and accosted the angler with insinuating friendliness, and with the air of a man who had no ulterior motive.

"W'y, hello, Jake! dat you-all? Howdy!"

"Howdy," answered Jake, without taking his eyes from the water, — his ears had recognized the speaker.

"Havin' any luck?" pursued Uncle Smiley. "I 'spec' not, f'om de 'pearance."

He stooped and picked up from the grass, where it lay gasping, the only prize Jake had succeeded in landing. As the creature wriggled in his hands, and finally flopped itself back upon the ground, he exclaimed, "You ain't gwine t' eat dat kind o' fish, Jake?"

"Mos' likely, 'f I don't git no cat-fish," was the laconic answer.

"He ain't nuffin' but bones! You eat dat fish up, 'n' you cyan't pull yo' shirt off oveh yo' head fo' week."

The appalling suggestion made no impression upon the phlegmatic Jake.

Uncle Smiley regarded him silently for a moment, and then changed the conversation.

"Sun gittin' pu'ty neah down," he remarked casually, squinting at the red western glow through the trees. "Mebbe you-all 'd like to ride home, I's got de wagon down hyeh?"

No answer.

The intruder stood with knotted brows. Presently his face lighted up.

" Look hyeh, Jake, — "

He was about to make the obdurate fisherman a handsome proposition. But in a flash Jake was upon his feet, in threatening attitude.

" I 's a good min' t' pitch you-all oveh de bank ! " he cried angrily. " You scared all de fish out'n de bayou wid yo' gab."

He was a young fellow, of gigantic size and furious temper.

Uncle Smiley discreetly backed away from the river and gave up his futile efforts.

" If he know'd C'listy 's up hyeh, he 'd come along, sho' ! " he muttered as he trudged back toward the landing ; " but I 's not gwine t' give 'im de info'mation."

Calisty had started to meet him. " Whar' you-all been, Unc' Smiley," she called out indignantly, " leavin' we-all stan'in' roun' hyeh, waitin'? "

" I 's jes' tryin' t' git Big Jake t' gimme a lif' on dem boxes," said the old man apologetically.

" Well, you cyan't ; Big Jake 's de on'ries', lazies' niggeh on de plantation," returned Calisty. " Come 'long hyeh, I 'low dis chile kin tote one en' dem boxes."

She started off impetuously. Uncle Smiley followed as nimbly as he might, feebly deprecating the necessity of accepting such assistance from the weaker sex.

CHAPTER IV.

DO old houses shrink and dwindle when the life within them has gone out? If so, the La Scalla homestead on the Têche has shrunk and dwindled.

Surely, it is not merely an optical illusion !

When Beatrice, a little wondering creature, sat in a corner of the carriage as it rolled up the long magnolia avenue, and looked out, at Evalina's bidding, to get her first view of the mansion at the farther end, its white, symmetrical proportions were colossal. The great chimneys at the gable ends loomed up against the sky and mingled the pale blue smoke of their wood fires with the clouds.

Now the house is not grand or imposing at all ! It is low and flat and insignificant. The Grecian columns supporting the immense roof upon three sides, and lending the structure so much dignity and grace, are scarcely more than posts !

It is a dead house. Then it was abundantly and gloriously alive. Its hospitable doors opened to some of the brightest men and women of the time, — statesmen, poets, military heroes, renowned singers, and celebrated beauties.

House parties were of frequent occurrence, when guests from New Orleans, New York, and even Paris, met and mingled in delightful social freedom, all contributing their respective shares to the general pleasure. For Madame La Scalla would not cheapen her hospitality by inviting stupid, or surly, or uninteresting people, — except, sometimes, as " appendages " to exceptionally desirable husbands or wives !

There was great variety of entertainment ; hunting and fishing expeditions, long drives, horseback rides, and moonlight sails upon the bayou, out-of-door luncheons, and visits to neighboring plantations, where perhaps similar parties were gathered.

And there was much fine conversation on all sorts of subjects, and delicious idling, and pleasant gossip, and love-making. Impromptu musicales were gotten up, and dances, and private theatricals ; when the gleam of white necks and arms, the glow of youthful cheeks, the flash of bright eyes, and the entrancing mystery of women's toilets played havoc with the hearts of the men.

There was also the teeming, busy under-life ; as full, as joyous, as important in its way as the life above.

It was slavery, but slavery in its least repulsive aspect. Its evils, whatever they may have been, melt together now into a dim and indiscriminate background, against which only the sweetest, tenderest memories stand out in high relief, — making the hearts of two or three old, bent, black creatures who are lingering their days out there to ache with longing and regret.

It may be only sentiment on the part of these superannuated old crones, — they are women, all of them ; but it is sentiment that throws the beautiful glamour over the childish recollections of us all, and persuades us that the present is barren and matter-of-fact and insipid, compared with the spicy and romantic past.

Behind the gardens, at the back of the house, cluster a hundred negro cabins, gone to ruin; each as empty, as desolate, as a bereaved heart. Their chimneys have tumbled down, their batten shutters have dropped off the hinges, the gates of their tiny enclosures are broken, and the little paths which led to their doors are choked with weeds.

Years ago, these cabins yielded up their inmates to the thrifty village which surrounds the lumber-mills and various factories a mile or so below.

A little to one side, and screened from the mansion by a dense pine grove, stands the plantation sugar-house; and near by is a goodly gathering of stables, sheds, offices, shops, and storehouses. For La Scalla Place was a whole commonwealth within itself.

These buildings speak with mournful eloquence of the dead past. The tools are rusting on the benches, the barrels and buckets have gone to staves, the last vestige of grain has been eaten by vermin.

The grand family carriage — the same in which Beatrice rode up from the landing, thrilling with a thousand new delights and apprehensions — stands in its old accustomed place, curtainless, cushionless, windowless; covered with dust and cobwebs.

One sort of life and growth has gone on; the magnolias have reached a statelier height, the wide-spreading oaks crowning the little green knoll which used to be the picnic ground of the La Scallas have added to their massiveness and strength.

The beautiful Cherokee hedges, with their long, graceful, willowy branches, encroach unforbidden on many a rood of the neglected land. So dense are these hedges that a bird may not burrow through them ; so high that a mounted horseman cannot look over them.

Cutting straight through the plantation, from end to end, is a long, narrow lane with one of these mobile walls upon either hand, its emerald green thickly powdered with large, white-petaled, yellow-stamened blossoms ; the sweetest, loveliest, loneliest drive in the world !

A hedge of this same incomparable shrub surrounds the once famous flower-gardens — now a tangled waste, an almost impenetrable jungle. Though you may still find, if you pick round among the rank growths, a few of the delicate, sweet-scented English violets, whose refined and subtle perfume seems like a tender reminiscence of the dreams, the loves, the *dolce far niente* of bygone days.

Or, here or there, you may pluck a superb red rose, which proudly blooms amid all the desolation, to assert the beauty and the glory of the past.

CHAPTER V.

A SURPRISE awaited Madame La Scalla.

As she alighted from the carriage, a lady of about her own age appeared upon the lower gallery, in slippers too delicate to press the white shelled walk. She advanced no farther than the steps, and stood smiling and fluttering her lace-trimmed handkerchief with great animation.

She was followed by a young girl, a little taller than Evalina, who flew down to the carriage, crying : —

" Oh, Auntie Corinne ! are n't you surprised to see us ? "

" Surprised and delighted ! " replied Madame with gracious hospitality.

Helen and Evalina wound their arms about each others' necks and gave vent to little exclamations of delight.

" I never *dreamed* of your being here," said Evalina.

" Of course not," returned Helen, " people do not dream things that are true. We wrote to you, though, but you were not here to get the letter."

Her eyes fell upon Beatrice who had climbed down from the carriage, and stood regarding her with a perplexed, uncertain gaze.

Evalina explained that this was her new little maid,

at which Helen laughed, — unpleasantly Beatrice thought, and her nebulous opinion concerning the young guest crystallized into a sudden bitter antipathy. It was all the more bitter because she saw that Helen was extremely pretty. And one hates a supercilious pretty person much more than a supercilious homely one.

Madame La Scalla had gone on and greeted her cousin with some warmth, — tempered as she usually tempered her affectionate demonstrations.

" I really am glad to see you, Constance," she admitted. " You can't imagine what a doleful time I have had ; I think I should be glad to see anybody ! "

She laughed, and Constance, who had laid a small plump hand upon either shoulder and reached up for a kiss, gave her a little shake.

" The same old Corinne ! " she cried, " spoiling her pretty compliments in her own sweet way."

They went into the house together, and Corinne threw off her things.

Just then a joyous shout from Evalina attracted her attention, and she stepped to the window.

M. La Scalla was riding up the avenue at a gallop, and Evalina was flying to meet him. He threw himself from the saddle as supplely as a man of twenty-five, though he was twice that almost, and clasped his daughter in his arms. Her yellow curls were like sunshine against the blue of his coat.

" How Maurice loves that child ! " exclaimed Mrs. Vincent. " He has just been *aching* to see her, he could hardly speak of her without tears in his eyes."

Madame made no answer. Something came into her face which the keen-eyed Constance had noted before, when this topic was under discussion; not jealousy, but regret and a touch of surprise perhaps, that she herself, with all her personal attractions, had failed to inspire such tenderness on the part of the only man she had ever loved.

He loved her, in a way, — he admired her grace and beauty, and her peculiar intelligence; but the deepest springs of affection in him she could not touch. Maurice, however, was wholly satisfied with his family life, and his family ties. It seemed to him that no man on earth had more to be thankful for than himself, — modestly, sincerely thankful.

Madame La Scalla called her cousin's attention to Beatrice, who was still standing outside on the walk. She was bare-headed, and her rippling hair fell about her face and upon her shoulders.

"*Mon Dieu!* who is she, where did she come from?" exclaimed Mrs. Vincent; and when she was told, she sighed, "Alas! the evils of slavery! to think of as lovely a little creature as that — "

"Excuse me," interrupted Madame, "but you would better save your comments upon our southern institutions for your northern friends, — or for Maurice, he would appreciate them!"

"Oh, yes, I have had some very interesting talks with Cousin Maurice," replied Mrs. Vincent. "It is surprising what ideas he has on the slavery question! Do you know, I am beginning to be quite enlightened on that subject, we talk of little else at home; I mean Aunt Cynthia and I; James does not concern himself about politics very much. Aunt Cynthia, you know, is a terrible abolitionist, reads the *Liberator* and the *Independent.* Of course I always take issue

with her; but I think I see things a little differently
from what I used to. Really, Corinne, when we
were children, you and I, we scarcely looked upon
the slaves as human beings, did we?"

Madame La Scalla did not take time to reply
but hastened to the door to meet and embrace her
husband, to whom Evalina was still fondly clinging.

Mrs. Vincent and Madame La Scalla had the
same family name, Deschamps. They were both
born in New Orleans and had both been educated
in Paris. The former had met and married abroad
Mr. James Vincent, a wealthy banker of New York,
and their home was ostensibly in that city. But
Constance was too cosmopolitan to be able to settle
down contentedly in any particular spot. For the
first few years of their married life they had been, as
her husband phrased it, continually on the wing,
flitting from place to place like birds of passage, —
north in summer, south in winter, — and only halting
at their nominal abode between seasons. He had
finally rebelled. Constance drooped and pined.
After an uncomfortable interlude a compromise was
effected, by which she was able to resume her rov-
ings and he was permitted to remain quietly at
home.

Both he and his house were thriftily looked after
by his Aunt Cynthia. This good woman had so little
respect for her nephew's southern wife that it almost
did violence to her stern New England conscience
even to treat the volatile creole with civility.

But Mrs. Vincent could afford to ignore her hos-
tility, since the presence of so efficient a manager in
her house left her at liberty to " go gallivanting " —

as Aunt Cynthia expressed it — whenever she chose, besides relieving her of domestic responsibilities when she was at home.

Accompanied by her daughter, she made frequent visits to La Scalla Place; inviting herself whenever the fancy seized her, and being invited whenever Madame La Scalla thought her presence might add to the pleasure of other guests, or help to assimilate the various elements she desired to bring together in a house party. For the vivacious Constance was a universal favorite in society.

Comparing her with her more brilliant and beautiful cousin, men said that she was a rest to the intellect rather than a stimulant.

The two women were not devotedly attached to each other, they disagreed continually; but neither of them took any account of their differences, and both prized the tie of blood. Mrs. Vincent thought M. La Scalla adorable, and had an unbounded admiration for Burgoyne, whom she called the " perfect blossom on the topmost bough of the La Scalla tree."

On the other hand, Madame had a great fondness for Helen Vincent, whose pink and white loveliness she could not help contrasting with Evalina's plainness.

A colored woman came in and lighted the candles and stirred the great wood fire into a ruddy blaze. The little party seated themselves in a friendly group around the hearth; and Beatrice, still standing upon the white walk outside, could look in, through the lace-curtained windows, at their pleased, animated faces, and observe the cheerful pantomime of their conversation, though she was too far away to hear what was said.

Evalina was nestled upon a sofa beside her father, with her hand in his, wholly absorbed in watching the expression of his countenance, and listening to the sound of his voice.

Beatrice could not have told why it was that her eyes suddenly filled with tears, and her heart seemed ready to burst.

She was not yet self-conscious enough to contrast her forlorn lot with that of the two happy girls within, who were enjoying, without a thought of its blessedness, the luxury of warmth and light and love !

She turned from the bright fireside scene, but without any bitterness of envy or poignancy of self-pity, and looked about with the alert poise and quick glance of some frightened wild creature seeking cover.

There were a hundred places where she might have hidden herself, — but wherefore? It was herself, or the awakening consciousness of herself, as an identity, as something apart, which startled her. She was beginning to lose the serene confidence of childhood, to feel the instinct of self-protection, and to realize her helplessness. A sense of strangeness and isolation was upon her like that she had experienced in the cathedral at Miss Rosamond's funeral. She seemed not to touch the universe at any point, but to be spinning off into voidness, — that awful sensation one sometimes has in a dream.

The sun had gone down, but there was still the soft pink afterglow in which grass and foliage are greenest, and in which shadows are blackest.

Some clusters of cape jasmine bushes were a-bloom in front of the gallery, and there was not breeze enough to lift and bear away their heavy perfume.

A young moon, as slender as Diana's bow, hung low in the mellow sky, and a resplendent star shone above it. All over the heavens other stars were peeping out more timidly.

The only distinguishable sounds were the loud croakings of frogs somewhere in the neighborhood. There seemed to be a million of them, all doing their best, as conscientiously as a faithful orchestra in the tedious *entr'actes* of a play.

Beatrice did not mind the apparent, almost appalling, nearness of the vocal multitude, or the incredible volume of the chorus, — which included the whole gamut of sound, from the hoarse trombone of the lowest basso to the high, shrill piccolo of the attenuated treble, — except that they intensified her loneliness.

Presently the sight of the wagon far down the avenue, in which sat her grandmother and Calisty — black silhouettes against the fading horizon — almost made her cry out, so great was her relief, so joyful the reconjoining of herself with human kind.

She ran forward to meet them; but the wagon turned into an alley, and disappeared in the dark shrubbery. She paused a few moments that her ear might follow its rumble, and then turned and flew round to the back of the house, but stopped abruptly, and stood panting in the shadow of a syringa bush.

A bright light had dazzled her eyes. It came from the kitchen, a long, low structure connected with the rear of the mansion by a latticed corridor, over which a honeysuckle vine was carelessly trained.

The door stood wide open, showing by the light of a glowing wood-fire three aproned and turbaned negro women leisurely busying themselves about the dinner, which was evidently soon to be served. Enticing odors came from the steaming pots and kettles and from the great oven, when Aunt Riddy, the head cook, opened the door to peep into it.

Very soon the wagon drove up, and the sound of it brought all three women to the door, with fork or spoon or dish-cloth in hand. They nodded, and cried "Howdy!" to Calisty, and looked curiously at old Salome, as she climbed down stiffly, back foremost, having declined Uncle Smiley's proffered assistance.

Calisty also curtly waved the old man aside when he reached up his hands to her.

"G'way, niggeh," she said; "dis chile don't requi' any yo' help out 'n dis yeh buggy."

She raised her arms slightly, as a bird about to soar raises its wings, and with a little spring cleared the hind wheel, and alighted airily but firmly upon the ground.

Uncle Smiley ran off in pretended fright, and the women jeered him with soft yah — yah — yahs!

He came back presently, and dragged from the farther end of the wagon Salome's old chest. One of the women good-naturedly helped him to set it on the porch, — "fo' de present," he explained, "til we sees whar' dey's gwine t' lodge."

The porch, which was almost on a level with the ground, ran the whole length of the kitchen, and was furnished with rough benches and clumsily mended old chairs. It was shaded by China-berry trees, and was the rendezvous of the house servants and their "company," on warm afternoons when they were not at work, or when their work was such as could be carried on there.

Uncle Smiley clambered into the wagon again, and drove off. Calisty entered the arbor-like passage leading from the kitchen to the back hall of the mansion, and Salome was left standing alone, a desolate old figure in a black gown and turban.

Beatrice, with a little cry, darted to her side.

The women, who were still grouped in the porch, uttered surprised ejaculations, and drew near to look at the child. One of them raised her eyes to Salome, and asked respectfully, "Am she relashun o' you'n?"

Salome made no reply, and the woman, who bore the fine name of Cleopatra, concluded she could not hear, and again turned her admiring attention to the child.

"My! she 'm jes' like a li'le white lily," she commented, as Beatrice turned her face upward and regarded her. "What's yo' name, honey?"

The child took her cue from her grandmother and was silent also.

"Fo' de lan' sake!" exclaimed the questioner impatiently, "am bofe o' you-all deef 'n' dumb?"

Aunt Riddy, who had gone back into the kitchen to note the progress of things there, called peremptorily to her assistants, —

"Come 'long in hyeh, Lexy 'n' Cle'patra, 'n' 'ten' t' yo' business, don't be idlin' roun'; dis yeh dinneh all bu'n up!"

A few moments later she herself shuffled over to the door again, in her down-at-the-heel galoches, and said hospitably to the new-comers, " You-all betta' step in hyeh 'n' set by de fi' ; you git yo' def o' col' out dah in de damp.''

The great, warm, capacious kitchen seemed to repeat the invitation, and they went in and seated themselves on an old wooden settee near the fire but out of the way of the cooks, who were beginning to dish up the savory messes and to pass the smoking platters and tureens to the dining-room maids, as they flirted into the kitchen in starched petticoats and smart *tignons*, with a fine superior air.

Beatrice, whose cheeks were reddened by the heat of the fire, watched them drowsily, and listened to their simple joking with a deep sense of comfort, — the relaxation from the strain of a few minutes before.

Presently she and Salome were provided with a luncheon of sweet potatoes and corn-bread, which had been kept hot in the oven ; and after that she drooped over and fell asleep in her grandmother's lap. Salome herself leaned her head against the brick jamb and dozed ; and her face softened into an expression almost as untroubled as the child's.

Both these human creatures were as unknowing and irresponsible respecting their future destiny as the cattle roaming in the fields. Beatrice was of course ignorant of the complicated relations of life, and the laws of custom and society. Salome, though enlightened, had no apprehensions, and indulged in but few speculations concerning the treatment they were likely to receive in this household.

The La Scallas were people of quality, whose manners, and in most cases characters also, were formed upon the royal principle of *noblesse oblige.*

All of them whom she had known had been men and women of patrician dignity, of courteous demeanor and kindly feeling.

Even Miss Rosamond, soured in her last years by suffering and disappointment, had always been humane. In her early life, though haughty enough with her equals, she had been gentle and considerate toward her dependents. Salome had acquired enough respect and affection for her in those days to last through all the subsequent years of trial, and to keep her at her post in the face of glittering temptations. Even now she clung to the memory of her imperious mistress as a loyal wife clings to the memory of a husband who has not always merited her devotion.

Of Maurice La Scalla, as a young man, she had the most agreeable recollections. He had been the standard of comparison among the colored people, who were wont to say, respectively, of other young gentlemen who visited at the La Scalla house in New Orleans, "He's 'mos' 's good 's Marse Maurice;" or, "He cyan't hold a can'le to Marse Maurice."

She had recalled these things vaguely during the long, tedious voyage, and they had softened the gloom, a little, in which her soul was enwrapped.

Now, as she slept, or half-slept, she dreamed of him. And suddenly she opened her eyes and he stood before her!

She started and would have risen, but a slight motion of his hand toward the slumbering child compelled her to keep her seat.

She looked up at him with the smile of other days,

as though in the flood of recollection her youth had momentarily come back to her.

"Lawd, Marse Maurice! is that you?" she exclaimed. "Time's been lettin' you alone, fo' sho'; jes' de same young gen'leman I remembeh twenty yeahs ago!"

M. La Scalla threw back his head and laughed. It was a laugh that was pleasant to hear, as unreserved and merry as a boy's.

The firelight shone full upon him, but Salome's sight was too dim to note the fine lines radiating from the corners of his handsome eyes, or the streaks of silver in the dark locks brushed back from his forehead.

His face was smooth-shaven; it was a face that could bear exposure, — the chin was fine, and the expression of the mouth winsome, but, perhaps, lacking a little in firmness, or in that bull-dog determination to have one's own way which is often flatteringly miscalled firmness. Yet it was not a weak mouth: you would expect the man to achieve his object, — but by patient, persuasive, convincing argument, not by sheer force of will. He had mastered a secret; had learned that it was better, easier, nobler, to rule through the intelligent co-operation of those he governed than by his own might; and he did not think the time wasted which was spent in enlightening the meanest slave.

He had never been a great traveller, like his wife and her cousin Constance; he was a man of quiet tastes and conservative habits, but his thoughts took a wide and rather bold range.

Corinne and Evalina, the latter through the

patient coaching of Miss Speedwell, the governess, spoke the most approved English. But M. La Scalla made little effort in that direction. His southern tongue clung affectionately to its smooth native dialect, and slipped a cog at every rough *r* or jagged *g*.

Most of the La Scallas were tall and elegantly slender, but Maurice was of medium height. He was a trifle stout; but his complexion was colorless, and his physician had repeatedly warned him to avoid undue excitement and violent physical exertion.

It was the custom of the La Scalla household to assemble in the back parlor after dinner, and amuse or entertain themselves as they chose, severally or collectively. In this they were governed by the spirit of the hour, — which might be a quiet brooding spirit, or a lively sociable one. Often an evening passed with scarcely a word spoken. There was unlimited freedom in this respect. No one's sensibilities were so delicate that the others must be on their guard for fear of wounding them. But yet there was harmony and geniality. They were not an intensely self-centred family; they did not grudge either their time or their talents, when it was a question of making themselves agreeable. If any one of them happened to be charged with a particular idea or impulse he might give direction to a whole evening's occupation in which all joined heartily. Thus music often filled the hours from dinner till bed-time; or games, or reading aloud, or conversation, or mere lively frolic.

On this particular evening the ladies, including Helen and Miss Speedwell, had gone directly to the piano to try a new song which Mrs. Vincent had brought from New York. And Evalina had her beloved Papa all to herself.

They sat together upon a deep high-backed sofa, apart from the others, and she described to him the tedious stay in the city, the funeral, the journey home, — and Beatrice !

The last was the most interesting topic of all, and M. La Scalla got an exhaustive and flattering description of the new little piece of property.

Evalina had formulated some plans in her mind relative to her maid, which she laid before him in what very much resembled his own clear and gently persuasive manner. She wished Beatrice to be her very own, and she wanted to have the entire responsibility of her training and bringing up.

M. La Scalla considered the proposition for a moment or two, and then assented to it, — with a proviso.

" Of cou'se, my deah," he said, " this law must be subject to repeal if at any time, or in any way, my little daughta' abuses her authority or her privilege."

" Papa ! you know I never will," she answered reproachfully. " I mean to be *very* good to Beatrice, I like her so much ! "

" I hardly thought you would err on that side," said he, " but you might upon the otheh. You may spoil yo' little maid by oveh-indulgence, so that she may become an annoyance to othehs, — yo' motheh, fo' instance."

He glanced at Madame La Scalla, who was going over her part of the song alone, with Miss Speedwell playing the accompaniment. It was the suggestive glance of one accustomed to conforming to another's ways.

Evalina smiled. "Oh, I know Mamma!" she cried archly. "I shall take care that Beatrice does not trouble her, — or any one else. She shall have a little cot in my dressing-room, and I will keep her quite to myself. I do not intend to have her associate with the other servants; for, really, Papa, she is too nice!"

"Oh!" he returned, lifting his brows quizzically. "And what about old Salome, she is ratheh nice, too, is she not? She was to Cousin Rose jus' what you want this girl to be to you, I infeh. By the way, something has just occu'ed to me," he added. "Do you know that we had a funeral heah while you were away? Old Aunt Nancy is gone at last; she was buried last Sunday."

"Oh, dear, the poor old soul!" exclaimed Evalina, "and I was not here to look after her and see that she had things!"

"She did not need 'things,' my deah, she jus' died quietly, of old age; she was gettin' towa'd ninety, you know."

Evalina was silent. She sat with her hands clasped round her knee, her eyes upon the fire. Presently a little smile, half-humorous and half-tender, touched her face.

"Was she laid out in her patch quilt?"

"I think so," he replied; "she looked fine. She had a new red silk tu'ban on her head. What I was about to say is that Aunt Nancy's cottage is vacant now; none of the servants have been near it since the funeral, except the women who went down undeh

Cosette's protection to put it in ordeh. You don't suppose Salome is too supe'stitious to go into it, do you?"

"I hope not," Evalina answered. "Papa, don't you want to see Salome and Beatrice? Let us go and find them."

She was up and had him by the hand, and he made no demur. One of the dining-room maids had told her Salome and Beatrice were safely housed in the kitchen.

After the brief visit was over Evalina went to hunt up the housekeeper Cosette, and beg her to have the cottage put in readiness for its new occupant.

The little French-woman was taking her tea in her own room alone. Evalina sat down patiently and explained matters to her while she finished the bit of toast she had just browned over the coals at her side, and drained her little china cup. She was always heartily in sympathy with anything that Evalina promulgated ; and her small black eyes sparkled as she listened.

When she had cleared her little table and set the dishes upon a tray to be carried down to the kitchen, she took off her house slippers and put her feet into thick shoes.

"I go right 'way myse'f," she said. "I'm vair' glad ze li'le cottage have 'nother occupan', it seem too bad to let it go to wrack 'n' ruin, lack houses will zat are not lived in. I'm sho' ole Nancy's flowe's need waterin' by zis time. She water'm herse'f ze vair' day she die, I been down dere 'n' see her doin' it."

Evalina sighed. She had a vivid picture before

her mental vision of the little old woman pottering round with her tin pail and dipper, peering at the new buds and carefully scrutinizing the leaves and stocks for vermin.

Cosette, when she was ready, summoned a maid to go along with her and carry some clean bedding. Evalina herself accompanied them.

The moon had disappeared, but the stars were numerous and brilliant enough to light their way, which led down through the flower-gardens.

The dew sparkled on the grass, and the air was filled with the perfume of hundreds of blossoms.

A little gate was set into the hedge at the farther side of the gardens, almost hidden in greenery; and the gateway was arched over with long pendent branches.

A short path running obliquely from the gate led to the cottage, which stood quite by itself in what might be called an annex of the gardens. It was snuggled in amongst the trees and shrubbery as cosily as a bird's nest, and its little portico, running the whole length of the front, was wreathed with climbing roses of many varieties.

Cosette went ahead fearlessly and opened the door, whose simple fastenings were worked with a string.

The maid, "Stasie," followed; shuddering as she crossed the threshold over which a dead body had so recently been borne.

In the starlight the few pieces of furniture had a grewsome and rigid look, as if they too were dead.

But Stasie had brought along in her apron some sticks of fat pine, and she soon had a blaze in the large brick fireplace, which illumined the entire room, and went a long way toward driving out the horrible hobgoblins with which the place was, to her mental apprehension, numerously peopled.

In the farthest corner of the room stood a high bedstead; and who could tell how many unholy spooks were skulking beneath the huge feather-tick and pillows, or practicing their diabolical antics behind the gay calico valance!

The two white persons, who seated themselves unconcernedly before the fire, had no conception of the terrors that shook the frame of the young colored girl as she approached that uncanny corner with her bundle of sheets and blankets.

Everything in the room was incredibly clean. The bare floor, the little square pine table, and the rude cupboard filled with Aunt Nancy's carefully preserved stock of cracked dishes and tumblers, all testified to unnumbered scourings.

Aunt Nancy had once been head cook at the mansion. When she grew too old for that responsible position, this little cottage — formerly the gardener's lodge — had been fitted up for her. And here she had lived for nearly a score of years, — expressing herself to the last in the thrifty ways that had characterized her all her life long. She had cooked her simple meals, and scrubbed and cleaned, and knitted and spun, and tended her flowers and her little patch of ground; and had executed between-whiles her one grand piece of needle-work, her patch quilt, in which she had long ago stipulated that she should be buried. And she had collected such odds and ends, rejected or thrown away by others, as had helped to give to her humble abode an air of comfort and a touch of beauty; or that indefinable something which makes a house, great or small, seem homelike.

Many gay pictures were pinned upon the walls, together with some old letters carefully smoothed out, whose chirography, in blue and violet ink, was both beautiful and mysterious to her. A battered but bright brass candlestick adorned one end of the mantel, and upon the other was a broken china vase still capable of holding flowers, and of making a splendid appearance when its crippled side was next the wall, — as, of course, it always was.

Evalina and Cosette looked about and talked while Stasie made up the bed. Both of them had been fond of old Nancy; but their talk and their thoughts had more concern with the prospective than with the departed mistress.

"She surely will like it," argued Evalina, "it is such a quiet, peaceful place for an old person."

"Yes, if ze ole person been fond of ze quiet 'n' peaceful place!" retorted Cosette with a shrug.

Salome did like it, — at least better than she would have liked anything else on the plantation.

The sight of "Marse" Maurice had broken up the lethargic state into which she had lapsed after the death of her mistress, and she was able to take some little interest in her surroundings.

She had Beatrice with her the first night, and after that she was alone. But she did not mind; Aunt Nancy's ghost did not trouble her. Though possibly that old creature's thrifty spirit may in some occult way have guided her; for very soon she unconsciously slipped into the well-worn grooves of a daily routine as regular as the rising and setting of the sun.

The cottage resumed so much of its former air as to thoroughly deceive old Robespierre, Aunt Nancy's big gray cat. On the night of the wake he had been so terrified at the unusual goings-on that he precipitately fled through the cat-hole in the door and went into hiding for a fortnight.

But a few days after Salome's advent he came reconnoitering with cautious sniffs and plaintive calls; and finally, as if persuaded that the frightful orgies which had driven him forth into the darkness were but the foolish chimera of a dream, and that there had really been no change, he stole tentatively in and took his accustomed place on the hearth.

However, Robespierre might have observed a great many changes if he had not been an uncommonly stupid cat, dozing in his chosen corner all day long. Salome had opened her chest and brought out her few belongings; a little clock which she set upon the mantel, a few books, a framed picture of Miss Rosamond, a looking-glass, — the same that had hung on her kitchen wall in New Orleans, — and two musical instruments, a banjo and a mandolin.

She was sadly out of practice and could not make much music upon either of them; but the little thrumming she was able to do afforded relief to her feelings sometimes as she sat by her lonely fireside and recalled the gay and the sorrowful scenes of the past.

Robespierre, astonished at first and resentful at having his personal comfort ignored, — as the overindulged always are, — grew presently to like the tuneful sounds, and to exhibit signs of pleasure and animation whenever one or other of the instruments was brought out.

All mankind like an audience ; and it was surprising how Salome's stiff old fingers limbered up the moment the cat began to take an interest in her performance. She played livelier airs, and kept time with her foot, and quite lost herself in the enthusiasm his flattering attention inspired.

CHAPTER VI.

BEATRICE adapted herself to the new life with the happy facility of pliant childhood. She was almost constantly in Evalina's presence except during the latter's school hours, when she was permitted to visit her grandmother, or amuse herself in the gardens, or take little strolls beyond the immediate premises of the mansion.

Salome did not constrain her in any way; she was free to flit in and out as she liked, and to occupy herself as suited the whim of the moment, — a privilege of which she availed herself with careless abandon, singing, dancing, chattering about a hundred different things that interested her; plucking fresh flowers for the china vase on the mantel, — which still kept up appearances by hiding its injuries from the public eye, as all elegant natures must; arranging the humble furniture in new ways, cultivating Robespierre's surly acquaintance, and practicing little self-taught airs on the old Spanish mandolin; and in all filling the old woman's heart with unspeakable joy and unspeakable sadness. In herself, in her pretty, gay, debonair ways, she was the brightest bit of sunshine that had ever come into Salome's life. But who could foretell the fate of a slave-child! The possibilities were all of the darkest.

Beatrice loved to wander alone in the narrow lanes, whose lovely green walls, full of sweetness and bloom, divided the plantation into vast fields, now alive with busy workers. And she had an especial fondness for the woods, in which she sought out many a deep secret place, safe from the eyes of hunters and choppers.

This larger, freer life had its inevitable effect upon her. In the satisfying fullness of the present she grew less speculative about the future, less silent and abstracted though not less thoughtful. She took note of all about her, and there was scarcely a live thing on the plantation, except the servants, with whom she did not quickly establish friendly relations.

Two blood-hounds belonging to Burgoyne were chained in the back-yard, — enormous creatures supposed to be hostile toward every one save their master, who had petted and trained them from their early puppyhood, and Big Jake, whose business it was to feed and exercise them in Burgoyne's absence.

Helen and Evalina shuddered at the mere sight of the gigantic brutes, with their red mouths, their panting sides and uneasy movements. But Beatrice felt only admiration for their beauty and sagacity, their great strength and incredible speed. She was entirely without fear respecting animals, but diplomatic in her advances to them, whether they were disposed to be ferocious or were simply shy. She cautiously ingratiated herself with Fleet and Prospero, as Burgoyne had named his pets, and began experimenting with their dog intellects, and by patient and painstaking application to the task she succeeded in carrying their education to a point just short of speech. It was an exciting occupation, one that gave her an exultant sense of power and mastery. She delighted in their attentiveness and quickness of apprehension, and in their boundless affection, which they soon began to express in wild demonstrations of pleasure whenever she appeared.

The dogs had considerable liberty of chain, and she loved to frolic with them, and twine garlands round their brass collars and parry the rough caresses of their great paws. Sometimes she accompanied Jake in his rambles with them over the fields.

She admired Jake somewhat as she did the dogs, — for his massive strength, and for a vein of kindliness and intelligent appreciation running through his rough nature.

She was quite as fond of the horses as of the dogs, especially the fine thoroughbreds that were brought prancing and caracoling from the stables every pleasant morning, for Madame La Scalla and her husband, and sometimes Mrs. Vincent and Helen, to ride.

Her favorite of them all was Madame's magnificent chestnut, Ilderim, whose steps were as daintily firm as the step of a high-bred lady, whose eyes were brilliant but soft, and whose flowing mane and tail were like spun gold in the sun. It filled her with exquisite delight to be lifted and swung into the saddle now and then by the strong-armed Jake, and to feel the motion of the beautiful, powerful animal under her.

She stole into the stable sometimes and fed Ilderim a bunch of sweet-grass or a stick of sugar-cane, — young and tender growths pulled up in the fence corners, — and smoothed his satiny flank with her little hand; attentions for which he returned unmistakable and hearty thanks.

Evalina was timid about riding, but she had a pair of 'Cajan ponies which she was not afraid to drive, — though they were far less intelligent and reliable than the princely Ilderim. Formerly she had Miss Speedwell or Cosette to accompany her, but now she took Beatrice, and gave her lessons in the technique of driving.

But Beatrice's introduction to Nature's dumb nobility did not lead her to forsake or ignore her humbler acquaintances, — the tiny things that carried on the busy operations of their transient life among the bushes, or under the leaves, or in the grass. She sought for them in the gardens, and looked about in the lanes and meadows to find their abodes. The sprightly little denizens of the wood were the most elusive. At first she could not get more than a flashing glimpse of them, for at the slightest sound, no more than the crackling of a dried twig under her foot, they were up and away with whisk of tail or whir of wing.

It was not until she had learned, like Thoreau, to steal quietly into their haunts, and sit so still that the shy creatures might mistake her for a bit of the dim wilderness, that she got to know anything about the private life of a squirrel, a rabbit, or any of the cunning dwellers of the solitudes.

Nothing afforded her greater felicity than to slip into a thicket and spy upon the love-makings and family quarrels and nest-building operations of the charming under-world; or to have a coy songster alight upon a pendulous bough not three feet away and rehearse its brilliant solo in happy unconsciousness.

Multitudes of birds nested in the groves about the mansion, and Beatrice was soon familiar with every species, recognizing them both by their voices and their plumage. A great intimacy sprang up between herself and a pair of mocking-birds who built their annual home in a bunchy orange-tree near the house. She could imitate their notes perfectly, and the sociable little fellows appeared to accept her as one of their kind. They made no secret of the location of their nest with her; and sometimes, after many tentative approaches and quick little movements and twitterings, and confidential whisperings between themselves, one or the other of them would hop down and snatch a morsel of food from her hand.

Helen Vincent happened to witness this performance one morning, and as the bird flew away with its booty, she came running up and exclaimed, —

" How do you ever manage to do that, Beatrice? It's simply wonderful; I cannot get within gunshot of a bird."

Beatrice looked at her with a frown and did not reply. The presence of this beautiful girl at La Scalla Place was the only cloud in her sky.

" Say, Beatrice, I would like to ask a favor of you," Helen went on insinuatingly. " I wish very much to take one or two of these mocking-birds home with me. Will you catch them for me? I know you can, you could have caught that one just now."

She waited a moment, and then repeated her request still more persuasively, thinking the child's silence was only due to bashfulness.

But Beatrice, with a storm of indignant surprise gathering in her dark eyes, startled her with an explosive " No ! " and added, as if launching an overwhelming argument against the proposed outrage, " They 's got li'le young ones in the'r nes'."

" Oh, have they ? " said Helen.   " Well, then," with a derisive laugh, " you need n't mind.   I 'll take the young ones ; that will be better.   Thank you for the information ! "

She swept the little bird champion a mocking courtesy, and started off to look for the nest, which there was no great difficulty in finding, for the father-bird was proclaiming his domestic happiness from the topmost bough of the orange-tree.

Beatrice stood and watched her for a moment, her whole body tense with rage, and her soul filled with the anguish of helplessness and that white heat of feeling out of which inspiration bursts like lightning from a black sky.   A sudden fierce resolve kindled her eyes, and chiselled a new and dangerous expression on her childish features.   She turned and flew round to the back-yard, as if equipped with Mercury's wingéd heels, and quickly unfastening Prospero's chain, since he was nearest to her, she laid her hand firmly upon his collar and led him swiftly back to the scene of the proposed robbery.

Helen had discovered the nest, and was on tiptoe, reaching up and parting the branches ready to lay hold of it, when she caught sight of the approaching pair.

She gave a terrified shriek, and letting go the branches darted out from under the tree.

Instantly the dog leaped forward, bristling with

ferocious instinct, and opened his great jaws for the thin flounces streaming out behind the flying girl. But a sharp command from Beatrice brought him reluctantly back to her side, quivering with excitement and eagerness and beating the air with his tail.

Helen escaped into the house, and Beatrice, well satisfied with the result of her prompt action, convoyed Prospero back to his complaining mate.

The lower rooms were vacant, and Helen ran upstairs and betook herself, white and trembling and almost in hysterics, to her mother's room. Mrs Vincent listened to her story, brokenly told between sobs and shivers, with astonished and wrathful eyes. As soon as she had comforted her a little and persuaded her to lie down upon the couch, she rushed off in great excitement to relate the tragic occurrence to Madame La Scalla, who, to her indignant surprise, did not appear to be moved by it.

Madame was lounging in her dressing-room, absorbed in George Sand's latest novel, and could not immediately bring herself to take much interest in an unpleasant actual happening, particularly as no damage had been done. "Really, Constance," she said, with a frown on her brow which her lips tried to apologize for with a faint smile, "I believe we have always been too apprehensive about those dogs. The fact is, they cannot be so very dangerous, else why do they not molest Beatrice herself? She plays with them as if they were a pair of harmless kittens."

"She is not like anybody else," retorted Constance ; "she seems to have a kinship with all the brute creation."

"Well, at least she has perfect mastery of the

7

dogs," said Madame; "and I presume she only meant to frighten Helen to prevent her from taking the birds. Beatrice is very fond of the birds."

"Well, simply to be frightened like that is bad enough," complained Constance, and turned to leave the room. "My poor Helen's nervous system has received such a shock as she is likely not to recover from very soon."

Madame threw down her book, and sprang up.

"Oh," she exclaimed, "the dear child! Is there anything I can do for her?"

"No," said Constance shortly; "I have done what was necessary. All there is for you to do is to see that that little heathen receives the punishment she deserves. To think of the impudence of it, leaving out the question of danger! Corinne, do you know what your father, or mine, would have done in such a case as this?"

Madame shrugged her shoulders.

"There is a different *régime* at La Scalla Place," she said; and passing out of the room, she swept down the long corridor ahead of her cousin, who bustled after her with short, quick steps, and entered Helen's room.

The young girl, still presenting signs of the recent rencounter, sat by the window examining her delicate hands. She looked up with a rueful smile as the two women approached.

"I jerked my hands out of the tree," she explained, "and scratched them on the horrid thorns; I had n't time to be particular!"

"You poor, frightened child!" said Madame, bending over and kissing her, and inspecting the ugly wounds. "Why, how dreadful! Your Mama did not tell me you were hurt. Cosette must bring you something to put on these places."

She heard the story all over again from Helen's lips, this time with more feeling, as Mrs. Vincent was gratified to see, and with some severity of judgment respecting Beatrice's conduct. Then she went out and sent for Cosette, and hastened on to the school-room.

Evalina, who was diligently studying her lessons, looked up in pleased surprise at the unusual honor of a visit from her mother, but turned pale and let her books slide to the floor as the object of the visit was disclosed to her. Her lips had barely fashioned the question, "What are you going to do to Beatrice, Mama?" when she burst into tears.

"I do not know," replied Madame, seating herself in a temporary attitude on the edge of a chair; "don't cry, my dear! What would you suggest? It is really a pretty serious matter, looked at from all points. The most important thing, perhaps, is the question of discipline."

"I — I would take the punishment in her place if I could," sobbed Evalina, "for I'm sure she did not know, she did not mean — "

She suddenly took her handkerchief from her wet eyes, and said eagerly, "Mama, you know I am responsible for Beatrice."

"Yes, I remember there was some such absurd arrangement between your father and you," returned Madame. She rose and her eyes swept the room with a sort of alien glance, — she hated the sight of maps and slates and text-books. "Perhaps we should better leave this matter to your father; he usually finds a way out of such difficulties."

Evalina's heart leaped with joy. She raised her head and smiled with quick thankfulness through her tears.

Madame stooped and kissed her.

"I fear you compliment your father's judgment at the expense of your mother's," she said with a laugh, and before Evalina could frame the proper sort of answer she glided from the room. Ordinarily her manner was languid and sinuous; but she had the art of moving swiftly without seeming to, — the very consummation of grace.

M. La Scalla was out somewhere on the plantation and returned late in the afternoon. He was not apprised of the unfortunate affair until dinner was over and all were assembled in the back parlor, with no servants about.

He had observed that Evalina's eyes were red, and that she only made a pretense of eating.

When the story was told to him — with the bitter accent of prejudice, for Mrs. Vincent was the narrator — Evalina winced painfully, and watched his face with an expression that touched his heart.

"Well," said he, "I should not have thought Beatrice was such a little tempest! You were fo'tunate, Helen, in getting away from the brute."

"She could not have gotten away from him," said Mrs. Vincent, "if the little savage had not seen fit to call the dog back, — and it's a wonder she did, for she seems to have a particular antipathy to Helen. She's a dangerous child, and if she belonged to me I'd either sell her or put her to work in the cotton fields."

Evalina shuddered, and looked anxiously at her father.

"As to that," said he, "Evalina mus' be the one to decide; Beatrice is her prope'ty." He turned to Evalina and said kindly, "You know, my deah, that you undehtook the entire responsibility of yo' little maid. And I should not be treating you fai'ly if I took away yo' authority the firs' time it is put to the test. You shall deal with the offenda accordin' to yo' bes' judgment. And you must also make what amends you can to yo' Cousin Helen."

"All the amends I care for," laughed Helen, "is to have the birds."

"And Beatrice ought to be made to get them for you," put in her mother, "if only to give an additional sting to her punishment."

"That is hardly a Christian sentiment, my dear Constance," said Madame, with her light ironical laugh. "Only barbarians punish an enemy through his finest feelings, — and Beatrice can have no finer feeling than her tender solicitude for the helpless little birds."

Mrs. Vincent's wrath at the seeming indifference of her friends bubbled almost to the surface, but she kept it down until she and Helen were safe in their own apartments, and then it broke forth.

"The idea of letting a child like Evalina decide about a matter which really involves life and death! for there is no knowing what that little wretch will do next," she cried, throwing herself into a chair. But what can one say to a man like Maurice La Scalla? These quiet, calm people, especially if they get sentimental notions into their heads, are stubborn

beyond everything.   For my part, I'd rather deal
with a fiery temper than a mild one, — you can
mould a hot crow-bar but you can't bend a cold
bodkin !   One would think," she went on scornfully,
"that Corinne would have a word to say in a matter
of this kind, but I have noticed that when Maurice
puts his gentle foot down she never peeps."

"Well, Mama, isn't that the better way?" ventured
Helen.

"It isn't my way, — as your father learned some
years ago," returned Mrs. Vincent.

She sat a few moments, steeped in angry medita-
tion, winking rapidly and tapping the carpet with the
toe of her pretty shoe.

"I have a good mind to pack the trunks and
leave," she said finally, as the outcome of her
cogitations.

"Oh, no, Mama !" protested Helen.   "We want
to see Burgoyne, and you know he'll be here in a few
days now."

"That is true," sighed her mother, "I don't like
to go without seeing Burgoyne.   Well, we'll wait
and see how Miss Evalina settles this dog business.
I shall not stay at the risk of our lives."

Evalina settled it in this wise : Beatrice was made a
sort of prisoner on parole.   Certain limits were prescribed for her, beyond which she must not go without special permission during the remainder of the
Vincents' stay.

This severe sentence was prefaced by a thought-
fully prepared and tearful little lecture on Evalina's
part, which — except that Beatrice was moved by the
distress of her young mistress, even to the point of

begging her not to cry, and earnestly assuring her
that she should not very much mind the restriction
put upon her — had but little effect.

The child had been used to looking at things from
the purely natural and immediate standpoint, and
knew nothing about conventional standards.

" Mis' Helen was go'n' to steal the li'le birds 'way
f'om the'r nes'," she eagerly explained.

" Yes, I know," said Evalina, " and I do not think
that was right, though people do such things very
often and nobody minds, or at least nothing is said
about it. It is not a crime to steal or hurt animals,
you know. It is only when you do harm to
people that you are considered wicked and must be
punished."

Beatrice regarded her with a puzzled gaze. Clearly
she could not comprehend the subtleties of statutory
law.

" Do you know, Beatrice," Evalina added im-
pressively, " that if Prospero had killed Miss Helen
you would be called a *murderer* ? "

It was a horrible word and it made her flesh creep
to utter it, but she felt that strong terms were needed
to arouse the child's dormant conscience.

" But I did n' let Prospero kill her," said Beatrice,
" I made him come back when she stopped tryin' to
get the li'le birds. He jus' scared her."

" Well, suppose you could not have made him
come back? Dogs do not always mind."

" Oh, Fleet and Prospero always mind," returned
Beatrice with perfect assurance.

They had much further talk about the matter,
which Evalina faithfully reported to her father ; and

it was settled between them that the only thing to be done was to treat the unregenerate maid as a dangerous person until she should learn to discriminate between the rights of animals and those of men.

Beatrice had the freedom of her mistress' suite of rooms, including the school-room, and of the upper galleries, and also of Cosette's apartments. She was a great favorite with the house-keeper, at whose little table she took her meals, — at first after Cosette had finished ; but that was an unsociable arrangement, and the little Frenchwoman, who had no race prejudice, soon changed it and had the child sit down with herself, and was vastly entertained by her quaint gossip about the world of thought and feeling and of intimacy with humble things, in which she lived. For though usually reserved and self-contained, Beatrice would sometimes pour herself out with extraordinary volubility under the genial influence of her elderly companion's friendly interest and enthusiastic appreciation. But she never made the mistake of unveiling this delicate side of her nature to unsympathetic eyes, or an obtuse understanding.

Much of Beatrice's time was spent in the school-room where she was allowed to busy herself with books and a slate and pencil. The latter she particularly delighted in. She had a great facility for drawing pictures, and made quite wonderful birds and cats and horses, — so wonderful that Evalina often exhibited them to other members of the household with much pride.

Books she cared less about, particularly the arithmetic and speller. But very soon she began to take an interest in Evalina's lessons, listening to the recitations, and to Miss Speedwell's careful elucidation of obscure points, with the closest attention. Now and then, in entire self-forgetfulness, she broke out with a question or a comment so pertinent and keen as quite to startle the governess, who, however, always returned a kind and encouraging answer.

Miss Speedwell, who was an Englishwoman, regarded slavery as an abomination, but she never offered a remonstrance or even expressed an opinion upon the subject in that southern environment. Her good taste would have withheld her from such a violation of good form if her timidity had not. Her sympathy with the oppressed race, which was very great, was shown only in furtive kindnesses to those members of it with whom she came in contact.

She need not, however, have observed so much caution, since M. La Scalla himself made no secret of his dislike for the system, and often expressed the hope that it might some day be uprooted from the land.

Miss Speedwell was obliged to confess to herself, and in her letters to her friends in Devonshire, that her prejudice had been considerably modified by her association with the La Scalla household. Though, as an offset to this admission, she always added that the principle and the awful possibilities of the institution could not be gotten over by simply citing the customs of this one intelligent and charming family.

Evalina had already begun to teach her charge the rudiments of the English tongue, and, prompted by the lucid illustrations, Beatrice, whenever called upon, read glibly, in the high staccato of those times, the succinct primer legends about A Cat, The Hen, and other familiar objects.

Her imitative faculties were perfect, and her senses quick to seize upon any facts presented to them. But she was not yet ready to grapple with abstractions. The alphabet was tiresome to her, figures were more tiresome still, and prayers and sermons were incomprehensible. She was generally fond of hymns and psalms, some sense of poetry in her responded to their rhythm and mystery; but her imagination was so lively and her sensibilities so delicate, that to hear Miss Speedwell naïvely sing, —

> " There is a fountain filled with blood,
>
> .   .   .   .   .
>
> And sinners plunged beneath that flood,"

always made her shiver and turn pale with nausea. It was entirely too figurative for her childish apprehension, and altogether frightful.

She had been taught the Apostles' Creed, and liked the majestic roll of the awe-inspiring words, especially when she attended catechism at St. Martinsville with Evalina and heard the children repeat them in chorus, led by the venerable priest.

Miss Speedwell threw out the apparently casual remark one morning, " What a fine scholar Beatrice would make if — if she were not a colored child ! "

" What difference does it make about her being colored ; that does not affect her brain, does it ? " asked Evalina with a smile. " Would you object to teaching her, if Papa would consent? — you English and French people do not feel as we Americans do about the negroes."

" Oh, no, I should have no objections to teaching her," replied the sly governess, who had been revolving the matter in her mind for days. " I really think it would make our school more interesting to have another pupil."

" Especially when the other one is so very bright," laughed Evalina.

She carried the proposition to her father and was not surprised when he assented to it. It was quite in keeping with M. La Scalla's own views. He believed, and earnestly advocated, that some system for the general education of the slaves ought to be instituted ; that they should receive a money compensation for their labor, should be taught thrift, self-respect, and self-reliance, and should eventually be made free.

His wife laughed at him, called him visionary and a dreamer. She could not conceive of such a change in the domestic economy of the South as the abolishment of slavery, or she thought of it only as one thinks of the final destruction of the universe, the remotest of all contingencies. Things to which we have always been accustomed seem rooted in the eternal rock.

Madame La Scalla had a theory which she loved to set up against the convictions of her husband, — often for the sake of mere dilettant argument, but which, if the whim seized her, she might urge to the bitter end. She argued that slavery must and would continue to exist, co-extensive with American civilization ; it was preposterous to conceive of anything different. And upon this assumption she built a tolerably logical superstructure, and reasoned so eloquently as to convince herself at least, and sometimes others, that she was expounding the fixed principles of her faith, instead of elaborating in a most graceful and womanly way a mere ephemeral sentiment.

"When one's liberty," she asserted warmly, "is circumscribed by unalterable conditions, education, which enlarges one's comprehension of life and the world, and increases the capacity for enjoyment, is a cruel thing. It is like stimulating a man's appetite when there is no possibility of his being able to gratify it."

Had the subject of Beatrice's education been broached at a time when she happened to be indulging in one of these periodical pseudo-philanthropic heats, she might have embarrassed matters by interfering, for she was not always the yielding wife her cousin Constance had represented her to be.

But the time, fortunately, was opportune.

The severity of Mrs. Vincent's judgment upon the child's impulsive misdemeanor had caused a slight leaning in the opposite direction on Madame's part. It was not a moral but a constitutional leaning; she was always rather more prone to be irritated than conciliated. And besides, she was fond of Beatrice, in a way. She loved to feast her beauty-loving eyes on the child's exquisite face and form. Almost every day she sent for her to come and spend an hour or two in her dressing-room; and gave her albums and illustrated magazines to amuse herself with, or set her to doing a bit of simple needle-work, or to piling up books and papers or dusting the furniture.

Evalina's well-trained maid was very neat and thorough and industrious in all this, except perhaps the needle-work, which was distasteful to her.

Madame usually reclined in an easy-chair with a novel, or a piece of embroidery which she was not very diligent about, and regarded her with somewhat of the same deep and contemplative satisfaction with which she herself was wont to regard the fussy birds and squirrels when they were not cognizant of her presence.

She was such an unconscious, ingenuous, interesting little body, and had such a firm delicious way of doing things, not quite like other people, that it was a pleasure simply to follow the motions of her active feet and busy hands.

Beatrice no longer stood in awe of Madame La Scalla, as she had done on first seeing her, but she did not cease to have a profound admiration for her queenly figure, and fine imperious manner, — which with respect to her small self was touched with a capricious kindness. She thrilled under the touch of Madame's soft white hand, and delighted in the delicate perfume of her garments, and all the elegancies of her dress and belongings, and she loved the sound of her peculiar, drawling voice.

Perhaps it was the child's frank adoration which made her company so agreeable, for Madame La Scalla, like many beautiful women, was fond of the incense of praise, no matter how humble the censer.

M. La Scalla came into the room one day just as Beatrice was leaving, and his wife turned her face toward him with a smile, and remarked, " It was a fortunate thing that I happened to go down to New Orleans, was n't it, dear? "

"Well, I do not know," he replied, seating himself upon the sofa, and regarding her with an unconvinced air, "it remains to be seen."

"You do not know?" she echoed. "What do you mean, — did I not tell you that Cousin Rose would have freed that child if I had not been there to interfere?"

"That is the point," said he; "that is why I said I did not know. If you had not inte'fered, and Rose had carried out her project, we should not have so much to anseh fo'."

Madame elevated her chin slightly and closed her lips, with an air of putting up the bars before her understanding, a proceeding which always provokes the opposing party to force the issue a little harder.

"Accordin' to yo' showing, my deah," her husband continued, "we might jus' as well have gone out and kidnapped a free child."

"Maurice!"

He made a slight deprecatory gesture.

"I do not say that it is not all the betta' fo' the child," he explained, "but that it is a great responsibility fo' us. Beatrice is the one to be consid'ed chiefly, not ourselves. So, when you ask me if it is not fo'tunate that you went oveh to New Orleans and secu'ed her, I am fo'ced to anseh from her standpoint. And I say, I do not know. She is an exceptional child. Miss Speedwell tells me her unde'standing is something ma'velous. Nothing is plainer than that she ought not to be a slave. Nature has marked her fo' a higher place."

"I hope you are not indulging in the fantastical notion of freeing her?" demanded Corinne, and added in a tone which seemed to accuse him of an injustice to her motive, " It was really out of consideration for the child herself, and the old woman, that I first thought of interposing."

" Yes, yes, I know, I remembeh ! " he answered quickly, making amends. " Yo' intentions were excellent, my deah. And now we mus' try to justify yo' action in the matta' by looking afteh the consequences of it."

He sighed and ran his fingers through his hair. Corinne's eyes were upon him, but he was not looking at her.

" How gray you are getting, Maurice," she said, with a touch of regretful tenderness, noting not only the silvered locks he had brushed back from his temples, but the extreme pallor of his forehead. The rest of his face was a deep tan, for he spent a large part of the time out of doors looking after his crops and workmen.

" I do not know what to do," he said, not heeding her remark. " This child ought to have her chance, the chance which every one with brain and talents such as she possesses is entitled to."

He was silent for a time, and by and by he said, as if interrupting a train of thought which could lead to no satisfactory conclusion, " It is a vexatious question. We have a good many men and women on this plantation who ought to be free, by right of their unquestionable ability to take their place in the world and fight their own battles. And then, there are othe's too old, or too stupid, or too dependent to shift fo' themselves. It would be a cowardly and cruel act to set these latter adrift."

Corinne, who had always a haunting fear that Maurice might some day take it into his head to make a clean sweep of the slave business so far as his own personal possessions were concerned, gave a sigh of relief.

"Yes," she returned, with a laugh, "those Northern abolitionists do not know, or do not take into account, all the complications of the problem they are so eager to tackle, — complications which affect the slaves quite as much as they do us."

"But in the case of this one particular child," said Maurice, "our duty, it seems to me, is clear. We, La Scallas, owe her not only her freedom, but everything else to which the young of our own flesh and blood are entitled."

"The law scarcely interprets our obligation so broadly," said Corinne drily.

"There is a law above law," he returned.

"Well, even that does not provide a remedy for the greatest of her misfortunes. Free the child if you will, educate her, elevate her; with every step of her advance she will become a more distinct target for poisoned arrows, and more susceptible to their sting."

CHAPTER VII.

A N unusual event of any consequence, occurring in an isolated country mansion in the quiet times preceding the great war, produced a commotion whose concentric circles vibrated to the farthest limits of the plantation. Especially might this be expected to happen at the home-coming of a young collegiate at the close of his school year.

It was known one morning at the breakfast table that Burgoyne would arrive that day. The news had come in a roundabout way, for Burgoyne had not been able to give the exact date of his return in his last letter.

M. Condé, at St. Martinsville, had been notified the evening before, by a stage-coach passenger, that his young friend was on board the " Arlington," due the following day, and had kept himself awake half the night in order to get his indolent, irresponsible factotum, Ebenezer, off for La Scalla Place in good season with the message. The result of his faithful vigil was that Ebenezer, astride the only beast he was ever permitted to mount, whose patrician name of Bonaparte he had contemptuously reduced to " Bony," for obvious reasons, was faring along on his way with a remnant of his breakfast in his hands before the first blush of dawn.

8

It was a six-mile trip; but as Bonaparte had little flesh to carry, either of his own or the rider's, and as they met no one at that early hour with whom Ebenezer could squander time, which he was always prone to do, they covered the distance with reasonable despatch.

A single incident broke the monotony of the ride. Despite his general worthlessness, Ebenezer enjoyed to some extent the confidence of his master, and he was informed of the object of his matutinal jaunt. When he was nearing the journey's end, he espied through a fringe of trees the overseer of La Scalla Place making ready to cross the *coulée* which cut through one end of the plantation; and unable to forego the satisfaction of communicating with that high functionary, and incidentally availing himself of the prestige which attaches to the trusted courier, he drew up as near to the *coulée* as he could get, for the swampy ground and thick jungle of palms, and called out his interesting news.

The overseer, though glad enough of the information, and of being the first to receive it, crushed the unlucky messenger with the rude advice to " push on and deliver his cargo at headquarters instead of peddling it out along the way." " Crushed " is the right word, for poor Ebenezer had a spirit as delicate as a mushroom, — a persevering spirit that reared itself anon from the mellow soil of his gentle simplicity, to be reduced to impalpability by any careless foot that chose to tread upon it.

A bright black boy who accompanied the overseer on his rounds from field to field, holding himself ready — as is often the sorry office of boys — for any service that might be required of him, found means unbeknown to his master to spread the tidings all over the plantation before the sun was in the zenith; causing the whole air to palpitate with a pleasant excitement, — for which, after all, there was no substantial foundation. Burgoyne would not scatter golden guineas among his father's slaves, nor would his coming change the routine of their laborious, monotonous lives. But the young heir of the La Scallas had the gift of popularity. He was one of the royal scions of Nature born to receive the generous, free-will homage of the multitudes, — a homage that depends not so much upon what a person does as upon what he is. He stood for ideals. But to see him crossing the fields with his dogs, or dashing along the lanes on his beautiful black mare, Dauphine, was an agreeable event worthy of remembrance. It was as if one beheld, not merely a young man engaged in exhilarating pastime, but Young-Manhood itself, haloed by all the bright possibilities of glorious, free, untrammelled life.

The slaves, great and small, rejoiced in him; though the joy cast an indefinable shadow upon their own hearts, like the shadow, tender, and glad, and sad, which falls upon the heart of age when radiant youth passes by.

Though it was broad day, and the mists were rolled into soft white clouds and lifted a little above the landscape, and the birds were piping their sweet early songs in the dewy trees, there was no stir at the mansion as Bonaparte ambled up the avenue.

But at sound of hoofs on the hard shelled drive, Big Jake came out of the stable door, curry-comb in hand, and peered down through the files of magnolias. He recognized both horse and rider at a glance, — for they made frequent appearances at La Scalla Place, — and called out, " Hi, Eb ! wah you boun' fuh ? Mus' be somebody daid, or some kine urgen' business transpiah, t' see you canterin' oveh hyeh s' early in de mawn'n' ! Hope 't ain' Marse Condé? He 's mighty fine man, he make plenty fine gif's roun' hyeh."

" Nobody ain' daid," replied Ebenezer, reining up in the stable yard and regarding Jake with a passive, uncommunicative gaze.

" I 's glad t' hyeah that," said Jake, and paused. After an interval of inquisitive silence, which elicited no response, he remarked with cold courtesy, " Ain' you gwine t' 'light? "

Ebenezer, whose mind worked as slowly as his body, except when it involuntarily let loose some guileless thought, sat still and considered. He liked company as a rule, but was not fond of Jake's, and he balanced his general liking for society with this particular dislike, and was undecided.

Jake eyed his skeleton steed with a fine air of connoisseurship, and asked with cruel levity, " When you gwine t' plaster dat hoss, Eb? I see you got de lath on."

Ebenezer grinned helplessly. At best he had but the modicum of dignity which attaches to the shiftless ; mounted upon old Bony his self-respect shrank to the smallest proportions. Jake's heartless banter hit the tenderest spot in his composition, the susceptibility to ridicule, and made him wince. He slid out of the saddle with unwonted alacrity and, leaving the despised beast to take care of himself, advanced toward the stable door, hoping by the value of his news to indemnify himself for the humiliation put upon him.

Jake had stepped inside the stable and resumed his morning task with pretended indifference as to the object of Ebenezer's visit, — the quickest way, he believed, to precipitate the information.

" I 's got a letter hyeh, f'om Marse Condé," Ebenezer hastened to say, fumbling in his pockets and bringing the missive to light.

Jake dropped the curry-comb, and wiping his hands on his trowser-leg, reached for it.

" Impo'tant?" he asked, with a grave manifestation of interest.

The word seemed to impart somewhat of its quality to Ebenezer's limp manner. He straightened himself up, until his centre of support struck the true anatomical axis, and replied, "I espec', suh, dat letter gwine t' tell you-all, leas'wise yo' marse 'n' yo' mis' dat yo' young Marse Burgoyne 'rive home dis evenin'."

" Dat so?" said Jake. He looked at the yellow envelope, which he held gingerly by one corner, and suddenly his black face expanded with a generous smile. "Golly! I 's pow'ful glad you tol' me, Eb'neza, it gimme de chaynce t' polish up Marse Burgoyne's mar' a li'le mo'n common."

Ebenezer edged inside the stable door.

" Don't ainy 'em look lack dey requi' polishin'," he remarked, but not with the intention of being complimentary. He spoke sadly, as if mentally contrasting the sleek fat creatures, who at sound of his strange voice turned their intelligent eyes toward him inquiringly, with his own scrawny beast.

His humble spirit could barely support the gaze of these four-footed aristocrats, and he was almost on the point of taking off his hat to them when his attention was diverted by an angry exclamation from Jake.

Bonaparte, accustomed to relying chiefly upon himself in the matter of food and drink, had taken advantage of his liberty and wandered off on what proved to be a successful foraging expedition. He had found a small door ajar in one of the out-buildings and had his nose deep in a feed-bin. Ebenezer's heart sank.

"Git out'n dar, y' ole stack o' bones!" shouted Jake, running toward the thief and shying a piece of pine-board at his thin flank.

"Hyeh, Jake, don't scar' 'im 'way," besought Ebenezer, "I 's got t' be movin'."

He made haste to capture the animal, who had got his foot entangled in the halter-strap, but led him beyond the range of Jake's contemptuous gaze before mounting him, — complaining bitterly the while, and laying the blame of his self-disgust and all his other woes upon the luckless but not depressed Bony.

Bony, in fact, had no susceptibilities; he was tough both in his feelings and in his hide. Even now, upon the heels of his ungracious rebuff, and when his delicate-minded master was bowed to the earth with mortification on his account, he was making calculations about certain green things he meant to snatch just a little farther down the road.

"Yer al'ays gittin' me inte' trouble, y' ole skinflint," muttered Ebenezer, trudging along beside the unconscionable beast and eying his uncouth anatomy with baleful but harmless resentment, "wid bofe yo' 'bom'nable 'pearance 'n' yo' greedy jaws. An' Big Jake 's dat stingy he would n' give you moufful 'f you 's starvin' to def! An' you ain' got no mo' sense, 'n' no mo' regyards fo' youself, 'n' *my*self, 'n' to go 'n' poke yo' ole haid in de co'n-crib 'n' confuse bofe we-all wid shame 'n' humidity. You mought jus' 's well esplain de esplanation to Big Jake dat you ain' got nuffin t' eat t' home! which am a lie. De Lawd knows," he went on, cuffing a persistent fly that had settled on Bonaparte's neck, "if you had n't al'ays been saddled onto me f'om de beginment, eveh since you was an on'ry, long-legged, yaller-hided colt, I mought 'a' been somebody mo'n I is. You 's tuk all de speret out 'n me, an' all de ambishum, 'n' I ain' no — hyeh, don't swalla' dat mulberry-tree!"

He pulled the animal back into the road and mounting him continued his journey and his complainings.

CHAPTER VIII.

GOOD news in which all are interested creates a general feeling of good-will. When it was known that Burgoyne was really coming home that day, there was bustle and excitement and joyous animation all over the premises. The house had to be put in holiday trim with flowers and green festoons, and preparations set on foot for an extra good dinner.

Uncle Smiley hitched his mules to an old cart and drove into the woods for a load of rattan vine, a species of decoration of which Madame La Scalla was particularly fond.

Cosette sent the maids flying hither and thither, with special directions about Burgoyne's rooms. She herself went into the kitchen to discuss the important affairs pertaining to that department with Aunt Riddy ; and finally put on her sun-bonnet and trotted down through the gardens to consult Salome about some of her famous pudding recipes, — a circumstance which had a most revivifying effect upon Salome's spirits. She went to the old chest and got out her French cook-books and turned their hallowed leaves with something like the thrills one feels in opening old love-letters that have long been locked away.

The two old women sat down and bent their heads over the yellow pages, and fell to talking of Paris and the past, — their hearts warming toward each other as they reconstructed, in imagination, the scenes with which both had been familiar in their youth. And thenceforth Salome had a friend, — with whom she could chat on equal terms, and smoke cigarettes on her little portico of a quiet evening.

Late in the afternoon, when the whole place had begun to wear an air of preparedness and delightful expectancy, Evalina sent Beatrice out to cut a few more flowers for the finishing touches. M. La Scalla, with his wife and Mrs. Vincent, had gone for a drive, intending to meet Burgoyne at the steamer landing. Jake also had gone to the landing leading the splendidly groomed Dauphine.

Beatrice had filled her apron and was tripping round the house, as eager and interested as any of them, when the sound of galloping hoofs arrested her attention, and she stopped short.

Burgoyne, with Jake behind him, was riding up the avenue. He was dressed in the uniform of his school, — which included a good many brass buttons. A jaunty cap rested on his thick black hair; he carried a steel-ringed riding-whip and wore spurs of polished silver.

Already he had passed the chrysalis stage of callow, ungainly boyhood, and was a tall, symmetrical youth, with a rich coloring and a fine fearless glance.

He dismounted and walked rapidly toward the house, gazing inquiringly and admiringly at the small figure on the walk.

Beatrice had not moved. The rhythmic hoof-beats and the picturesque rider with the slanting sunbeams glancing from all the bright points in his dress, had brought to her mind a confused medley of recollections made up of the glittering carnival, with its throbbing of drums and fanfare of trumpets; the handsome young uniformed officers whom she had seen dancing in the brilliant hall and talking softly with their beautiful partners on the star-lit gallery overhanging her little court in the French Quarter; and above all the many glorious visions she had conjured up out of her own innocent consciousness about the great, gay, processioning world, — whose *avant-coureur* the young rider seemed to be. She looked at him as one looks at a picture that has fathomless meanings, and stirs the soul to uneasy longings and vague but high aspirations.

Burgoyne supposed her to be the child of some guest of the house, which was not surprising, for Evalina dressed Beatrice in her own outgrown clothing, always fine and pretty.

Her neck and arms were bare and there were bows of ribbon on her shoulders. Her abundant hair hung in loose half-curled masses, and she wore an odd-shaped cap with a tassel, which Madame La Scalla regarded as a highly artistic decoration.

Burgoyne stopped in front of her. "How d' ye do, little Miss?" he said. "Would you mind telling me who you are, — what your name is? There, look out, you are spilling your posies."

He dropped upon one knee and began picking them up, calling their names as he replaced them in her apron: "Roses, verbenas, japonicas, amaryllis, — there you are, now hold your pinafore up so."

At that moment Helen appeared upon the upper gallery, attracted by the sound of his voice, and called out, "Oh, Evalina, come, quick, and see Burgoyne on his knees to Beatrice!"

Burgoyne straightened himself, looked up and raised his cap without the least embarrassment.

"Is it not the proper thing to bend the knee to beauty?" he demanded, and added with smiling gallantry, "I might have done the same if it had been you, instead of this little Miss."

Helen tipped her chin saucily. Evalina rushed out and threw her brother a kiss, and then both she and Helen disappeared from the gallery and came flying down the stairs.

"And so your name is Beatrice?" said Burgoyne. "Well, I should like that if I were you; it's a fine name."

He turned to greet the other two girls.

"Why, don't you know? — she 's Evalina's maid!" exclaimed Helen, as she shook hands with him.

"You don't expect me to believe that," said he. "Does she, Eva?"

"Oh, yes," Evalina replied; she was clasping him around the neck and pulling his face down to hers. "She is my new little maid, that I wrote you about; and she 's the dearest little thing, — Mama thinks so, too. But —" she added in his ear, "Cousin Helen and she are not on — pleasant terms."

Beatrice had stolen away and gone into the house with her flowers, wondering why Helen's explanation should have angered her so, and why Burgoyne's incredulity made her feel like crying. She had thought it a very pleasant thing to be Evalina's maid!

In a moment the carriage drove up. Burgoyne had greeted the party at the landing, but Dauphine was too restive to be kept down to the sober pace of the carriage horses, and had galloped on with him in advance. He helped the ladies out, giving his mother a second embrace, and his father and Mrs. Vincent another hand-shake. There was the usual clatter of tongues, the noisy intoxication of delight, which characterizes a happy reunion.

" I thought that steamer was never coming," declared Mrs. Vincent, " we must have waited there an hour! We got out and walked up and down the bank and looked, and listened, and — "

" My dear Constance, it was scarcely half an hour ! " said Madame.

" Oh, well, I measured the time by my impatience, not my watch," laughed Constance. " We were all dying to see you, Burgoyne. *Mon Dieu!* how you 've grown."

Burgoyne took this as a compliment and bowed.

" I was the first to see him," said Helen.

" Oh, no, Beatrice was the first," returned Evalina.

Helen curled her lip. " That does n't count," she said.

" And how are the dogs?" asked Burgoyne, making a move for the back yard. They all went with him, curious to see whether the animals would recognize him. Madame said she would hardly have known him herself.

Burgoyne gave a peculiar whistle, and the great creatures started to their feet, hesitated a moment, quivering from head to tail, and then leaped forward to the full length of their chains, scattering the flowers wreathed round their necks.

Evalina explained that Beatrice had begged leave to decorate their collars in honor of their master's return.

"Beatrice!" exclaimed Burgoyne.

His mother took it upon herself to explain Beatrice's friendly relations with the dogs, and their tractability under her hands, and related the bird story by way of illustration.

Burgoyne's eyes sparkled with surprise and admiration.

"The plucky little pigeon!" said he. "I should hardly have dared to risk so much myself, especially with Prospero; he is much more unmanageable than Fleet."

"Oh, Beatrice did not consider the risk," said Mrs. Vincent, affronted that the subject had been mentioned; "that cut no figure with her."

"Of course," returned Madame, "she is only a child."

She linked her arm in Burgoyne's and headed the procession back to the house.

He looked about, noting with lively interest all the little changes that had taken place in his absence, and all the familiar things. He raised his eyes to follow the twinings of a honeysuckle vine, which he himself had planted, running up one of the great pillars of the mansion, and espied Beatrice among the leaves, leaning over the railing of the upper gallery looking down upon them. He smiled and waved his hand to her, and repeated, "The plucky little pigeon!"

Beatrice disappeared as a squirrel disappears at sight of a hunter.

Cosette marshalled all the house-servants into the hall to be noticed by the "Young Master" as he went out to dinner.

His manner of meeting them — simple, kindly, courteous, and with some special look or word of recognition for each — seemed to take away the perfunctory character of the ceremony. But it was a ceremony that did not lack in dignity on his part or in respect on theirs. The line between master and slave was as clearly drawn at La Scalla Place as elsewhere, but on a plane where tyranny and abject humility could not meet.

The enlivening influence of Burgoyne's presence was not a mere temporary effect, passing away as soon as the household and himself were again familiarly adjusted to each other, but an unfailing elixir. He carried about with him an exhilarating atmosphere, — as strolling players of ancient times carried their "properties," ready to set up a stage for the delectation of an audience on any village green or city common; though Burgoyne was not given to making amusement, — he had no particular talents or accomplishments, and no disposition to shine. But, and this is a singular fact, he was never regarded as the inferior of those who had talents and accomplishments and who did shine. He was one of those to whom genius appeals far recognition, — one of those royal judges who cannot themselves compete for prizes, but whose gracious office it is to award the laurels.

He had had no great personal ambition since the relinquishment of his early desire to be a pirate. But at school he was always ready to back his aspiring friends for college honors in any field of contest, intellectual or athletic. His particular associate at school, chiefly because circumstance had thrown them together, was a young man named Hugh Connelly, four years his senior, a budding poet, ambitious but poor.

Burgoyne candidly avowed that he cared not a rap for all the rhymes that ever were written, and understood the ethics of poetry as little as he understood the technique of the Old Masters ; but he had, during the past year, saved enough money out of his liberal allowance to pay for the first edition of *A Tiara of Dewdrops*, as Hugh's thin little maiden volume of verse was delicately entitled.

Burgoyne believed in Hugh, and therefore believed in his poetry. He did not think it possible for a man like Connelly, endowed with both sense and sentiment, to be mistaken in his gifts and acquirements. He even gave his friend the credit of rousing in him some sense of the beauty of word-melody. For Hugh, fired with the enthusiasm of self-appreciation, rendered his poetic effusions with a spirit, a fervency, an exquisiteness of interpretation, that could not fail to awaken the dullest imagination, — if that imagination had not been tempered by the discriminating judgment which is the fruit of years and culture. But the fruit of years and culture is not so sweet and luscious as the fruit of youth and inexperience, and Burgoyne came to the feast with an unpampered appetite, — an appetite which was only an instinct, as of hunger in the new-born.

He had brought home a copy of the work, and the first time he visited his mother in her private apartments he carried it with him and proudly presented it to her with his friend's compliments, calling her attention to a few things which he had delicately bracketed. "The twinkling of fairies' star-shod feet," he thought was particularly fine. Hugh had repeated that to him one night when they were out walking, with such pauses and silences, and subtilties of meaning in his intonations, that it had seemed to him as if the whole universe above and below was alive with dancing sprites. "The moonbeams glinting on the crusted snow," was equally alluring to the fancy.

Both these lines occurred in a poem entitled, "To Cruel Lenore." The poet, after describing all the frozen beauties of a winter night, broke into the bitter apostrophe, "Thou art as beautifully fair — and as cold !"

Burgoyne knew nothing about the pangs of un-requited love, but his young soul approved mightily of this avalanche of scorn hurled at the Cruel One, — an avalanche, Hugh pointed out, rolled into one crushing phrase.

Considering that volumes of poetry were used chiefly as ornaments on center-tables, Burgoyne had been very particular with the publisher about the quality of the paper, the kind of type, and the style of binding. He was pleased that his mother, in whose taste he had unbounded confidence, approved of all these features. There was a fountain of pure feeling underneath Madame La Scalla's cynical hardness, and into this fountain he had unconsciously dropped a plummet. A humid softness overspread her eyes as she turned the thick creamy leaves, with their little oblong blocks of print and elegant wide margins.

"And you paid for this?" she asked.

Burgoyne replied with delicious simplicity: "I advanced the money, but Hugh insists upon calling it a loan; he will pay me back out of the first sales."

They were sitting side by side, his head inclined to her. She made no answer. The thought drifted through her mind, as his bright steady gaze held hers, "That is the true La Scalla look. Maurice has it, and Evalina, and — Beatrice."

But it was a look which was liable to break up differently in the different individuals, if the confidence it implied were ever outraged. In Evalina's case it might melt to tears and pity; in her father's, change to disappointment and sorrowful rebuke; but with the other two, it was more likely to flash into swift anger and measureless scorn.

Madame mused, "He is only sixteen. And what does one know about poetry — or anything ! — at sixteen?"

She put her hand up to his cheek, dashed with rich color, and ran her fingers through his hair, every crisp glossy curl of which seemed to be charged with an electrical vitality of its own.

"You are growing into a man, my son," she said, with the half-sad sigh of a mother who sees her

9

fledglings developing the self-directing wings of maturity; "you will soon be shaving!"

For already the down was on his chin.

Burgoyne had not yet begun to notice the color of girls' eyes and hair, or to thrill at the touch of their hands. Sentiment was a thing almost unknown to him, and he had never given a moment's study to his own emotions. He was of an active temperament, which does not signify that he was restless or nervous, or impatient of hindrances to action. He had the true Southern spirit of leisureliness, the faculty of waiting serenely for the turn of events, for the ebb or the flow of the tide. If it rained and he could not gallop over to St. Martinsville, or go hunting with his dogs as he had planned, he could content himself very well in his rooms, watching the downpour from a window, the sudden forming of little pools and rivulets, the scrambling of poultry for shelter, the weak submission of the dispirited cows. Or he could sort over his miscellaneous possessions; could tinker at his guns, or entertain himself with his violin, of which he was fond, though his persistent sawing was never productive of remarkable results. He enjoyed certain kinds of books, and he had two or three friends to whom he now and then wrote a letter if he had any definite thing to say. He did few things for the mere sake of doing them, or to cheat himself with the notion that he was industrious, or that he was discharging a duty. What he thought was worth doing he did as well as he could; what was not worth doing he would not trouble himself to do at all.

The Vincents remained some two weeks longer. During that time Burgoyne saw very little of Beatrice;

but not because of her imprisonment. She interested him somewhat as she interested his mother; and he often sought for her where she was the most likely to be found.

But Beatrice was painstakingly shy of him. She shared in the general delight his presence inspired; but the contemptuous looks his playful kindness toward her evoked from Mrs. Vincent and Helen filled her with a bitter rage and humiliation, and constrained her to keep well out of his way.

"Where is the Little Pigeon?" he would inquire, coming along the corridor, and putting his head into the school-room.

But she was seldom to be found. Her ear, keenly alert as to his voice and movements, usually caught the sounds of his approach, since his steps were never cautious, and he was often whistling or humming softly to himself; and she vanished so adroitly that neither Evalina nor Miss Speedwell was aware of her flight or could tell whither she had gone. But notwithstanding, he managed to establish a relation of *camaraderie* with her, based upon their mutual interest in the dogs, — a relation, however, in which there was always the unconscious condescension of master to slave on his part, and acquiescence on hers.

Beatrice had come gradually to realize that she was a slave, as much a slave as the ebony creatures she daily saw bending their backs under the burning sun in the cotton fields, — to which Mrs. Vincent would gladly have had her consigned.

Evalina had kindly and conscientiously made the fact clear to her; and the Vincents had branded it upon her understanding whenever occasion offered. Mrs. Vincent was righteously persuaded that in very justice Beatrice should be taught to know her place ; and Helen was actuated by the natural desire to avenge the atrocious indignity which she herself had suffered.

Some of the colored people, also, with whom Beatrice was not allowed, and had no desire, to associate, missed few opportunities of reminding her that she was numbered with themselves.

A slow process was going on within the child, corresponding with this moral environment. It was a detaching and withdrawing of herself from the people about her, above and beneath. She occupied a middle ground, and gradually, unknowingly, she fortified her position in it. She had a subtile conviction, the heritage from her free white forefathers, that she was not wholly a slave. Her body belonged to her masters, and she rendered the willing service of her hands to those who had the right to require it. This she never questioned. But that which was peculiarly herself, that which we all recognize as the " I " in a human being, was under no man's control. Her reason played no part in this theory as yet; she simply acted upon it as the birds of the air, as the beasts of the forest, act upon their natural instincts.

She took a valiant stand for her rights as a Free Spirit.

One evening Burgoyne brought Fleet and Prospero round to the front of the house to exhibit them before the family who were assembled in the gallery.

After he had exhausted their répertoire so far as he

knew it, his mother made some reference to the feats Beatrice had taught them to perform.

" Oh, I 'll run up and have her come down," said he, and bounded up the stairs. He found her on the upper gallery, but to his amazement she refused to go down.

" What," said he, " you won't go? Well, we 'll see, my little Miss." He took hold of her arm, — not very gently, for a rebellious slave was a new thing in his experience. But she clung desperately to the railing.

He frowned, commanded, coaxed, but nothing availed. He demanded a reason, but none was forthcoming. Beatrice could not tell him it was her dread of the Vincents' cruel derision. Madame La Scalla smiled when he reported with much chagrin his unlooked-for failure. Mrs. Vincent laughed exasperatingly.

" Perhaps you could get her to come down, Eva? " Burgoyne suggested.

Evalina shook her head. " No, if Beatrice said she would not come, that ends it," she replied.

" She is a curious study, that child," remarked M. La Scalla. " She discriminates with wonde'ful intelligence and fai'ness between her duty as a servant and her rights as a person."

Mrs. Vincent sniffed. " Slaves were not ' persons ' in my day," she retorted, " nor did they have ' rights.' "

" Alas, no ; the world moves ! " said Madame.

" The child's discrimination seems to be fineh than our own," said M. La Scalla. " She realizes that her power oveh these brutes, fo' instance, is something apart from her condition as a slave. And she has the same right to decline to exhibit this power at our request that these young ladies have to decline to play or sing fo' our ente'tainment, — as they sometimes do."

He smiled indulgently upon the two girls, who exchanged glances in acknowledgment of his gentle rebuke.

" Papa, we don't often decline," protested Evalina.

" Well, no one denies that you have the right to, my deah," he replied.

" It will be interesting for you, Burgoyne," said Mrs. Vincent, " to make a study of these nice points, and learn just how far you may command your slaves and to what extent their peculiar rights will justify their disobedience."

" Fortunately, I have no jurisdiction over this little rebel," answered Burgoyne. " Truly," he added, " I can't help admiring the grit of her. You should have seen her eyes, they blazed like coals of fire when I took hold of her and tried to drag her away from the banister."

The following morning Beatrice saw M. and Mme. La Scalla and the Vincents ride away on horseback, and begged Evalina to let her run down stairs.

Burgoyne was in the back yard with the dogs. He had taken off their chains and was about to start to the woods with them. Seeing Beatrice, they bounded toward her in joyful recognition. Burgoyne knotted his brow in recollection of the scene of last night. But the touch of displeasure vanished as he stood looking at her and watching the dogs leap about her, licking her hands and kissing her face. There was nothing stubborn or rebellious in her appearance now.

"Would you like to show me what you can do with them — me, alone?" he asked.

She complied, not only willingly, but joyfully. He was amazed at the wonderful things she had taught the animals, at the ease with which she controlled them, and at their almost human intelligence in interpreting her pretty gestures and tones. They understood the soft modulations of her voice quite as well as they did Big Jake's explosive vociferations, or his own sharp commands.

When the performance was over, Burgoyne turned to her and said, half-playfully, half-authoritatively, — the playfulness to cover his retreat in case she refused, — "Now, little maid, I want you to tell me why you would not come down and give us this exhibition yesterday evening."

She dropped her eyes to the ground and made no answer. He regarded her for a few seconds in silence, wondering how so inflexible a will could be enshrined in a thing so soft and round and fair.

"You are very stubborn," he said.

The charge made no visible impression, — not the quiver of an eyelash, nor slightest movement of the well-closed, rosy lips. He felt an impulse to take hold of her white shoulders and shake her great eyes open, that he might look down through their liquid depths and find out the secrets which she guarded with such invincible determination.

"You do everything your mistress tells you to, do you not?" he asked.

She nodded.

"Well, why won't you do what I tell you, — is it because you belong especially to Evalina and not to me?"

"No."

"Why, then?"

"She don't tell me to do things I cyan't do."

"Well, neither do I. You could have done what I asked you to do last night, easily enough."

There was a flush like the tint of dawn on her face, but still she did not raise her eyes. A wave of admiration swept Burgoyne's breast. He had never seen anything so lovely, and again he wanted to take hold of her, to make her look up, — as one turns the face of a flower upward to drink its sweetness. But he folded his arms and stepped back a pace.

"Could n't you?" he urged.

There was still no reply, and he turned on his heel, snapped his fingers at the dogs and strode away.

Beatrice buried herself in a nest of shrubbery and burst into tears. Burgoyne's authority, which seemed more positive even than Madame La Scalla's, had a quality which made obedience to it a delight. It was her soul's desire to please and obey him. But her soul held something stronger than this; a divine particle of self-value, which is a precious attribute to be paid for sometimes with tears and sacrifices.

Before going into the house she pulled some blades of grass and went into the stable and fed them to Dauphine and stroked her sleek nose. Hitherto she had not paid much attention to Dauphine, but now she was interested in all the Young Master's possessions. Burgoyne's possessions seemed to take upon themselves a touch of his own personality. His coats and his caps, even his riding-whips and fishing tackle had a peculiar way of confessing his ownership.

Evalina sent Beatrice every morning to cut flowers for Burgoyne's mantel. To Evalina his rooms were only a boy's rooms, somewhat disorderly and queer, his things only a boy's things usually the worse for wear. But to Beatrice, going into these rooms with her offering of flowers was almost like going into a hallowed place.

Sometimes Helen dropped in when Evalina was arranging the flowers, and Beatrice wondered at her irreverent handling of Burgoyne's books and knick-knacks, and her audacity in taking his precious violin out of its case and scraping some dreadful wails out of it, against Evalina's earnest remonstrances.

When the Vincents took their departure Beatrice was restored to full liberty, and again enjoyed her long rambles, her frolics with the dogs, and her visits to old Salome. And soon all thoughts of the unpleasant visitors left her mind.

Burgoyne was fond of rowing and sailing, and he often took Evalina and Beatrice with him when he went on the bayou. He seemed to forget, as did they all sometimes, that Beatrice was a slave. He taught her how to manage the rudder and handle the oars, and before the summer was over she could sail a boat almost as skilfully as himself. He also instructed her in horseback-riding and in the use of fire-arms, — both of which accomplishments Evalina was too timid to undertake, — and she was always ready for spirited racing and contests of marksmanship, but could never be induced to point a gun at any living creature.

All this was to Burgoyne the play and pastime of an idle summer and soon forgotten. To Beatrice it was an advance, the fulfillment of some past vague forecastings about the future; an outlook, a radiant promise of things to come.

CHAPTER IX.

THE Vincents did not revisit La Scalla Place for some years. Mrs. Vincent, though a legitimist — a Bourbonist — in opinion, was by nature cosmopolitan, liking any society that afforded her agreeable entertainment. She had fallen in with a gay New York set, and was content to remain at home for a time, — or rather to make her home the *point d'appui* for social campaigns within a narrower radius than had formerly been her wont. Saratoga, the White Mountains, and Washington, — which she liked for the official ceremony and the presence of the *corps diplomatique* and their families, — were the farthest points she touched. For the rest, New York satisfied her for the nonce. She shrugged her shoulders at the theatre and opera, but delighted in the balls and parties, especially when there was somebody to be lionized and impressed, — some foreign celebrity, some scion of royalty or nobility over whom the intoxicated metropolis went wild. She herself was not behind in the social race. Her brown-stone mansion in Madison Square was the scene of such reckless festivities as kept poor Aunt Cynthia in a constant state of surprise and breathless dismay. Her decorous imagination could not keep pace with the dazzling whirl of events Mrs. Vincent set in motion ; and the good woman often found herself sighing in secret for the quiet old times when her erratic niece-in-law was "gallivanting" from one end of the country to the other, and absenting herself for months at a time. " When she is away," Aunt Cynthia reflected, " one only sur- mises what she is up to ; but when she is here, one is in hot water every minute about what she is doing or is likely to do."

It was not a wholesome life for Helen. Her mother had no compunctions about interrupting her studies, or about letting her into the questionable secrets of the fashionable world. " I have plans for you, my dear," Mrs. Vincent frequently hinted. And Helen idled over her books or threw them will- ingly aside, and looked forward vaguely but with pleasurable confidence to a change in her life which would raise her above the necessity of plodding. She had an inkling of what the change was to be, for her mother talked a great deal about the superiority of old established institutions, — as if these held the secrets of culture as Aladdin's lamp held the secret of wealth, — and drew fascinating pictures of foreign convent life. Helen fancied that in a foreign con- vent, whose walls were saturated with the culture and learning of ages, as it were, one could somehow imbibe education and accomplishments without the dull slow routine of work.

The years passed quietly and uneventfully at the Plantation, — and very happily for the two young girls there, whose constant association brought them nearer and nearer to each other in affection and sympathy. They studied together, played and sang, walked, rowed, and drove about the country together,

and had intimate talks and sweet confidences growing
out of the " long, long thoughts " of youth. The life
at La Scalla Place was so far removed from the cen-
ters of conventionality, where the lynx-eyed sentinels
challenge individual conduct, that Evalina, pursuing
her studies with conscientious industry, seeing little
of the neighbors or even of guests in the house, and
free to do as she liked, — guided only by the gentle
wisdom that presided over the whole Plantation life,
— could not be otherwise than simple and natural.
With respect to Beatrice she held, it is true, to the
little ceremonies of etiquette as between mistress and
servant, which was a part of her breeding. But her
affectionate heart took no account of the peculiar
relation. The two were comrades and friends, with
boundless trust on either side. Beatrice, competent
and courageous, assumed the leadership in all their
games, exploits, and explorations, and finally in their
lessons and musical performances, and even in matters requiring the exercise of judgment. " Assumed "
is hardly the word. Leadership was the rôle that fell
naturally to Beatrice. Evalina never gainsaid it,
never tried to set her little authority above the
higher law which gave to each her own unmistakable
place.

She was timid about many things, and Beatrice
exercised a curious guardianship over her ; keeping
close to her side in the dark, putting her arms affectionately about her when the terrific coast-line thunder-
storms tortured her sensitive nerves.

All Beatrice's instincts were docile and tender ; but
they went hand in hand with a sense of justice made
of tough — though delicate — fiber, and a sense of

wrong that might easily kindle to revenge. She was made up of the qualities in which lie all the risks and chances of life. But her kind young mistress had nothing to fear, for gratitude was one of her strongest traits.

Burgoyne's visits were few and brief. Once at his mother's request he brought Hugh Connelly home with him, and at another time a young Canadian whom he took off on a deer-hunt. As a trophy of that expedition he brought home a young fawn and presented it to Beatrice. It was her first important possession, and the joy of it marked a new line in her experience. She named the little creature Doudouce.

Every summer the family, with the agreeable addition of M. Condé, spent a few of the hottest weeks down on the coast somewhere, usually on one of the Gulf Islands. Beatrice was always taken along. Her delight in the vast stretches of sky and water, the one reflected in the other, and the whole resembling the inside of a great iridescent bubble, passed all bounds. Especially was it an infinite rapture to her to sail a little boat with her own hands. Madame La Scalla, who was always studying with a curious, half-amused interest the child's face and movements, exclaimed one evening as she stood with her husband and M. Condé on the beach, watching the gay life on the water ; there was a stiff breeze at the moment, —

" Look at Beatrice, Maurice ! Her management of winds and waves is like her management of dogs and horses. She seems to understand them in the same way, to have the secret of mastery over them."

" In other words she is a sensible girl, and does not lose her head," laughed M. Condé.

" No," objected Madame, " your description is inadequate. The child has genius, a perception and judgment amounting almost to divination."

No one, not even M. La Scalla, appreciated Beatrice's finer qualities as did Madame. To the others she was an extraordinarily bright child, abounding in health and good humor, fearless and strong, and with a capacity for doing many things. Madame alone was aware of her spiritual force. She had noted the sudden transfiguration of her face, and a something elevated and glorious — an *aura* — radiating from her supple body, in times of danger, — as when a horse became unmanageable, or a vessel careened before a heavy sea, or an appalling storm sent women into hysterics. She believed that it was in such a nature to rise to the supremest heights, and triumph in the last extremity. Beatrice might be another Joan of Arc. Sometimes her contemplation of the child filled her with superstitious shivers and made her half regret having interfered in the matter of old Rosamond's will.

The third summer after the Vincents' visit, M. La Scalla's health demanded a change of climate, and the family, including Miss Speedwell, went north, Burgoyne joining the party at Saratoga Springs. It had been the intention to take Beatrice, but to Evalina's grievous disappointment she fell ill with the measles as they were on the point of starting, and had to be left behind. Evalina charged Cosette with numberless, and as Cosette thought, unnecessary instructions about the care of her; and begged

Beatrice to obey the housekeeper's orders implicitly and get well as quickly as possible, and to send a letter by every boat as soon as she was able to write. And with many tears and kisses she bade her "darling Betty" good-bye.

During the governess's absence there were of course no lessons; and Beatrice, recovering quickly under Cosette's skilful doctoring, was at liberty to occupy herself as she saw fit. Her pretty Doudouce, which she prized dearly as a gift from Burgoyne, and ardently loved for its own sweet sake, was always at her side. She had, with considerable difficulty, taught Fleet and Prospero that they were not to molest the little animal, and the four of them often took long rambles through the fields and woods. Beatrice's liking for picture-making had developed into a passion. Miss Speedwell had taught her the first principles of drawing and perspective, and after that she seemed to grasp intuitively what it often takes years of patient application to learn. She made sketches of the various animals about the place, notably of the dogs, of Doudouce, and old Robespierre, and of Uncle Smiley and other picturesque characters, and pinned them on the walls of Salome's cabin. Old Mauma found great entertainment in studying, admiring, and wondering at these pictures. She knew enough of art herself to feel that they had merit. Now and then Beatrice illuminated a page of her letters with effective little illustrations, which brought tears to the eyes of the oft-times homesick Evalina, and called forth surprised and approbative comments from other members of the family. Some cartoons of the dogs, sketched on rough paper, were claimed

by Burgoyne to hang up in his rooms at college.
Her letters were of course childish and crude in construction, but they were oddly original in substance,
and aflame with a quaint humor. Madame smiled
at the little flashes and sparkles, and declared that
the sense of humor was the touchstone of genius.
Without this sense she herself would have looked at
life with a wry face. Beatrice gave brief but luminous accounts of all that happened on the Plantation; and M. La Scalla pronounced her letters
far more satisfactory than the overseer's verbose
reports.

Shortly after the family returned home, in the
autumn, Madame La Scalla received a letter from
her cousin Constance, saying that she and Helen
were about to sail for Europe. Mr. Vincent had
business in London and would accompany them, and
Aunt Cynthia would shut up the house for a brief
season and visit her relatives in New England.

Following this gossipy preamble, Mrs. Vincent
wrote : —

"If I can manage it, Helen and I will remain abroad
for a couple of years. I wish to place the child where
she can have suitable advantages. Certainly with our
means, as I tell James, who has always been absurdly
opposed to it, you know, — this is my imperative duty.
And, pardon me, Corinne, I think it is yours, too, with
respect to Evalina! You know how it was with us when
we were girls, — we would have thought it a monstrous
deprivation if our parents had not sent us abroad to be
finished. A young person really cannot acquire true
culture, the *crème de la crème* of style and manner, in a
new raw country like ours. The Northern people do not

10

feel this as we do. We are Americans the same as themselves. *Mon Dieu!* I hope we are patriots as well.
But I believe we are more loyal to the traditions of our
race. It seems to me that patriotism means something
more than love of one's country, — it means love of one's
kind, of the particular stock from which one springs.
You know what the feeling was among our ancestors
when Louis XV. made a gift of Louisiana to His Catholic
Majesty of Spain. And again, when Napoleon ceded
our beautiful province to the United States ; and English
— or American — customs, even American dances, were
introduced into New Orleans! Do you remember how
our dear old *grandpère* used to rage about those dances,
and about a governor who couldn't speak a word of
French? I can very well understand the feeling of some
of our proud old Creole families, — your cousin Rose was
a good example! — who have never set foot on the
modern side of Canal Street. We have a general antipathy to the Anglo-Saxon race. Circumstances overcome it in particular cases, like mine, but the rule
holds. I mean that my daughter shall be educated in
the old French traditions."

Madame La Scalla was not surprised when, a few
weeks later, she learned that Mr. Vincent had returned
to New York alone.

Mrs. Vincent promptly placed Helen in a high-
walled convent, picturesque with age and ivy, in the
environs of Paris, there to absorb the dim grandeur
and high-bred elegance of the older civilization.
And she herself proceeded to enjoy the large liberty
and luxury, the social and intellectual delirium of the
gay and brilliant capital, — then on the eve of the
Coup d'État. Her money and her connections gave
her access to every desirable coterie, and introduction to whomsoever she cared to meet.

Her letters to Madame presented wonderful kalei-
doscopic pictures of the various phases of society of
that changeable epoch. Descriptions of balls, receptions, presentations, *soirées*, the opera, elegant dinners
and delightful conversational breakfasts, where one
met, almost *en famille*, the most distinguished celebrities, — artists, poets, composers, *littérateurs*, — and
listened to sparkling, epigrammatic talk on a bewildering variety of subjects.

" It is a tournament," she wrote, " where every knight
may have his chance, if he have a lance. One starts up
a covey of partridges, as you might say, and then you
should hear the shots and see the feathers fly! Every
one takes his quick turn — at the bird on the wing. No one
is interested in a tame hen! In other words, trite topics
are tabooed. Everything is bright, glancing, daring.

" I know of no one better adapted to this sort of touch-
and-go game than yourself, my dear Corinne, and I long
for you every day. And so do a good many of these
people, — who remember the beautiful Mademoiselle
Deschamps, and others whom I have talked to about
you. For my part in conversation is generally to quote
your brilliant *mots*. Beyond this I can only sit and be
thrilled."

In a way Mrs. Vincent's letters were cruel. They
stirred disquieting memories and made Corinne's
soul burn with longing for the great world, — which
still moved, though she, about whom it had once
appeared to revolve, was not of it!

Thus far she had accepted with reasonable content
her life at La Scalla Place, — freshened so often by
the presence of agreeable guests and broken by summer outings and brief seasons of winter gayety in the

city; to say nothing of St. Martinsville, the Little Paris of Louisiana, which had received her with enthusiasm as a bride, and which had never ceased to honor her with distinguished consideration. There were days when she wandered restlessly about, or sat and mused, dreamy-eyed, self-absorbed, filled with the discomforting thought that she was simply wasting her life, her splendid powers, the fruits of her rich ripe years. What did it matter that she was beautiful, that she knew how to dress, that she had a tongue to match the most brilliant talker in Paris? Maurice did not mind, — or not greatly. He cared more for the prattle of Evalina and her maid than for the brightest things she could say. Alas! she might lose the faculty for saying bright things, — the knife must be whetted if it would cut. There was no longer the sparkling friction of newness betwixt the people of St. Martinsville and herself. They held no surprises for her, nor she for them. And both were necessary to keep up her interest. She liked society rather more for what she could give it than for what it could give her. In this she differed from her cousin Constance, who was like a gourmand at a feast, — caring only to eat. But, exhausted as she felt herself to be, as empty of interest to her neighborhood, there was never a time when Madame La Scalla was not prominent in the thought of the community, and when she was not welcomed at public and social gatherings with a brightening of eyes and quickening of pulses. She was the first person thought of when any new festivity was proposed, — not that she would be expected to lead actively, but the grace of her presence was always needed to give tone and spirit.

M. Condé, sly old gallant, who sometimes found himself growing ennuied in tame old St. Martinsville, charged her with defrauding the world by isolating herself on an out-of-the-way Louisiana plantation. To which she laughingly replied, — for whatever she thought she kept her own counsel, — "I have my husband, you know. He is quite worth spending my munificent self upon !"

"Ah, but the gift might be made still more munificent," he said. "Women are like jewels, they need to be befittingly set. You, Madame, are a jewel of many crystalline facets."

Corinne blushed as at the sudden *exposé* of a secret. She herself knew her own value, and that her "setting" was inadequate, her stage too small. She was not a vain woman, any more than the man who values his intellectual gifts is a vain man. She separated herself from herself and felt, with a certain disinterestedness, that she was one who ought to be seen in large perspective ; that her image should be multiplied in myriads of eyes, her words echo in the innumerable human cells that go to make up a vast society. Of course, these were mere irresponsible phantom fancies floating through the impalpable ether of Madame's dreamy consciousness, not fully acknowledged by herself, not of sufficient substance to make thought.

Souls cry for appreciation in various ways and from various quarters. In poetry, in music, in art ; from the pulpit, the rostrum, the stage. Why should not a beautiful woman with an accomplished mind and a heart athirst for sympathy ask for the same wide recognition? But beauty is shamefaced and will scarcely confess its desires even to itself. Madame's longings were not clearly defined, but they were dimly outlined ; if Maurice would give up Plantation life for at least a part of the year, as many of their wealthy neighbors did, and go abroad with her and live in the mighty world, and see the world focused in those " many crystalline facets " M. Condé referred to, life might be worth the living ! After all, her husband's judgment was the final tribunal before which she would present her claims, — backed by the testimony of the world. But Maurice, she feared, could never be induced to leave the plantation. He had turned missionary of late, and was educating his slaves for something he saw, not with the eye of faith but the eye of conviction, in the distant future. He was a believer in the science of progress, and was marking the signs. He was resolved to get his little fraction of the world in line for the next new movement.

Constance wrote : —

" Do come over ! Come and bring Evalina. It would delight the girls, I am sure, to be together in school. And it would be a prodigious joy to their mamas. Paris was never so charming as now, — such life, such gayety, such reckless extravagance ! Or, perhaps, I have just reached the point where one begins to enjoy life. Whichever it is, you, *ma chère*, would be in the seventh heaven, you always had a talent for *le beau monde.*"

Corinne replied that she should not think of living abroad without her husband. And as for putting Evalina into a foreign convent, Maurice would not hear of it, nor did she favor it herself. They desired that their children should be well grounded in Ameri-

can principles and ideas, and after that there would
be time enough for old-world polish.

If the social life of the Gallic capital was more
than a realization of Mrs. Vincent's anticipations,
convent life was a cruel disappointment to her
daughter. Poor Helen had been fascinated by the
air of mystery and romance which hangs round old
cloistered institutions, and by the poetic and alluring
phraseology in which they are described. But neither
the miraculous legends nor the aristocratic exclusiveness of which this particular convent boasted gave
any compensation for its dullness and hopeless monotony to the heart of the disenchanted and homesick
girl. The placid faces of the nuns, discharged, as
it seemed to her, of all human expression, annoyed
her by their unvaryingness. The spotless cleanness
of the place had the effect of coldness and austerity.
Accustomed as she had been to every luxury, and to
profuse tokens of wealth and culture, the convent
seemed to her as clean-swept of beauty and sentiment
as the grassless dooryard of a remorseless housewife.
The air of surveillance, the noiseless footfalls and low
voices, made her feel as if the very walls were heark-
ening. There was even something uncanny about the
demure maids in pinned-up frocks, moving silently
about with their buckets and brushes eternally scrub-
bing, — their big bright eyes following her with the
wondering awe which the lowly young feel for the
more fortunate of their own age and sex. For it was
immediately known throughout the place that Helen
was an American heiress. The janitor was the only
person who did not fear to wake the slumbering
echoes. He stamped noisily about the halls and

corridors, and tended the fires and opened and closed the windows and doors with uncompunctious rattling and bangings.

At the close of the first week Helen besought her mother to take her away. She protested that her nerves could not bear the pressure of such an atmosphere. Mrs. Vincent was in despair. By this time she had completed her own plans and could not endure the thought of cancelling them and going tamely home, — after all the eloquence she had expended upon her husband to carry her point! A happy inspiration sent her to the Mother Superior. Mother Alphonsine, who had the face of a Madonna — of the Sistine Madonna, Mrs. Vincent reflected as she sat fronting her — and the brain of a diplomat, replied with a single sweetly spoken word, " Wait."

Old Father Time himself has no better or wiser advice to offer to distracted souls. The word and the angelic smile which accompanied it fell like a benediction on the visitor's perturbed spirit. She went away with a light heart, though she left her daughter in tears. But gradually the magic little word worked its charm. It is a barren soil indeed in which a young life may not take root and flourish in some fashion. Helen's rebellious soul quieted itself and began to cast about, half-suspiciously, half-resentfully, for indemnification, — as an angry baby crying for the moon compromises with its nurse for a bit of cake or a toy.

Wherever human beings, or any other beings, congregate, there is variety and there must be affinities. No doubt there are special friendships in an ant-hill. Helen's first feeble thrill of interest in her surroundings came of the discovery that the monotonous ranks of pupils were composed of real girls, with individual traits and characteristics, and with more or less pronounced attracting or repelling powers. Her first choice of a mate fell upon Mabel Pembroke, a young girl, homesick like herself, from her own native city. They were familiar with the same places in and about New York; they had sailed in the very same boats up and down the Hudson River; they had attended the same concerts, and both had taken lessons of the eccentric old music master, Herr Mathias. Upon these slender grounds they set up an ardent friendship, — a friendship which expressed itself in constant association and intimate confidences.

Mother Alphonsine smiled indulgently upon it. " The dear demoiselles ! their sorrows will melt away in their mutual sympathy," she said to her favorite companion, Sister Felicia, who returned with a sigh, "Ah, yes, the young have sorrows like the little icicles which form on the eaves, — the first bit of warmth dissolves them."

During one of their arm-interlocked promenades in the high-walled enclosure surrounding the great buildings, Mabel confided to Helen that an aged relative of her mother's had made her the legatee of a large property, conditioned upon her attending this particular school, where she herself had been educated, " generations ago." " My own mother is dead," explained Mabel. " I have a step-mama and two half-sisters, Kitty and Nell. This old auntie who left me her property was a Creole. She died lately in New Orleans."

" Have you ever been in New Orleans ? " asked Helen.

"Only once. Mama took us down there to pay a visit to my aunt, who was very anxious to see me; that was before she made her will."

"Evidently you impressed her favorably!" laughed Helen.

Mabel related her experiences in New Orleans, and among other things mentioned the very beautiful little girl whose acquaintance she and her sisters had made on the rear gallery of her Aunt d'Aubigné's old mansion. "Beatrice something, — I forget what," she said.

"Beatrice!" exclaimed Helen, "I wonder — no, it can't be possible! what did she look like?"

Mabel described her.

"I declare! I do believe it's the same," said Helen. "And what a joke! If it is the same, she is a little colored girl and my cousin Evalina's maid."

"Oh, I'm sure that can't be," Mabel returned, "she would still be quite small for a maid; and besides I remember she told us she was white."

"Yes, that was the ridiculous part of it, the impertinent little thing supposed she was white because her skin happened to be fair, and because her silly old grandmother deceived her. But she has learned her mistake!"

"Oh, how dreadful, I can hardly believe it! she was the dearest, loveliest, brightest little thing!"

"Y-e-s, if one did not know what she was! My aunt, Madame La Scalla — "

"La Scalla! that was the name, Beatrice La Scalla."

"Beatrice nothing! slaves have no surname," retorted Helen.

"Is she well treated?" asked Mabel.

"Well, I should say so! They almost make her one of the family. She studies under a governess with Cousin Evalina, and is not allowed to associate with the other servants. Mama thinks it is wrong, and that it will go all the harder with her some day."

From the date of this conversation the intimacy between the two girls began to wane. Exploration of each other's moral territory showed that they had little in common, and both yielded easily to influences that drew them apart. On Mabel's side it was sweet Sister Felicia, who taught needle-work, for which art Mabel had a *penchant;* and on Helen's it was another girl, Fifine Cardonnet.

Fifine was a revolutionary spirit, generally at war with the established order. She was deeply enamored of the daring poetry and fiction of the time, and she introduced Helen into this proscribed but entrancing realm. Helen had never cared much for reading of any sort. But in the nihilistic state of mind engendered by her disillusion, anything which meant infringement of convent discipline had attractions. Very soon, however, she was swept into a new existence as delicious as the opium-eater's dreams, — an alluring world of which Madame Sand, Dumas, Alfred de Musset opened the portals.

While other girls were quietly pursuing their studies these two were moving through elysian fields, thrilled to ecstasy by imaginary joys and sorrows, steeping their young souls in imaginary passion, and thinking the real world well lost in such a dream-world as this! Even their own quiet lives were turned into romantic dramas, for which the convent walls furnished a lurid but fascinating background. The attachment between them was a poem in itself, they declared, and raised them above their uncongenial surroundings.

Toward the close of the second year Mrs. Vincent wrote her husband : —

" Dear Helen is so happy and doing so well that I think it would be a great mistake to remove her from this lovely school, where I am sure she is daily enriching her mind, improving her manner, and perfecting her accomplishments. She has a really queenly carriage, and her complexion is charming. She sings very sweetly, and dances with grace. I know you will be proud of her when she returns home with all her laurels ! "

Mr. Vincent had the discretion not to turn this letter over to Aunt Cynthia. When she questioned him about Helen's school-work he replied with an inscrutable smile, " Her mother seems satisfied with her progress."

CHAPTER X.

WHEN Helen's convent course was completed, Mrs. Vincent naïvely suggested to her husband that six months, or a year's travel, in the British Isles and on the continent would give just the touch, the purple bloom of culture, necessary to a young girl about to enter society.

It was a matter concerning which she had some misgivings, and she was not greatly surprised when Mr. Vincent objected.

"Bring the child home," he wrote curtly; "let me have a glimpse of my girl again before you turn her out a full-fledged woman of fashion."

This was cruel, insinuating, and it brought a flood of tears; but there was a comforting clause at the end of the letter: "You can make the tour you speak of next year if it is a matter of so much importance. One quiet year at home will not make a superannuated spinster of our daughter."

"How ungracious men are," sighed Mrs. Vincent. But she dried her tears. Next year Paris would have her grand *Exposition Universelle.* Already the diplomatic Emperor was making preparations for the unprecedented *fête.* Perhaps James had taken this into account. It was like him to do a pleasant thing in a brusque way. If the shell was a little rough, the kernel was sweet, and one could put up with a bit of rudeness.

She sketched a rapid plan in her mind, and decided to postpone Helen's début until after her post-graduate course of travel.

This arrangement would suit her husband above everything; and while it would be equally agreeable to herself, she could make a virtue of it with him. And poor Constance felt that she had little enough capital of that sort.

She packed her trunks cheerfully and came home.

But an attempt to resume her former pleasures and occupations, and renew her relations with former friends, very soon convinced her that she could not conveniently fit herself back into her old niche in the American metropolis. The discovery was a tonic to her vanity, though a bitter one. It is pleasant to grow only when one has room.

She wondered how she could ever have endured such cramping, as a little chick might wonder how he could have compressed all his young importance into a shell.

But, in reality, her expansion was a mere matter of fluffiness and feathers. She was the same volatile, capricious Constance, eager only for flight and change.

She compared New York society, as she found it now, to unfermented wine; and it was most unpalatable after one had been sipping of the old vintages of France !

"A society so 'recent' as this," she wrote Corinne, "has no *bouquet*. There are no traditions, no subtleties of meaning in anything, or poetical significance.

No hallowed lavender-scent of a *past,* — in a word, no Gobelin Tapestries ! "

Madame smiled at the idea of the worldly-minded, pleasure-loving votary of fashion and modern luxury affecting so fine a nostril for *antique arome,* so devout a worship for the heroic ages.

After a barely decent length of stay in New York, Mrs. Vincent set off for La Scalla Place to supplement her voluminous letters with verbal recollections of her experiences abroad. She declared that she never got the full flavor of anything until it had been sifted through the luminous understanding of her clever though satirical relative !

Helen of course accompanied her.

An unlooked for pleasure awaited them on the journey. At the moment they were setting foot on board a Bayou steamer, — the "Arlington," as it happened, — a young man detached himself from a group on the deck, and advanced toward them with the eager pleased air of an acquaintance.

Mrs. Vincent's eyes challenged him for an instant, and then she exclaimed in a voice almost shrill with surprise, " Burgoyne La Scalla ! "

Burgoyne, his figure developed to fine manly proportions and his face matured by a luxuriant silky first mustache, acknowledged his identity laughingly. But his alert young man's glance passed by the elder woman to the slim gray apparition in her wake, stepping lightly over the gang-plank.

He spoke her name hesitatingly and with a note of surprised admiration, than which nothing could have been more flattering, half doubting whether it could really be Helen Vincent, the somewhat listless girl, whose much lauded prettiness had always failed to appeal to him in by-gone times.

This girl, with her slender beauty, her graceful *aplomb*, her thousand bewildering charms of young-ladyhood, attacked him at every point of his masculine consciousness, and made him feel with a kind of delicious fear that she possessed some strange, awful, but most sweet power which it was impossible to withstand.

He felt that she might be such a girl as Hugh Connelly had raved about in his lines to The Cruel One, — a girl capable of inspiring and rebuking a man's passion in one and the same glance. But no matter, it was worth a thousand throes of pain to feel one such exquisite sensation as surged through his soul when their eyes met.

She seemed to have the advantage of him somehow, to rise above him like a young goddess. He felt timid, unlike himself, in her presence. She gave him her fingers, not her hand, to clasp, and permitted a smile to her lovely lips reluctantly, as though it were too precious a thing to bestow lightly.

Her whole manner seemed to say, "We meet on a different footing now, you know."

"How much you have changed!" he said, in vague explanation of what he feared was too prolonged a look.

A cruder girl might have provoked an easy compliment. Helen was not crude, though a novice in the ways of real young men.

She had played Lady to many an imaginary Knight, and was an adept in her rôle. But here, now, was an actual knight with a part of his own to perform, and to which she must fit hers. How exciting, how delightful !

She had quite expected to enter upon just such a real drama as this when released from the convent, though with *un autre thèâtre, et un entourage différent !* Garish daylight, a common river steamer, a gang of colored roustabouts, were not the most desirable or romantic accessories. But the *dramatis personæ* would go a long way toward making up for deficiencies in the *mise en scène !*

After her excited and voluble greeting, Mrs. Vincent hastened on to speak to the master of the boat, and the youthful pair fell into step side by side.

"I am some inches taller than I was five years ago," said Helen demurely, "and I wear my dresses some inches longer."

The personal references thrilled him deliciously.

"Oh, it is not that exactly !" he returned, glancing down the line of her trim figure, from the feathery *aigrette* topping her pretty head-gear to the hem of her plain gray skirt.

A ravishing, daintily-booted little foot peeped from beneath the skirt, and a ravishing little gray-gloved hand clasped an ivory-handled parasol.

Burgoyne had always admired his mother's hands and feet, but they had never stirre'd deep emotions in him. Here were a hand and a foot that Hugh Connelly might write sonnets about. But what then of her eyes, her throat, her whole entrancing personality? They would fill cantos !

"You have changed, too," Helen remarked, giving him a brief measuring glance.

"I? Oh, yes; somewhat, I suppose."

They found seats on the shady side of the boat, and presently Mrs. Vincent joined them. She plied Burgoyne with questions about himself and his family, and interspersed bits of information about herself and Helen, which he found marvellously interesting, especially the bits that concerned Helen.

She deferred to Helen a good deal, appealing to her for confirmation of this or that, and kept her always in the current of the conversation, which gave him excuse for continually turning his eyes in her direction.

He was loath to lose a single one of her words, or attitudes, or gestures. He treasured them all, and thought about them afterwards, turning them over and over in his mind and finding the loveliest meanings in them.

He began to find lovely meanings in many other things to which he had never given much thought before, for love is a wonderful eye-opener. All about were the lavish charms of spring, — bloom and fragrance, far-away deep blue skies, the sheen of water, a thousand tints of green. He seemed to see them all for the first time. And he recalled scraps of poetry he had learned, for the musical rhythm in them, and found in them a real and exquisite significance.

Mrs. Vincent was a considerate mother; in the evenings she allowed the young people to sit apart in the moonlight and the soft wind !

They did not talk much, there was no need; their souls held silent communion. When they did speak, it was on vast subjects, — the starry heavens, the universe, life, love, and the meaning of all; other things seemed too trivial.

A new faculty was developed in them; they had no need of eyes to determine each other's presence, no need of speech to know what each other thought and felt. They commented upon this wonderingly, as a remarkable phenomenon, and their own peculiar gift!

Burgoyne bought a bunch of flowers of an urchin who came on board with a basketful at one of the landings. He placed one in Helen's hand as he bade her "good-night," and murmured, —

> "So hush, and I'll give you this sweet white rose;
> See, I clasp it inside of your cool soft hand.
> There, that is our secret, go to sleep;
> You will wake, and remember, and understand."

"Our secret?" She looked up at him with eyes big and tender in the moonlight. But he went away without a word.

Helen did not go to sleep. She sat up in her little white bed in her state-room, and looked out into the starry night and revelled in her sensations. She had been so many times enamored of imaginary heroes that it was difficult to tell how much of her present experience was real feeling, and how much unconscious rehearsal of things learned from books.

It is not an easy matter for the sincerest of us to separate intrinsic feeling from the sentiment which education, conventionalism, and a thousand extraneous influences weave round the heart.

Whenever Helen had a little time to herself she scribbled bits of letters to her friend Fifine, describing and analyzing her beautiful emotions, usually in the jargon of the heroines of romantic fiction. But she meant all that she wrote.

"DEAREST," she began once, and drew a line through the word. "No, a thousand pardons, *mon amie!* Not even to you can I evermore apply that sweet superlative. It belongs henceforth to One only, the one who of all the world is the hero of my dreams and of my life; my — oh, dare I say it? my — *lover*. Yes, dear friend, for it is true, *true*. I cannot mistake the language of those eyes. Fifine, believe me, the most glorious eyes that ever beamed with the light of love! . . . And all this wonder has happened in three days! Three days? One day, one little minute, so long a space only as it takes a glance to telegraph its message. It is true, I have known him all my life nearly. But our two souls, like two spheres circling in space, have just now touched. And oh, the deliciousness of the shock! It thrills, it thrills to the center of one's being! Madame Sand knows what love is, and describes it beautifully, wonderfully; and one seems to know from the reading. But it is like knowing the steps and figures but not knowing how to dance, or like learning the theory of music without being able to play a single instrument. . . . Last night we sat out on the deck. The sky was the sweetest blue sprinkled with stars, — other worlds, *he* said, — and little pink scarfs of cloud floated near the moon, transparent; you could see the blue distance through and beyond them. Woods on both sides of us, and the glistening river between. And all sorts of queer sounds, bird-calls, and the like, could be heard. And over all such a throbbing stillness. Oh, of course the steamer was puffing, and the boat-hands were talking down below. But *for us*, sitting apart and alone, it was still and sublime. We scarcely spoke. But we lived, Fifine, *we lived* to our finger-tips. I turned my face toward him and asked, 'Of what are you thinking, Burgoyne?' 'Of you,' he answered quickly, with a divine

look. And suddenly it seemed as if some irresistible
force was drawing us together, and that our lips must
meet in one long, long, long kiss, and our souls, steeped
in rapture, die away into the blue, blue night! That was
the sensation, dear, mine and his — yes, I am sure it was
his, too. But he is strong, strong even in love, where
most men are weak. He drew a long breath and moved
away a little, and the spell was broken. For we have
known each other such a little while, and he would not
take advantage. I feel sure that is why he did not
speak then and there. Or perhaps — yes, I think he is
a little bit afraid of me — in awe of me, as if I were a
superior being! Men have such amazingly high ideals
of woman. And when they fall in love with us we must
perforce stand for those ideals. And really, Fifine, I do
feel a little saintly when I am with him — really! Is that
hypocritical, or do we positively become for the moment
what people believe us, be it saint or devil? I know that
for some reason or other Mabel Pembroke dislikes me;
and I always feel at my very worst in her presence. I
suppose I am very sensitive; people play upon me easily.
Well, thank Heaven, the tunes in me are not all bad!
When the right sort of hand touches me, I flatter myself
I am capable of a little melody. And just now, *ma chère*,
I am singing, ringing with a most joyful sound. Oh,
Fifine, love, *love*, in the imperative mode! You must
love if you would know what love is. No one can tell
you, not even the author of 'Lucrezia Floriana.'"

Burgoyne's experience was absolutely initiatory.
And naturally it was intense, tremendous. He had
come to the period in young manhood — a movable
period occurring sometimes at a tender and sometimes
at a mature age — when the Grand Passion, under
provocation, must break out in its first blind stormy
chaotic phase, the emotional.

The provocation is not always necessarily great,

but in this case it was considerable. Helen was indeed very pretty, — with a wonderful pink-and-white complexion, an arch glance, a delicate grace of movement, and the trick of knowing how to use her charms, — which is much. But it is possible the result would have been the same if she had been sallow and angular. There is a mighty potency in the mysterious charm of sex, propinquity, idleness, moonlight, and languorous breezes.

It would have been a sad blow to the girl's pride to be made aware of how small a part her precious individuality played in this important affair : a necessary one, however, — as necessary as the part of the wick, whose simple office is to conduct the oil to the flame.

There is a great deal of sentiment yet in the world about birth and love and death. Science cannot explain away the wondering joy of the new mother, or convince the enamored swain that it is but a simple function of his nature to love and mate, or dispel the awful mystery that broods over life's ending.

Burgoyne and Helen drifted naturally, inevitably, to the climax of their amazing love, and their lips met finally in that " long, long, long kiss," the seal of happy betrothal. They believed and declared with perfect faith that the flame of this splendid torch they had lighted would illumine their joint pathway adown the whole journey of life and even into the great Beyond. For love links souls with immortality, with infinity, with God.

Burgoyne, delirious with his new strange happiness, went straightway to Mrs. Vincent. She was both delighted and perturbed. She had always cherished a secret wish that this thing might happen : and so, she believed, had Madame La Scalla, though no word had ever been spoken ; but it had happened too soon. Helen was a mere child yet, and what could she know about love? And how had it come about so quickly? The girl was altogether ignorant of the world, of society. And so, for that matter, was Burgoyne. Well, they must wait, — that was the easy solution.

Burgoyne, the most generous of lovers, was willing to promise anything, — even a secret engagement for as long as might be desired.

"For, after all," he reasoned royally, "nothing matters much to love *but* love."

CHAPTER XI.

IT was a radiant party that alighted at La Scalla Place one fine evening. The young people were brimming with a secret that leaked out in every glance and gesture, and Mrs. Vincent herself was almost as transparent.

"It is so comfortable," she reflected, "to have a child's future so beautifully settled at the very outset." And this complacency showed itself continually in her contemplation of the happy pair.

A few mornings after the arrival, Burgoyne and Helen went off for a gallop, and Madame La Scalla, who was paying a lengthy visit in her cousin's apartments, drifted over to a window-seat. She could see the riders far down the lane, Helen's gauze veil floating on the wind like a delicate gray cloud.

Mrs. Vincent, who was busy taking things out of her trunk, with the help of a French maid, came and stood beside her to exhibit some dainty garment she had brought from Paris. She was talking with her usual vivacity, but as her eyes took the direction of Madame's she broke off and exclaimed, "Aren't they a beautiful pair?"

Corinne looked up and said dryly, "How far has it gone?"

Mrs. Vincent flushed.

"You surely can have no objections, Corinne ! "

"I did not make any."

"But you spoke strangely, — perhaps you think nothing should have been done before you were consulted ? "

"*Bien entendu,*" said Madame, with a shrug.

"Well, we are even on that score ; they did not ask *me* if they might fall in love, — young people have a way of taking these matters into their own hands."

"It occurred under your own eyes, however. You should have staved it off for the present, I think. They are absurdly young, especially Burgoyne."

"I wish to Heaven you had had the case to deal with instead of me," returned Constance, impatiently.

"It might have been better," coolly admitted Madame. "There is always a way to manage these things. But *quelque soit*, we will not quarrel. I have no fault to find with my future daughter-in-law ; I have always had a great fondness for Helen. If all goes well, I shall be satisfied."

Mrs. Vincent returned to her task, and presently Madame joined her, and the two went over the contents of the trunk together, interestedly as women do in such matters, and fell into pleasant chat about old friends and familiar places. Madame La Scalla had a piece of news to tell. Maurice was planning for the whole family, himself included, to visit the Paris Exposition, and perhaps spend the entire season abroad.

Mrs. Vincent was in ecstasies, and immediately began supplementing the arrangement with plans of her own. They would travel *tout ensemble*, take quarters together in the gay capital, and Burgoyne and Helen would have the felicity of each other's companionship !

"How did you ever manage it, Corinne?" she asked. "I thought Maurice could never be induced to go abroad."

"I think M. Condé managed it," said Madame; "he thinks the world ought to be treated to a glimpse of me now and then."

"Ah, M. Condé, your life-long admirer !" laughed Constance. "He will go too, I suppose?"

"Surely."

"Perhaps I can persuade James also, — I can hold up Maurice to him, you know. *Mon Dieu !* We shall have grand times in dear old Paris next year."

Madame was not the only one who divined the Great Secret. Beatrice too was conscious of it in a dim way. The attitude of the lovers toward each other fascinated her, and filled her with a strange pain. She liked to watch them covertly, and then steal away and brood over the inexplicable hurt in her heart.

Doudouce was always at her side looking up at her with soft, innocent eyes, serenely unsympathetic. One day, in a sudden and most unusual fit of exasperation, she struck Doudouce a sharp little blow. "You are a stupid, unfeeling thing," she cried; and then, in swift repentance, flung her arms round the astonished creature's neck and burst into tears. It was the first time she had ever deliberately — if this act could be called deliberate — inflicted pain, and the reaction was an intolerable hurt to her own feelings.

There was a volcanic force in her which must have an outlet whenever there was an internal commotion. The internal commotions were seldom fits of anger. Sometimes they were the flaming up of a mighty creative fervor, when she must seize her paint-pots and brushes and produce something on canvas; or they were the restless stirrings of an active, over-flowing spirit, and she must take a flying gallop on the back of a spirited horse, or sail her boat in the teeth of a gale, or row furiously up and down the bayou. Expression was the great need of her soul.

Gradually more and more liberty had been accorded to her. The knowledge of the secret of her birth made a profound impression upon Evalina, to whose love for Beatrice was added an infinite tenderness and compassion. Like her father, she felt a deep sense of obligation toward the child, and a longing to make reparation. The latter could only be accomplished in one way, and she and M. La Scalla had held long consultations about that.

As before, when the Vincents were at the plantation, Beatrice kept out of the way. The first time Burgoyne met her — in his blissful absorption he had scarcely more than inquired about her — was one morning when he and Helen were strolling in the garden, whose tall hedges and other tangled growths made a kind of lovers' seclusion infinitely agreeable to the pair.

Beatrice came down the walk on her way to Salome's cottage. She was startled at the unexpected encounter, but made a quick obeisance and passed on. She was barely as large as her fourteen years would warrant, and lithe and agile as her own little fawn.

Burgoyne's eyes followed her until she disappeared through the gate.

"How handsome Beatrice is," he remarked. "I think she has the vividest beauty of all the girls I ever saw."

"Really!" said Helen.

He caught the sharp note in her voice, and replied, with a smile, "I am not partial to vivid things, I prefer the softer tones."

She flushed angrily. "I hope you do not presume to compare us," she retorted.

"Why, no, except in the matter of — coloring, perhaps," he said, regarding her with amazement. Here was a new phase in the character of his beloved which he did not comprehend, and did not know how to meet.

"I do not choose to be compared with a *negress* in any way," she returned, drawing up her slender form, and regarding him with a haughty eye.

"Why, my darling!" he exclaimed.

But she turned on her heel and walked away statelily, thrilling with the delicious pangs of a first lovers' quarrel, and satisfied that she was conducting herself after the manner of her favorite heroines of fiction.

But she was a little conscience-smitten at the look of agony on Burgoyne's face, — as though he believed all must be over between them. She smiled inwardly, and thought how tragic it was, and how fearfully delightful so to test one's power over a man! She went straight to her room, and wrote it all out to her dear Fifine.

However, she suffered a good deal that night. In

the darkness — which was always peopled with terrors to her — the thought came that perhaps Burgoyne would not "make up!" Perhaps a real lover was altogether different from the amiable heroes of romance. She had made a gallant show, but was not strong enough to hold her ground; long before the dawn she decided to go to him, confess that her performance had been three-fourths acting, and ask his forgiveness.

But Burgoyne was not at breakfast; and soon afterwards — from the south gallery, where they often sat together of a morning, and whither she hoped he might come to seek her now — she espied him striding across the fields, his gun on his shoulder and the dogs at his heels.

Her heart fairly stood still. What had she done! — blighted the sweet prospects of her young life forever? And for a caprice, a mere vain, mean wish to test her power and experiment with her emotions!

She ran upstairs and locked herself in her room and wrote Burgoyne a letter, a rather tragic and foolish letter, blotted with a tear or two, — not purposely, but since they were there, she let them stay; they would vouch for her sincerity.

As it happened, the day was very quiet. The whole family had been invited to pay a visit to M. Condé at St. Martinsville. Helen pleaded a headache, and was regretfully excused, and Burgoyne had evidently forgotten the engagement.

Miss Speedwell, as usual, retired to her room after luncheon for her siesta. Beatrice, visible from Helen's window, was quietly sketching on the north gallery.

Late in the afternoon Burgoyne returned. Helen's heart throbbed wildly as he passed along the corridor to his own apartments.

She took her letter from the table and stood with it in her hand, wondering how she should get it to him.

Beatrice, absorbed in her work, began trilling a little song. Helen stepped to the window and called to her. She laid down her pallet and brushes with a frown, and came in.

" I wish you to take this note to Mr. Burgoyne ; he is in his room, I think," said Helen, mustering a non-chalant air.

To her amazement, Beatrice drew herself up proudly, and replied, " I will not ! "

" What, you will not, you — *slave ?* "

Quicker than thought, Helen's white hand flew out and dealt her a stinging blow on the cheek.

It was incomprehensible to her then and ever after-wards how she could have so far forgotten herself, and how she managed to get out of the room and away from the terrible look in Beatrice's eyes.

Beatrice turned and flew down the stairs, and down through the gardens, and burst like a hurricane into her grandmother's quiet cabin. She threw herself upon the bed, and writhed and moaned.

Salome thought the child was in convulsions, and got down by the bedside and rubbed her hands, and lamented and contorted her old face sympathetically.

" What is it, honey, what is it, dahlin? Cyan't you tell yo' old Mauma what the matta' is? Did anybody hu't yo', sweetheart? "

After a time Beatrice broke out, — not so much in

answer to Mauma's solicitations as to relieve her own feelings, apparently, —

" She struck me, she struck me, oh, oh ! and called me a slave — *a slave !* "

" Who struck you, — Mis' Evalina? "

" No, no ; Mis' Helen. Oh, I hate her, I hate her, *I hate her.*"

She sat up suddenly, and clenched her small fists. Her eyes blazed.

" I could kill her, — I *will* kill her some day."

" Hush, hush, honey," replied her old grandmother ; " the Lawd 'll punish you fo' those wicked wu'ds."

CHAPTER XII.

IT was days before Helen could get sight of Beatrice ; though she tried, without making the effort appear conspicuous. Her sense of justice compelled her to feel that she owed the girl at least a shadow of apology. It was more the desire to ease her own conscience than the wish to make reparation ; she disliked being on uncomfortable terms with any one in the ordinary relations of life. But with Helen there was always the question of her own dignity to consider, — an easy, graceful attribute, if one is not over-conscious of it ; cumbersome if one is.

She went down into the garden one morning to find a fresh rose for her hair, — a decoration to which she was very partial. The reconciliation with her lover had been effected to her entire satisfaction, and she was in a charming mood. As she turned down the path leading to her favorite bush, she espied Beatrice bending over a bed of violets. A stiff white sunbonnet concealed her face, and prevented her from hearing the step on the walk.

Helen stood for a moment or two watching the delicate white fingers selecting the purple blossoms and laying them carefully, one by one, in a tiny basket. Then she touched Beatrice on the shoulder.

"I am very sorry I struck you the other day,

Beatrice," she began, with a pleasant little patronizing air; " I was too hasty, I — "

Beatrice sprang to her feet and flung off the conciliating hand. Her sun-bonnet, tied loosely, fell back upon her shoulders. An angry color flamed in her cheeks and an indignant light in her eyes. She faced Helen for an instant, and then turned and vanished in the shrubbery.

Helen could not forbear the mental comment: "How magnificently handsome she is!" And then she smiled, remembering that a similar remark on Burgoyne's part a few days before had brought about that ridiculous quarrel. She added aloud, " The little savage is angry with me yet ! "

" Who can possibly be angry with my darling? "

This was Burgoyne's voice, of course, charged with the delicious, subtle quality which lovers put into their tones, and which permeates the soul of the loved one like a divine essence.

Helen wheeled round, surprised and startled but in an instant radiant. " Oh, Beatrice," she answered.

" Impossible ! Beatrice is the most amiable little creature in the world," said he.

" So you all appear to think," pouted Helen. " I believe it is only to me she shows her disagreeable side. I wonder why? "

She looked up at him pathetically. Her eyes were the loveliest blue, with an agate-like clearness in their rayed depths.

Burgoyne took her face in his hands and kissed her on the forehead and on the lips. " All your imagination, dearest," he said, lightly, " unless you have happened to offend her in some way? "

A dash of pink came into Helen's cheeks, but she made no reply.

He slipped his arm through hers, and drew her gently along down the walk, his head inclined toward her, his brilliant glance — no longer timid and apologetic — openly delighting in her beauty.

"Tell me," he said playfully, "what have you done to the little pigeon?"

"Why, I — I struck her."

"What! you struck Beatrice?"

He stopped short, and dropped her arm, and seemed to rebound from her.

Beatrice sat looking out at them balefully from a little arbor-like place in the hedge. Her heart leaped at his words; it was worth all she had suffered to have Burgoyne champion her with such an air and such a tone, for at the moment all the La Scalla hauteur and the La Scalla temper rose in him.

"Oh, Burgoyne! please, *please* do not look at me so!" implored Helen.

"I supposed you were aware that no slave is ever chastised on this plantation," he replied coldly.

Beatrice started. "Slave, *slave*," she gasped, "oh, I am nothing but a slave — like the others, the black people. It would have been the same if she had struck Stasie or Black Dick. I am no more than they."

She crouched lower and lower amid the dense green until her face touched the hard ground, repeating over and over, "A slave, a *slave!*"

"Burgoyne, let me explain," said Helen. "I did not mean to do it; it was an accident, believe me! it happened the day we had the — the misunderstanding. I was so wretched when you went away that morning — without a word, as if you did not care; and I wrote you a letter, and asked Beatrice to carry it to you in your room directly after you came in. There was no one else about, or I would not have asked her. I suppose I should not have asked her anyhow, — nobody seems to consider that she is merely a servant. Well, when she refused, — impudently, as if she despised and defied me — "

"Which I do, I do, *I do!*" cried Beatrice in her heart —

"I seemed to lose all control of myself. The impulse came upon me so suddenly; I had no intention — no foreknowledge of what I was going to do. I suppose it was because I had been so wrought up, my nerves were — were — "

Her voice faltered and stopped.

After a moment she gathered a little self-control and went on. "I was so sorry the instant it happened, and so ashamed. I have been trying to get an opportunity to apologize to her ever since."

Burgoyne's face softened, a smile dawned in his eyes.

"You were going to apologize to Beatrice?"

"I did apologize to her just before you came up, and she resented it."

His smile broadened. "She's a spirited little wench," said he. "But Evalina must teach her better manners. I presume she has spoiled the girl by over-indulgence. As you say, nobody regards Beatrice as a servant, and it is quite natural she should forget the fact herself."

They moved on down the path, side by side, the

little cloud that had thrown its shadow upon their hearts disappearing in the sunshine of their love.

Beatrice lay writhing in her misery. She was going through a tremendous experience, unique and terrible for one of her sensibilities and powers, — an experience which must make a profound impression upon her character, which would deepen though it could not change the current of her life. Its channel was cut through solid rock, and it must go on, gathering much and holding all within its strong, firm walls; but it would have its cataracts, its dashing foam and spray, its plunging, irresistible torrents, as well as its deep, cool, quiet places. She had often before this felt her peculiar position in the blind, grieved way of a child. Now she realized the awfulness, the abjectness of it to the last bitter dreg, — realized it because, though still so young, a woman's heart was beating in her bosom.

Beatrice had during these days at La Scalla place come under the same refining influences that had gone to the up-building of Evalina's character. Naturally her character had been up-built in the same way. In no respect had nature discriminated against her, but the reverse. She had a stronger intellectual fiber than Evalina, even a deeper and keener moral apprehension. She far surpassed her young mistress in imagination, — not of the fantastical but the prophetic sort, which pierces the black darkness lying everywhere athwart the path of truth, blasting the rocks, inserting the wedge, lighting the way for new discoveries. This was Beatrice's peculiar talent, — to see things clearly, to comprehend facts, to grasp realities. She could not cheat or deceive herself. She was even insensible to the tragic picturesqueness of her condition, — a circumstance in which a weaker or more romantic nature might have found relief, considering that her sufferings were all of the moral, not the physical sort. She could not complain of ill or even of inconsiderate treatment, except it were accidental.

The child — the girl with the woman's heart — had not attained to her true balance. She was passionate, impatient of wrong, not prepared for the injustices of the world, not accomplished in endurance. It was the awful machinery of society that was crushing her, but she revenged it upon individuals, — a mistake that wiser people are continually making.

A long time ago a sense of separateness had begun to grow in Beatrice, and a reticence of which Evalina sometimes gently complained. Now it seemed to her there was complete isolation. She could have no fellowship with her intellectual and moral equals ever again, — not even in books! She remembered, in this new illumination of her understanding, that there were no delightful stories written about people in her condition, that history itself took no account of slaves. All the circumstances and characteristics which writers set forth and made much of were the circumstances and characteristics appertaining to free people, or to the noble captives of war. Many of the people in books were poor, were afflicted, were cruelly treated; but she felt, this child who had never known hunger or bodily suffering, that she would gladly have exchanged places with the most miserable if only she might have the one thing they possessed and forgot to prize, — liberty.   There was one other passion that lived side by side with the passion of liberty in her soul, — the passion of sympathy.   But in this she was cut off as effectually as in the other.   She could not go down into the kitchen or out into the busy fields and find companionship.   She was a young creature set apart in a profound moral loneliness.   Her love of Nature, her eager pursuit of knowledge, her passion for books, music, art, — of what avail were all these to a slave?   Despair and deep humiliation took possession of her, but only for a time.   Whatever else might be taken from her, there was one thing to which she would cling as long as she had breath, — her self-respect, and with it the indomitable pride of the La Scalla blood.

Helen and Burgoyne sauntered on to the end of the walk, and then turned and retraced their steps. As they again neared the place where Beatrice sat, Doudouce came trotting toward them.

"Isn't she a *dear?*" exclaimed Helen, brushing the animal's nose caressingly with a flower-spray she had just picked.

"For a fact!" laughed Burgoyne.

"I am not punning, sir," she replied saucily, and added: "I would give anything if the lovely creature belonged to me."

"Would you?" said he.   "I was not aware that you were fond of pets."

"I am not fond of ordinary pets, — cats, and canary birds, and the like; but who could help wanting such a sweet thing as Doudouce?"

"Beatrice may give her to you," said he.

"Impossible!   I would never think of asking her."

"Nonsense! I can get her another fawn the next time I go on a tramp, just as pretty as Doudouce, and younger. The woods are full of them. And she would like the practice of taming it."

They passed on and left the garden. Beatrice sat fairly stupefied by this new outrage. What, take away her Doudouce, her pet, her *bien-aimée* — and give her to Helen — to *Helen*, her enemy? *Never!*

She sprang up and hurried out of the garden. Doudouce ran joyfully to meet her. She went into the back hall and took down her small gun used for target shooting, — a gun Burgoyne had given her as a reward of marksmanship a long time ago, — and went quickly down through the garden again. She sped past Salome's cottage and entered one of the narrow, quiet lanes. Douduce, excited and playful, kept close at her heels. She reached the most secluded spot, — one of her favorite retreats, — and wheeled round, her gun at her shoulder.

"Stand still!" she commanded.

The pretty creature obeyed, regarding her with innocent, unsuspecting eyes, — and the next instant dropped, straightened her delicate limbs, and died without a moan.

Beatrice threw down the gun with a heart-broken cry and knelt over the body of her beautiful beloved, whose warm blood was oozing out upon the grass.

Some hours later Big Jake came into the kitchen porch with the dead animal across his shoulder. Aunt Riddy sent a maid to apprise the household, every member of which had been fond of Beatrice's pet.

Beatrice herself was sought for, but could not be

found. She must have gone off to the woods, the servants said, — her gun was not on the rack.

Late in the evening she returned. Evalina met her with a sad face.

"Betty, something very, very dreadful has happened," she said, throwing her arms around Beatrice affectionately and drawing her close. "Your pretty Doudouce is dead."

"I know it," replied Beatrice; "I killed her."

"*You* killed her? Oh, Beatrice, how dreadful! How did it happen?"

"It did not 'happen;' I killed her on purpose."

"Beatrice!" Evalina fell away from her, shocked and frightened.

"She was mine!" said Beatrice, with hard, bright eyes.

CHAPTER XIII.

BURGOYNE, eager for an interview with the father of his *fiancée*, accompanied Helen and her mother to New York. And a few days later the remainder of the La Scalla household set out for their favorite summer resort, — L'Ile Dernière, — the loveliest and most celebrated of all the Gulf islands.

It was still early in the season, but already the place was thronged with wealthy and aristocratic Southerners. There was also a small party of guests from the North, whose native love of adventure and keen Northern curiosity had been excited by flattering reports of this remote and beautiful island, — its remarkable healthfulness, and its delicious coolness, even in midsummer, in spite of its far southern latitude. Dilettant pleasure-seekers these, who took a great deal of pains for their pleasure, yet could not give themselves up to the simple and hearty enjoyment of life ; who were in the habit of roaming over the world in search of new scenes and new sensations, pausing here or there, wherever the fancy seized them, and then up and away again like ships that touch at many ports.

The Southerners, on the other hand, — who travelled with a vast amount of luggage and a retinue of servants, — settled themselves as comfortably and with

as much of an air of permanency as though they expected to spend a lifetime on the island. With most
of them it was an oft-repeated story, this summer
sojourn on L'Ile Dernière. A few like the La Scallas
managed to secure, year after year, the same suites
of apartments in the great hotel. They had their
favorite boats and boatmen. They knew the best
horses for riding and driving, the best fishing-grounds,
and most desirable bathing-places; and they were
familiar with every nook and cranny in the village,
and with all the delightful drives and promenades.
Naturally they took precedence, not only with the
natives and hotel people, but with the new-comers.
They had the prestige of familiarity, of — in a measure
— belonging to the place. And even the clown on
his own hearthstone has the advantage of the king.

But there were other reasons why these rich
Southern planters and merchants were the acknowledged Grand Seigneurs of the island. They had
the courtly, self-respecting and respect-compelling
manner of princes. They were large-hearted and
high-minded, — men of fine leisure. They dispensed
largesse among the attendants and hangers-on with
unquestioning generosity; and they were accustomed
to deference and service. The women belonging to
them had the counterpart of these traits. The chief
fault the critical Northern visitors had to find with
them was a certain polite exclusiveness. They were
satisfied with themselves, with one another, and with
their familiar haunts and diversions. They had little
curiosity and no craving for novelty.

When the steamer containing the La Scalla party
— which as usual included M. Condé — ploughed its

way up the bayou on which the village was located, the wide hotel galleries above and below were gay with women's toilettes.

The sun was going down, with much pomp of color, and children who had just been let out of doors were running about on the ground shouting and playing. Men were strolling, singly or in pairs, and puffing aromatic cigars, as only true-born Southerners can, — not vigorously, or as if in haste to be done with it and ready for another; but slowly, caressingly prolonging the life of the slender brown cylinder as if there might never in the world be another like it, with such a flavor, such a divine spirituality of fragrance ! Lovers were promenading in the myrtle-shaded lanes, and a few carriages were rolling noiselessly over the sandy drives.

There was still greater activity on the beach, where crowds of eager young people — and old people renewing their youth — were making ready for boating and surf-bathing. The smooth glassy surface of the water, suffused with the day's last blushes, was beginning to rock and sway a little as if beckoning to the white sails.

Beatrice, catching the spirit of the lively and familiar scene, and filled with the joy of boundless space and motion, could hardly wait for the lowering of the gang-plank. With her feet upon the sand, her eyes sweeping the vast horizon, the cool keen breath of the sea blowing in her face, and the recurrence of a thousand delightful memories of days past, she again forgot that she was a slave. She turned a laughing face to Evalina as they went up the board walk to the hotel steps, and remarked upon the wild antics of the children, whose white legs and feet were temporarily freed from the bondage of shoes and stockings, — their nurses standing by with these garments in their hands, broad grins on their dusky faces.

Evalina smiled back and said, "What makes you look so happy, Beatrice? Are you so glad to get back here again?"

"Yes, are not you?" returned Beatrice. "One can breathe here better than anywhere else; it seems as if one's very *soul* breathes! I don't want to go in yet, do you?"

"I think I want my supper," said Evalina.

"May I go out alone then — I am not hungry?"

"Do you mean on the water?"

"Yes."

"As you like; but I should think you had had enough of the water!"

"It is different to be in a little boat," Beatrice answered, and turned and ran off toward the beach.

Several Northern people, grouped on the gallery, overheard this little dialogue, and one of them — a somewhat distinguished-looking lady — remarked, "Is it not a burning shame that that beautiful child is a slave?"

She glanced about her, and spoke in an undertone.

"A slave! is it possible?" exclaimed another lady.

"Why, how do you know, Mrs. Thompson?" demanded a third, a young girl with bright, inquisitive eyes. "I was just thinking of the charming contrast between the two, and of how lovely they were to each other, — supposing they were sisters!"

" They are lovely to each other," replied Mrs. Thompson ; " but one is mistress and the other maid. I met those people, the La Scallas, here at this same place last year when I took that long voyage with my brother, Captain Jack. That is the girl I told you about, Harold," she added, turning to her husband.

" I remember," he said, his eyes following Beatrice's rapidly retreating form with lively interest. " What a damnable thing it is ! "

Mrs. Thompson smilingly condoned his profanity to her two friends, with the remark, —

" Harold feels so strongly on the slavery question."

" Who would n't feel strongly about such an infernal institution ? " he retorted, resenting as he often did his wife's calm attitude.

" Well, you have my permission to say as many naughty words as you like on the subject, Mr. Thompson," laughed the young girl; " my sex prohibits me. But, beware ! we are in the enemy's country."

" We are still under the American flag," he replied, " and have the right of free speech."

" Oh, might makes right, you know, and we are wofully in the minority ! "

" No might on earth shall ever make me hold my tongue in the face of a gigantic wrong," he answered, raising his voice.

" Hush, hush, Harold ! " cautioned his wife, " you always get so excited ! "

" The occasion justifies it," said he.

"Oh, the occasion may justify it, but we must consider whether any good can be accomplished by it.

It is rather Quixotic of you, my dear, to attempt storming so large a castle single-handed."

" ' Little drops of water, little grains of sand'," quoted the young girl, laughingly.

" Yes," exclaimed Mr. Thompson, " you are right, Grace ; it is the little agitations, the little single-handed attacks, here and there, that finally provoke great revolutions."

" Do you wish to provoke a revolution ? " asked his wife.

" Well, a reform, at least."

" And I am with you, dear ; we differ only as to methods."

The amiable pair had been differing as to methods, and trying to convince each other of their respective errors of judgment, for twenty years or more, and both had conspicuously failed. Nature had cast their characters strongly, and in different moulds. Mrs. Thompson had the diplomacy of wisdom and charity, her husband the rashness, narrowness, and intensity of fanaticism. No fault could be found with either of them in the matter of principle, and both were animated with the spirit of benevolence.

" I see how we may do one little thing in the way of reformation," said Mrs. Thompson : " let us purchase this young girl's freedom ! "

" I do not suppose they would sell her," returned her husband.

In the course of a day or two, Mr. Thompson was introduced to M. La Scalla ; but the two gentlemen had not much in common. There was, rather, a mutual antipathy, — half-unconscious on the one side, positive and aggressive on the other. To Mr.

Thompson, La Scalla was the suave embodiment of enormous offences against modern civilization. He resented the Southerner's gentleness of manner, his courteous and dignified bearing, and denounced him for a hypocrite and soft-handed tyrant.

Mrs. Thompson differed with him broadly and frankly. She declared that M. La Scalla was quite her ideal of a gentleman ; that he might be the victim of his education and social influences, but that no impartial student of human nature could look into his face, or observe his conduct, and doubt either his kindliness or his candor.

One morning there was a threatened rainstorm, and a few gentlemen who did not care to risk getting wet were collected in the hotel office, — among them Mr. Thompson and M. La Scalla. The conversation took a political turn, as conversation among men in those days was almost certain to do, and there was some rather warm talk relative to the next Presidential election, and to certain important matters pending in Congress. Mr. Thompson was in the minority of course, but held his own with angry fearlessness ; and had the satisfaction of being argued with and not frowned down. The Southerners observed the etiquette of discussion with many an " I beg yo' pardon, suh," and " Permit me to correct you on that point, suh," and the like : which polite formalities of contradiction were almost unbearable to the out-spoken New Yorker.

In the midst of the talk, Beatrice came along the corridor with a message from Madame La Scalla to her husband. He was standing near the counter in the act of lighting a cigar. Beatrice paused, expecting in a moment to catch his eye. A young fellow lounging on the gallery sauntered up and addressed her with impudent familiarity. At that instant M. La Scalla threw away his burnt match and glanced up. He took the cigar from his lips and stepped quickly out, his usually serene eyes flashing and the color mounting to his pale face.

The fellow, whom Beatrice herself had rebuffed with a surprised, indignant stare, slunk away.

Some one in the office happened to cast an eye at Thompson, who shrugged his shoulders and muttered with a sneer, "What exquisite courtesy these lordly slave-owners show toward their handsome female chattels!"

M. Condé, who sat near, caught the import of the words and sprang to his feet, livid with anger. M. La Scalla had sent Beatrice away and re-entered the office. He glanced inquiringly at his old friend, and then round upon the other persons present, with his accustomed calmness and gentleness of manner, which however never disguised the force that lay behind it.

There was a sensation; but Mr. Thompson, though evidently somewhat disconcerted, met his gaze doggedly.

"Take that back!" thundered M. Condé; but his old voice quavered, and Mr. Thompson turned his back upon him.

"What is it?" demanded M. La Scalla. His form seemed to rise to a kingly height; the expression of his face — paling again, but with eyes brilliantly alight — was singularly lofty and beautiful. The quiet majesty of the man impressed every one. A thrill ran through the hearts of his friends: it was as though he stood for the honor and dignity of the whole proud South, her champion and defender.

"That man — that *cur*," exclaimed M. Condé, pointing a long thin finger at Thompson, "has grossly insulted us — you, me, every Southern gentleman!"

Thompson's face flamed, and his eyes sparkled defiantly. His courage, at all events, was equal to his imprudence ; and he was supported by the conviction that he was *right*, whatever came of the affair.

"I spoke the truth," he said, straightening up and planting himself firmly. "The whole world knows of the practices of you Southern *gentlemen!* You cannot disguise it; that girl's beautiful face tells the story plainly enough!"

He suddenly remembered his wife's proposal to purchase Beatrice's freedom, and with a masterly reversal of himself, as it were, he hastened to apologize. "I am a radical," he said, "and you are radicals ; and we are on opposite sides of the field, and ought not to throw stones at one another. But after all, gentlemen, facts are facts, and I have never been in the habit of evading them. Honest men, I take it, are willing to stand by their facts."

"We are, by heaven!" cried M. Condé, "and with the sword!"

Mr. Thompson turned to M. La Scalla. "I beg you to believe that I meant no offence to you personally, sir," he said. "Whatever may be your opinions, or the faults of your particular section of the country, according to my view — I — "

"You lie!" shouted M. Condé. "It makes no difference that M. La Scalla did not hear your vile insinuation: *I* heard and understood!"

Mr. Thompson, still ignoring him, continued, "I have a proposition to make to you, M. La Scalla, — a proposition of my wife's. She has become very much interested in that young girl, and desires to purchase her freedom. What will you take for her?"

M. La Scalla looked as if he had not heard aright; his manner was frigid. "What will I take fo' — "

"Beatrice, I think you call her?"

"Suh! she is not fo' sale."

"I thought as much!" returned Thompson, with a sneer and a new tide of anger.

"Suh, you insult me!" The lightning played in M. La Scalla's eyes.

"That is as you may take it," the other answered.

"You are perhaps not unmindful of the consequences of an insult offe'd to a man of honeh!"

"I have not forgotten the accursed locality I am in," replied Thompson; "I am aware of the consequences you refer to, and ready to abide by them."

"Very well; Monsieur Condé, will you have the kindness to attend to the matta' on my behalf?"

The infuriated old soldier bowed as though the most distinguished honor had been conferred upon him.

M. La Scalla turned to leave the room. The pallor of his face was deathly, and he moved uncertainly and put out his hands as if he had suddenly been stricken blind. He staggered as he reached the threshold, and leaned against the door-post. Every one in the room, even Mr. Thompson, started forward with the impulse to save him from falling. But they were too late; he sank heavily to the floor.

Madame La Scalla and a physician were summoned;

but he was unconscious when they reached him, and he did not rally.

The Thompson party took passage on the out-going boat the following morning, bidding a sorrowful adieu to the Island. As they steamed away, the flag above the hotel was lowered at half-mast, and the sound of a tolling bell came to them over the sparkling waves.

CHAPTER XIV.

WHEN M. La Scalla's will was opened it was found that to Beatrice and her grandmother had been bequeathed the priceless legacy of freedom. But old Salome did not live to realize the fulfillment of her long-cherished and finally abandoned hope. For many months her health had been failing, and she passed away within a week after the return of the family from L'Ile Dernière.

In the preamble of the will something of Beatrice's history was set forth, together with her peculiar claims upon the La Scalla family; and to her were left the proceeds of Miss Rosamond's estate, which had been placed in the hands of Mr. Vincent for investment in Northern enterprises, — a disposition M. La Scalla had made of his own surplus income for many years past.

It was left to Evalina to break the glad tidings to Beatrice. Some time had elapsed since their return to the plantation. Evalina had been terribly prostrated by her father's death, and she was lying upon a couch in her own room, and Beatrice was ministering to her with the most tender and delicate sympathy.

"Beatrice," she said, holding her companion's hand in her weak but sensitive clasp, and looking up into

her face affectionately, " I have something very important to tell you. Papa's will — " her voice faltered,
but in a moment she went on — " Papa's will has
made you free. And now — "

Beatrice started up, her lips parted, her eyes filled
with a strange wild light. She wheeled round, threw
her clasped hands high above her head, and made as
if to rush from the room, but stopped midway and fell
upon her knees with face upturned in the involuntary
attitude of prayer.

Evalina flew to her with a cry of self-reproach for
her abruptness, hesitated, and then retreated a step
or two and stood regarding her with an awe-stricken
gaze.

Beatrice was in the habit of repeating daily the
prescribed formulas of praise and supplication, —
perfunctorily for the most part, but with occasional
flashes of mental questioning as to the real purpose
and efficacy of it all. She was familiar with the
Christian doctrines as they are usually set forth in
quiet country places, by quiet country priests, where
habit takes the place of belief, and where the majestic
church service, mumbled Sunday after Sunday by a
drowsy congregation, becomes as commonplace as any
of the marvellous, steadily recurring phenomena of
Nature. It was her impression, or theory, — if a
child's vague, incoherent ideas may be construed as
a theory, — that Christianity was one of society's most
elaborate and august conventionalities, too splendid
and remote for practical application to every-day life ;
to be taken *au grand serieux* in a way, but not
positively believed in, any more than the geometrical
birds and trees stitched into our grandmothers'

samplers.   The Creed, the Ten Commandments, the
Lord's Prayer were a kind of moral sampler, patterns
of the thought and conduct and culture of by-gone
generations.   She had, however, a very real reverence
for sacred emblems and for customs consecrated by
the faith and practice of the long Past, — due, perhaps, to Evalina's gentle but decided influence.   Life
— the life of the world — was becoming more practical and more artistic and more vitally religious.   It
was past the seed-time, and in the blossom.   Squares
of neatly embroidered canvas were not needed as
vouchers for young ladies' skill in needle-work.
Their taste manifested itself in subtler and more
useful and more telling ways.   And men no longer
measured their actions by Rules of Conduct ; honorable and kindly motives found means of expression
independent of mere etiquette.   All the virtues and
graces were insisting upon a larger and freer
interpretation.

These things Beatrice could see in the conduct of
the people about her.   They had been especially
conspicuous in the conduct of M. La Scalla.   Art
and morals were linking themselves more intimately
and significantly with life ; even a child listening to
the legends of fifty years ago could understand that.
But art and morals are not mere erratic air-plants,
attaching themselves like graceful parasites to the
social structure.   Their apparent beginnings lie in
the samplers, in the Rules of Conduct, in men's
earliest conceptions of the Beautiful and the True ;
but back of these there is something else, — something real, something vital, something eternal.   A
something that came to Beatrice now in one supreme

burst of revelation, sweeping aside all that men have tried to teach from the throne of intellect about the soul and its immortal destiny, and thrilling her heart with an unutterable rapture of recognition and thanksgiving : "God, I thank Thee ! God, I thank Thee ! " She took no account of the kindly human agency that had wrought the great change in her condition. She realized nothing, — nothing but God, the Infinite, the Omnipotent. It was a triumph of the spirit over physical consciousness, — such as martyrs have felt, and heroes on battle-fields ; such as poets feel in moments of great inspiration ; such as any soul may feel that scales the heights and holds communion with the Eternal.

But such moments cannot last, they do not belong to time. Beatrice arose and turned to Evalina.

"Won't you lie down, dear? — you look so white ! " Evalina entreated.

Beatrice laughed. Her whiteness was the pale radiance of supreme joy. " No, I would rather go out of doors," she said, " out into the open air. Oh, I am so happy ! I am *so happy !* "

Evalina's face lighted up with the reflection of her gladness. " Go, then," she answered, and Beatrice kissed her and vanished.

Evalina felt strangely lonely when Beatrice was gone. She had opened her hand, and let the dearest of birds fly away, — the wildest, the most untamable of birds, she mused, and yet the gentlest ! There was a sense of moral as well as social loss. She was pained and disappointed that the first use Beatrice made of her freedom was to escape from her presence. She had pictured a different scene ; had thought they would sit down quietly together, and talk it all over and discuss their future. She had many more things to tell, — plans her dear father had made for them both respecting their education. But far across the fields Beatrice was flying, towards the woods.

"Ah, she loves the woods!" murmured Evalina, gazing wistfully from the open window. "She wants to pour out her joy to them. She thinks the birds and the squirrels can understand — better than I perhaps. Or she may just want to be quite alone with herself, and get a little used to her freedom. How strange it must seem to her! And yet she was never treated as a slave. She has been my companion, — my friend." She sighed, and a little twinge of wounded love gripped her heart. Would Beatrice care for her now, as before? But she pulled herself up sharply. "Oh, what am I doing!" she cried. "Thinking first of myself, — of how Beatrice's good fortune is going to affect *me*. And because she has accepted my father's gift in the fullest sense, and with a joy that shows her deep appreciation, I have — in my innermost heart — half accused her of ingratitude, vain little egotist that I am!"

Her mother came down the hall and stopped at the open door with a hand upon either doorpost. She wore a long, white, clinging gown unrelieved by any touch of color. She was extremely pale, but lovely as a delicate white flower that the rain has washed but not crushed. Her beautiful hair was massed on the top of her head, little rings curling at the temples.

Evalina ran to her and drew her into the room and coaxed her to be seated.

Madame La Scalla had been singularly affected by her husband's death. She could not accept it as a fact. She was like a tree that has been felled, and whose leaves refuse to wither. Maurice dead? Oh, no, it could not be : he was ever-present to her, only that her eyes — her physical eyes — could not see him. But she was continually hearing his step, his voice, his pleasant laugh, and could feel the touch of his hand, — which was like no other touch. If she closed her eyes he was always there, seated in his accustomed chair, or coming in at the door, or crossing the fields with the overseer, or riding up the avenue. Or if her eyes were open he was approaching from behind. The seeming actuality of his presence was continually forcing her to look up, to turn her head ; and the vanished illusion left a poignant sting. " I wish I were blind," she said to Cosette one day ; " then my Maurice would stay with me : my eyes banish him."

During her husband's lifetime she had never been wholly satisfied with his calm affection and unimpassioned admiration. Now it seemed to her that their relations had been ideal. She could not remember that he had ever given her one unkind word or rebuking look. All her recollections of him were sweet — poignantly sweet. She would not go into mourning : Maurice had not approved of mourning, though he had once said that it should be a matter of personal feeling. He was entirely without prejudice or arbitrariness. She could recall but few expressions of his opinion. Looking back upon his life it was apparent that he had been singularly reticent, though no one had ever been in doubt respect-

ing his views and principles: he had not given bond
for them in words but in conduct and character.
There were few written records of his thought even.
He had never been given to letter-writing. When
she had been away he had kept her informed about
simple home matters, — that was all. She had preserved almost all his letters, carelessly putting them
aside here and there. She gathered them up now,
and read and conned them over and over. She
spent a great deal of time in retrospect and in studying the theory of his clean, simple, independent life.
How thoroughly he had lived his life, how whole-
somely, how sincerely! She realized that now, and
lived in a kind of rapturous memory of him. And
she was not unhappy; except in those bitter moments
when she could not deceive herself, when the awful
finality of death forced itself upon her. Sometimes
she dressed herself elaborately in the toilettes he had
liked, and sometimes — as now — spent whole days
in negligee.

"Where is Beatrice?" she asked.

Evalina explained that she had gone to the woods.

"Does she know — have you told her?"

"Yes, just a little while ago," said Evalina.

"And how did it affect her?"

"Oh, Mama, you should have seen her, — her
face was positively glorified!"

Madame sighed, then she smiled, and said in a
musing way, "We differed about Beatrice, — your
father and I. He thought we might make reparation.
I feared we should only increase the mischief by at-
tempting to remedy it. It remains to be seen."

She arose and moved up and down the room, her

cheeks beginning to flush with excitement. "It remains to be seen," she repeated. "Your father thought a peculiar injustice was suffered by such persons as Beatrice, — persons with rare talents and fine sensibilities, whose wrongs and not their crimes put them at the mercy of a cruel world. He thought the world ought to join hands with Nature to right these wrongs instead of making them an excuse for continued oppression. It was a peculiar theory — for a Southern man," she added. "But your father did not belong to a type or a clique. He believed in one thing, — Eternal Justice."

She was silent for a time, and then went on. "I intend that Beatrice shall have her chance. If there is such a thing as social redemption for one of her unfortunate class, she shall be redeemed from the taint of blood of which she is the innocent victim. Your father's will must be carried out in spirit as well as in letter. Beatrice has gone to the woods, did you say?"

Evalina, who had been for some moments nervously anxious to divert her mother's thoughts, replied in cheering tone, "Yes; and just before you came in I was standing here pitying myself because she had taken her happiness and gone off to tell it to her particular friends the Brownies and the Fairies, instead of sharing it with me!"

"You would have done differently, of course," returned her mother, stopping abruptly in her walk as though arrested by a new thought.

"Indeed I would," said Evalina. "I should have wanted human sympathy. But Beatrice is not like anybody else."

"No, and should not be judged by common standards. She has not conformed to the stereotyped pattern of humanity. She is consistent, however; she does — what she does; not what you would do, or I, or any one else. I have always remarked the child's singular independence, — which is not rebellion, or defiance, or egotism, but an unconscious noble poise of herself upon a pedestal her very own. Let her alone, my dear; do not constrain her by so much as a thought."

"I can hardly help my thoughts, Mama," said Evalina, smiling.

"You must remember there is a larger liberty than the personal independence Beatrice has acquired to-day, more essential to happiness. You love her, but love may become the worst of tyrants. Be patient. Give Beatrice time to adjust herself. I think you may depend upon it that she will be true."

"Oh, I know that, — I know it," said Evalina, with conviction.

There was a spot that Beatrice knew, — a bit of a *chênaie* in the midst of the cypress swamp, — that was entirely isolated. She had to cross the *coulée* to reach it, but there were points where she could do this by taking a gallant leap. She cleared it to-day at the first approach, and landing safe on the other side parted the long curtains of silvery moss suspended from the trees and stepped into the place, into its cool deep stillness.

A thick carpet of leaves covered the ground, — leaves that had been silently falling for years, packed layer upon layer. Overhead was the vast emerald vault, and far away through the ranks of cypress-boles and swaying banners of moss were shining glimpses of the bayou.

In all the many times Beatrice had visited this spot she had never met a human being. She had no fears of meeting any now. She might have shouted at the top of her voice in the confident assurance that there was none to hear. Her movements were unguarded, her face made no concealment of the joy she felt, — a purely human delight now, rather than a spiritual exaltation. She laughed aloud, and leapt upon fallen trees and flung out her arms in wild free gestures. She threw back her head and looked up through the net-work of boughs, through swarming myriads of leaves twinkling against the blue sky. A few birds began twittering in the pale green light as if it were evening, and a few small four-footed creatures were scampering about. She clapped her hands.

"O birds! O squirrels!" she cried, "I am free, I am free! O trees and sky and leaves and flowers I am free, free, free! Oh, if I had but wings! I feel so light, so swift, so strange, — as if I might almost lift myself up and sink into those billowy white clouds yonder and float away, away above the world. . . . I wish I were on the sea in my boat, with the wind blowing and the waves rolling high. Or I wish — I wish — Oh, it is too still here, I want life, *life!* Oh, you are stupid creatures, that look out at me with your scared eyes. You too are free, but you live in holes and nests. You know nothing of life! And freedom and life should go together, — freedom and life, freedom and life!"

When this wave of ecstasy subsided Beatrice sat down upon a mossy log and gave rein to thought, — rapid, tumultuous, exultant. And first of all — alas for human vanity ! — her freedom was a salve to her sorely wounded pride. She was a personage now, entitled to consideration. People would no longer condescend to her, but treat her as an equal. She would have a right to respect, to companionship, to love, — not conditioned upon the grievous circumstance of her birth. Her talents, her genius, her many accomplishments, so worthless a little while ago, had suddenly acquired value. She was ambitious. She would win a place for herself in the world ; would join the Great Procession, the echoes of whose triumphant marching had filled her soul with longing when she was but a little child. There was nothing to hinder now ; she was free, free ! — and life all before her. They should see, they who had scorned, — or, worse yet, had ignored her, — they should see ! And Burgoyne, too, whose by-gone kindness was a pain to remember, who had taught her so many things, and who for the sake of another (whom she hated) had lightly robbed her of his own beautiful gift — he — they — all the world should recognize her claims to high respect ! Her cheeks burned, her eyes shone, her whole body throbbed with anticipation of her glorious vindication of herself.

She fell into a long reverie, — such a reverie as ambitious youth delights in, — from which she at last started up with a sigh. Ah, but how does one begin to be great ? What is the first step ? A blank wall seemed to rise before her, a smooth blank wall, with no niches for her feet. Would things be so very different after all, — would she not go on here at the plantation quite the same as before? In reality there could be but little change in the conditions of her life. "What then is freedom?" she asked. It was not a question for the intellect, which undertakes the solution of so many difficult problems not within its province; which deals with inflexible material that bends only in angles; which is like a voice incapable of inflections, a medium through which the finer meanings of life are sifted and lost. Intellect is arrogant and as stubborn as stupidity. A subtler consciousness in her shaped the answer: Freedom is equality, dignity, boundless opportunity, everything that noble souls aspire to in this world.

When Beatrice left her sylvan retreat and started homeward, it was with a slower step but with a heart full of joy, — like the joy of new love, that turns everything to beauty and delight.

CHAPTER XV.

A TRANSCENDENT experience awaited Beatrice a few weeks later. M. Condé, to whom the tragic death of Maurice had been a shock and a horror, was much concerned about its effect on Madame La Scalla, and took it upon himself to consult the old family physician in St. Martinsville, who did the most natural thing in the world, — recommended a change of scene. And Burgoyne, before whom — as being now the head of the family — they laid the matter, proposed to his mother that they immediately start on the contemplated journey abroad. He mapped out a plan : they might spend the autumn in Venice perhaps, — since she had always expressed a great liking for that unique city, — and the winter in Rome, and join the Vincents the following spring in Paris.

Madame La Scalla listened with an indifferent ear, though without opposition, merely stipulating that Beatrice should accompany them. "Of course," she added, as if it were a matter which admitted of no question, "Beatrice must now take her place on an equal footing with us."

"Will not that be a little awkward, mother?" Burgoyne demurred.

"Oh, let us put conventionalities aside," she answered impatiently, "and stand upon the simple truth. I suppose you think society will disapprove. Let it. The La Scallas surely are not accountable to public opinion ! For myself, I have but one purpose left in life, — to be loyal to your father's principles."

Burgoyne was not thinking of public opinion, but of the Vincents. What would Helen say, and in what terms would Mrs. Vincent couch her indignation? But he offered no further remonstrances. He saw his mother's eyes filling with tears. She was seated at her desk, where she had been writing. The pen was still in her hand. She let it drop, arose and moved about, unable to control her emotion.

"Oh," she cried, "he is gone, gone forever ! He can nevermore raise his voice in gentle protest against wrong and injustice, — never, never, never ! My son," — she wheeled round and came toward him with a passion of earnestness in voice and gesture, — "let us carry out his will effectively, *effectively*. The dead are so helpless ! Oh, they are so helpless ! Do you remember how he lay there, his eyes closed, his lips still, his dear hands folded? How expressive are dead hands, — expressive of work finished ! "

She broke down utterly ; and Burgoyne, overcome by the picture she had drawn, folded his arms about her and said huskily, "Don't, mother ; I can't bear to see you suffer so. I will do what I can — all I can, anything you wish."

At that moment everything else in the world seemed trivial in comparison with his mother's grief and the awful fact that caused it.

The terrible event had changed the whole com-

14

plexion of things on the plantation, and Burgoyne, putting his own personal affairs aside, had devoted himself entirely to his mother and sister, and to the care of the estate. Like his father, he had little talent for letter-writing, and his communications to his betrothed were such as called forth continual complaints and appeals. Could he not find time to write more than *three pages*, even though they *were* the largest letter-size? And would he not tell her more about his own precious self, and the dear thoughts that were in his heart of hearts?

Such importunities annoyed him. He was a youth possessed of a good deal of spontaneity. He could be tender in voice and look, could say and do charming things on the prompting of the moment, but he could not be ardent at long range; and he was too much occupied with the business in hand to sit down and compose voluminous letters of the kind to delight a romantic girl with an insatiable appetite for such sweets. A most unsatisfactory lover a thousand miles away! As a matter of fact Helen's image was pretty nearly always with him, floating in that dreamy sea of sub-consciousness which constitutes the half, or more than half, of life to us all; and often, in the intervals of activity, he found himself thinking glowingly of her, but in the unshapen way of reverie.

Some faint reflection of these thoughts did occasionally light up his broad page, as when he said, " I got off my horse this morning, down by the *coulée*, and picked a blue flag and pinned it on my coat. The color of it, and the light and dark rays, reminded me of your eyes; and then I remembered that you said you liked large loose flowers such as that, rather than the kind of things that have regular petals set round a centre, — like inverted wine bottles round a circular garden bed! You said they were more artistic. And I, too, think they are."

This was not very direct love-making, but a girl must have been obtuse who could not find in it the most exquisite of compliments.

Burgoyne's apprehension respecting the view which the Vincents might take of Beatrice's new dignities proved to be well-founded.

The La Scallas were to coast up the Atlantic seaboard and sail from New York. Mrs. Vincent and Helen were at a watering-place, but they promptly declared their intention to come home and open the house in Madison Square in order to entertain them while in the city. The house was not actually closed, only swathed in linen and otherwise protected from moth and dust. Mr. Vincent and Aunt Cynthia had managed to live in it all summer.

Burgoyne thought it wise to apprise Helen beforehand of Beatrice's social elevation, in order to avoid any unpleasant *contre-temps;* and Mrs. Vincent, without taking a moment's time to consider, seized her pen and wrote a letter of remonstrance to his mother : —

" You cannot do this thing, Corinne," she said; "people will never forget that the girl was born a slave, or that she bears the additional disgrace of illegitimacy, — enough of itself to bar her out of respectable society. I do wish you would wait a little, my dear; your great sorrow has unsettled you. I am sure you are not in your normal, healthy state of mind. You were always so clear-headed

in these matters, — much more so than dear Maurice, if
you will allow me to say so.   But of course, if you insist,
Helen and I will put by our personal feelings and 'receive'
Mademoiselle Beatrice.   But fancy the dudgeon of my
Irish maids if they should know they were asked to wait
upon a person tainted with colored blood!"

Corinne wrote back that their stay in New York
would be very brief, — in all probability not longer
than a day or two, — and it would not be worth while
to put their friends to so much trouble.   She had some
shopping to do, and she wished to take the girls for
a sail to West Point; and if Constance pleased, they
would prefer to stop at a hotel.   Burgoyne would of
course make his own arrangements.

But, notwithstanding, Mrs. Vincent proceeded to
carry out her intention.   She was on the alert for the
New Orleans steamer, and met them at the landing
with her carriage, her manner overflowing with cordiality and welcome.   She was kind enough to shake
hands with Beatrice and to shower upon her a little
volley of congratulations, — rather incoherent, and
delivered so rapidly and cut off so abruptly as to
leave no chance for reply, so that Beatrice was spared
all save a passive part in the sham friendliness.

Mrs. Vincent bustled about, giving orders to the
footman and the coachman, making inquiries about
the baggage, getting Calisty and her bandboxes into
an omnibus, and altogether carrying things with such
a high hand that Madame La Scalla's suggestion
about going to the hotel was quite borne down and
overridden.

Helen, looking lovelier than ever in a smart
summer costume, was seated in an open carriage —

which she drove herself — waiting for Burgoyne. Her recognition of Beatrice had the sting of cool, patronizing superiority, that rankles cruelly in a proud heart.

Beatrice was surprised that *now* any one should have the power to wound her, that her new grace of liberty and equality was not proof against the petty arrows of a young girl's careless contumely! But her self-respect, wounded by both Helen's discourtesy and Mrs. Vincent's strained politeness, was restored by the genuine kindness of Mr. Vincent and the anxious friendliness of Aunt Cynthia, whose sympathies for the "oppressed race" had but lately been profoundly stirred by Mrs. Stowe's powerful romance; though in any case Beatrice's interest in the new scenes unrolled before her, in the surprising activity and intensity of the great Northern metropolis, would have banished the unpleasant sensations of those first moments from her consciousness and set them in the dim palimpsest of memory, to form a part of the summary of her life-experiences. The vivid beauty of the Hudson and the Highlands — so different from Southern rivers and landscape — was simply a delightfully novel aspect of a beloved face. She had not been all her young life a lover of Nature without gaining Nature's confidence, without being able to bring to her aid Nature's sweet consolations.

Helen declined to participate in the shopping, and on the day of the excursion to West Point she excused herself to go with Burgoyne to meet his old college friend, Hugh Connelly.

Hugh had recently fallen heir to an obscure baronetcy in Scotland, and had written to Burgoyne that he was going over to the Old Country *incognito,* to find out whether he had better accept the legacy or escape from it. In response to Burgoyne's request, he had delayed his journey in order to take passage in the "Baltic" with the La Scalla party.

Helen invited him up to dinner, and he came with a radiant manner and a fine flower in his button-hole. He was a good-looking young fellow, with curly hair and smiling blue eyes, and an expression that indicated a perpetual play of humorous fancy. There was nothing about him to suggest the sentimental poet. When Madame La Scalla made friendly inquiries concerning his muse, he replied with a blush that the fickle goddess had forsaken him.

"I have not attempted any poetry," he said, "since I visited at your house several years ago."

"Really! And how are we to construe that?" she asked.

"Oh, it only means that I am older and have shifted my point of view a little," he replied. And then he added, "I have been at work trying to better my fortunes."

"Hugh has turned politician," said Burgoyne with a smile. "You received the nomination for representative, did you not?"

"I declined it."

"Indeed!" exclaimed Madame, to whom that honor seemed of more consequence than the Scotch baronetcy.

"I can't afford to go into politics yet," said Hugh, and then with clever modesty turned the conversation into another channel.

During the little personal discussion Evalina afforded an interesting study of conscious maidenhood.

Ever since her eyes first rested upon Hugh's handsome face, his lively existence had found an echo in her pure young heart. But it was a secret guarded with vigilant modesty. Sometimes, during his visit to the plantation, she had fancied with a shy girlish instinct that his glance challenged her particular interest in what he was saying; that what he said was intended more for her than any one else, so delicately did he seem to shape and color his thought to harmonize with hers. But cool reason had always forbidden the indulgence of such sweet thoughts. Now, however, instinct again got the better of reason and planted its crimson banner in her cheeks, and made her whole sensitive face respond to the blue lightning of his glance when it chanced to meet hers.

The following day the party embarked. The Vincents went on board, as did the friends of hundreds of other passengers, to take their final leave, — a culminant rite, whose grace depends on brevity. They had not given themselves much margin of time, and in their case the fine flavor of parting — for every important moment in life, whether of joy or sorrow, has its fine flavor — was not lost in a protracted waiting fraught with dreary platitudes and vacuous silences. The hoarse cry, "All 'shore not going !" cut short their farewells and hurried them off on the pier, where the crowd of wistful stay-at-homes lingered, looking up at the thickly peopled decks and singling out familiar faces with smiling or tearful eyes, fluttering their handkerchiefs and calling, " Good-bye, good-bye, good-bye !"

Beatrice, standing near Burgoyne, was jostled by the throng surging to the front, with the brutal heedlessness of humanity *en masse.* He took her hand and helped her to mount upon a coil of rope, which brought her face almost to a level with his. The ship moved away, and Helen waved him her last kiss and put up her opera-glass.

"Oh, look, Mama, at Burgoyne and Beatrice!" she cried. "Do you see them standing there, side by side? Really, I think that is ominous!"

"Nonsense, you foolish, romantic girl!" said her mother. But even she did not soon forget the striking picture of the two splendid faces fading slowly in the mists of the sea.

CHAPTER XVI.

OUT in mid-ocean, in ideal weather, day after day, Beatrice revelled in the glory of space and motion and the wide blue light of sky and sea. It was not so much a time for thought as for sensation. Why should one fret the mind with thought in the midst of this vast peace? Was it not enough to live, to breathe, to feel that God was managing the world, and all was well?

But there were many diversions. If one would learn the atomic weight of individuals, let him go to sea. A ship is a little republic where every man, freed from his habitual environment and dependent upon his personal quality alone, has an equal chance; where individuals fall into their true relative positions by an unerring law of moral gravitation.

Madame La Scalla, here as elsewhere, unconsciously exerted her peculiar power of attracting whatever there was of intelligence or genius or refinement, — though now, in her widowhood, she was in a measure indifferent, lying back in her steamer-chair for long hours at a stretch, careless of companionship, or idly attentive to the conversation in which she took little part. Possibly the young people about her added to the charm of her *locale*. They seldom wandered far from her, and the little party constituted a center toward which the select of the steamer's company were instinctively drawn.

Beatrice came in for a share of this social distinction, and realized in a new and still more delicious sense the value of liberty and equality. Here there was no condescension except to her youth; and this, with her irresistible beauty and unspoiled character, seemed to entitle her to a protecting, indulgent kindness half playful, half caressing. She had her modest little share in the talk sometimes, — when she was directly appealed to, — under Madame La Scalla's encouraging eye. Naturally the conversation, though it never failed to stimulate her imagination, often rose above her understanding, — as when Madame La Scalla and a distinguished New York artist discussed and compared the several modern schools in his profession; or when a professor of English literature let loose a volley of comment and criticism upon authors whose names only (seen on the backs of books in M. La Scalla's library or on Madame's table) had a precarious lodgment in her mind; or when Hugh on clear moonless nights swept the sky with his field-glass and discoursed about the splendor of the constellations, calling them by name and referring familiarly to their respective habits.

All these things opened inviting and mysterious vistas in which Beatrice's fancy loved to revel. It had been planned that upon their return from abroad she and Evalina should enter a Northern school and begin a systematic course of study; and the prospect delighted her, — not that she so dearly loved study, but that she wanted so much to *know*. She was rather impatient of the tedium of books. Literature was nothing to her but a vehicle, valuable only for its cargo. Her mind was filled with three images, — Nature, Man, God.

Burgoyne, who still continued his violin practice, and had become fairly proficient, sat one evening softly drawing the bow, his eyes fixed inadvertently upon a particular bright point in the heavens, intent upon mastering a difficult strain.

"Are you performing incantations to Orpheus," asked Hugh, "or are you personating the gentle lyrist himself, and trying to beguile the fair Eurydice out of this Plutonic darkness?"

"Take care, or I'll personate old Boötes, and turn my Dogs loose upon you," answered Burgoyne, going on with his playing.

"No doubt they would be glad of a diversion," said Hugh, turning his glass to the north. "Poor little Ursa Minor! forever swinging round the Pole by his luckless tail!"

Beatrice, who was standing near, turned quickly and glanced up. "Here, look through this, Miss Beatrice," said Hugh, offering her the glass. "Do you know the story of the Bears, — the big Ursa Major (the Dipper yonder) and the Little Bear? No? Well, once upon a time there was a lovely young person named Callisto, with whom the mighty god Jupiter fell in love. Whereupon Jupiter's celestial spouse, Juno, who had a frightfully jealous temper, maliciously transformed Callisto and her young son Arcas into bears. Jupiter was terribly angry, for with all his power he could not undo the mischief; and for fear some unconscionable huntsman might slay the poor creatures, he caught them up and set them among the stars. And there they are to this day, proof positive of the truth of this story!"

"Did people ever believe such things?" asked Beatrice.

"Believe them! they were the pagan Scriptures."

' "That is what gives them their principal interest now," remarked the professor of English literature. "The beliefs of mankind have been the most important factor in the history of civilization."

"There are prettier stories than that in the stars," said Burgoyne. He got up and moved forward a little, and pointed with his bow toward the zenith. "Give her the glass again, Hugh, and let her examine Berenice's Hair, and tell her that story."

Hugh related the legend of the beautiful young queen with the golden tresses; and, encouraged as he afterward said by Beatrice's "intelligent ignorance," he went on from star to star and from story to story, illustrating with stanzas from old heathen bards and modern poets.

"You will find," he said, "when you get into the big picture galleries over in Europe, that the painters as well as the poets have made a great deal of capital out of these mythological tales. You will see the beautiful Andromeda chained to the rocks with the atrocious sea-monster coming to devour her, and the radiant Perseus flying through the clouds to rescue her. You will find the royal brothers, Castor and Pollux, immortalized on canvas and in marble as they are in literature and in the heavens.

' Fair Leda's twins, in time to stars decreed;
  One fought on foot, one curbed the fiery steed.'

And you will see Diana with her Hunting-Dogs, and the terrible Dragon that guarded the Golden Apples in the Garden of the Hesperides, — and no end of others."

The professor, observing the intense interest in Beatrice's eyes, — which rivalled the stars themselves in brightness, — could not let the matter rest here. "You understand, Miss Beatrice," he said, "that these ancient fables are not mere fairy tales, invented to amuse children, — monstrosities of the imagination, like the adventures of Sinbad the Sailor. They had a tremendous significance in their time, and still have, when we consider that they were the beginnings of religion, of the progressive system of beliefs and aspirations without which there would be no spirituality, no higher ethics in this world. Mr. Connelly has omitted one particularly interesting legend, the story of Virgo."

"Oh, yes!" said Hugh. "Well, there is more than one version; give yours."

"The story is illustrated in the cluster of which yonder brilliant white star is the leader, Miss Beatrice," the professor explained, taking his place beside her. "During the Golden Age the Virgin — whose real name is Justice — dwelt upon the earth as the queen of mankind. With the passing of that age she

'Winged her flight to heaven.'

It is said that for a time she occasionally revisited the scene of her former sovereignty; but as the consciences of men grew harder, and ambition and oppression and injustice took the place of brotherly love, her visits became less frequent, and finally she ceased coming altogether. I am not quite prepared to believe this last. I think I have more than once had an intimation of her presence in the heart of some good man or good woman whom she has prompted to a kind or generous deed. All such, I dare say, she eventually gathers to herself, and places them in her beautiful constellation, there to shine for evermore as a reward for their virtue."

The professor smiled, but Beatrice gave a little start, — as at a sudden, wonderful revelation, — and a strange flood of emotion swept over her. Could it be that this immaculate queen had descended to earth in her behalf, and that M. La Scalla's benevolent eyes were looking down upon her out of the serene heavens?

Burgoyne had ceased playing, and the whole little company had been listening to the professor.

Madame La Scalla rose and moved away with a sob in her throat. Evalina followed, and slipped an arm tenderly round her waist. It was one of those moments of spiritual supremacy, when thought transmits itself without speech.

At Liverpool the La Scallas embarked for the Mediterranean, and Hugh bade them a " good-bye " which had in it a much more poignant sting than the regretfulness of mere friendly parting, but without a word to prove the truth of Evalina's maidenly suspicions. He who had raved in rhythmic measure about a dozen adorable girls, who in turn had lightly touched his fancy, was mute in the presence of this one, toward whom, in reality, had set the strong current of loyalty and love. The boldest of sentimental admirers was the shyest of true-lovers!

Madame La Scalla remarked one day when they were entering the Mediterranean, "You young people will find much to interest you in Venice; I did at your age. But now I shall not care to look at churches and palaces and pictures. I do not wish to study Venice, but simply to enjoy it."

She adopted the Venetian routine, keeping to her rooms all day and emerging only when the tide of waking life began to set toward the Lido, or the marvellous illumination of St. Mark's drew the gay population into the great square. The smooth gliding through the weird streets, and the curious evening sights and sounds sufficed for her mood, — and for Evalina's too, the greater part of the time.

Evalina was preoccupied, wrapped in thoughts from which she could not free herself, and which made her blind and deaf to all the joyous life round about. This until one day a letter came from Hugh, who wrote that he was more than pleased with his little baronetcy, and intended to remain and see what he could make of it.

The letter was to Madame, and he begged her permission to write to Evalina, — which, after a little family consultation, was granted; and there began one of those delicious correspondences which absorb so much of a young girl's time and thought.

It fell out that Burgoyne and Beatrice were left to go about together; and it seemed a most natural as it was a most delightful thing that they should be going about together, prying into old churches, palaces, out-of-the-way shops and obscure little dens where untaught genius fashions its bits of art, of exquisite bric-a-brac, getting all sorts of curious and interesting information which escapes the ordinary, hurried tourist, and following the footsteps of civilization backward into the old, old past.

Burgoyne still looked upon Beatrice as a child dependent upon his protection and superior knowledge, — a child of such glowing and devouring intelligence that to be her companion and instructor, and driven by her searching, eager questionings, to remote investigation, was worth a course in archæology, in mediæval history. It was the same in Rome as it had been in Venice. Everything was so old and so significant and insistent, and old things were made so much of by everybody, — from the rapid tourists scouring every nook and cranny, and possessing themselves ruthlessly of sacred relics as they had opportunity, down to the ragged mendicants who went crossing themselves at every shrine, — that it came to seem as if the traditions of the past were the real life and business of the present ; and that all the modern inventions, pretensions, triumphs, and fashions were impertinent innovations and signs of an effeminate and morally degenerate age.

Beatrice felt as if she were in a dream, a long dream of wondering awe, — a dream in which the dead were walking about in the manly strength and serious dignity of the old Roman days ; and a dream sweetened by the most charming companionship in the world, for Burgoyne was still always with her, his kind eyes responding to her every emotion. The old spirit of *camaraderie* which had once existed between them, and had lapsed for a time, came back and deepened into a solid friendship ; and friendship is a lovely relation between two people of any age,

under any circumstances, in any condition of life, but
especially when both are young, and one a man and
one a woman, and there is a moral or a legal bar to
tenderer attachment !

Suddenly she awoke in Paris. Paris ! the City of
Life ; the city of beauty and art and equipage and
splendor ; of song and literature and light morality,
and glittering new royalty and somber old nobility,
and wit and fashion and careless flirtation ! In
Rome she had felt herself in sympathy with the pale
enthusiasts of the brush, dragging their easels through
the long galleries, and dreaming and worshipping and
trying to catch inspiration from the immortal canvases
rather than from the great original source from which
all true genius draws its life. She would have liked
to join their ranks ; but Madame poohed laughingly.
" I might as well put you in a nunnery to spend the
rest of your days counting beads," she said ; "wait
until you have seen the living world."

And the living world was Paris. Madame took her
to visit art galleries and famous studios ; and it was
with something of a shock that she first saw the development of new methods, new ideals, new technique. In Paris the divine Muse, the muse of a
Raphael, an Angelo, was certainly prostituted to very
common uses ! But how beautiful ! Might the Old
Masters have been too exclusive then? Was any
part of life and human experience more sacred than
the rest? Ah, was not all life, all passion, all feeling
worthy the labor of genius? Her young soul, which
had been for months under the spell of the stern,
jealous, fiercely religious spirit of a by-gone era, leapt
into sudden harmony with the wide freedom of

15

modern art and modern thought. It was a new birth, a new baptism of liberty !

Here Beatrice had little of Burgoyne's company. Much of his time was spent with the Vincents, who had come over in the spring as they had planned. Mrs. Vincent had secured her old quarters in a place near the Madeleine, and the La Scallas took rooms at the Hôtel Meurice in the Rue de Rivoli. But Madame La Scalla devoted herself quite generously to the two girls. For one thing, she had them sit for portraits to Delacroix. He made a " likeness " of Evalina and a " picture " of Beatrice, as he quaintly described the difference to a friend.

Beatrice had a little talk with him one day, and informed him that she too would like to paint, and finally confessed that she had made some modest attempts. He put a brush in her hand, and bade her sketch the profile of a bust that stood on a pedestal before her.

" Good ! " he cried, as he watched her. " You have the sure stroke ; you do not smear and you do not hesitate ; and your eye is true. You may be a painter if you wish. Would you like to study under me ? " But he smiled as though he were not in earnest.

After hearing Madame Alboni she thought no more about painting. For days she was conscious of nothing else but that marvellous voice, which stirred new aspirations and seemed to evoke new powers within herself. She sat down to the piano one morning to imitate certain remembered strains, and Madame La Scalla came in and clapped her hands. " Bravo, Beatrice ! " she cried ; " I thought the great prima donna had stolen into our rooms! Your voice has a quality similar to hers."

Beatrice blushed with self-consciousness.

" How would you like to be a great singer?" went on Madame, lightly. " It is a wonderful gift, and as personal and as fascinating as beauty, — and as fleeting! It has its little hour of triumph, and then all is over. Which would you prefer, a brief blaze of glory or a quiet little glow of life-long satisfaction?"

It was one of those questions to which Madame seldom expected an answer, — a kind of half-soliloquy.

" Do you think I might ever sing like Alboni?" asked Beatrice, as cold as marble at the thought.

" Who knows?" answered Madame. " You might try."

CHAPTER XVII.

MADAME DEROUEN, a lady of less than medium height, and of plump figure compressed at the waist and bulging a little above and below, trailed the wide sweep of her handsome morning gown out upon a semicircular balcony jutting from the upper story of a broad-fronted red-brick building on Brooklyn Heights.

The building, which had begun life as an aristocratic family mansion, was now devoting itself — without much change of character — to the uses of education. It was a commanding edifice, possessing certain structural elements of nobility which are sometimes seen in men and women who have been deflected from a career of opulent indolence to busy occupation. There was a little different tone, but no actual letting down. Still exclusive to a degree, it yet had a livelier air, with its open windows and numerous young smiling faces looking out from them, than in the stately days of yore. With the proud modesty of conscious worth it stood well back from the street, its ample grounds environed with an elaborate wrought-iron fence rising into a high, arched gateway in front. The legend, " Lust en Rust," set into the arch in beautiful open letters, not only bespoke the happy serenity of the place, but clinched the idea of its knickerbocker character in the mind of any possible doubter.

The main entrance to the building was through a substantial portico, whose massive roof obviously required the support of the sturdy marble pillars underneath. On either side the stone steps — broad and safe and easy of ascent — leading up into the portico reclined a peaceable granite lion. A fountain in the front yard shot its crystal column high into the air, and fell back in iridescent spray upon the lovely shoulders of a group of naked imps whose crouching attitudes and gleeful grimaces testified to their unwearied enjoyment of the fun. Even when a cutting north wind or a chilling blast from the sea should have turned their merriment to shivers they kept up the brave show; even when Old Boreas muffled their curly heads in caps of snow and hung icicles on their dimpled elbows they crouched and grimaced still. A carefully trimmed hedge supplemented the fence, and made the place still more secluded and exclusive. The generous spread of greensward was sharply punctuated here and there by a pyramidal evergreen or a well-kept flower-bed of geometrical pattern. Everything was as precise and conventional as court etiquette, and with something of the same venerableness, without decay. Age, which had softened the tints of brick and paint, had increased the luxuriance of the vines and foliage, and given additional dignity to the kingly trees.

Madame Derouen's School for Young Ladies had a reputation for caste, and jealously guarded it. It made no overtures to the *bourgeoisie*, — in fact, never entertained propositions from the vulgar commonality except, perhaps, for reasons of the most cogent expediency. Its patrons were carefully selected from the *crème de la crème* of eastern cities, — the rich, the fashionable, the delicately bred.

Though it was mid-autumn, the warmth and sweetness of the morning justified the delight of the laughing imps and of the lingering warblers that came to drink at the fountain, and flirt and flutter in the shimmering spray, and pay tribute of song for these gracious privileges.

Madame Derouen, who had just taken her light *premier déjeûner* in her dressing-room, laid a small firm hand upon the iron railing that guarded the balcony, and sent her bright quick glance up and down the shady street, — at one end of which there was a narrow prospect of the Bay, with a sail or two in the misty distance.

To step out upon this little balcony at this hour was Madame's unfailing habit the year round. It was her invocation to Dame Nature, a goddess she much adored, though she had little time for her worship. Two or three rapturous inhalations of the pure air, a comprehensive sweep of the eye over the charming scene, and rapid absorption of every bright detail and enchanting effect of light and color, a thought of the beauty and glory of life and the world (with both of which she was much in love), and perhaps a sigh heavenward, and her prayer was ended and she was ready for the arduous and numberless duties of the day, — duties to which she brought a large fund of enthusiasm and energy, an electrical brain and a deft wit. Her mind was as quick to take impressions of men and women as her eye of a landscape ; and she was as sure in her judgment of social conditions and possibilities as a Wall Street broker of financial winds and tides. She was a somewhat daring manipulator, ready to take large risks if there was a reasonable chance of large returns ; as when, some years before, she had accepted two western pupils of quite unknown pedigree, — the one because she was enormously rich, and the other because she was a genius. The former had eventually married a foreign nobleman of distinction, and the latter had become a famous sculptress. Both reflected high honor upon the school, and one, My Lady, had conferred substantial benefits, — which Madame was not above accepting. In fact she was quite proud of saying, "This beautiful grand piano was a gift from my beloved pupil, the Countess of Paxon ; " or, "That exquisite thing — a real Van Dyke you see — was sent me by dear Lady Matilda." Nearly all her speculations had resulted just as advantageously, and success had inspired her with confidence.

The Madame had spent the greater part of her life in New York, but certain eccentricities of speech and gesticulation betokened her Parisian birth.

While she stood in conscious pleasurable contemplation of the scene around, beneath, and above, a carriage dashed round the corner of the square and pulled up at her gate. The driver sprang down and opened the door, and a lady of elegant figure and bearing stepped out, followed by two young girls. The whole party had an unmistakable air of gentility, and there was that peculiar harmony and fitness in their dress which denotes the power of choice as well as the ability to choose ; all of which was not lost upon

Madame Derouen. She stepped back into her room, and from behind a window-curtain watched them coming up the walk. When they disappeared under the roof of the portico, she turned round and stood waiting and wondering. She was not expecting any new pupils, and had received no intimation of a visit from a possible new patron. *Parbleu !* she was not usually approached by possible new patrons with so little ceremony.

When she heard the light step of the maid in the hall she darted across the room and threw open the door. Celerity of movement was one of her peculiar traits, and she had a lightness of step which often characterizes people of considerable avoirdupois. The maid handed her a card and a letter. The name on the card was unfamiliar. The letter was from Mrs. James Vincent, introducing her dear cousin, Madame La Scalla, of Louisiana, who desired to secure for her daughter, Miss Evalina, and her ward, Miss Beatrice, a young relative, the very superior advantages of Madame Derouen's charming and celebrated school. The letter, dated at Paris, was brief, for Mrs. Vincent was pressed for time ; but besides being profusely garnished with compliments for the recipient, it adroitly conveyed an impression of Madame La Scalla's social and financial importance and the value of her patronage. There had been a little jesting about this between the two cousins, and Mrs. Vincent said she knew with whom she was dealing !

Madame Derouen read the letter standing, and her lively face beamed with satisfaction. A cousin of Mrs. James Vincent ! *C'est très bien.* Mrs. Vincent's own daughter had been her pupil for a time, and Mrs.

Vincent was a power in the fashionable world. But, *ciel !* how early ! what a horrid hour to see visitors ! Her first impulse was to rush down stairs ; but she bethought herself, and wheeled round in front of a long cheval-glass at the other side of the room, and catching up a brush made a pass or two at her black, lusterless, kinky hair, which never looked much the better for a dressing, but which, however, was always picturesque and becoming. She held out her hands, and scowled at the lace in her sleeves, which was fine but not immaculately clean.

" *Diable !* but Susanne should look after me bettaire," she ejaculated. There was a soiled spot on the front of her gown ; but this she deftly caught over in a fold with her left hand as she entered the parlor, and neatly doubled the score by the exposure of a richly embroidered petticoat underneath. In the hurry and scurry of her busy life she could give but little time to her toilette. She was punctilious about her early morning bath, but as for dressing, she caught up the first thing that came to hand, or that Susanne the shiftless saw fit to produce ; and as she was a woman of expensive tastes there were sure to be elegancies about her somewhere, even though they were not always *faciles à découvrir.*

The two women — the stately, gracious, graceful Louisiana Creole, and the alert, sparkling, keenly intelligent and intuitive little Frenchwoman — confronted each other with extended hands and smiling, attentive regard.

Madame La Scalla, who was half an inch the taller, and looked more, inclined her head, and apologized charmingly for the unconventional hour and for not having sent Mrs. Vincent's letter and arranged for the visit beforehand. They had just returned from abroad, and she and her son were in haste to get on home. If Madame would kindly pardon these apparent rudenesses, and if she could be persuaded to consider the matter referred to in the letter, which of course was the object of the visit —

Her beautiful eyes conveyed far more of deprecation and persuasion than the politely worded speech; and if Madame Derouen had had misgivings of any sort they must have been routed completely, for she had a weakness for the eloquence of beauty. But the letter itself was talismanic, and her mind was made up almost before entering the room. She swept aside all apologies with expressive shrugs and pretty gestures, declaring herself honored by Madame La Scalla's distinguished visit and gracious choice of her modest *établissement.* Then her glance settled upon the two girls with a most engaging geniality, and she said something about the happy addition of two such *jolies demoiselles.* And had they all just come from Paris? *Que Paris est beau!* And had witnessed the Exposition Universelle? *Mon dieu!* what joy! She struck her hands together ecstatically and raised her eyes heavenward — or ceilingward, where in an elaborate stucco center-piece some Dutch nymphs were diligently plucking flowers to scatter, perchance, upon the heads of whosoever might come beneath. But in a moment she recovered herself and came back to the business in hand. Providentially there were vacancies in the school just then; some Baltimore young ladies had cancelled their contract because their father had been honored with an important foreign appointment, and they were going abroad with him. There had been other applicants in plenty, but —

There was a delicacy of flattery in the "but" which Madame La Scalla acknowledged courteously.

"*Parbleu !* in my position one cannot be too careful," returned Madame Derouen. "I have a vairy great regard for the tone of my little *pension*. And, besides, it is one of the conditions imposed by *la propriétaire*, whose home this charming place used to be, and who still will not part with it for any consideration. You perceive, Madame, that it maintains yet the character of a Dutch palace."

And in fact much of the *mobilier*, — the pictures on the walls, the pots of Delft on the mantel, and the little blue and white tiles set into the chimney-piece, — as well as the solid walls themselves and the massive ornamentations in the architecture, bore out the statement.

"Madame Vandever's precise words to me when she was last here," went on Madame Derouen, "were, 'I pray you let nothing lower the respectability of this dear old house !' And I hope I have kept the faith, according to my light."

The two women smiled, as two well-bred French women may smile behind the back of a good Dutch lady, — not with discourtesy, but with a mutual recognition of the difference between her social ethics and theirs.

"There is nothing in the language better fitted to describe Dutch ideals than the word 'respectability,'" said Madame La Scalla, perhaps in extenuation of the smile, or perhaps with that unconscious deference which maturity pays to youthful innocence and sincerity.

Madame Derouen glanced at once to the two girls, who were paying respectful attention to the conversation of their elders.

"And a vairy good word it is ; " she said, "and the quality makes an excellent backbone for society."

"But scarcely meets all the needs of society," smiled Madame La Scalla.

"*Eh bien !* it lacks *esprit* of course."

Madame La Scalla embraced the opportunity to say something fine and significant about the happy results of engrafting French *esprit* upon Dutch respectability, and Madame Derouen blushed through her swarthy skin and swept an elaborate courtesy. She presently proposed that the party explore the place a little before making final arrangements ; and Evalina almost rivalled her mother's suavity in refuting the suggestion of a doubt about the ultimate decision, since all they had seen was so lovely.

A tour of the lower rooms satisfied Madame La Scalla ; and an under-teacher, a Miss Avery, was sent for to conduct the two girls through the upper regions. The ladies were left alone in the library.

"We would bettaire rest here a moment," said Madame Derouen, thinking to provide her visitor an opportunity for any special instructions she might wish to give concerning the new pupils. She pushed back the heavy portières on either side the room to make sure — and to let Madame La Scalla perceive — that the alcoves were deserted, and pulled forward two comfortable chairs.

But Madame La Scalla only laid a hand on the back of hers.

"I have an explanation to make to you, Madame Derouen, before we go any farther," she said, in such an impressive manner that Madame Derouen who had seized the cord of a window-shade, intending to soften the light that streamed dazzlingly in from the east, paused with an inquiring "Yes?" "Explanations as a rule are insufferable, but I desire first of all to be perfectly candid and honorable with you in this transaction. What I have to say is this: The young girl Beatrice, who is related to my husband's family, — by ties which the law takes no cognizance of, however, — and who, please bear in mind, is a beloved member of my household and my daughter's dear companion and friend, belongs to a most unfortunate class of beings. She is of mixed blood, — you know what that means in the South, — and was born in slavery. If these facts make any difference to you — "

Madame Derouen let go the cord, and the shade flew to the top of the window with a sharp click.

"My God!" she cried in strong English — the French expression in which she habitually indulged was inadequate — "is not Madame jesting? Surely, one nevair sees a fairer skin, a more exquisite creature altogether. I sayed to myself when my eyes fell upon that young girl, 'the *charmante* brunette has the color of the lily and the rose, and a carriage like the daughter of a king.' What a pose she has, and what a step, — so light, so elegant! One would know by the walk that she has the foot *aristocratique*. And those eyes, ah, superb!"

"Yes," returned Madame La Scalla, "Beatrice is beautiful; Nature has tried to compensate for the sins of men in her case. I wished you to see her before making this explanation, — I wished her to have that advantage."

"Ah, you were right, Madame; she is herself her own best advocate. Who could withstand such loveliness? But yet, alas! I am sorely pairplexed. I have my patrons to consider, — my patrons, you are aware, are *de la vieille noblesse.* I fear me to bring my *académie* into disrepute, if I may be pardoned such plain speaking!"

"Certainly. But could that be possible here in the free, democratic North?" asked Madame La Scalla, with a touch of her old-time irony. "One would suppose that it would be quite the reverse; that in the land of a Phillips, a Garrison, a Mrs. Stowe, a beautiful young girl in Beatrice's position would have prestige, and command distinguished consideration."

"Ah, me! I fear it is not so, Madame, except in sentiment. Pairhaps it is the artistic, the dramatic representation which stirs the emotions, not living facts. Alas! how unhappy I am not to be pairmitted to follow the *mouvement* of my heart. But the world, society, is one grand system, and one may not transgress with *impunité.* The young girl is so vairy beautiful, and beauty appeals to me with extraordinary force."

"Beatrice would be an ornament in more ways than one : she is as talented as she is beautiful," returned Madame La Scalla, but still not insistently. Her manner was almost indifferent. "It was my husband's desire," she continued, "that the two girls should be educated here in the North. But I myself think it would be far better for Beatrice to be sent abroad, where race prejudice is not so pronounced. The only objection is that where she goes my daughter will go also. They are inseparable."

"Your daughter is angelic," said Madame Derouen, fervently. She dropped her eyes to the floor, but in a moment raised them again, twinkling with a shrewd light. " This unfortunate fact would not be generally known here?" she said.

" Obviously I have mentioned it to you as a matter of fairness," returned Madame La Scalla, coldly.

" Pardon ! My question was stupid. You spoke of race prejudice, Madame ; I have none. *Parbleu !* are we not all God's children? To myself personally it would make no difference whatever, and if others are not informed — as why should they be? *Mon Dieu !* it is not a case of leprosy ! — what harm is done, and what is to hinder me from availing myself of so promising and brilliant a pupil? " Underneath this fair reasoning was the reflection, " especially as the rejection of this promising and brilliant pupil involves the forfeiture of Madame La Scalla's illustrious and profitable patronage altogether."

" Even though this unfortunate, remarkable child *is* of mixed blood," she continued aloud, and with a shrug, " *Toutefois* she might pairhaps match pedigrees with some of the vairy select if the truth were known ! "

Madame La Scalla said not another word. When a woman begins to argue a point with herself the upshot is a foregone conclusion.

Miss Avery's position in Madame Derouen's fashionable *pension* was that of coach to dull pupils. She was very entertaining in a guileless, gossipy way, and as she led the two girls along the corridors and into the pretty suite of rooms now vacant by default of the young ladies who were going abroad, she let fall many delightful little legends about the fine old house and its owners and original occupants. Years ago she had been a governess in the Vandever family, and her remarks concerning this one or that one set them livingly before the mind, and made one feel a sort of intimacy with them and a friendly curiosity to meet them face to face. There was Miss Sophie the brunette, who was wildly gay, though as sweet and innocent as a dove ; who broke the hearts of dozens of young gentlemen before she accepted one of them : and Miss Annie the delicate blonde, and Mr. Roger, and Mr. Augustus, and Mr. John, — the last her favorite without doubt. Mr. John was a musical genius, with a heavenly voice and a talent for playing upon any instrument — but a gentleman for all that !

"This was Miss Annie's bow-window," said Miss Avery. "She used to sit here with her portfolio on her knee, and watch the ships sail away, and write little verses of poetry, and dream, and wish that she too might sail away. And one day she got her wish ; she sailed away a bride, — the happiest and the loveliest bride ! Here is where she stood for us all to come and look at her when she was dressed ready to go down and meet her bridegroom, who was a young gentleman from The Hague. She was as white as a snow-drop, and her eyes shone like two beautiful sapphires, and her dear little hands held the sweetest bunch of roses that could be found. . . . And this is the hall where the children used to dance. A piano stood there, which I played. Madame herself danced sometimes — in the minuet — as a rare favor, and there was always a scramble among the boys as to who should have her for a partner. She was a very small lady, and full of fun with the children; though they could never take any liberties with her any more than as if she had been a giantess, — she was so quick to see and to rebuke an impropriety. In company she was always stately; and yet — well, they said it was easy to see where Miss Sophie got her spirit! She was the moving spirit in whatever was going on. But you may be sure that whatever went on in her presence was perfectly proper. I have never seen a queen, but I always thought she must be like one."

Miss Avery spoke of the whole Vandever family in the past tense, though all of them were living except the father. But they were scattered to the ends of the earth, all except Mr. John, — called Jack by his intimates, — who lived in bachelor quarters over in the city, and spent his money with splendid lavishness, and was much courted by society.

It hardly seemed as if Miss Avery was telling all this, she was such an artless tattler; it oozed out of the fullness of her affectionate heart, which was like a little spring bubbling over. She was romantic, and as appreciative as a Boswell, and much attached to people she was intimately associated with, finding a lovely significance in everything they did and said; and when they were gone from her the memory of them lingered in her gentle soul, and gathered sweetness and hallowedness as the years went on. She was all

alive this morning, taking impressions of the prospective new pupils, one of whom aroused her intensest
admiration.

But it was not due to Miss Avery alone that in
course of time Beatrice herself — listening now with
so much interest to reminiscences of vanished youths
and maidens and the little .Dutch lady of queenly
character — became, with her beauty and talents and
sad romantic history, one of the most enchanting
traditions of the old place.

The house was all astir, and now and then some
fair girl gliding across the corridor in high-heeled
slippers and dainty morning-dress turned her haughty
young head for a casual, indifferent glance at the
approaching trio, and was constrained to give another
quick look of surprised admiration; for Beatrice made
an incisive impression upon strangers, — not by her
beauty alone, but by some untranslatable quality as
interesting as a mystery.

These fair girls are elderly matrons now, but they
will give you, if you should happen to run across some
one of them anywhere on this little globe, a clear-cut
picture of Beatrice as she looked that morning, — of
the one superb figure standing out in high relief
against the dim background of their jumbled recollections. They will tell you her dress was all of rich
dark reds and browns, like certain combinations of
autumn foliage; that her skin was of a transcendent
whiteness, touched with the faintest rose-hue in the
cheeks and deepening to carnation in the finely cut
lips; that her expression was both sweet and firm,
and full of a pleased interest as she looked about.
Above all, they will recall the splendid radiance of

her dark eyes, which yet had something shadowy lurking in their velvet depths. Was it a reminiscent or a prophetic sadness? It was a something that touched a chord of tenderness in every one of their young souls, — so they say now; but one cannot be altogether sure of retrospective testimony.

The only question Beatrice asked Miss Avery pertaining to Madame Derouen's *pension* was, " Have you a singing master? "

" The best in the city," replied Miss Avery, — " Herr Wilhelm, who comes over twice a week. Everything we have here is of the very best, you know," she added, with the tone and manner of one proudly conscious of being an integral part of a great institution.

Madame Derouen's school was distinctively of the *élite*, — in the accepted sense of the term, which is not always the best sense, nor always the truest to the original idea. The life there was not confined to books. Madame herself had liberal views on education ; or, as she was pleased to call them, practical views. She took into consideration the peculiar condition of her particular constituency, and conformed to it. It was her boast that her young ladies were in training for the highest social rank. It was not to be supposed that they were fitting themselves for governesses or accountants, but for the elegant functions of fashionable life ; to contract advantageous marriages ; to preside over fine establishments ; to dance, to play the piano-forte ; to pass judgment in graceful phraseology upon art, music, the drama. A taste for literature was cultivated, and the art of conversation much encouraged, — especially light and airy conversation. Madame abhorred stupidity. A girl must know how to use her tongue, must be prepared for emergencies. She must know, if overtaken by a subject about which she is uninformed, how to cover her ignorance or carry it off with grace, — a really fine accomplishment. For a fact, it is not all smooth sailing in the fashionable world, where even wealth, rank, splendid environment cannot atone for dullness.

Madame's recipe for quickness of apprehension was attention; and for facility of speech, practice. Every one at the proper time must take her part in the touch-and-go of light talk; and she took care to show due appreciation of every *bon mot*, however feeble, and every little rill of intelligent pleasantry. And all this had its effect: careful and persistent training of any sort cannot altogether fail of results.

Dinner each day was a magnificent function, from the superb service and elaborate *menu* down to the last detail of decoration and the newest fads and fancies, — for it was a part of Madame's curriculum to keep her school in touch with the fashionable world, so that a graduate from the knickerbocker palace was always the most accomplished of *débutantes* in society. The young ladies were expected to dress and deport themselves at dinner or at a reception as though it were a state occasion, — as in fact it often was, for Madame entertained many celebrities. If parents demurred at the frightful expense, she shrugged her shoulders and replied, "*Eh bien !* I have my system. I do not advertise one cheap school, but a high cultivation. It takes money, — Oh, yes, I am vairy well aware; but what can you expect ? "

The attitude of the two new pupils was unconsciously

opposed to this sort of superficial training. Both had
a positive love of knowledge, and certain convictions
of duty respecting the value of time and opportunity.
They took rather serious, at least very earnest, views
of life. They liked pretty gowns it is true, and beautiful surroundings, and all the elegancies of refined
civilization, — but in the artistic sense ; never for
vulgar display, and never for mere luxurious indulgence. If ever two young creatures were blessed with
sincerity and singleness of heart, these two were.
But yet no fault could be found with them from
Madame Derouen's extremely worldly view-point. It
would have been strange if a daughter of Corinne La
Scalla had not been able to show elegant breeding !
With the La Scallas elegant breeding was like a fine
polish on good hard wood, an ingrained grace and
finish.

Beatrice had come now to the time to which she
had looked forward with such burning eagerness, —
the time for preparation for that vague Greatness
which had haunted her all her life, — and she found
the new experience delightful beyond her wildest
expectations. She went at every task like a workman
whose tools are all bright and keen and clean, and
who has zest for his task and a long and glorious prospect ahead of him ; and there was such a lovely un-
folding of the prospect day by day that sometimes she
could hardly believe in the reality of it.

"My heart is like those merry imps down at the
fountain," she said to Evalina, — "it laughs all the
time."

Every additional individual in a society, large or
small, high or low, modifies the tone of it more or

less, as we all know. The new ingredient either dilutes or strengthens, or discolors or clarifies, or in a thousand other ways affects the quality of it; and Beatrice, with her infinite gladness diffusing itself always and everywhere, made buoyant the whole spirit of this place.

Her companions were fond of discussing her.

"I envy her her happiness almost more than her beauty," said one.

"Perhaps she is happy because she is beautiful,' rejoined another. "I should be."

"No, for she is entirely unconscious, or — well, of course she knows she is beautiful, but she makes no capital of it somehow, as you or I would, Kate."

"Speak for yourself, beloved. *I* am not vain," answered Kate.

"I should think we would all be mortally jealous of her, but we 're not. I simply admire her without a thrill of malice."

"There is a point where envy ceases, you know. Is the moon jealous of the sun by whose light she shines? I like to sit next Beatrice in the theatre : people are always putting up their glasses toward our box."

"And yet you are not vain, Kitty?"

"If I were going to envy Beatrice," said Kate, "it would be for that quality which somehow makes everybody take a keener interest in life when she is present. She is the oxygen, the ozone, of our social atmosphere. I think Miss Avery is going to write a book about her."

"Indeed?"

"Well, at least she is putting her down in her diary ;

and she makes little water-color pictures of her, —
goes down to the beach and sketches her in her sail-
boat, with her beautiful hair blowing in the wind ; and
the other day she journeyed all the way to the riding-
school to take Beatrice on horseback."

" Dear little enthusiast ! She has sketches of all
the Vandevers pinned upon the walls in her room. I
wish Mr. Jack could see some she has of him ! "

" He wouldn't mind ; he is awfully kind to Miss
Avery. By the way, I wonder when he is coming
over here to sing for us again."

" Soon, I hope. What a pity he is rich ! He
might have made a fortune for himself on the stage ;
and then the world would have had the benefit of his
talents."

" It has, anyhow ; does n't he contribute his talents
to dozens of charitable entertainments ? "

" Not dozens, — he is very choice of himself, they
say."

It happened that Mr. Jack came over that very
evening, and delighted the school with his charming
voice and his exquisite flute-playing. Miss Avery, to
her great felicity, accompanied him on the piano, as
she had done when he was a boy. A few evenings
later he came again, invited by Madame to one of
the school receptions. He brought with him a
Mrs. Priestly, called the finest amateur singer in the
city, — a large, handsome woman, with a voice of
wonderful compass and power.

" Did you ever hear anything so grand ? " asked
Kate Kavanagh of Beatrice.

" I have heard Madame Alboni," said Beatrice, and
unfortunately Mrs. Priestly caught her answer, and

flushed angrily. She too had heard Alboni, and imagined herself the equal of the famous prima donna,
— with something of an advantage, perhaps, in the
one respect that *she* did not sing for pay; and if
public recognition was a little tardy it was some
satisfaction to feel that it had never been unduly
stimulated by an extravagant commercial valuation of
her talent.

CHAPTER XVIII.

IN the panic winter of 1857, New York society took an uncommon interest in the poor, — perhaps because society was depressed by the financial gloom, and could hit upon no other means of enlivening itself. But let us believe it was something more disinterested and humane. It might have been that women — by "society" one generally means women — who could not buy so many diamonds that year, or give so many parties, or order so many Paris gowns, were constrained to think more pityingly and benevolently of those other women who could not buy so many loaves of bread and sticks of wood to feed and warm their little ones. At all events, the ultra-fashionables awakened suddenly and bestirred themselves with great enthusiasm to raise a relief fund ; not as men raise money, with a passing of the hat and a diving into the pocket and a "See here, boys ! there are a lot of people starving over yonder at Five Points, — chip in ! " No, women are more delicate and roundabout ; they do not come at you with the cool demand for a dollar, but hand out a neat little ticket, perhaps, which is a guarantee for an elaborate evening entertainment ; and you pay your dollar, and have the satisfaction not only of getting a dollar's worth of pleasure for yourself, but of knowing that you have contributed a dollar's worth of comfort to the miserable Five Pointers. There are few other ways in which a man can double his money and come out of the transaction with such a clean conscience, — nay, with such a righteous feeling of self-approbation.

And then there is all the excitement, — the boiling and bubbling of the social kettle stirred to its very dregs by a noble motive. Such a furore among the women to make good the promise of those little tickets ; to achieve success and win a certain kind of renown for themselves, to say nothing of the ulterior object. Such a rushing round in carriages and on foot, seeing this one and that one ; organizing committees ; skirmishing for talent and new ideas ; shopping, stitching, attending rehearsals, and withal sustaining little shocks of grieved surprise and anger at the revealed weaknesses of one another ; and finally losing the whole beautiful perspective with which the project was set on foot in the *mêlée* of distracting preparation, and the dreadful possibility of a complete fiasco ! But when it turns out to be a splendid success, there come a glow and radiance of good feeling all round ; congratulations and compliments are freely exchanged ; bruised hearts are flushed of petty spites and jealousies, — and a neat sum handed over to the finance committee. A great deal of restless feminine energy is worked off, the social conscience satisfied, and the poor made happy for a day.

Mrs. Harold Thompson was one of the half-dozen or so women in the city who had a talent for charity entertainments, an intuitive know-how. This winter she happened neither to be travelling with her husband, — who was gone on a protracted tour to the

East Indies with a party of English gentlemen, — nor cruising in southern waters with her brother, Captain Jack ; and it was expected that she would do something splendid in that line before the season was over. She had her friend Grace Convers with her, always ready to supplement her efforts in any direction, social, benevolent, or whatever. Grace, who was several years her junior, admired her ardently and loved her devotedly, but was as independent a spirit in some ways as Mrs. Thompson herself.

Mrs. Thompson was a woman of resources and ingenuity. She was charged with a vast amount of noiseless energy, and there radiated from her a serene consciousness of power which was the joy of her associates and the despair of her friendly and unfriendly rivals. People who did not understand Mrs. Thompson, or were jealous of her popularity, said she "spread herself out," — which was true, and unavoidable. She could not help diffusing herself in a gracious, luminous atmosphere almost palpable enough to fill space. She was a tall, ample woman, with a fresh complexion and an abundance of wavy chestnut hair, which she dressed simply. The same delicate, elusive perfume always accompanied the soft *frou-frou* of her garments, and seemed a part of her agreeable personality. She was very generous to the rival managers, very sweet in her appreciation of their efforts and successes. She left off her gloves at the various entertainments in order that her large white hands might be free to applaud, and provided herself with quantities of beautiful and costly flowers to throw upon the stage. One could always see her leaning a little forward in her box (if the place of entertainment happened to be a theatre), a smile upon her lips, her large, comprehensive glance taking in the whole effect, — not critically, but with an unmistakable kindly interest.

There had been balls, lectures, parlor talks, private theatricals, and the dear knows what all, until it would have seemed there was nothing more to be thought of. But Mrs. Thompson maintained her customary superb tranquillity while waiting for her turn and time, merely replying to a friend or two when questioned about her plans, "Ah, I fear you have exhausted all the resources." But this they knew was mere chaff.

The Thompson residence was not one of the newest brown-stone fronts, but an old-fashioned home-like place, commodious, and in the interior handsome, filled with luxuries and elegancies from all quarters of the globe. It was but a little way from Madison Square, and Mrs. Thompson might have viewed the chimney-pots of the Vincent mansion from the gable windows of her attic, if she had been curious about the chimney-pots of the Vincent mansion. But she was not; the petty private affairs of her neighbors interested her very little. Her attitude was cosmo-politan, her eye took a wide range. She declared that people the world over were kept in order by certain laws, customs, opinions, and creeds of their own human making, or which have been the natural, gradual outgrowth of their respective mental and moral organisms and climatic conditions; and that the nearer the various laws, customs, opinions, and creeds approximate to the simplest rule of justice be-tween man and man, the more perfect they are, and the nobler, gentler, happier are the men and women who live and labor in the faith of them. She belonged to the broadest church in New York; but, unlike her husband, who was that curious anomaly, a bigot on the liberal side, she was tolerant, indulgent even, toward all the others.

One crisp, clear morning in the latter part of January Mrs. Thompson was sitting at the piano in an up-stairs room, going over a multitude of musical compositions; not for practice nor for her own or Grace's entertainment, but to test their respective merits with reference to a specific object. Large flat books and unbound sheets were scattered round upon the floor and on tables and chairs. Mrs. Thompson was neat in her methods, but not fussy; she could endure a pleasant litter of things when there was an excuse for it.

Grace was nestled in a wide divan in the big bow-window, with one slippered foot tucked under her and a bit of practical needle-work in her hands, — a fine silk stocking, with the premonition of a hole in its toe. Her occupation did not hold her attention resolutely, and her glance was continually wandering down into the street, merry with bells and gay with life and color. Fine flakes of frost detached from the skeleton trees sparkled everywhere in the cold, bright air. Now and then she saw some one she knew, dashing by in a cutter or a sleigh. Once a gentleman looked up and touched his fur cap to her. She nodded, smiled, and found herself blushing a little.

From time to time Mrs. Thompson, without taking her strong flexible fingers from the keys, broke out with an exclamation or a question: "Listen to this, Grace!" or, "How does that strike you?"

Miss Convers expressed her opinion freely. "Very pretty, but it seems to me it would not be particularly effective," she said once; and again, "Beautiful! but whom can you get to sing it? Of course you count on Mrs. Priestly — and Jack Vandever? Lucky for you Mr. Vandever has been away all these weeks, Emma; they would have had him all worn out. He went by just now looking extremely well, — or it may have been the cold, — he had a fine color."

"Oh, he is back then," said Mrs. Thompson, dropping her hands and turning round with an expression of interest. "I must see him immediately. I wonder if the bride and groom came with him?"

"I suppose so, of course; but they were to go on out to Chicago to visit the bride's family. Did you know the Pembrokes, Emma?"

"Somewhat, but they went west shortly after Mabel was sent abroad to school. Mabel, you know, inherited a fortune from some ancient relative of her mother's."

"Yes," said Grace, and added with a smile, "Roger Vandever probably did not marry her for that."

"Hardly," said Mrs. Thompson, and turned again to her playing, but in a moment stopped and listened.

A rich foreign voice was audible in the hall below. It was the hour Mrs. Thompson had appointed for an interview with Herr Wilhelm. The servant had had orders to show him up-stairs, and in due time he appeared, — a breezy little man with a ruddy complexion, shifty black eyes, a mammoth mustache, and a dot of beard just under his lower lip. His hair was rather long, though not conspicuously so, black and oily and combed straight back from a not particularly intellectual forehead. He was dressed like a gentleman, not like a professional.

"Goot-morning, Matame! goot-morning, Mees Graze!" he cried cheerfully, as though he were hailing them from across the street. "I hope I see you bote vell dis fine morning? Lofely morning, blenty off schnow, schleigh-bells jinkling, everyting merry as a Christmas ball."

His quick eye, darting round the room like a humming-bird, alighted upon the coal fire glowing genially in the grate, and he strode toward it — with the stride of a little person possessing the corporeal ambition of a giant — and planted himself before it man-wise, his small pointed-toed shoes sinking deep in a white bear-skin rug. He gave a snort of satisfaction as he took in the *ensemble* of the well-appointed room — it was the first time he had been received there — and felt the warmth of the fire stealing over his body.

"You haf it very comfortable here, laties," he remarked approvingly. "It is glorious oudtside, as I haf observed, but cold, cold! An atmosphere such as dis suits me better."

Mrs. Thompson replied that she supposed it was pretty cold, but she had not been out. Miss Convers, who had put both feet on the floor when the professor was announced, dropped her work in her lap and sat regarding him with an amused interest. He was not conscious that his dignity was compromised by her smiling attitude, — and indeed Grace had no intention of being disrespectful, it was simply that Herr Wilhelm always affected her like a comedy.

"Vell, and vhat haf you decided upon?" he asked abruptly.

The question was so manifestly directed to Miss Convers that she felt obliged to answer.

"*I* have not decided upon anything," she said; "I am only an adjunct, you know, — the fifth wheel."

"I beg your pardon," he returned quickly, "I supposed you vas de mainspring."

"I have been thinking, professor," interrupted Mrs. Thompson, who was busy with her music, putting the right sheets together, "that we might make up a program of selections from various operas, — put them on the stage with the proper settings, you know. There is *Fra Diavolo*, for instance, and *Semiramide*, and *Lucia di Lammermoor*."

"And the *Bohemian Girl*," put in Grace; "nothing could be more fetching than 'I dreamt I dwelt in marble halls,' unless it is the exquisite duet in *Norma*."

"You are ridt, Mees Graze," the professor assented with deference. "For simple melody de *Bohemian Girl* is unsurpassed. And *Norma* is grand!"

"Mrs. Priestly could sing the *solo* with great effect," said Grace, "providing — " Mrs. Thompson looked at her, and she broke off.

"Ah, Mrs. Briestly! she can sing anyting, mitoudt a prowiso," exclaimed the professor with unction.

Miss Convers laughed. She was about to say, "providing there was a *lover* to her taste."

"But not everything — on this occasion," said Mrs. Thompson; "we want variety in singers as well as in music. I wish we had a brand-new voice that nobody has ever heard, — a voice that would be a revelation ! "

" Hah, I know a voice vhat vould be a refelation," cried the professor, slapping his thigh. " Vas you ever acguainted mit von Matame Derwine who keeps a Yong Laties' *pension* over in Brooklyn yonder? "

" Madame Derouen? Oh, yes, everybody knows Madame Derouen," replied Mrs. Thompson.

" Whom not to know argues one's self unknown," murmured Grace.

" Vell ! dere is over in dat school a yong girl mit a vonterful voice, and a brand-new voice, as you say, Matame ; vhich, if my modesty vill excuse me, I haf myself made."

" Oh, then it must be unique," said Grace.

" You are quite ridt, Mees, it is unique ; I know no oder voice mit vhich it to compare."

Mrs. Thompson asked who this prodigy was.

" Her name, it is La Schalla, Mees Be-at-rice La Schalla," answered the professor. " She is from Louisiana, a Greole, you know."

The two women looked at each other in lively astonishment, but immediately corrected the glance.

" Do you think she would sing in our concert? " Mrs. Thompson asked.

The professor shrugged his shoulders and slanted his eyes upward. " Oh, vell, dat depends. I might possibly intercete for you."

" But I know Madame Derouen very well ; perhaps I might better see her myself."

" As you like, Matame." The professor bowed deeply.

17

An hour later Mrs. Thompson ordered her carriage, and she and Miss Convers drove over and called at the Knickerbocker Palace and asked to see Madame Derouen. Madame treated the proposition with some coolness. "These French Creoles are vairy exclusive," she said ; "they hold themselves — well, you know, not common. It is rather *bourgeois*, is it not, to sing for public entertainments? "

"Some very elegant people think it is not beneath their dignity to sing for charitable entertainments," returned Mrs. Thompson, affably. "There is Mrs. Priestly, you know, and Mr. Vandever."

"Ah, to be sure, and vairy gracious of them. But, *parbleu !* both are so well known."

"There is something in that, of course ; but — have you any objection to our seeing the young lady, Madame Derouen? "

"*Mon Dieu !* why should I object? " Madame stepped out and sent a maid to summon Beatrice.

"She will recognize us," said Grace, "and it may be awkward for her."

"She will soon see that we are friends," answered Mrs. Thompson.

It was not awkward for Beatrice in the least. She came into the room with a little natural air of expectation, and acknowledged the introduction courteously, and immediately afterward exclaimed, with a brightening of glance which betokened quite unembarrassed recognition, "I have seen you at L'Ile Dernière ! "

"Yes," replied Mrs. Thompson, "I was sure it must be you when Professor Wilhelm mentioned your name. La Scalla is not a common name."

" No," Beatrice answered, " I suppose not ; they are all related, all the La Scallas."

" What an inscrutable young person," thought Miss Convers.

" I am very glad to meet you again — here," said Mrs. Thompson, with the kindest manner, — a manner which almost expressed sympathy and invited confidence, but so delicately that only one who was in need of a friend would so interpret it. Miss Convers glanced at her quickly, as if to say, " That is quite thrown away, Emma ! " For Beatrice only thanked her, without appearing to note the slight emphasis on the last word. The expression of her face had changed a little, however, and Mrs. Thompson divined what memories had been stirred by the thought of L'Ile Dernière.

" We have come to see you on a matter of business, Miss Beatrice," she said animatedly. " We are getting up a musical entertainment to raise money for the suffering poor in Five Points, and we are in need of a voice, an altogether out-of-the-common sort of voice. And the Herr Professor under whom you are studying — and who therefore is qualified to judge — has recommended yours."

" Mine ! " cried Beatrice, a red tide rushing to her face. It was plain to see that pleasure mingled with her astonishment.

" Yes ; will you loan it to us — remember, it is for sweet charity ? " smiled Mrs. Thompson.

" Oh, if I could ! " said Beatrice, with kindling, dilating eyes, but a kind of shrinking in her manner. " But I cannot ; oh, it is impossible, indeed it is impossible ! You are very kind, Mrs. Thompson, and it was kind of the professor; but I have never sung in public, never at all."

The thought frightened her, yet it tingled through her body deliciously. Was it not her summons to the ranks of the great moving, marching world? In a quick introspective flash she seemed to see again the magnificent French theatre with its splendor of light and color; to be conscious of the pulsing, throbbing, thrilling vibration of the warm, perfumed atmosphere; to listen to the subdued, pleasant rustle of a forest of fans and of women's dresses, like a soft wind among the pines; to feel the ineffable *rapport* of the mighty audience and its intense concentration upon a single wonderful figure, — a radiant woman, smiling, self-possessed; alive to the supreme distinction of her position, but supremely simple, divinely gracious, and with a voice that might have been chosen out of the choirs of heaven ! " Oh, Alboni, Alboni ! if I could ! " she thought, and in her deep secret soul she felt that she could if she dared.

"You might at least try," persuaded Mrs. Thompson, as though the thought was legible in her face.

"You see, that is all they really ask of you at present," broke in Miss Convers, with her humorous smile. " These little cliques are fiercely jealous of one another; they will turn themselves into perfect barbarians rather than risk a failure. I assure you they would sacrifice you without the slightest compunction if they found you inadequate ! And this, looked at in the right way, is greatly to your advantage, Miss Beatrice, if you happen to be fostering a secret ambition. Make the trial, and these unscrupulous benefactors of the poor will let you know in short order just where you stand."

"My dear, we are not infallible," corrected Mrs. Thompson, with mild rebuke.

Beatrice was conscious of a slight feeling of resentment. "They would not find me inadequate," she thought, with deep conviction, which had not its root in vanity, but in an intuitive understanding of herself, that genuine self-consciousness which must come sooner or later to all persons endowed with special gifts.

The same thought was in Madame Derouen's mind, and she expressed it with a laugh in which there was a harsh note. Beatrice and her voice she had come to regard as one of the "features" of her School, and Miss Convers's remark had the effect of an unpleasant reflection.

"Oh, I am sure they would not," Grace hastened to say. "I merely suggested the possibility, in order to make it more difficult for Miss Beatrice to refuse ! "

She had in fact made it impossible for Beatrice to refuse. It was arranged that Herr Wilhelm should come over and give her a little preliminary drill.

"*Se soumettre à l'épreuve !*" said Madame, with a shrug.

"Oh, no," returned Mrs. Thompson, good-naturedly. "I fear Grace has put me in a bad light."

"But, however, I am to sing only on condition that you are perfectly satisfied with me," said Beatrice.

"I am safe," laughed Mrs. Thompson, rising and pulling her big fur cloak around her.

When the ladies left, Beatrice ran upstairs and shut

herself in her room. Self-contained as she was, there was something in the present situation which made her long for sympathetic companionship, and she wished Evalina was there. But the Northern winter had proved too severe for her delicate constitution, and she had returned home in the midst of the holidays. Just now she and her mother were in New Orleans visiting the Chevannes. In her last letter she had given a detailed account of all that she was seeing and doing. Some parts of this letter had moved Beatrice deeply : —

"Old Aunt M'rye, you must remember her," Evalina wrote, "took me out on to the back gallery this morning to show me the curious shut-in court where your dear little childhood was spent! There was the broad, low door-step where you used to sit and look up at the sky, and think those wonderful thoughts you have so often told me about; and the great mulberry-tree, and the honeysuckle-vine, and the rose-bushes, and the big cistern. But I did not see a single chameleon, or grasshopper, or any of your pets! There were only a few bees droning, and a toad or two, — you did not care for the toads, did you? I can't remember. But just as we were about to go back into the house who should pop out of a door directly opposite us but your funny little old wig-maker, with a lot of nicely dressed wigs which he proceeded to try on, one after another, exactly as of old, — standing before the tiny looking-glass tacked to the door-post. I wonder if he has been at that all these years! I suppose so, of course. But it just seemed as if he was doing it on purpose — as they do in a play — to make good the traditions of the place. I confess that if it had not been for him I should have been disappointed. Somehow the little court did not seem like your charming descriptions of it; it looked very empty and desolate. But I know why; it is because the distinguished little Personality which gave it life and interest is not there! You *are* distinguished in a way, *bien-aimée;* there is no one else in all the world like my darling Betty, and any place where you are is sure to be full of life and interest."

Evalina also wrote about the cemeteries, abloom with roses though it was midwinter, and about attending service in the old church near Jackson Park. And Beatrice shuddered at the revived memory of Miss Rosamond's dismal funeral and the terrors she had experienced on that day. Ever since reading the letter she had seemed to be living her lonely little past all over again. And it was a relief, a joy to turn to the future, opening before her like the rosy dawn of a glorious new day. She sat down and wrote a long letter to Evalina, pouring out her heart to her as she could to no one else, and yet reserving much.

Herr Wilhelm came with the music the following day, and immediately hastened to make his report to Mrs. Thompson. "She vill do!" he cried triumphantly. "I knew dere could be no mishtake about dat voice! Ah, it is von glorious gift Mees Be-at-rice La Schalla haf! You should hear her take dose high notes, — schlick as a foxhound clears de fence in a shace! And de low vons sveet and mellow and sympathetic. It is a — vot you call? — *pénétrante* voice; it find oudt all vhat you feel off pain or plessure, or vhat not!"

Mrs. Thompson listened with delight, and Miss Convers remarked, "You are always in luck, Emma. People say you have a talent for success, but I contend that you were born under a lucky star."

"Vhich is de same ting as genyuse, Mees Graze," said the professor.

They were still talking of Beatrice, when Mr. John Vandever was announced and shown up into the music-room. Mr. Vandever was always welcome wherever he chose or chanced to present himself. His musical talent was by no means his most important or most agreeable characteristic. You thought first of the man and then of his gift, which was putting a high value upon his individuality. While he spent his ample income in a free and easy manner, there was yet considerable attentiveness to the question of an equivalent; and he looked after his investments with a shrewd eye. He was versatile in light accomplishments, a graceful dancer, and very clever in private theatricals, — a man, in short, whom society could not well do without. He had been the hope and the despair of new belles and managing mammas for ten years past. Just now society was coupling his name with that of Grace Convers; but Grace herself maintained a non-committal air. She could not help brightening a little, however, when he came into her presence, — but for that matter no one could. Mrs. Thompson got quite up from her chair and held out her hand to him.

"I am glad to see you," she said, with a straight, cordial look. "We are going to arrange for the rehearsals right away. The professor has found us a new singer, — why, you must know her, Jack, one of Madame Derouen's pupils; her name is La Scalla?"

"Oh, Miss Beatrice," said Jack. "Yes, I know her, as I know the other young ladies over there, which is to say in not a very personal way. And she is going to take part?"

" Yes, and what do you suppose she is going to be, for one thing? The Daughter of the Regiment, — with you for the Sergeant ! "

" Oh, you have got the work all cut out," said he. " The 'Daughter of the Regiment !' Are n't you a little ambitious? "

" Ambitious, but not presumptuous," she returned, "unless you think I have been presuming in putting you down without consulting you? "

" Make your peace with the injured public," said Jack. " I am always humbly at your service."

" What consecration ! " laughed Grace.

" Vhat fooling ! " scoffed the professor, stamping round on the white bear-skin rug.

After the two men went away, Miss Convers — who was seldom without a needle in her fingers — sat stitching in silence for some seconds. She was thinking hard and fast, and finally her thought broke away from her.

" It seems to me it is a ticklish business for Beatrice's pedigree to have been kept a secret here."

Mrs. Thompson, who had gone over and sat down by the fire and pulled a big Maltese cat up into her lap, whose fur she was stroking, replied, " Perhaps ; but clearly it is none of our business, dear."

" You can never be charged with meddlesomeness, Emma," Grace answered, with a laugh. " But it is my besetting sin. Oh, I don't mean that I shall interfere, or that I ever do interfere in other people's affairs maliciously ; but my mind can't help busying itself, that is all. I was just thinking that if anybody — say Jack Vandever, though he is not more likely than any one else, I suppose — were to fall in love with Beatrice ! Jack looked mightily pleased when you told him he was to sing with her."

"If Jack Vandever falls in love with any one," said Mrs. Thompson, rocking gently to and fro and enjoying her little hour of idleness, " take my word for it, it will not be on account of pedigree, supposed or real. Jack has pedigree enough of his own."

The two women had discussed this matter of Beatrice's pedigree immediately after their interview with her. They knew it was a secret, otherwise Beatrice would not have been where she was.

" It does n't seem quite honest," Grace insisted, going back to the beginning of the subject ; " and the child carries it off with such an air."

"You would not have her placard herself, would you? " said Mrs. Thompson.   " Her ' air' indicates to my mind simply a grand self-respect.   None of us, my dear, go round advertising the disgraceful things about ourselves, — if you call this poor child's misfortune a disgrace."

"Oh, I do not blame Beatrice," answered Grace ; " but it is n't quite fair on Madame La Scalla's part. She knows better: that is a shrewd woman, Emma. I should not wonder if she is laughing in her sleeve at this moment for having foisted her handsome exslave girl upon New York aristocratic society ! It is a situation which a Southern woman, with a turn for the humorous, would enjoy at this particular time, I fancy."

"You forget how all the La Scallas appeared to love Beatrice," said Mrs. Thompson ; " that it was really in defence of her that M. La Scalla lost his life. No ; if they have any design, it is simply kindness to

Beatrice.   And perhaps they think as I do, that it is a private matter, nobody's affair but their own."

" But that is not true, Emma ; suppose, as I said, some man of caste should wish to marry her? "

"Then it would become *his* affair.   ' Caste ' is a word I do not like.   Social distinctions *as* social distinctions do not exist for me.   How often have I told you, Grace, that, other things being equal, a civilized Hottentot is just as respectable in my opinion as any other creature with a soul ! "

" Oh, I know ; you want to reduce the whole human race to one big happy family," retorted Grace ; " but God never meant it to be so ! "

" How do you know?   God filled the earth with germs, coarse specimens, crude material ; and left it to man to work perfection."

" Well, man works perfection by a process of careful selection, not by indiscriminate mixing up," said Grace, triumphantly.

A maid came in with Mrs. Priestly's card.

"Oh, don't have her up here," begged Grace, and Mrs. Thompson let the cat slip off her lap and rose to go down, — but took time to answer.

"There I agree with you, Grace ; but in making our selections, let us look to it that we do not discriminate against the most exquisite specimens because they happen not to be found in a particular class."

CHAPTER XIX.

A FTER the first general rehearsal, Mrs. Thompson had no hesitancy in placing Beatrice's name on the program and making it one of the strong features in advertising. She did this judiciously, with reference to the reputed jealousy of musical people, — who perhaps are not more jealous than other people after all.

But in spite of her delicate management there was a slight jar now and then. Miss Convers thought it originated with Mrs. Priestly; but Mrs. Thompson ridiculed the idea: Mrs. Priestly was only too happy of the opportunity to win fresh laurels from an adoring public, and why should she wish to make a disturbance? But Grace had a keen insight, and a more acute faculty for detecting the frailties of human nature than her amiable friend. The trouble, she thought, was either about Beatrice or Jack Vandever, — or both, since they were to sing together. There was no disguising the fact, at least from as intuitive a person as Grace Convers, that Mrs. Priestly — though she had a worthy husband of her own — was exceedingly partial to Jack. Not in the broad, frank, open way which characterizes the partiality of married women for unmarried men in these rapid end-of-the-century days, but none the less culpably perhaps, and with no less keen delight in the situation which awards to the unblushing matron the flowers of chivalry that should bloom only for the modest maid. Doubtless there was something even more delicious and sinful in the situation then than now, because a woman's conscience was more tender, and the risk of losing caste was greater.

Miss Convers was right. Mrs. Priestly would herself have liked the rôle of Marie, with Jack Vandever as the Sergeant, notwithstanding her mature years and matronly figure. She still felt equal to light and graceful playing, on the stage or off; and she had not forgotten the unfavorable comparison of herself with Madame Alboni which Beatrice had unwittingly made. She fancied that she was the victim of a "scheme," and that Grace Convers was at the bottom of it. On the surface all was smooth, but there was secret war between these two. They smiled, but stabbed each other with their eyes,—and both knew the cause, but neither was in a position to confess it to a living soul.

Mrs. Priestly and Beatrice were to do the celebrated duet in *Norma*, with appropriate tableaux. Their voices harmonized exquisitely, and at the last rehearsal the spectators declared with enthusiasm that you might search the world over in vain for two persons who could better look, act, and sing the parts.

" *Gott im himmel !* " exclaimed Herr Wilhelm to the leader of the orchestra, " if I could injuce dose two laties to go upon de stage mit me for de manager, my fordtune vas made."

" Can't you ? " asked the leader, with a smile.

" *Donner !* " returned the professor ; " I might as vell propose dat scheme to Queen Victoria ! "

"I never heard that Queen Victoria could sing," said the man; and the professor looked at him in disgust, and disdained explanation. "De tam schtupidity of dese Yankee fiddlers!" he muttered, and stalked away.

In Madame Derouen's *pension* there was a furore of excitement over the coming event. Every girl there — and Madame herself — felt an almost personal interest in it. For was not Beatrice representing them all, in a way? It was their little coterie against the best talent of New York. That was the way they put it. There was not a pang of envy, but only pride, admiration, and the most affectionate and inspiring sympathy.

Beatrice had never been more entirely happy than in those days, never more full of that sweet and gay delight which had come to be one of her most lovable characteristics. She seemed suddenly to have acquired a more mature look and bearing, to spring from simple, blithesome girlhood to adorable, mysterious young-womanhood. Her companions noted it, — as they noted everything about her, — and said it was because she was associating with such "swell, grown-up folks," young gentlemen and all. "If I were to be handed into a carriage by Mr. John Vandever," said Kate Kavanagh, "as he hands Beatrice into Mrs. Thompson's carriage, I should feel myself twenty at least."

Madame Derouen attended to Beatrice's costumes, which necessitated many consultations with Grace Convers, who had the supervision of those things. Beatrice's allowance was liberal, and she could have whatever was thought desirable. In amateur theatricals there is usually *carte blanche* in this respect, for every one likes to look her best regardless of the situation and of the character she personates.

When the beautiful garments came home and Beatrice tried them on, with all the girls standing round to admire her, and going into raptures over her, Kate Kavanagh exclaimed quizzically, " I wonder if the entertainment will net as much as those things cost ! "

Another girl chimed in, "Oh, there 's always more than one axe to grind ; and sometimes the little axes are of greater importance than the big one. What chiefly concerns us is that Beatrice shall score a tremendous success, and beat Mrs. Priestly all hollow ! "

There was laughter and clapping of hands ; but Beatrice had not heard. She was listening to Miss Avery, telling her that it reminded her so much of the night Miss Annie was married and the household all came to look at her in her wedding dress. " A virgin's dress looks very much like a bride's dress," she said admiringly. Beatrice at the moment had on the Duet costume.

There were tears in Miss Avery's eyes, and some one asked her jokingly what she was crying about.

"Oh, I don't know," she answered, with a smile that made her face like an April day. " It always affects me so to see a lovely young girl dressed all in white."

Some of the girls had felt tears in their eyes too, and perhaps none of them could have given any better reason for them : so many things that touch the emotions are too delicate for analysis.

" The situation is getting too strained," some one exclaimed. " Beatrice is so splendid that we are all melting in her rays like ' snaw wreaths in May ! ' Do go and take off your finery, Beatrice ; it will be enough for you to dazzle us to-morrow night ! And Miss Avery, please go to the piano."

In a twinkling the whole roomful of girls were circling and swaying to rapturous waltz music, and the evening wound up in wild merriment.

Soon after Beatrice went upstairs, Madame Derouen came to her door to apprise her, with many apologies, of a fact she had forgotten until that moment : Mr. Burgoyne La Scalla had called that afternoon while she was at the rehearsal. He was greatly disappointed at not seeing her ; he would be leaving the city almost immediately, and had embraced the only opportunity he was likely to have of coming over to Brooklyn.

" But," said Madame, " I gave him a program, and told him he must surely stay long enough to see you in grand opera ! "

" Oh," exclaimed Beatrice, with a thrill of joy which ended in a pang of regret, " how sorry I am ! " She had known Burgoyne was coming to New York. Evalina had written that her mother had invited Mrs. Vincent and Helen to spend the Lenten season at the plantation, and that Burgoyne, who had not seen them since their recent return from their prolonged foreign travels, was going North to fetch them. The marriage, so long deferred, was to take place soon after Easter.

Beatrice had not seen Burgoyne since she had first entered Madame Derouen's school ; but she had had many kind messages from him, through Evalina, and her relations with him were still of the friendliest. Burgoyne was her unconfessed beau-ideal, the standard by which she unconsciously measured all other men. Lately she had thought Mr. Jack Vandever resembled him somewhat, not in appearance or in character, but in a certain kindliness and attentiveness of manner. He was helpful to her about her music, as Burgoyne had been about the antique architecture of Venice and the paintings in the Vatican. There was nothing in the history, the development, the technique of music which Mr. Vandever did not know, and he had both the confidence and the modesty appertaining to perfect knowledge. Already she looked upon him as a friend. Besides seeing him always at the rehearsals, she had met him at a good many little suppers and luncheons at Mrs. Thompson's. Other people besides the girls at Madame Derouen's were beginning to observe his chivalrous attitude toward her, and to throw out the usual suggestive little comments.

18

CHAPTER XX.

THE night preceding the Entertainment was one
of Beatrice's wakeful times. She often had
them, — times when she would lie awake for hours,
looking up into the night sky. She felt more intensely alive then than at any other time ; to have the
fullest possession of herself ; to comprehend her place,
her relations, her moral attitude toward the world,
toward God, in whose divine but remote existence
she believed ; in a word, to know herself better.

The shutters were open and the curtains pulled
back. The house was quiet, the street sounds all
hushed ; there were only the mysterious little ghostly
noises which steal into the solemn silences of night,
— the little creaking, cracking, snapping noises of a
winter night. The brightest and coldest of moons
looked down upon the whitest and coldest of worlds.
The stars had taken their places in the great blue
field to form those wonderful, never-varying constellations which always reminded Beatrice of the voyage
on the " Baltic," when they all sat out on deck and
Burgoyne played his violin, and Hugh discoursed
about the heavens, and the professor and the artist
paid deferential court to Madame La Scalla. All
these memories and many more stirred in her consciousness. She had so many things to think about,

— her perfect life here at Madame Derouen's, with the delightful companionship of a host of warm-hearted girls; Evalina's affectionate letters, and Burgoyne's visit which she had unfortunately missed; Mrs. Thompson's enveloping friendship, and Miss Convers's curiously capricious kindness; Mr. Vandever's marked courteousness, Mrs. Priestly's chill politeness (which she could but attribute to that lady's haughty temperament), and the frank cordiality of her other musical associates. With respect to the Entertainment, now so close at hand, she felt, strangely enough, not the slightest trepidation. She knew she should not fail. She had had a few great moments in her life when it had seemed as if nothing could harm her; when a marvellous spiritual buoyancy, a fine frenzy of exaltation seemed to lift her above material conditions and circumstances. And now, upon the eve of her début before a great and critical New York audience, she felt herself circling toward one of these rare culminant moments, as an eagle circles toward the commanding crag.

It was a magnificent audience that filled the Music Hall for " Mrs. Thompson's Charity Entertainment," as it was called, — not only in numbers but in quality, for the best people turned out. The affair had been thoroughly advertised, and then it was the very last thing before Lent.

In one of the most conspicuous boxes sat Helen Vincent and her mother, with Mr. Vincent and Burgoyne back of them. The box to their right had been secured by Mr. Jack Vandever for his brother Roger and his bride, who had just returned from the

West. There was a little stir of curiosity as they made their appearance. Roger, like his bachelor brother, had been a popular beau in New York society some years previous, and his erstwhile admirers were eager to see what sort of a choice he had made. Mabel bore the inspection well. She was a tall, handsome girl, with a charming manner. She was dressed in white as became her brideship, and wore exquisite jewels. Her husband when he looked at her gave one the impression of not having as yet fully persuaded himself that he was the actual possessor of so much loveliness. He himself was getting a little bald, a little thick-waisted, and had a suggestion of crows'-feet round the eyes. The belles of a dozen years ago noted these cruel changes, but to Mabel he was still an Adonis, — but then Mabel had not known him at twenty-five ! She thought Jack magnificent.

Jack put her into her chair, and arranged her satin-lined opera cloak in such a way that she looked like a pearl rising out of a pink sea-shell (he knew so well how to do these things), and then disappeared.

The orchestra was beginning its grand overture, an incomparable medley arranged by the leader himself, and made up of pleasing airs from all the operas drawn upon for the singers' program, — a résumé, or a suggestion, of the whole evening's performance.

During the progress of the overture people rustled into their seats, greeted one another in cordial undertones, and nodded and smiled at everything and everybody ; and there was that delightful flutter of excitement and expectancy which betokens the deepest interest in what is to come. The bride and Helen Vincent caught each other's eye, and exchanged elaborate bows in the face of all New York, as one might say, for all the opera glasses were levelled at these two conspicuous beauties; and then both settled back into their places and surveyed the happy scene with serene content, conscious that they were young and lovely and the center of attraction.

The curtain came up on a rousing chorus from *Fra Diavolo*, which enhanced the good feeling, if that were possible. The audience applauded generously, — as had been their good-natured intention, — but with a burst of spontaneity too, for it was worth it. Grace slipped into one of the stage boxes for a peep at the house, and reported to Mrs. Thompson that this was no mere tin-whistle enthusiasm! The chorus of course came back in response to the encore, and sang a humorous selection with some good hits in it, which raised a prodigious laugh. This was followed by a quintette of male voices, something more dignified and serious to keep the balance even. And then came Mrs. Priestly as the Bohemian Girl. The moment she appeared there was that quick, unhesitating recognition with which an audience greets a well-known favorite. There was not much curiosity, — they knew just what she was capable of; and certainly she did not fall below the mark. Some said that she even surpassed herself, that her voice had never before risen so full and clear: it was a ringing, metallic voice, with a sort of clarion note in it. She smiled upon her audience with a conscious graciousness which made them sensible of her great condescension. Ladies whispered gushingly to one another, "Is n't it just lovely of Mrs. Priestly to give herself out so for the benefit of the poor?"

After her song and recall, there was an *entr'acte*, and then the orchestra tuned up for another masterpiece. Mrs. Priestly drew a mass of downy fluffiness round her bare, white shoulders and asked Jack Vandever to take her out to his brother's box to meet the bride whom she was dying to know, and also that she might see a little of the entertainment from a better vantage-ground. She was not to come on again until the very last thing. The worst part of being in a show, she said, was being behind the scenes.

Mr. Roger Vandever had been one of Mrs. Priestly's early lovers, before she was married. There was no embarrassment in their meeting, however, — neither of them was so unsophisticated as that. Roger introduced her to Mabel, who made a place for her where she could see and be seen, and gracefully complimented her singing and her generosity. " We all know that true charity does not consist in the mere giving of money," she said sweetly. Mrs. Priestly thanked her with much feeling and breathed a complacent little sigh, and began to look round with a slow turning of the head and eyes to see who were in the other boxes.

The orchestra made an adroit transition into " The Light of Early Days was Breaking ; " the portières at the back of the stage were drawn apart and The Daughter of the Regiment stepped out and walked down toward the footlights.

And now there was an intensity of interest which had been lacking when Mrs. Priestly sang. Necks were craned this way and that, and everybody was on the *qui vive* to catch the first glimpse of the remarkable young girl about whom so much had been said.

There was a little perfunctory clapping, which subsided immediately and was followed by a rapidly rising sensation like the wide sweep of an on-coming wind. Marie opened her lips, and at the first sound of her marvellous voice the gathering volume of applause was hushed into breathless silence. People leaned a little forward in their seats, and put all the energy of body and mind into looking and listening. What was there in that voice which sank so deep, so deep, which searched out such strange and sweet emotions, such undreamt of tendernesses? And why did those glorious eyes kindle an ecstasy in which joy and sorrow mingled?

Beatrice had not miscalculated; it was one of her great moments — her greatest ! Like Raphael Meng's Virgin in the act of mounting heavenward, one delicate foot poised upon the earth, unconsciously spurning it, she seemed poised above this multitude, a sublime and youthful figure, with a face of infinite beauty, with a form of matchless symmetry, and a grace unspeakable.

The girls from Madame Derouen's clutched one another's hands and wondered, " Is this our Beatrice ?" They had never seen her look like that before. Miss Avery was dissolved in tears, of which she was blissfully unconscious. Even Mrs. Vincent was moved, and Helen was thrilled in spite of herself. She glanced at Burgoyne, and felt a fierce pang of jealousy, and encouraged the sensation because of the delicious element of tragedy in it. She had not yet ceased to play with her emotions. Nothing had ever yet gone very wrong with Helen, so she could afford to do this.

Suddenly, in the midst of the romantic ballad and when the orchestra is thinning down to a mere thread of an accompaniment, another voice is heard in the distance piping a very different air, the jolly, rollicking *Rataplan*. Marie breaks off, listens, a transcendent light leaps into her eyes, and, turning, she catches up the strain and bounds forward to meet the gallant Sergeant; and together they continue the song, and describe as they sing the beautiful military evolutions of the Regiment, as they have never been described in any camp or upon any stage! The effect is tremendous; people look at one another with shining eyes and exclaim, "Oh, how beautiful!" "Oh, how delightful!"

The performance ends, the last flourish of trumpets sweeps the graceful pair off the stage, and the curtain falls and will not go up again in spite of the thunders of applause. But finally the Sergeant steps out from a wing leading the beautiful Marie by the tips of her slender fingers, and they smile and bow, and bow and smile again, and disappear and cannot be brought back. "It is dreadful they did not have an encore," Grace complained. But Mrs. Thompson had not permitted it; she wished to economize Beatrice, she said. "She is going to sing again," some one exclaims, — "look at your program." And, sure enough, her name is at the very bottom of the page. Mrs. Priestly's name is there too, but that does not matter so much.

Mabel Vandever, with glistening eyelashes, turned to her husband and Mrs. Priestly. "Oh, isn't she wonderful?" she said. "But, then, one would know: she has the gift of her race, — the melody, the pathos,

the rhythm, the very poetry of music and motion !
You see it all through the South, crude of course in
most instances, and — " She broke off; Mrs. Priestly
was staring at her with eyes as hard and bright as
steel.

" What do you mean, Mrs. Vandever," she cried,
" that Beatrice is *colored ?* "

Mabel's face turned as white as her gown. " Why,
did you not know — does not every one know ? " she
asked. " Surely, it cannot be a secret ! The Vincents
know, and the Thompsons, — why, it was Mr. Thompson who offered to purchase Beatrice's freedom, down
at L'Ile Dérnière only two or three years ago, and it
resulted in a quarrel which was the cause of M. La
Scalla's death. Helen Vincent's friend, Fifine Cardonnet, told me the story. You remember Fifine,
Roger ? You have simply not been informed, Mrs.
Priestly," Mabel continued, recovering herself a little ;
" and you gave me a dreadful fright. You see, it is
utterly impossible that these facts should not be
generally known. How came Beatrice here ? Did
the Thompsons finally persuade her to come away
with them ? "

" I know nothing about her," said Mrs. Priestly,
icily, " except that she is in school here."

" Dear, unfortunate girl ! " said Mabel, " so beautiful, and yet with such a curse upon her ! "

Mrs. Priestly's emotions were very different. She
was furiously indignant. To think that she, Mrs.
Priestly, had been asked to sing in public with a
colored slave girl, — and by people who *knew !* It
was an unheard-of affront. She could not be very
angry with Mrs. Thompson, — it was simply another

of her philanthropic freaks. But Grace Convers! —
there was the sting. Grace would sit back and be
hatefully amused. Oh, the ignominy of it! Another
thought occurred to her, and she laughed a malicious
little laugh to herself: "It is a great joke on Mr.
Jack!" She excused herself, and got up hastily and
found her way back to the Green Room, but did not
go in. Beatrice was there, with the light of her great
triumph shining in her eyes, and Jack Vandever
was looking at her adoringly, and Mrs. Thompson
was congratulating her. Herr Wilhelm stood a little
to one side, a daring proposition burning on his
tongue.

Presently the Vincent party made their appearance,
and Beatrice sprang forward, — exactly as she had
done on the stage when she heard the Sergeant's
Rataplan, — and Burgoyne caught both her hands,
and seemed as glad as she.

"Beatrice," he said, "you don't know how proud
I am of you! What do you suppose Evalina will say
when I tell her?"

Jack Vandever stepped quietly out, and encountered
Mrs. Priestly in the ante-room.

"Oh, you here?" he said. "I thought you were
going to stay in the box until time for you to sing
again?"

"I shall not sing again to-night," she replied, with
a tightening of the lips over her pearly teeth.

"What! you are not ill?" He scrutinized her
face, apprehensively.

"No, but I have made a discovery." She told
him in cruel words and with crueler comments what
it was. But it was an unbelievable story.

"Oh, there is some mistake," he said. "It is preposterous, incredible ! Why, look at the girl ! You can very readily see — "

"There is no mistake," she interrupted impatiently ; "ask your sister-in-law ; ask Mrs. Thompson, or the Vincents, — they all know, everybody knows except a few dupes like you and me !"

Jack looked at her helplessly, hopelessly. "And you will not sing with her?" he asked.

She gave him a glance in which there was a confusion of emotions, — anger, appeal, wounded self-love, — and turned her back upon him.

CHAPTER XXI.

JACK went straight to his brother's box and began
to question Mabel, who told him all she knew
of Beatrice's history, beginning with her own early
acquaintance with the little isolated child.

Nothing had ever come into Jack Vandever's life
which moved him so deeply as this pathetic story, —
pathetic in its facts, if not yet in its effects upon Beatrice.
Indeed, there was all the more pathos because of
her innocent unconsciousness. She was like a skater
gliding gaily over thin ice, which might break at any
moment; though she was not daring, she did not
seem to know the ice was thin. She was a girl of
spirit, too, and of quick and delicate sensibilities. He
had seen manifestations of this in her attitude toward
the arrogant Mrs. Priestly, — a little touch of offended
dignity blending felicitously with the grace and beauty
of her youth. How carefully the La Scallas must
have shielded her, then, in order that she might not
feel the sting of her cruel position! Of course she
must feel it somewhat, and this accounted for the
deep mournfulness he had sometimes noted for the
space of a moment or two in those brilliantly beautiful eyes! He had wondered at this fugitive shadow;
had fancied it might be merely the effect of the long
dark lashes drooping a little lower than their wont.

Whatever the secret of it, it had drawn him to her each time with an inexplicable tenderness. He understood now, and the tenderness was increased a thousand-fold. He felt a strong impulse to go and take her in his arms and carry her away somewhere, away out of this brutal society, which would sooner or later crush her beneath its velvety foot. Ah, if he could but take her before she knew, before anything horrible happened! He knew his world and what it was capable of. Mrs. Priestly had coarsely voiced the sentiment of it.

Jack himself had as robust and haughty a prejudice against the colored race as it is possible for a well-born and well-bred American gentleman to have, — a prejudice which expressed itself in an attitude of cool, unconscious superiority and a not unkindly condescension. *The colored race!* Good heavens! was not this peerless Beatrice white; was there another woman in New York with so flawless a skin? What mattered a drop of African blood? It was the greatest absurdity, this race prejudice! Who had drawn the lines, — and were they parallel lines which might never converge? Where was the root, the far-back beginning of this deep-seated, cruel prejudice? Could nothing reach it; was our boasted civilization no more than skin deep?

So he sat and talked to himself, or let himself be penetrated by these questions which he could not answer. His eyes were upon the stage, following the motions of the singers as they came and went with their bows and smiles and recalls, not seeing them and not hearing them, and taking no note of the applause conscientiously awarded to each successive

performance. But finally when the stage manager
stepped before the curtain and announced that
owing to unforeseen circumstances the duet from
Norma would have to be omitted, he excused himself
hastily and got up and went back behind the scenes,
wondering whether anything had happened, whether
Beatrice had been insulted. No; there had been a
scene, Mrs. Thompson said, but she had kept Beatrice
out of it: she was still in the Green Room, and Miss
Convers was with her "like a lioness on guard."

Mrs. Priestly had gone home. "I found her in the
dressing-room putting on her things," Mrs. Thompson explained; "she was furious about the impo-
sition which she declared had been practiced upon
her."

"Did anybody hear her except you?" asked Jack.

"Oh, yes; Mrs. Priestly said, in reply to my
caution, that she did not care who heard her."

Mrs. Thompson spoke in her usual quiet way, and
with almost her usual serenity of countenance; and
Jack wondered at a philosophy so deep and calm as
not to be disturbed even by such a terrible catastrophe
as this.

"It is dreadful, but we must make the best of
it," Mrs. Thompson added, without so much as the
contraction of her eyebrows.

"What do the other singers say?" he inquired.

"Oh, they are dumfounded of course, but none of
them feel as Mrs. Priestly does. They are all dread-
fully sorry. But you and I know, Jack, that people —
even those who are the most kindly disposed — will by
and by adjust themselves to the discovered facts, and
their attitude toward Beatrice will not be the same.

It is human nature ; our feelings are modified more than we know by conditions and circumstances."

" Not yours," he said, with an affectionate look.

" Yes, mine, too ; I am no exception. But in my case there will be no adjusting here ; my strong attachment for Beatrice is of long standing, and there is no danger that I shall neglect or desert her when she most needs a friend ! "

Mrs. Thompson gave a little "spread" at her house after the entertainment was over, to which the participants and a few others were invited. Madame Derouen had her young ladies in charge, and was obliged to decline ; and Mrs. Thompson promised to send Beatrice home later.

Everything had been planned beforehand with extreme care ; and Mrs. Thompson and Grace, assisted by Jack, — who rather overdid the matter, — made noble efforts to have the affair pass off pleasantly ; but the spirit had gone out of the evening, and no persuasion could bring it back.

Jack escorted Beatrice home. It was rather a silent drive. He was painfully preoccupied, and Beatrice was undergoing the natural reaction from her recent high excitement, and perhaps unconsciously feeling the pressure in the moral atmosphere. Once she asked, —

" Do you know why Mrs. Priestly did not sing? Some said she was ill, and others that she was angry ; she went away, you know : I did not see her at all."

" She may have been offended about something," he replied. " The people were greatly disappointed ; they wanted to hear you again."

" And her, too, of course," Beatrice answered ;

"what a splendid greeting they gave her when she first came out!" Then added, with a sigh, "It is a beautiful duet."

Jack made no reply. When the carriage stopped, he helped her out and went up the walk with her and stood beside her on the steps until the door was opened. She wondered at the severe gravity of his face as he bade her "good-night." She wondered also why he had had so little to say about the concert and her singing. It was a little disappointing. Somehow it had all ended in disappointment!—no, Burgoyne's pride and delight in her compensated for everything! This was her last thought before she dropped asleep.

Jack returned to his hotel and passed a restless and troubled night. The whole aspect of life had suddenly changed for him. His mind went back and dwelt continually upon every event of the past days and weeks which had any connection with Beatrice, and he saw with a mingling of surprise and pain and pleasure how entirely she had come to occupy his imagination and his heart. "If only the knowledge of what occurred to-night could be kept from her!" he said to himself over and over. Ah, but this was not all: there were the hard and cruel facts. If it was only to protect her, he felt that he could do that: he *would* do that if she would allow him. But he could not remove the rock against which his own soul beat helplessly.

In the morning, while he sat indifferently toying with his breakfast and wondering—while his eye roved over the telegraphic news in the "Morning Messenger"—how humanity had contrived to muddle things up so in this world, he recollected that he had a brother newly wedded, and a lovely young sister-in-law to whom certain courtesies from him were due. He got up from the table and prepared to walk down street. Nothing in the familiar sights and sounds interested him in the least as he threaded his way through the blockade of jostling humanity. He entered a florist's little shop on Broadway, and examined from force of habit the various samples displayed in pots and vases, and selected an elegant pink rose of a new and fashionable variety, and gave his order.

" I will see if we have enough of those," said the young man in attendance, and stepped into the supply room.

Jack took his newspaper from his overcoat pocket and opened it out for a look at the city items. At the head of a column on the society page his eye fell upon some startling headlines : —

A YOUNG LADY OF THE BON TON SINGS AT A FASHIONABLE
CHARITY CONCERT, AND IS DISCOVERED TO BE AN
EX-SLAVE GIRL OF MIXED BLOOD !

There followed a sensational description of Beatrice and her singing, with an extravagant account of her " past lamentable condition and present good fortune," — in which connection Madame Derouen's " high-toned academy " received a conspicuous and flattering notice.

The writer went on to say : " When the secret leaked out among the participants in the concert, one of New York's most popular and talented singers, a lady of exalted social station, flatly refused to go upon the stage with the beautiful young quadroon, or octoroon, or whatever the degree of color may be ;

and the disappointed audience was obliged to forego one of the choicest gems on the program."

Thus the enterprising public press pilloried the rare and lovely girl to whom Mr. John Vandever had secretly, and with much pleasure and a good deal of trepidation, contemplated making a proposal of marriage! He had gone as far as that, and the thought had touched all his little attentions to her lately and given them a tender and delicate significance. In his own mind he had almost committed himself. Should he draw back now? Ah, that was not the question, — should he relinquish the dearest hope he had ever cherished? This was the point. It was not likely that a girl so young, so innocent, so unsuspecting had given a thought to the significance of his attentions. It was only himself who was interested so far ; he had only his own feelings to consider. Well, what should he do? The man came back with the roses, neatly packed, and he paid for them, gave the address, and passed out. Instinctively his thought turned to Mrs. Thompson. There was a woman to whom a man might go in any emergency and be sure of wise counsel and generous sympathy ! He started off briskly in the direction of her house.

Mrs. Thompson received him in the down-stairs sitting-room, standing beside an immense night-blooming cereus which had just been wheeled in from the conservatory. It was about to display the wonder of a blossom, and a few people, she told him, were coming in the evening to watch the phenomenon, — would not he like to come? She looked at him as she asked the question, and observed that he was not interested either in the flower or in what she was saying, which in a man of his quality would have seemed discourteous to any other woman but this woman. She could see that something was wrong; that there was some new cause of disturbance, or that the occurrences of last night affected him even more than she had supposed.

"Come over here and have a seat," she said, moving away from the plant.

He crossed the room, but continued to stand. "I — have you seen the morning papers?" he asked.

"I have seen *a* morning paper," she replied.

He pulled the "Messenger" from his pocket and watched her as she read the hideous article, and was gratified to see that her face grew grave over it.

"Oh!" she cried, "how unfortunate, how dreadful!" And then in a moment, "What shall we do?" It was not a mere emotional exclamation, but a practical facing of the question looking to prompt action.

"It is the most monstrous piece of effrontery I ever heard of!" Jack broke out. "There ought to be a law to punish such offences and put a stop to them."

"Yes, perhaps; but we have not time to lobby with the legislature just now, Jack, — we must take up the case in point. The question is, would I not better go over and see Beatrice? Maybe the ' Messenger ' has not penetrated to the Knickerbocker Palace."

"Oh, there is no doubt of that. Madame Derouen takes it every morning with her coffee, to see what is going on in the social world."

Jack walked to a window and stood looking out for a moment or two and then came back. "Mrs.

Thompson, you don't know how this cuts me up," he said appealingly.

" Yes, I know — I know," she replied, in a way to show that she understood but did not invite his confidence. She had been the recipient of enough confidences to know that they are usually a mistake when other people are involved.

" It is awful, horrible," she went on. " Some time, when this old world is thoroughly fraternized, people won't suffer half as much as they do now. We have come up ' through great tribulation,' but we 'll reach the Perfect Day by and by."

" I can't wait for the millennium," he answered ruefully.

" It may not be so far off as you think," she returned, with the sweetest of optimistic smiles.

Jack hastened his departure in order not to delay hers.

Mrs. Thompson did not invite Grace to accompany her, but went alone. She asked first to see Madame Derouen, and was taken up to her private room. Madame was manifestly in great distress. Her kinky, lusterless hair was more unkempt than ever, and she made no concealment of various shortcomings in her dress. She caught up an exquisite point-lace handkerchief from the chair where she had dropped it the night before, to wipe her tear-stained cheeks, and broke into a torrent of lamentations and invectives against the vile, *exécrable* newspaper. This scandalous *exposé* would be the ruin of her School, — her School, which she had been at such pains to raise to the highest pitch of respectability. And why did the wretch of a reporter have need to mention her School at all? She would go to her lawyer and see if it was an actionable offence, and, if so, would bring suit for damages against the "Messenger." Ah, *Père céleste!* how horrible it was! She was quite unreasonable, almost hysterical.

Mr. Thompson tried to reassure her. "My dear Madame! no one can blame you in the least. You were as ignorant of the facts in the case as any of your patrons, and they will not hold you responsible. I do not see how any harm can possibly come to you or your School."

Madame Derouen's swarthy skin grew a degree swarthier, but she was silent.

"I do not suppose," went on Mrs. Thompson, "that Madame La Scalla realized what an embarrassing position she was placing you in. I am somewhat acquainted with her, and she seems to me to be a woman incapable of a mean or deceitful act. There is something about this matter we do not understand. However, there is little profit or satisfaction in retrospect. Tell me how the situation is here, — how is it with Beatrice?"

"Ah, Beatrice!" returned Madame, bitterly, "you might know — but, *ouf!* there is in that young girl the *élément sauvage;* one nevair could have foreseen such *conduite extraordinaire!* You might think she would hang her head, weep. *Les bons cieux!*" A shrug expressed what could not be put into words.

Sitting in Mrs. Thompson's large-hearted presence, under the light of her frank eyes, Madame Derouen told rather an evasive, incoherent story about the occurrences of the morning. But Mrs. Thompson was able to gather the main facts. It appeared that

Madame, the moment she had glanced through the sensational article in the "Messenger," had rushed into Beatrice's room with the newspaper in her hand. Beatrice was up and dressed, and turned to her with a smiling face and exclaimed, " Ah, good-morning, Madame ! how kind of you to come and see me the first thing ! I got home all safe and sound, but it was after midnight. Mrs. Thompson had a beautiful little supper, but everybody seemed tired, and I really think we should all have felt better if we had come home when the concert was out — as you did." All this in one happy burst of words before Madame Derouen could open her lips. But there was the paper held out to her, and she took it with a quick blush and pretty confusion of manner, expecting without doubt to see a complimentary notice of her singing.

As she read, her face took on a deadly pallor, and she raised her eyes, dilating with a kind of terror, and gasped, " That was why Mrs. Priestly would not sing ! " This thought was the first that presented itself, but a dozen others instantly flashed through her brain. She remembered certain curious looks which had been directed to her by the other singers at the close of the concert. She understood now why Mrs. Thompson's supper had been such a failure ; and comprehended the compassionate friendliness of Mrs. Thompson and Grace — yes, and of Mr. Vandever ! But there was no time to dwell upon these things, for suddenly she became aware — as a knight in the tournament stunned by the shock of encounter becomes aware that his adversary is again bearing down upon him with even a more tremendous charge — that Madame Derouen was talking to her, was telling

her that she should expect her immediate departure
from the School !

Madame declared, with feeling, that she had not
meant to be unkind, and Mrs. Thompson understood that ; she had simply been totally blinded by
self-interest. For once her shrewdness had failed,
and her tact went with it.

" But the way Beatrice looked at me ! " said
Madame. " *Mon Dieu!* nevair shall I forget ! I
feared she would in one moment fall dead at my
feet. I screamed and ran toward the door, but she
was before me ; she sprang and locked the door,
crossing the room at a bound. ' No, you shall not
let any one in,' she cried. ' God help me ! ' I sayed,
for I was frightened for my life. The strength forsook
my limbs and I fell into a chair. And then it was
as if my presence were forgotten. She did not notice
me, but raged round the room like a tigress, a wild
tigress which had just been trapped and caged. Her
beautiful costumes, about which I had taken so much
pains, were lying over the backs of chairs, carefully
smoothed out and ready to be packed away ; and the
magnificent bouquets thrown upon the stage to her
last night were all in vases just as the girls had fondly
placed them after we came home. We brought her
things all back with us, you know. And they were as
fresh and sweet as though they had but just been
cut, — the flowers. Well, she snatched them up, one
bunch after another, and even the pretty baskets in
which some of them had been carefully arranged, and
crushed them in her hands and dashed them upon
the floor with the greatest violence. And she tore the
lovely costumes into shreds and stamped upon them.

And all so quickly that I had not time to interfere.
Bien-entendu, I should not have dared! And all the
time she uttered not a word, but at last threw herself
face downward upon the floor and moaned like a
dying creature. I unlocked the door and slipped out
and sent Miss Avery in. Miss Avery came and informed me a few moments ago that Beatrice was up
and was beginning to pack her trunks, so I suppose
she has recovered her senses, — surely they had deserted her! I cannot understand, — one would infer
that she had nevair known who and what she was,
and that it was as much of a surprise to her as
to any one else! How do you account for it, Mrs.
Thompson?"

"The secret probably lies in her point of view,"
returned Mrs. Thompson. She asked what the feeling was among the girls, and learned that they had
immediately drawn up a petition, signed by every one
of their number, praying that Beatrice might be
permitted to remain in the School.

Miss Avery reported the proceeding to Beatrice, at
Madame Derouen's own instigation; and Beatrice, as
Madame had wisely foreseen, furiously rejected the
friendly overture. "Which relieved me of a great
pairplexity," said Madame; "for though the dear
young ladies were so vairy sweet and gracious in the
matter, the parents would doubtless take a different —
a more practical view. I of course let the young
ladies suppose that their petition was granted, after
assuring myself it would be pairfectly safe to do so.
Now the blame lies with Beatrice herself."

Mrs. Thompson rose abruptly and asked, "I wonder
if Miss Beatrice will see me for a few moments."

Madame could not say, but sent a messenger to ascertain. Beatrice hesitated at first, but finally consented.

When Mrs. Thompson entered the room, Beatrice stood in the midst of trunks and boxes and scattered garments, her great somber eyes and smileless lips giving abundant evidence of the storm through which she had passed. The change in her was so dreadful that Mrs. Thompson, with all her self-command, could hardly control her voice and features. But still there was an unquestionable dignity in Beatrice's look and bearing, for which she breathed a fervent " Thank God ! " She went up and put her arms round the slender erect figure, which shook but did not yield.

" I have come to advise you, dear," she said, in a voice as soft and caressing as a mother's. " Would you not like to return to your old home in Louisiana for the present — with the Vincents and Mr. La Scalla ? Mrs. Vincent told me last night that they expected to start this evening. I can go and see them, and make the arrangements for you."

" Oh, no, no, not there — not with them ! " Beatrice answered with a shudder, as if seeing in this awful calamity the vision of Helen's fateful hand.

" Then there is just one alternative — and I like it the better ! you must come home with me."

Beatrice raised her eyes. " With you ? " And Mrs. Thompson took advantage of her moment of surprise and hesitation, and threw off her cloak.

" I am going to help you pack these things, and then we can send a man for them," she said. " You can ride back in the carriage with me."

She began to fold up the garments that were lying

on the tables and chairs, but Beatrice stopped her. " Mrs. Thompson, I cannot — I must not go with you. I — I will find some place, some place where no one knows me, where — "

Mrs. Thompson drew her to the sofa, and sat down with her arms around her. " Now, dear, just listen to me a moment," she said. " You are not the one to judge in this matter. You need a friend who is older and more worldly-wise than yourself, and I wish to be that friend. Let me tell you something : I was attracted to you the first time I set eyes on you down at L'Ile Dérnière ! I wanted you then, and tried to purchase your freedom so that I might bring you away with me and adopt you as my own. You were practically free at that time, as shown by M. La Scalla's will, but I did not know that ; and since meeting you again, here, I have loved you every minute, and it seems as if a kind Providence has at last given you to me ! Do not thwart the kind Providence, — come with me, come ! "

The tension of Beatrice's body relaxed a little, but she answered, " If it is a disgrace for me to be in the School, and if it would have been a disgrace for Mrs. Priestly to sing with me, it would disgrace you to take me into your home. I — I *must* go away; there is no place for me here — or anywhere in the world. I have no right to live, I had no right to be born. I do not belong *anywhere !*"

She shook with sobs, though her eyes were tearless ; and Mrs. Thompson held her closer, and felt that she had need to rally all the forces of her generous philosophy.

" Dear child, we do not live by the consent of

men," she said. "You are thinking only of the little cobweb conventionalities of society, — of a very limited society, bound up in its narrow traditions. There is a universal law, as high as heaven, as broad as infinity, which gives you just the same right to live and be happy that any other human being has."

"But I — I love society," Beatrice answered, "and I believe in tradition, and — and respectability. It is this which makes it so hard — to be shut out."

"Beatrice, let me tell you something: There is going to be a new society made up of liberated spirits, of people who have come up through all the stages of civilization and learned the real meaning of independence; and they may come from Africa, India, Japan, and the isles of the southern seas; and a Saint Peter will stand at the gate and admit them only on their personal merits. Think of it, — an aristocracy of souls! And you, and such as you, are needed more than any others in this new régime. Perhaps you were created, with all your rich gifts, on purpose to show that the time for race conflict and race prejudice has gone by! I prize our traditions, too, — they mark the long course over which humanity has toiled and fought; but we must not wrap ourselves in our ancestral cloaks, and rest content with the legacies of the Past, and fancy there is nothing left for us to do! We, too, must make traditions for the coming generations. We have a new gospel, the gospel of Brotherly Love; but this grievous experience of yours shows how far we are from its preaching and its teaching. Will you forgive me, dear, if I tell you that you were occupying a false position?"

Beatrice started, and opened her lips to speak,

but Mrs. Thompson went on: "You did not mean to deceive anybody, I know. You simply accepted the conditions that came to you, as we all do, if the conditions are pleasant. We should always meet the facts of life courageously, as courageously as our fore-fathers met their foes on the battle-field. Though in a certain narrow sense you may have no background, remember that just as much of the culture of the ages has gone to the making of your mind and character as of any other in this land! Just keep fast hold of your self-respect, my dear! As a matter of fact, by nature, and by moral and intellectual law, you rank with the best. Be brave! The earth is just as full of beauty and brightness to-day as it was yesterday, and you will not lack for friends; and the friendships you make henceforth will be as good as gold!"

Mrs. Thompson's voice had a soothing and hope-inspiring quality. She spoke slowly, and with many pauses which were full of tender meaning, and her words were like drops of oil trickling on a grievous wound. Beatrice allowed herself to be comforted for the moment, because she was already so weary of her burden of sorrow; but she felt that there was a fallacy of some kind in this new preaching, — that no per-sonal triumph, or vindication of herself as an individ-ual, or of the peculiarly unfortunate class to which she belonged, could compensate for the terrible desolation which had swept her beyond the pale of all that she most loved and longed for. She made no further remonstrance when Mrs. Thompson again turned to the packing of her trunks. When this was finished, they put on their wraps and went quietly out. Beatrice refused to see any one. But many a tearful face was pressed to the frosty window-panes for a last look at her. As she passed under the iron arch, Kate Kavanagh glanced at the motto above her head and exclaimed, —

"'Lust en Rust!' we ought to tear that down; it has served its time!"

CHAPTER XXII.

THAT same morning, about the time Mr. John Vandever got up from his sumptuous but unappreciated breakfast, Herr Wilhelm briskly invaded the semi-fashionable restaurant where he was in the habit of regaling himself with a piece of stale rye-bread and a cup of coffee. His hearty greeting of one or two persons he knew made all the other occupants of the place look up or turn round in their chairs, and the moral barometer recorded a cheery change in the character of the hour. People began to thaw out, and talk to one another a little. It was as if each said to his neighbor, "Come, what is the use of being surly?"

The professor sat down at a little table which he had all to himself, signalled a waiter, and opened a German-American newspaper.

At the farther end of the room the leader of the orchestra which had played at the Charity Concert was partaking of a much more elaborate meal, and glancing from time to time at the "Morning Messenger" spread out on the table at his left. When he had finished his breakfast he came up and laid the paper down beside the professor's plate, directed his attention to a particular article, and passed out.

Herr Wilhelm read it through with many explosive

grunts and snorts and half-suppressed ejaculations of astonishment; and jumping up from the table he crushed his hat on his head and rushed out into the street and looked up and down, wondering audibly "vhere dat fiddler vas disappeared already!"

A Yankee acquaintance passing at the time hailed him jovially, "We gates, professor?"

"*Wie eine Gans auf zwei Beinen!*" snapped the professor. He went back into the restaurant, muttering to himself, "It is our schance, de schance off a life-time! Dis exposure vill seriosely affect de yong laty's social standing, off course. Oder laties vill feel de same as Mrs. Priestly, vhy not? But vhat is socially objectionable vould be professionally a tremenjose advantage, — de schtrong card. It vould be sensational, and de great Northern public vould be immensely piqued. I haf de prophetic instinct; I vas sure somet'ing vould sometime come my vay, und here it is, *hein!*"

His eyes danced with the pleasure of his anticipated success, and he swept a look round the room as he rose to go out, which carried cordial good-will to everybody.

Herr Wilhelm had a few urgent matters to attend to, and when these were despatched, he took a cab and went over to ask an interview with Beatrice, — only to learn that she had gone away with Mrs. Thompson. He betrayed his chagrin like a disappointed child, and was about to depart when the maid Susanne came to summon him to Madame Derouen's presence. Madame's object in wishing to see him was simply to spread the news of Beatrice's withdrawal from the School: she was considerate enough to state it in that way. In reply to the professor's very direct questions she admitted that she knew but little about Beatrice's affairs, but supposed her to be entirely dependent upon the La Scallas; and she thought a girl of her spirit, and with her talent and ambition and her peculiar history, would be only too glad to avail herself of the opportunity to win fame and fortune for herself, since these were the only things she could now ever hope to have !

The professor was much encouraged. "I vill make her sing dat de whole vorld goes t'underschtruck ! " he declared, fairly intoxicated with his magnificent idea. Some hours later he presented himself at the Thompson residence with a request to see " Mees Be-at-rice La Schalla."

Miss Convers came down to receive him and to excuse Beatrice.

His beaming smile turned to a scowl. "Vhat ! she vill not see me ? But it is a matter off great importance ; I beg your pardon, but I must insist — "

" If it is your bill — " began Grace with a twinkle of amusement, but he interrupted her with a gesture of scorn.

"I haf no bill, and I am not in de habit off personally presenting my bills — like a green-grocer, Mees Graze ! " A green-grocer was the farthest antipode to a professional gentleman that he could think of at the moment, in the English tongue.

Grace promptly apologized, and put him in such good humor with both himself and her that he immediately proceeded to make her acquainted with his project, and begged her to intercede for him.

" Very well ; I will see what I can do," she replied,

and added, smiling back at him over her shoulder as she left the room, "I don't see how any girl in her senses could look with indifference upon a prospect so utterly dazzling."

"Dat is so," he responded, his eyes following her graceful figure with unctuous admiration. He sighed, and shook his head as she disappeared, and confessed to himself, "Mees Graze is a vil-o'-de-visp; her vays I do not comprehend, she is so full off — off caprice."

Grace returned in a few moments, and informed him that Beatrice not only declined to see him and emphatically refused to consider his proposition, but declared absolutely that she should never sing again.

"Vhat! Not sing again — never at all?"

"I take it that she means in public."

The professor fell into an attitude of the deepest dejection. "Ach, mein Gott, mein Gott! Vhat a rash resolution! Never sing again — and such a voice! Gott im him — hah! if I might haf von vord mit her myself, Mees Graze?"

"Y-e-s, your eloquence might prevail where mine fails."

"I beg your pardon! Belief me, I meant no disparagement; it vas simply dat I might be able to present to her dis matter in oder vays, — from de professional schtandpoint."

"I understand; but she has made up her mind, and her will is adamant."

He dropped his head and was silent. Turning the subject over and over in his mind a new view presented itself, and he looked up again: —

"I suppose Mees Be-at-rice vas much pained by vhat occurred last night; Mrs. Priestly, I understand — "

Grace had a mental picture of Beatrice lying upon a bed upstairs, her arms thrown out upon either side, her dark eyes full of an unfathomable sorrow, her lips drawn and colorless.

" Pained ! " she repeated, her eyes flashing and then filling with tears. " She is *killed !* "

The professor started.

" Not bodily — that would have been kinder."

He was shocked ; he wondered why he had not thought of this aspect of the situation before. " Vill you please kindly convey my regards and — sincere commiseration to Mees Be-at-rice ? " he requested, with profound feeling, and took his leave.

For the hundredth time, perhaps, the crystal cup of fortune was dashed from his expectant lips ; but his despair was only momentary, and did not interfere with the regular performance of his professional duties. He was likely, within a week or so, to have some other scheme afoot, equally propitious.

Beatrice had looked so faint and weak when they reached home, that Mrs. Thompson insisted upon her going to bed, and she did not refuse. It was not that she felt a disposition to yield ; she simply had no power of resistance left in mind or body. It was a large and beautiful apartment in which she lay, really the most beautiful she had ever seen. It was one in which Mrs. Thompson had expressed her finest art-feeling,

Grace was surprised. " I thought the Golden Room was too sacred for occupancy," she said when she was told that it was to be Beatrice's room.

" Yes, for any other occupancy," Mrs. Thompson

answered. "I have been waiting for Beatrice, you see; she is the finishing touch, the most beautiful thing that has ever gone into the Golden Room."

"Oh, had Beatrice's coming been heralded by one of your remarkable premonitions?" asked Grace, with a smile.

"Perhaps, unconsciously; I was prepared for her — and she came."

"You dear Emma! You are so practical and yet so visionary, — so entirely matter-of-fact even in your vagaries!"

"Vagaries?".

"Well, do you not say, yourself, that this faculty of second-sight is too delicate to be clothed even with thought? If I lose my ring and you try to think where it may be found, you are as helpless as I or any other mere ordinary mortal. But if you let your mind weigh anchor and sail away into the sublimated regions that lie beyond thought, you can go and put your hand upon it. If I had your peculiar gift I would not be satisfied to exercise it only in little everyday affairs as you do, I should turn it to account in more telling ways; but that is the lovely thing about you, — humble things and humble people get the best part of you!"

"*You* are not an humble person, Grace!"

Grace laughed. "No, thank Heaven!" she said. "But I keep so close to you that you cannot overlook me. Do you know that I should be jealous of Beatrice, Emma, if I did not know that you have such a big heart?"

"Grace!"

"I am just a little bit jealous as it is. Oh, I am

aware how contemptible it is, how mean and petty and degrading! but it is a fault of my nature, — I can't help it. I bring my mighty intellect to bear against the feeling, armed with the most excellent reasons, — reasons that would convince a jury of twelve. But feelings are like ghosts, they will not down at your bidding. Did Beatrice approve of the Room?"

"She did not appear to take any notice of it, though she was not entirely oblivious, — at least I think not, for she asked me to fetch her prettiest cambric wrapper to put on before she lay down."

"You took that to be her delicate way of complimenting her surroundings?"

"I took it that she wished to be dressed in keeping, — a mere mental habit; the poor child is too entirely stunned to think or to care about anything at present."

"Well, if she can only keep her mental habits."

"I have no fears for her mind, it is her body I am concerned about; the nervous shock was awful. But she is young, and the young rebound easily from sorrow."

"Yes, they rebound toward the hopeful future; but do you think Beatrice has a hopeful future?"

"Not from the old standpoints, of course."

"There are no other standpoints, Emma, — at least none in force. You cannot wrench yourself away from the old ideals — or prejudices, if you prefer the word — without a deadly struggle."

"I expect there will be a deadly struggle. But the old ideals are crumbling now, many of them. If the ballot could be operated in social affairs, and people had the courage of their convictions, and were guided by reason instead of prejudice, Beatrice would be elected to as fine a position as — Mrs. Priestly herself."

Grace curled her lip.

" I mean only in one sense," Mrs. Thompson explained. " Morally her position is far superior, in my opinion, — and that proves the weakness of our social system. Individuals," she went on, " are not cruel as a rule ; but the social machinery is cruel. Each one says, ' Oh, *I* should not object, but of course society has its restrictions ; ' and, ' I pity the poor young girl, not because *I* look down upon her, but because other people must.' And so we hold our individual suffrage in leash, and let ' public opinion ' — which is very often nobody's opinion, but a dead letter or an aggregation of supposed opinions for which no one is willing to be responsible — settle questions which mean more than life and death to our brothers and sisters."

" I think you are a little bit unfair, Emma, — and that is unlike you ! Society is not quite so frivolous and supercilious as you claim, if I may put my own inner consciousness in evidence. I can no more help looking down upon the colored race than I can help the color of my eyes or the height of my figure ! I love Beatrice ; she has qualities that commend her to my highest respect ; and I am just as keenly susceptible to the beauty of her face and her whole charming personality as you all. But, notwithstanding, there is deep down in the convolutions of my secret soul that sneaking little prejudice ! I don't know what it is, or why it is ; but I think it has come down to me from the beginning of time! Have you, *really*, no such feeling, Emma?"

Mrs. Thompson shook her head. "None whatever."

"Oh, well, of course not," said Grace, with a smile of affectionate admiration. "*You* are a genuine fanatic,—which is not so bad as it sounds: it puts you in the same class with Saint Paul and Savonarola, and all the heroes and martyrs who have died for an idea." She was silent for a moment or two, and when she spoke again her voice had a sharper edge. "Now, Jack Vandever is not a hero, Emma, though he may be led to commit martyrdom! He is just like a thousand other men who have veered square round from their inborn convictions under the spell of a woman's beauty."

Mrs. Thompson, who had the gift of silence when there was nothing to be said, made no answer, and the subject dropped.

Toward evening Jack called, and Mrs. Thompson told him she had brought Beatrice "home."

"Oh, that is kind! and it is like you," he said; "and one cannot pay you a higher compliment than to compare you to yourself!"

He wished to know how it had come about, and asked a dozen questions to which she returned discreet replies; and he gathered that matters were not quite so bad as he had feared, and ventured the suggestion, "She would not wish to see me, I suppose?"

He had hardly expected an affirmative answer, but his heart sank when she replied, "No, I think not; she will not see any one at present."

The following morning he sent a box of roses for

Beatrice, in Mrs. Thompson's care. In the evening he called again, and was surprised to see the roses on the center-table.

"I did not give them to her," Mrs. Thompson said.

"For any particular reason?" he asked.

"For obvious reasons."

He colored. "I do not understand; it was a simple act of friendship."

"Beatrice is a young lady, and you are handicapped in the matter of 'friendship' by being a young gentleman."

"But a mere box of flowers — "

"Oh, you must admit, Jack, that the situation is exceptionally delicate."

"But, Mrs. Thompson, it — it is something more than friendship. I — "

"Dear Jack, keep your own counsel; wait. You know what *my* sentiments are. Don't be rash, there is plenty of time; and — forgive me! but don't let the gossips — "

"Mrs. Thompson! I — you make me feel like a blubbering school-boy!"

"I only meant to give you a word of caution. You know, Jack, what a fierce light beats about such elegant and eligible young gentlemen as yourself!"

"You think I ought not to come here?"

"I do not wish to banish you, of course. But — did you know Miss Convers returned to Jersey City this morning?"

"No, I did not. To remain?"

"Yes, her mother is ill: I think the family will go South for a few weeks."

It was days before Beatrice came out of her room, and weeks before any but the members of the household saw her face. The girls at Madame Derouen's sent her notes and flowers, but she asked Mrs. Thompson to return them. She would not compromise with any of those sweet friendships on the new basis, but sacrificed them ruthlessly.

Mrs. Thompson quite suspended her relations with the fashionable world, and devoted herself to Beatrice with untiring and unobtrusive zeal. By and by they began to drive out together on little missions about the city; and Beatrice became interested in one and another of her friend's protégés, — youthful geniuses of both sexes, whom she was helping to their respective careers.

Mrs. Thompson never said anything to Beatrice about her own talents, but left her entirely free; and she felt as one might feel who has died and been resurrected to a wholly different life, — a life without aim or incentive. During those long days and nights when she lay motionless and wide-eyed in the Golden Room she had but one wish, — to die. Perhaps in some other world her destiny would not be so cruel! But still it was hard to give up this world. And, oh! to give it up — to be forced to give it up — and yet go on living, was unbearable! Her case was so hopeless: she was like a convict suffering an unjust sentence from which there is no appeal. But as time wore on, her naturally buoyant spirit asserted itself and refused to be held a constant prisoner to sorrow. At home and alone with Mrs. Thompson she had delicious little bursts of gaiety; but they were so plainly attributable to momentary forgetfulness as to be almost more pathetic than her habitual sadness.

Mrs. Thompson tried in all delicate and tender ways to win the girl's thoughts away from herself and turn them into other channels. She was a fine pianist, and Beatrice was very susceptible to her playing. One evening when she was more than usually inspired, and had filled the room with the sweet spirit of Beethoven, Beatrice, from the easy-chair in which she was reclining, said softly, —

"Oh, when you play like that I forget all my troubles ; I seem to be borne away into other worlds."

CHAPTER XXIII.

AS soon as the snow melted off the Highlands the Thompson household removed to a charming old place, not far from West Point, owned by Mrs. Thompson herself, and which had been the home of her childhood. The place was kept in order by "Aunt Melviny," an old personage round whom clustered many of Mrs. Thompson's early and happiest memories. She lived here the year round, busying herself with her chickens and her cow in winter, and in summer raising vegetables and cultivating marigolds and sweetwilliams and hollyhocks and morning-glories, and the whole race of homely, lovable, old-fashioned flowers. The change was a wholesome one for Beatrice. Here she once more came close to Nature's heart, and felt that peculiar, silent sympathy, more intimate than any other, which is like a soul speaking to itself. All her old loves came back, — her love of the water, of solitary places, of untamed creatures. She spent much of the time alone, rambling over the hills, or rowing or sailing on the river; and she began to sketch and paint a little, and re-acquired the power to lose herself in this absorbing occupation.

The city papers announced the approaching marriage of Miss Helen Vincent to Mr. Burgoyne La Scalla, who was ornately described as a "distinguished

representative of Southern chivalry." The marriage
was to be celebrated with great magnificence, at the
Madison Square mansion, and among the many expected guests from distant parts were the mother and
sister of the bridegroom-elect.

Beatrice was sitting alone one morning in the sunny
south porch, which commanded a view of the river
and its opposite bank, — all unmindful of the dimp-
ling water, the blue sky, the tender pinks and greens
of the new foliage, and the soft breeze that caressed
her face. Her hands lay listlessly in her lap, her
eyes were wide with a dreamy look of profound ab-
straction. "A distinguished representative of Southern chivalry," her thought repeated over and over.
Yes, Burgoyne was that; "a distinguished representative of Southern chivalry!" The description fitted
him. A whole troop of Burgoynes filed before her
mental vision; for she remembered him at every stage
of his life, from his uniformed, fascinating boyhood to
his noble and still fascinating manhood. How happy
Helen ought to be — and of course was! She would
be beautiful in bridal robes, and they would be a handsome pair. It would be an occasion full of dramatic
effect, — Helen would manage that; she would care
almost more about the dramatic effect, and what the
newspapers said, than about Burgoyne's love! Strange
that Burgoyne should love Helen! Could he not see
how shallow she was, how cold and how selfish? Oh,
more than that, cruel!

There was a little foot-path leading to the railroad
station a few rods below. A train whizzed by, close
to the water's edge, and a few moments later some
one was coming up the path, — some one in the

daintiest of spring costumes, walking very fast and eagerly showing a face rosy with the heat of exercise and wearing a pleased, excited, questioning look. Beatrice started to her feet and ran down the steps, crying, "Evalina! Oh, Evalina!"

It was a meeting in which old memories and new experiences were rolled together in an overwhelming flood of joy and pain. The two would hold each other in a tight clasp, and then fall apart, and each would search the other's face with loving eyes and with little bursts of tearful, hysterical laughter.

"Beatrice! why did you not come to us?" Evalina demanded.

"Because I could not — Helen was there," Beatrice unhesitatingly answered.

"But, as I wrote you, Helen does not feel unkindly toward you! She was as sorry as any of us. If they had only known of the trouble before they started, they would have waited and taken you with them. You do not mean that you are *never* coming home again, Beatrice, because of Helen?"

"Oh, I don't know, — I don't know," said Beatrice, and her face began to lose the light of joy which had flashed into it at sight of Evalina. But she rallied quickly. "Let us go up on the porch," she said, and they went up and sat down side by side, and with hand clasped in hand.

Evalina had only two hours to stay, but those two hours they had all to themselves. The conversation was chiefly about Evalina's affairs, and about matters and things at the plantation. Burgoyne was almost as devoted to the plantation as his father had been, and he and Helen were going to settle down there quietly after their wedding journey. Evalina did not know how Helen would enjoy that, she was so fond of travel and society,— and St. Martinsville was entirely too stupid for her. Of course they would go to New Orleans in the season, and Helen would doubtless pay frequent visits to New York. There had not been many changes at the plantation, but— had Beatrice heard that dear old M. Condé was dead? He had willed all his curios to Madame La Scalla, and a good many valuables besides. And Evalina had a secret to tell: she was betrothed to Hugh Connelly. Hugh was in the city now; he was going to be Burgoyne's "best man." Oh, they should not be married right away, she and Hugh, — Mama would not consent. And then Hugh would hardly like to take her to "the Castle" yet; he had not finished his improvements. He was very proud of the castle, and of the village where the tenants lived. They called him "the Laird," — a funny title for an American! When the time came for them to be married, Beatrice must come to the wedding — would she, *would* she? And Beatrice promised. She had never in her life refused a request of Evalina's.

Madame La Scalla was much affected by Evalina's report of Beatrice. "Oh, Mama, she has changed so, she does not seem like our Betty! She is like one standing apart, aloof, alone, — not crushed or broken or humiliated, but robbed of hope. There is a kind of silence round about her — I don't know how else to express it ! — as if the waves break at her feet and roll away without a sound. There is nothing in her to give back an echo; and once she vibrated at every touch ! But she is brave as ever. I had to talk and chatter all the time, — about Hugh and myself, and all of us, — for fear I should give way ; and it seemed as if I must not give way before her. And now I am afraid she will think I was heartless, though my heart was breaking every moment I was with her ; and I cried all the way home. Somehow, it takes all the joy out of life — out of one's own life — to see another so bereaved of happiness ! "

Mr. Thompson returned home while the family were still in the Highlands, and his coming fairly electrified the quiet hills. He was one of those social autocrats who claim sovereignty in conversation, and compel attention — even if they fail to create an interest — by sheer force of will, of vocal power and endurance, and through their own intense concentration upon an idea. He was endowed with a mind upon which a certain class of facts stamped themselves with great accuracy, — facts pertaining to the topography of countries, their industries, commerce, and political economy. And he brought back from the Orient a budget of information which threatened to prove inexhaustible. Fortunately he had one deeply appreciative listener. Beatrice dropped her sketching, her boating, her rambling, and literally sat at his feet, fascinated by his accounts of those far-off foreign lands, and those strange peoples among whom the missionaries of Christendom were endeavoring to displace religions of incalculable antiquity by a new faith. Every word he uttered was a vivid picture to her, carrying with it a significance that touched her fine sense of the mystery of human life and destiny.

The party had gone as far as Japan; and Mr. Thompson ventured many flattering predictions concerning the Flowery Kingdom, based upon his personal observation, which recent history has been kind enough to verify. They visited Benares — he brought away a pounded-brass cup in token — and Calcutta and Bombay, and a dozen other places which it was a wonder to have seen with one's own eyes. Little packages of teas and spices, tucked away in his steamer trunk, were produced in evidence. Java had contributed a tiny bag of coffee, a long fuse made of cocoanut fiber for lighting cigars, and some bits of perfumed grasses, — all valuable as texts for discourses and aids to description. Jack Vandever had some friends in Batavia, — Dutch merchants and government officials, to whom Mr. Thompson had carried letters of introduction. Shortly after Mr. Thompson's return Jack came up — as in duty bound — to inquire about these gentlemen, how they were prospering, how they liked the country, and so on; not that he was vitally interested in their fortunes and welfare, but that it made an excellent excuse for the visit. His coming had been pre-arranged; and Mr. Thompson brought out his Javanese trophies, and had the coffee roasted under his own personal supervision. When Jack arrived, the whole place was redolent of the aromatic berry. He was invited out into the kitchen, — a big, sunny, ideal country kitchen, with a sanded floor, deal tables scoured as white as a bone, and the whole paraphernalia of shining tin and copper utensils belonging to such a place. The coffee was made in the presence of the assembled household; and Jack was given a seat at one of the immaculate tables, and had the felicity of receiving a cup of the enticing beverage from Beatrice's hand. Mr. Thompson demanded whether he had ever tasted anything to compare with it, and he honestly admitted that he never had, and moreover that he never had drunk a cup of coffee under happier auspices, — the grace of which polite speech Aunt Melviny appropriated with the conscious blush of a proud housewife!

Mr. Thompson, prompted by Jack's perfunctory inquiries, launched into an ample delineation of the wonderful little island, so long ago captured and so securely held by the thrifty Dutch. He had tested every one of its half-dozen climates, from the sea to the mountain summits ; had visited the rice-swamps, the great fields of sugar-cane, the spice and orange groves, the marvellous forests. He had been entertained at the princely palace of a native " Regent," by request of a Dutch " Resident," — that he might satisfy a legitimate tourist-curiosity, — and had there learned something of the gentle courtesy of the followers of the Prophet. He had smoked a Manilla cheroot with the Governor-General in Buitenzorg, sitting in the shelter of amazing palms, and casting his eyes over the vast coffee plantations that covered the sloping hills ; and he had enjoyed some delightful days in the Capital with Jack's friends.

" Come out here under the trees," he said, when the cups were drained, " and I 'll show you how those gentlemen spend their time in that languorous climate ! " He lighted the fuse at the kitchen fire, told a housemaid to fetch his cigars, and went out into the yard.

Jack got up and started to follow him, but turned

on the threshold with an appeal to the two women, —
"Aren't you coming, too?" The prospect of a tête-
à-tête with his host was not alluring. Up to this
moment he had been immensely entertained. In
fact, it had struck him as he sat and looked at Beatrice holding her dainty cup and saucer in her lap,
and forgetting to drink, that Mr. Thompson was really
an admirable story-teller.

"Oh, yes, we are coming, too," replied Mrs.
Thompson; "I am sure Beatrice will not want to
lose a syllable of Harold's lectures on the Orient!"
She herself was not so entirely entranced by his descriptions, — perhaps because the scenes described were
not so new to her imagination. Once in the course
of his talk Mr. Thompson turned to her and said with
enthusiasm, "That is a journey which you and I must
take together some time, Emma."

"Agreed!" she replied, "and Beatrice shall go
with us." She took Beatrice's hand and laid it upon
her knee, and stroked it softly with her magnetic
fingers, as she sometimes stroked Herschel the Maltese
cat. The two occupied a low rustic settee. The men
sat in twisted willow arm-chairs, — Mr. Thompson, in
fact, had two, one for his feet.

"By all means," he assented. "Such a trip is a
liberal education for a young person like Beatrice!"

This was the only time during the afternoon that
Jack saw a flash of the old splendor in Beatrice's eyes.
It was a flash that fired a new thought in him, — a
thought which he amplified on his way back to the
city. "The world is wide," he mused, "and there
are places where accident of birth is not accounted a
crime. Why should this queen of women, this match-

less girl, remain *here,* where every day her heart must be pierced with barbed arrows? Why, if she cannot have a place in our little restricted, proscriptive society, may she not go elsewhere, where quality is the test, and not race or color?"

And then he dropped into more intimate and secret communion with himself, and put the mask of a scowl upon his face that no mind-reader might get at his soul.

CHAPTER XXIV.

THE first thing Mrs. Thompson did when they returned to the city was to have a studio fitted up for Beatrice in the attic ; and many of her choicest possessions found their way into it. A more artistic or better appointed workshop could hardly be imagined ; and Beatrice showed her appreciation of it by consenting to begin a course of lessons with Mr. Ford, the artist whose acquaintance she had made on shipboard. She had met Mr. Ford many times since the voyage, for he was in the habit of visiting Madame Derouen's School to inspect the drawings of the young ladies, whose teacher had studied under him. He had always been enthusiastic about Beatrice's work, and had earnestly advised her to cultivate her talent, to give preference to the study of art rather than music.

"Music ! Oh, that will do *pour passer le temps*, but what does it amount to?" he said. "It is a wind that blows hither to-day and thither to-morrow, and is lost in echoless space. Art is tangible and eternal ! "

Her lessons were private at first, but eventually Mr. Ford prevailed upon her to join a class of young women and study from the common model. She consented upon condition that the young women should be told who and what she was. Thanks to her inborn self-respect, enlightened by Mrs. Thompson's wisdom, she would henceforth stand by the facts of her history and abide the consequences.

"Dear, it is the only way," Mrs. Thompson said to her. "Be true, true, *true!* If we ever do rise above class distinctions, it will be through such as you. It is to you that the weaker ones of your race look with hopeful eyes."

In this case it made little difference. Bohemia is not over-particular in the matter of *caste*. It recognizes but one aristocracy, the aristocracy of genius; but one law, the law of the beautiful. Measured by both these standards Beatrice was entitled to cordial fellowship. Her position soon became exactly what it had been in the School. She was the idol and the ideal of the studio. Her personal characteristics were admired and imitated by this new set of devotees just as they had been by the old, and her opinions were quoted and adopted with the same unhesitating confidence. Not that she expressed them freely, — she was rather chary of her speech; but no one was ever much in doubt about what she thought and felt, and her original way of looking at things always piqued curiosity and interest. But even here, where kindness itself was so sincere as to be unobtrusive, she still felt that a circle was drawn round her which none might overstep; and she rebelled at the bitterness of her isolation. When Mrs. Thompson talked encouragingly, and with a beautiful enthusiasm illumining her dear face, Beatrice sometimes felt herself rising, expanding, glowing with the thought of her grand destiny. *Her grand destiny!* Oh, what mockery!

She was only a poor little spark, a waste particle thrown off the wheel of progress to perish amidst the rubbish of time, — a creature that had no right *to be*, whose wretched, unauthorized existence was a blot upon respectable, organized society !

There were times when Beatrice absented herself from Mr. Ford's studio for days, and shut herself up in her own, with the feeling that she would be glad to renounce the world altogether. But this was contrary to her nature ; she was bound to be tempted forth again into the sunshine of human association, to yield to the soft influences thrown round her with cunning and loving adroitness. A flight of stairs had been built leading from the music-room direct to the studio, in order that she might have the sense of companionship. And when she was in the lowest depths of despondency Mrs. Thompson beguiled her with the melodies of Chopin and Schubert and Mendelssohn. And sometimes Jack Vandever played in concert with her. This was irresistible ; Beatrice would come and sit on the top-stair and listen. On a few rare occasions she came down and sang with Jack, and betrayed ravishing glimpses of her old joyous self.

During the autumn Mrs. Thompson and Beatrice drove about a great deal in an open carriage. In Central Park and on the avenues they encountered many of Beatrice's former friends and acquaintances, but she never gave a sign of recognition. Naturally there was much curiosity about her. Her history was as well known as that of any celebrity in the city, and — because great beauty is the rarest and most wonderful thing under the sun — people were always on the *qui vive* for a glimpse of her face. Of course

she had her disclaimers, dull people who analyzed her
features and found no great wonder in them ; who
maintained there were numberless girls with forms just
as perfect and faces as handsome as hers, and nothing
said about it.   But Beatrice had something more
than a perfect form and a handsome face, — she had
genius.   It takes genius to be beautiful, as it takes
genius to write a poem or paint a picture.   And all
genius has its triumphant moments.   Any one who saw
Beatrice riding beside Jack Vandever in the park on a
fine frosty morning might have understood this definition of her.   These rides, which society regarded as almost a slap in the face, were of frequent occurrence.

Before permitting this "open confession" on Jack's
part, Mrs. Thompson had a serious talk with him.
He was very frank.   He told her that he had fought
a hard battle with himself, — or rather the battle was
between himself and all his preconceived sociologi-
cal ideas.   But he had conquered.   He had come to
believe, as she did, that old ideals must pass away and
give place to new.   The history of progressive civilization was the history of new thought sweeping over
decayed institutions.   He could see progress : why,
he could almost see the dawn of the millennium in
this change in his own individual attitude !   He had
been born in the patrician class, and the spirit of the
age demanded that from this class should come the
first practical recognition of the universal brotherhood
of man.   If the movement was from below upward, it
meant revolution ; if from above downward, it meant
union and sympathy, — it meant Christianity.   Oh, of
course he did not mean that he should like to hobnob
with every ebony sambo he met on the street, any

more than with a good many of his own race and color ! He claimed the right of selection. Universal equality was an impossible term in social life. You could not love every man as you loved your brother, — that was too literal an interpretation of the divine mandate. But there should be no arbitrary distinctions ; you should treat with men on the moral and intellectual plane, not on class lines.

Mrs. Thompson's eyes shone with a soft radiance. "Treat with men as if they had no bodies at all, black or white," she said ; "as if they had no earthly environment : treat with them as *souls*, classified only by Almighty God ! "

Society found itself in a painful quandary with respect to Mrs. Thompson's protégé. She could not be entirely ignored, and yet it was impossible to receive her on equal terms. The result was a compromise which would have made Beatrice' position even more painful than it was, had she accepted its terms. For this was what Society said in effect : " We are sorry for you, you poor unfortunate girl ! and we mean not to be unkind to you. We cannot recognize your class ; but as for yourself individually, we will give you a place among us as a curiously interesting human phenomenon whom one of our best families has seen fit to raise to prominence." Society ? Well, women ; men in such a case do one thing or the other without pestering their consciences.

Now and then Beatrice was invited to some modest function where only women — chiefly elderly women, or at least married women and advanced spinsters — were bidden ; a parlor lecture, or a meeting of some literary or charitable association where tea was served to mildly mitigate formality. But she rejected all these transparent overtures. She went only to public entertainments where she always seemed oblivious of the crowd and of the sensation which she created ; but to the keen student of human nature her reticent expression and proud, imperial bearing — as though she belonged to a superior rather than an inferior race — betrayed the most sensitive consciousness. Her feeling toward society crystallized into a bitter hatred, — all the more bitter because she was so helpless. She could only rage inwardly with a burning sense of the wrongs, the cruelty, the injustice which this bland world smiles upon, or at best takes no note of. She especially hated the spoiled daughters of fortune, of the type of Helen Vincent, — women enthroned upon the heights of social power and influence, and accepting graciously, or ungraciously, the homage poured out at their feet as if it were their right ! Why was it their right ; what had they done to deserve it ? How hateful they were with their pink-and-white faces, their coquettish glances, their light, frivolous, and supercilious ways ! And how little many of them really esteemed those things which made the awful difference between themselves and her, and which she would have prized above her life, — their family honor and their respectable names !

Mrs. Thompson was not disturbed at this mental phase, which she felt could be only temporary. Beatrice would rise high enough sometime, through her fine spiritual intelligence and good sense, to view the whole grand scheme of social ethics, and to look dispassionately even upon the hard conditions of her own life.

It began to be noticed that other elegant young
gentlemen besides Jack Vandever presented themselves at Mrs. Thompson's box at the theatre, or rode
gallantly alongside her carriage in the Park.   Beatrice
might have revenged herself upon Society for its scant
courtesy to her through a peculiar power she possessed, and which does not always go with physical
charms, — the "genius to be loved."   The evidence
of this power was shown in many pairs of unguarded
eyes ; and it carried temptations with it, for she was
young, impressible, a woman, lacking none of the
delicate intuitions or fine emotions of her sex.   The
blood tingled underneath her white skin at the ardent glances of handsome, chivalrous youths who
were ready to sacrifice everything — home, family,
and brilliant prospects — on the mad altar of passion.
It was not out of consideration for them or their distressed relatives that she refused to encourage their
adoration, — her obligations were to herself alone.
She would not, she could not, compromise her own
moral integrity.   She, standing alone, — without a
"background" as Mrs. Thompson had said, — held
her moral convictions as men hold their family honor
and national pride.

Beatrice did not object to having any of her friends
with her when she was at work in the studio.   Occasionally both Mr. and Mrs. Thompson spent a whole
morning there ; and Jack Vandever desired nothing
better than to sit and read to her, or lay the book
face downward upon his knee and watch her while
she worked, — talking little, thinking much, and real-
izing that his love for her was the grand passion of
his life.   She was making a likeness of Herschel, the

cat — posed in all his sinuous grace upon a rich Bokhara rug, which was also to go into the picture. It was nearly completed. One afternoon when the shadows were beginning to gather in the farthest corners, and she was deeply intent upon finishing the last of the graceful paws, Herschel got up, stretched himself, and deliberately walked out of the room and pattered down the stairs. Beatrice raised her eyes, glanced at the empty rug, and dropped her brush with a laugh.

" Like many of his class, your model is an irresponsible vagabond," said Jack, who was sitting at some distance from her, near a window. He rose and came over to look at the picture. " Do you suppose our friend Herschel will know himself?" he asked.

" No ; he will probably think he is somebody else, and try to pick a quarrel with himself," she answered.

" From pure jealousy ! you have more than done him justice. You have given him an almost human expression, — the expression of a pampered aristocrat. Was it intentional? "

" No, hardly intentional ; inevitable, perhaps. There are human traits in every animal, don't you think so? " He was about to make some light reply ; but before he had formed a word of it she looked up, and he began to tell her with rapid, unpremeditated eloquence that he loved her, that he wished to marry her, that he laid his life's service at her feet. He poured out all the impassioned vows that crowd upon a lover's tongue.

Beatrice had risen, and was standing before her easel. He took her hand, but she did not seem to

be aware of it until, interpreting her silence for acceptance of his suit, he attempted to draw her to himself. Then she snatched away her hand and started
back, looking up at him with eyes big and round with
surprise.

"You love me, *you love me?* Oh, Mr. Vandever,
I cannot marry you! I — I wish you would take
back what you have said!"

"Take it back? Oh, no, Beatrice, I can't do that!
Don't say you cannot marry me; there are no insu-
perable obstacles, believe me. Consider a little; do
not make your answer final; let me talk to you, convince you. I can — I can, indeed!"

His voice had the gentlest cadence, his eyes were
persuasive and tender; but he did not again offer to
touch her. He simply stood before her in manly
respectfulness, and waited for her to speak. Her
eyes were downcast, her lips closed with their usual
suggestion of firmness and reserve, and he could not
read her thoughts. He believed she was mentally
contrasting their respective positions in life. But
what could he do? In what delicate terms could he
convey to her the knowledge that in that higher philosophy of life to which he had lately attained, no
such contrasts were admissible? Surely his declara-
tion of love and offer of marriage ought to carry this
fact along with them! Could she not understand?
Well, he would not hurry her; he would wait. By
and by he could persuade her; he could explain
away all her scruples. There was something peculiarly touching in her attitude, — something that made
his heart ache with an infinite yearning and tenderness. Alas! that she could not lift that proud head

and acknowledge his love by the simple, royal right of womanhood ! that shame of her ignoble birth and lineage must thrust itself upon her in this supreme moment !

After a few seconds she looked up. "Mr. Vandever, I do not love you," she said ; "not as a woman should love the man she marries !"

He actually staggered. It seemed as if the earth were spinning from under his feet. It was his turn to keep silent, to look at her and find no words. She had rejected him ! and the arguments with which he had intended to meet this possible contingency— arguments which he had used to convince himself that he could afford to take this step—were not now available. For she did not love him — *not love him !* And he had been about to explain ; to say to this peerless woman who in her supreme nobility of soul had forgotten all but the fact that he was a man and she a woman, that he had carefully taken account of the disparity between them and cancelled it ! Had he abandoned all the instincts of a gentleman? But, thank God ! he had not betrayed himself ; he was spared the scorching rebuke which must have flashed into those grand eyes. He called himself a prig, an insufferable egotist, and even harsher names, and then tried to find excuses for himself, and repudiated them as fast as they came up, as being unworthy a man of sense and taste. Oh, there is no doubt that he was an egotist — women do their best to make egotists of such men as he ! The fact was plain enough that more than one young lady of his acquaintance would have been glad to add to her respectable family name the dignity of his. To tell the truth, he had thought more about his name, and what he could give Beatrice, than about his own personal worthiness. He had had but the one thought, — to take her to himself and surround her with his loving care ; to protect her, guard her, recompense her for the sorrows of her young life. Had she taken no account of these things — which must mean so much to a woman?

"Beatrice, have you nothing more to say to me?" he asked huskily.

"Oh, no, nothing, nothing ! Let us never speak of this again," she replied, with unmistakable finality.

Mrs. Thompson was sitting in the firelight with Beatrice's recalcitrant model on her lap when Jack came down stairs. He crossed the room and stood beside her.

She looked up with a smile and asked, "Is not Beatrice coming down?"

"I presume so, after I am gone," he replied. "I have just proposed to her — and been rejected."

"Jack ! you don't mean it?"

"Indeed I do."

"But I supposed — I supposed it was all clear sailing ! "

"So did I — and my presumption has been rebuked. Mrs. Thompson, there is a woman who is absolutely true to herself. I do not mean that my offer was a glittering temptation, — God knows it seems paltry enough now ! But I do not think Beatrice would sacrifice one jot of her self-respect for a kingdom ! "

"No, I don't think she would," Mrs. Thompson replied. "Won't you sit down, Jack?" She pushed him a chair.

"No, thank you, I am going now." He bade her

good-night and started toward the door, but came back again. " Mrs. Thompson, I don't mind if people know about this. You warned me against the gossips' tongues, but I did not heed ; and now I do not want Beatrice to be compromised. I do not want people to think I was trifling with her. I leave it all with you."

Mrs. Thompson got up, and in a tender, motherly way kissed him on the cheek, but said not a word. Her eyes were full of tears.

CHAPTER XXV.

IT had been raining for days in the Têche country. Sometimes it was an uncertain drizzle, after the manner of a person who does not know his own mind; and sometimes a steady, determined downpour, as if another deluge was imminent. The sky was so discouragingly opaque and dreary that only the most hopeful could conceive that the sun would ever shine again. It was nearing Christmas, and Evalina was to be married on Christmas Day. Hugh Connelly had already arrived, — he came just before the rain set in, — and Beatrice was expected on the next boat. Evalina was distressed about the weather chiefly on her account.

"Oh, dear, oh, dear!" she sighed one evening when the family — grouped round the great fireplace in the sitting room — were discussing this perennial subject; "it will be so dismal coming up the bayou, — nothing but black water everywhere. Mama, do you remember when we brought Beatrice home, and what a lovely voyage we had, — and how wonderful everything seemed to her?"

Madame La Scalla replied that the journey was one she was not likely ever to forget; and she added that most of the things with which Beatrice had been connected had left a vivid memory.

"It has been a long time since Beatrice saw the

bayou," remarked Burgoyne, and Evalina counted up on her fingers : " Fifty-five, fifty-six, fifty-seven, fifty-eight, fifty-nine, sixty, — six years ! I did not realize that it had been so long." She turned to her lover and said, " I am almost afraid she did not want to come to our wedding, Hugh ! But I had her promise and Betty never breaks her word."

" Why were you so particularly anxious to have her come, if you thought she did not wish to ? " Helen asked fretfully.

" Oh, because her presence is necessary to complete the supreme event of my life ! " replied Evalina lightly, with another glance at Hugh, — a sweet glance, full of pride and happiness, and which he apparently would have been glad to answer with a kiss.

Helen sneered, — whether at Evalina's reply, or at the frank fondness of the engaged pair, was uncertain. Burgoyne put the former interpretation upon it, and said good-naturedly, " My dear, you ought to be able to understand that ; I do not suppose we should have been married yet if your friend Fifine Cardonnet had not found it convenient to come over and give us her benediction ! "

" That was quite a different matter," Helen answered stiffly. " Fifine is — "

" Married herself, by this time, let us hope — if the Russian Count has done his duty," interrupted Burgoyne, to avert the unpleasant comparison which he was sure Helen intended to make.

But he had unwittingly jostled a sensitive subject. Tears from the fountain of injured feeling sprang to Helen's eyes. An invitation to Fifine's wedding — set for the middle of December — had come after the arrangements had been made for Evalina's ; and ever since then Helen had gone about with an aggrieved air, which even Evalina with her sunny temper found it hard to withstand. The situation was all the more aggravating to Helen because her mother was in Paris, and her letters as usual breathed the very essence and spirit of the gay French Capital.

Evalina was genuinely sorry, and had ventured to say to Burgoyne that he might perhaps better take Helen abroad, adding bravely that Hugh and she would not mind, since Helen was so anxious to go. He indignantly scouted the thought, but added upon consideration that Helen might go if she wished ; she was a good traveller, and knew how to take care of herself. But Helen declined, and even chose to regard the proposition in the light of an additional grievance. Her extraordinary sentimentality had developed into morbidness, of the kind that finds luxury in being miserable. The quiet plantation life was unspeakably dull to her, but she was not disposed to follow her mother's cheerful example and go about without her husband. She was quite martyr-like in her wifely devotion, and made no concealment of the fact.

" Beatrice must have changed a good deal ·since we last saw her," remarked Madame La Scalla.

" I hope she is happier than when *I* last saw her ! " said Evalina ; " and I think she must be, her letters have a brighter tone of late. She is so much interested in her painting. But is n't it strange that she will not sell a single picture, nor allow one to be hung in a public gallery ? "

" I do not think it strange," replied Madame ;

22

" her history would of course go with the picture, and she shrinks from every sort of notoriety, which is quite natural under the circumstances."

"Poor Betty! she had such a wide ambition, and now the theatre of her life is so small!" said Evalina.

"It is better not to have a wide ambition, is it not?" answered Hugh, with a smile. "Then whatever good comes to us has the flavor of unexpectedness."

Evalina took the force of this logic home to her own heart, and thrilled with happiness. She had been so timid in her demands upon life, and so much had come to her!

Down in the kitchen there was the usual dusky assemblage enjoying the roaring heat of a pine-knot blaze, — Aunt Riddy, Uncle Smiley, Big Jake, two or three coquettish housemaids, and one other, the melancholy Ebenezer, who was one of the "valuables" bequeathed to Madame La Scalla by the late M. Condé. Ebenezer had at last been dissevered from the cause of his many trials and bitter soliloquies. The redoubtable Bonaparte was dead. He had given up the discouraging struggle for existence just previous to M. Condé's demise, and his lean carcass had been dragged off to the swamp to furnish a Barmecide feast for the buzzards. Curiously enough, Ebenezer's chief comfort now was in dwelling upon the memory of the poor beast, which grew softer as it receded into the past.

The younger maids were washing the dinner dishes at an enormous table opposite the fireplace. Two or three tallow candles stood upon the shelf above the table, but their pale glow was shamed by the brilliant flame of the pine-knots.

Aunt Riddy sat with her back to the jamb where she could keep an eye on the dish-washers, and charge down upon them with a timely rebuke for any carelessness or delinquency. She was smoking a little lead pipe which had been fashioned at the blacksmith shop, and mounted on a honeysuckle stem and presented to her by Uncle Smiley one Christmas eve many years ago. Her right hand comfortably supported her left elbow, and her whole attitude bespoke luxurious ease. "Yais," she said, taking the pipe from her lips and clinching a statement she had just made by a repetition of it, " Mis' C'rinne she done give de ordeh herself. She say we-all mus' call Beatrice *Miss* Beatrice, like she 's w'ite folks."

" *Bonté !* w 'at fo' dat ? " inquired Uncle Smiley.

" 'Cos she done bin freed, 'n' got education," returned Aunt Riddy, and added with a chuckle, " You mens mus' jerk off yo' ole chapeaus w'en you meet huh, right quick."

" I don't min' dat, me," said Big Jake.

" Co'se not, you al'ays mighty sweet on dat li'le gal, eveh sence she fus' come hyeh," retorted Aunt Riddy.

" What you-all talkin' 'bout ? " demanded Calisty, who at that moment appeared in the doorway, having slipped away as was her nightly custom, to come and spend an hour or two in this goodly company.

Jake got up and gallantly offered her his chair.

" Keep yo' seat, niggeh," she said, with a disdainful twist of her shoulders ; and she went over and drew a low stool close beside Aunt Riddy and seated herself upon it, her voluminous flounces making a wide radius on the kitchen floor, — to the envy of the humbler maids.

"I jes' bin givin' Mis' C'rinne's ordeh 'bout *Miss* Beatrice," said Aunt Riddy, with a shrug; and then a crash of dishes attracted her attention. "Look out dar, Stasie! you brek dem china cups 'n' you git yo' ears boxed, you!"

Stasie giggled and muttered, "Reck'n ain' ainy 'm broke."

Aunt Riddy gave Calisty a poke in the ribs with the elbow which was not socketed in the palm of her hand, and said tantalizingly, "Don't you wish you's w'ite, honey, 'n' got yo' freedom, 'n' bin educated?"

"I 'low my education ain' bin neglected none," returned Calisty with a grand air.

A rumble of thunder was heard above the crackling of the fire, and Big Jake exclaimed with a start, "*Eh bien!* mebbe we gwine t' have de clair'n' off shower, now."

"Dat's what I bin waitin' fo'," said Uncle Smiley. "I mus' git in de timbeh wid de mules fo' dat green truck. Mis' Evalina she want de house all trim up fine befo' Beatrice come, dat's what she say dis mawn'n'; but she don't want nobody t' git dey daith o' cold bein' out in de rain."

"Bonyparte he neveh min' de rain," spoke up Ebenezer eagerly from out of the shadow into which his modesty had drawn him.

But Jake cut in upon his loyal eulogy without ceremony: "*Va au diable* wid yo' Bonyparte! cyan't you let dat 'bom'nable ole beast res' in his grave?"

" Yah, yah ! how you gwine find Bonyparte's grave, Jake ? " chuckled Aunt Riddy.

These sacrileges grated so upon Ebenezer's tender feelings that he got up and slid out of the kitchen-door sidewise, and sought his own lorn cabin.

Jake's prophecy was not correct ; the sky was just as unpromising the following morning as it had been for many days past. But, notwithstanding, at a hint from Burgoyne Uncle Smiley got out his mule-cart, and in company with Jake and Ebenezer started off through seas of shallow water in the direction of the woods, and returned in due time with a splendid load of green boughs, amidst which gleamed the scarlet holly-berries and pearly clusters of the mistletoe. Hugh and Evalina, assisted by Burgoyne, undertook the decorating, and made merry over the pleasant task. Helen watched them a part of the time, and occasionally offered a half-hearted suggestion. It all seemed cheap and homely to her pampered taste. How unlike the preparations for her own wedding, when the Madison Square mansion was turned over into the hands of professional decorators, — and even her Mama had been appalled at the bills which came in afterwards ! What a child Evalina was, to be so easily pleased !

Hugh dragged the step-ladder into the library, and mounting upon it hung an enormous ball of mistletoe under the high chandelier. " This is to be the kissing-place," he announced. " I give you ladies fair warning ! No matter who you are, old or young, married or single, any man who captures you in this spot has a right to a kiss."

" There is going to be a lot of pretty women here,"

said Burgoyne, "and a good many of them will be likely to stray this way."

"Of course they will, instinctively!" laughed Hugh, pushing the curly locks back from his forehead and looking round to see what was to be done next.

"Hark! I thought I heard the boat whistle," said Evalina, and immediately the carriage-wheels grated on the shell drive.

Burgoyne rushed out into the hall and began to put on his great-coat.

"Oh, my dear! are you going out in this awful weather?" cried Helen, "the water is coming down in *sheets!*"

"Some one should meet Beatrice," he returned hurriedly, "and under the circumstances it rather devolves on me." He opened the door, spread his umbrella against the driving rain, and stepped out. Helen watched him drearily from the window.

"Oh, come, now," exclaimed Evalina, excitedly, "let us light up, it is almost dark! We'll make everything bright inside, even if it is cheerless without. Run, Stasie, and bring some more pine knots, and light all the candles, — get some one to help you!"

Stasie had been making herself useful about the decorations. Hugh himself went round and lighted the candles in the lower rooms, and picked up scattered leaves and twigs and threw them upon the fire.

Madame La Scalla came down stairs in a handsome dinner-gown, and Evalina exclaimed, "Oh, dear me! I have forgotten to dress!"

"How could you? You have been too busy," said Hugh. He gave her an attentive look and added,

"That's a pretty enough dress you have on, so never mind."

Helen examined her costume in the long parlor mirror, and could not help wondering how she would compare with the expected guest. She was not as pretty as she had been three years ago. She had the delicate, clear-cut features which are so exquisite in youth, but tend to sharpness in maturity.

The steamer cut through the thick, sluggish water and puffed laboriously up to La Scalla Place landing. Beatrice, enveloped in a water-proof garment, with the hood pulled snugly over her pretty travelling hat, stood at a window of the cabin and looked out.

Swinging down the old familiar road came the old familiar carriage, with its curtains all down, and the black driver, muffled in shiny oil-cloth, sitting erect on his high seat. Not far behind the carriage came Uncle Smiley in his mule-cart.

"Ah! nothing changes here," murmured Beatrice, with the tribute of a sigh to old memories. She felt herself trembling with excitement as the steamer bumped against the little pier. A gentleman got out of the carriage and hurried down the plank walk.

"Oh, I did not dream Burgoyne would come to meet me!" she thought, a great joy leaping into her heart. How handsome he was! what a noble bearing he had! what a firm, sure tread!

During the first half of a life-time the changes are great, and the meeting of friends who have been separated for a few years may prove either surprisingly delightful or bitterly disappointing. Beatrice felt that this friend had kept pace with her ideals; that there was a moral grandeur in the man to correspond with his kingly form and superb physical power. He stepped upon the deck and met her as she came out, his black eyes flashing with the light of welcome.

"Ah! here you are," he cried. He clasped her hand and drew it within his arm, and looked down into her face with his fine, untarnished glance, which still had a touch of its boyish boldness, —a masterful, respectful, kindly glance, that came straight from a lordly soul.

Uncle Smiley had hitched his team and come down to take charge of the baggage, and stood watching for an opportunity to pull off his old white wool hat and say with great ostentation, "*Bon-jou'*, Miss Beatrice."

Burgoyne held his umbrella over her until she was safe in the carriage, then took the seat beside her, and tucked the robes round her where the curtain flapped and let in the rain. Their shoulders jostled together as the old coach lumbered along over the rough places and splashed through the little gullies; and Beatrice thrilled at this magnetic touch, and at the sound of his voice, to which time had added deeper tones. A wild delight throbbed in her veins; the pent-up emotion of years burst its bounds and flooded her soul with a lawless, sweet, savage joy, — Nature's own unhindered rapture. And Burgoyne's soul responded with a kind of vague surprise. Much as he had always admired her beauty, he was struck anew by the wonder of it. Through it breathed now that fine quality of womanliness which is the last grace of woman.

Their talk was sufficiently reminiscent to link the past with the present; but they touched only upon

the happiest experiences they had had together, —
the journey abroad, and their delightful wanderings in
the by-ways of old cities. And the same sense of
intimacy and fellowship which had entered into their
relations then, came back : and something more, —
a curiously tantalizing desire for some expression,
stronger than a hand-shake, of that which they both
felt. There was a great splendor in their eyes, a
softness in their voices, a tingling in their veins which
marked the critical high-tide of emotion. It was one
of those moments, those turning-points in the lives of
men and women, when a word or a look may break
down the guard of self-respect, and the shamed soul
step naked out of Eden, with the gates forever closed.

But it was a moment of victory. Beatrice moved
away a little, and parted the curtains and looked out.

" How familiar the sound of this splashing is ! " she
said. " It surely rains nowhere else in the world as
it rains in the Têche country, — don't you think so? "

" We prayed devoutly for fair weather before you
came," he replied, " but the fates were not propitious.
Evalina lamented continually ; she thought you would
have such a dismal journey on the water."

The whole household crowded into the hall to
meet Beatrice, — Evalina in the foreground, her sweet
face quivering with emotion ; Hugh and Madame just
back of her, and beyond them Helen ; and still
further back Cosette and Calisty, and Helen's French
maid, and a confusion of dusky faces. Beatrice could
not have been more warmly welcomed had she been
a real daughter of the house. Her eyes filled with
tears, and she could not speak. A genial warmth
was diffused through her whole being. Ah ! if there

was any spot on earth responsive to the home feeling in her it was here; it was this dear old sunny Southern mansion, with its great blazing fires, its wide halls and galleries, about which she had played in the long, long ago! For all was indeed bright within, as Evalina had planned; and there was the old spicy odor of fresh cut branches, — the dear holly and mistletoe, in all their glistening and mossy green, their lovely red and white berries! The same pictures were on the walls, the same massive furniture stood on the same rich, dark carpets; for nothing had been changed in these lower rooms since M. La Scalla's death. It was different upstairs: Helen's apartments were magnificent in modern elegancies, and innovations had crept into Madame's and Evalina's.

Beatrice, as in the old days, shared Evalina's rooms. The two white beds stood there just as they always had. When they went upstairs Beatrice threw herself down upon hers and laid her glowing cheek on the pillow caressingly, as if it had been another cheek. "Oh, it is so good, *so good* to be here!" she said.

"Betty! you don't know how glad you make me!" cried Evalina. "I was so afraid you did not want to come, — that you came only because you had promised, and to please me."

The men brought up the trunks, and Madame sent Calisty to open them and take out Beatrice's dresses; and in half-an-hour the two girls came down to dinner, — Evalina in a pink gown, with delicacies of lace and a bunch of violets; and Beatrice in white, severely plain, but infinitely becoming.

Beatrice was always characterized by an elegant

precision of dress, almost destitute of ornamentation. A fine jewel or two, a single superb flower, was sufficient decoration. There was nothing about her which it was needful to "favor." From every point of view the lines of her face and figure — if not true to the old models — were artistic. Her forehead was not high, her nose not positively straight, her waist not large. She was a new revelation in feminine beauty, something not known in the old Greek days ; something evolved by a new civilization, in a new world, through the mingling of types and races, — a new idea from Nature's infinite brain. There was little of girlishness about her now, for sorrow is even more ripening than years. She was of stately height, and had a superb and noble pose. Her face was radiant with the joy of this happy meeting ; the "genius of beauty " burned in her eyes and on her lips, and made these familiar friends wonder at the change in her, — a subtle change which evaded analysis ; for she was the same Beatrice still, grown a little taller, a little older.

After dinner Beatrice sang for them, and in this perfect accomplishment riveted the chain of her entrancing influence round the hearts that loved her. Helen's eyes continually sought Burgoyne's with a furtive look, to see how he was affected. His admiration was so frank as to have disarmed her jealousy if she had stopped to reason about it ; but her lurid imagination straightway began to weave a tragedy round this little fireside circle, of which she herself was the the heroine and the victim.

The day following, the sun came out in all his Southern splendor, the birds tuned up their jocund voices, the flowers lifted up their heads, the water, which had almost covered the ground, disappeared as if by magic. Other guests began to arrive, — some from New Orleans, some from Mississippi plantations, and a few of Hugh's friends from farther north; and there was instituted every form of Southern hospitality and Southern entertainment, for the whole neighborhood was interested in Evalina's wedding, and lamenting because she was going away.

Horseback riding and sailing on the bayou were the principal out-door diversions. Sometimes Beatrice participated in these. But when balls and dinners were given at neighboring plantations she was not invited. She had begged Evalina not to force a recognition of her in any quarter, even from guests in the house. "I have learned to live within myself, and to take care of myself," she said. "And do not," she added, with a smile that seemed light-hearted, "let any one make you unhappy about me: I wear an invulnerable armor!"

But for all this bravado, Beatrice had some bitter, rebellious hours, some of the bitterest she had ever known. Helen lost no opportunity to sting her with a covert word, or look, or sneer: her only retaliation was a royal scorn which spurned the petty weapons of a mean revenge. There was not the first element of coquetry in her; not by the turn of an eyelash would she compromise her womanly dignity. Her charm was legitimate and sincere. She was like a queenly flower, blooming in a garden, which all admired but none might touch, — so grandly she bore herself.

On the day before Christmas one of the old families in St. Martinsville gave a breakfast for the La Scallas

and their guests. Helen excused herself on plea of
a headache, but insisted that Burgoyne should go.

After the party had driven off, Beatrice strolled
down into the garden. Old memories crowded thick
upon her in that spot. She passed through the little
arched and vine-wreathed gateway, and went into her
grandmother's deserted cottage. No one had lived
in it since Salome's death. Most of the furniture had
been taken away, but the pictures Beatrice had drawn
were still hanging upon the walls. They were all
curiously interesting to her now. A life-like sketch of
Doudouce she took down and carried away, thinking
to paint a picture from it some day.

As Beatrice came back through the garden, picking
a flower here and there, and musing on many things,
she was suddenly confronted by Helen, who had evidently come down on purpose to meet her: her face
had a hard, set, determined look, and she stood
squarely in the walk. It was the first time they had
encountered each other alone.

"I want you to tell me what you mean," demanded
Helen, in a voice which she could barely control for
anger and hate.

"Tell you what I mean?" returned Beatrice,—
"you are mysterious."

"Oh, you need not pretend that you don't
understand! You — you are *designedly* winning my
husband's affections away from me."

Beatrice's lip curled with a smile. "You must be
jesting, Mrs. La Scalla," she said; "you forget who I
am, what I am! Could a slave aspire to your husband's affections? And if she did, would he stoop to
her level? You pay me too great a compliment!"

"But you know it makes no difference who or what such women as you are; men cannot resist your beauty, your evil spell. You are a wicked temptress!"

Beatrice stood speechless for a moment, with tense muscles, with a tempest of rage driving the color from her lips and cheeks, with clenched hands and quick-coming breath, and eyes in which a terrible lightning played.

Helen might well have feared her in that moment, but she was passion-blind to the awfulness of the storm she had evoked.

"Be more explicit; tell me what you mean, — in what way am I a temptress?"

The voice was low, but the words came sharp and clear and incisive.

"In the way you dress, in the way you sing, in the way you carry yourself: everything you do invites men's admiration!"

Beatrice laughed scornfully. "Oh, the Lord was too good to me, was He not? He gave me a voice, and a little measure of beauty! But He made me a slave, the child of a despised race, — despised through the injuries received from your race! Would you exchange places with me, — take my small gifts and relinquish your great ones? Oh, no! you want all; you would rob me of everything, everything! You would tear out my eyes, scar my face, shut me in a dungeon! In your heart you murder me. And I — oh, I could murder *you!* Oh, you have been cruel, cruel! Your hate has followed me all through my life like a horrible specter. You have cut me off from the world; you have killed every hope I had cherished ; you have poisoned my little cup of happiness, — you, *you* to whom God has been so good! And if the curse of a woman scorned, bereft of all that makes life sweet, avails, take mine ! "

Helen put up her hand as if to ward off this terrible malediction, and then reeled backward into a rustic seat.

Beatrice, unheeding her fall, and her blanched face, turned and moved swiftly away. Through all her blind frenzy of passion she felt a confused pity and contempt for the woman who had so demeaned herself, — the woman who had the proud privilege of calling herself Burgoyne La Scalla's wife !

CHAPTER XXVI.

THE marriage took place on Christmas morning in the little plantation chapel, with only the family, the visitors, and the house-servants present.

Long before the rest of the household were astir Beatrice had risen and gone out, once more to fill her eyes and her soul with the old familiar scenes. After a few hurried hours she must again bid adieu to them, — and this time forever ! Aunt Riddy was coming out of the kitchen door with a bucket on her arm. Beatrice was about to say "Good morning" to her, but the old creature turned her back saucily and went about her business. "Ah," mused Beatrice, sadly, "one who steps out of the niche in which she is born, either upward or downward, is buffeted upon all sides ; the whole world repudiates her !"

The bright sun struggled through the morning mist and everything glistened with the new varnish of a heavy dew. She plucked a few belated blossoms from the Cherokee hedge and listened to the notes of the early songsters, and consciously took impressions of all about. "I could paint it all from memory," she said, closing her eyes for a moment to make sure. How lovely, how peaceful, how quiet the whole sweet picture, as if Heaven's choicest benediction lay upon it ! — and yet homely. The rows of

white-washed cabins with the thin, blue smoke curling
up from their mud chimneys; a few bright-turbaned
heads bobbing round among the wood-piles; hens
cackling and scratching; a flock of sheep crowding
through lowered bars; horses neighing to be fed;
the great, level fields; the dense, encircling woods
with the mystic hanging-moss, — and over all, pervading all with its ineffable charm, and stealing into
the very soul with its balm and its caress, the soft,
luminous atmosphere! And there was security and
an air of changelessness, as though a thousand years
might not disturb a single feature of the place!
This was Beatrice's thought as she gave it the last,
long look. "Yes, I shall remember it all!" she said,
and turned back toward the house.

At dusk the old mansion — twinkling with innumerable lights, and showing itself all in proper trim
with flowers and new-cut greenery, and with an air
of holding its breath in joyous anticipation — began
to be invaded with guests for the wedding ball. Carriages from St. Martinsville and from neighboring
plantations rolled up the avenue and deposited their
occupants in the gallery. The ladies, muffled in
wraps, were spirited to the upper rooms, and presently
emerged on the broad crimson-carpeted stairs in all
the glory of new and fashionable attire, — their white
necks and arms flashing with jewels, their daintily
shod feet peeping from beneath flounces of costly
lace. The men likewise were dressed with punctilious elegance; for this was one of the rare and prized
occasions that demanded thoughtful preparation.

Evalina insisted that Beatrice should be present
and stand beside her when she received the congratu-

lations of her friends. It was a trial of fortitude, but Beatrice had had schooling in that. Usually she affected dark colors or simple white, but to-night her dress was of some cloud-like, silken, crapy material in Maréchal Niel yellow; and to complement this soft, lovely color she wore an emerald necklace, a royal gift from Mrs. Thompson. She was at the height of her beauty and of that singular magnetic power which, on rare occasions, seemed to radiate from her like light. Helen could not bear to look upon her; and yet she seemed to see no one else: she was in that highly-strung, super-conscious state in which the perceptions appear to work through a finer medium than physical sense. Beatrice, in her yellow gown and flashing emeralds, filled all her vision.

The grand dining-room had been cleared of tables and chairs, and a daïs erected at the upper end for the orchestra. At an early hour the leader drew his bow across the strings and the dancing began.

Helen, who stood indifferently listening to the conversation of a young Mr. Chevanne, from New Orleans, saw Burgoyne go up and speak to Beatrice and offer her his arm; and it seemed as if she could almost feel the shock of electrical delight that thrilled them both as Beatrice looked up and met his glance, — demurring a little, and then yielding as if through an irresistible impulse.

They moved away together; and Evalina and Hugh — and even Madame La Scalla — followed them with smiling, approving, admiring eyes. Were they blind, were they *blind?* Helen questioned in despair and anger; could they not see that those two were lovers, guilty and shameless? Or — oh, hideous thought ! — were they all conspiring against her, the wronged, insulted wife? She recalled the scene of yesterday in the garden, and thought with a shudder, " Beatrice will stop at nothing now. I have aroused the tigress in her; she will have her revenge, — she will drive me *mad !*"

" What a handsome pair ! " exclaimed some woman at her back. And another returned, —

" You know who she is, do you not? " and there was a whispering behind fans, followed by a jumble of exclamations and comments,

" Is it possible ! " " Wonderful ! " " What grace, what dignity, what *aplomb !* "

Burgoyne and Beatrice were caught up on a wave of waltz-music and swept away. Mr. Chevanne broke off the story he was telling and exclaimed, —

" Madame, are you ill? "

" A little faint," Helen replied. " It is very warm here ; let us go outside."

He gave her his arm. A few turns on the gallery revived her. As they were about to re-enter the parlor, Burgoyne came hurrying to meet them.

" What is the matter, Helen? " he asked anxiously ; " some one said you were like to faint a moment ago ! "

" I suppose I was overheated ; I am better now, thank you," she replied coldly. " Go — go and finish your waltz ! "

" The waltz is ended. I only wanted to give Beatrice a turn, — I taught her the steps when she was a wee bit of a girl. Do you feel equal to a polka now, — they have just started in, and that is your favorite dance? "

Mr. Chevanne had moved away and left the pair together.

"No," she replied, "I shall not dance to-night."

He scrutinized her face with much concern. "Well, perhaps you are wise," he said kindly, supporting her with his arm. "You certainly do not look quite yourself. You should not stand so much; I'll find you a seat."

"Oh, do not trouble yourself about me!" she retorted, with a harsh little laugh, and pulled herself free of him.

"Helen! what is the matter?"

"Nothing whatever, my dear! I am quite restored."

She left him and joined a group of ladies, and during the remainder of the evening she was almost tragically gay. Once or twice she met Beatrice's eyes for an instant, and their glances crossed like flashing swords.

The dancing lasted until midnight, and then a supper was served, — with plenty of champagne and strong, black coffee; and afterward there were some games and a little quiet talk among the old people, a little flirting among the unennuied young people, and a great deal of fun under the mistletoe bough. It was late when the guests began to make their *adieux*, — with many a "*bon voyage*" to the newly wedded pair, who were to depart the following day for their home abroad.

Before going upstairs, Beatrice stepped into the library on some errand. The servants had already put out the lights in that part of the house, and there was only the pale illumination of the moon through

the long French windows. She had crossed to the
opposite side of the room and was coming quickly
back, when she ran squarely into Burgoyne's open
arms.

"The mistletoe!" he exclaimed, with a laugh, and
held her fast and kissed her on the lips.

Over his shoulder she caught the reflection of
Helen's white face in the long parlor mirror; and she
sprang away from him, and ran upstairs with wildly
beating heart. Oh, this was cruel, cruel! Helen
might well despise her now, and call her a wicked,
designing woman! And she was innocent, and Burgoyne was only in jest, — it was the merest accident!
But Helen would not know this; she would think, in
her foolish jealousy, that it had all been planned, —
the meeting, the kiss, the embrace. But was it an
accident; was Burgoyne really in jest? Oh, that
kiss! it burned on her lips! it burned deep down
into her soul! It filled her with ecstasy, with a
strange, triumphant rapture like a soul's awakening!
She locked her door, and knelt down at a window
and looked out upon the silent, moon-bright world,
up into the starry sky. O sweet, sweet spirits of the
night! what is the greatest thing on earth, in heaven?
It is love, love, *love!*

For a brief hour Nature claimed this child of hers,
and obliterated from her thought the intermeddling
of men. Her passion was more of the spirit than of
the body; it lifted her upward into a great white
light, into a palpitating, rhythmic silence, above earth
and time and physical sense, and made her feel herself one with the universal, the infinite, the ever-
lasting!

A white figure flitted across the lawn, entered the magnolia avenue and melted into the shadow of the trees. For the moment Beatrice was no more surprised than one is surprised at the fantastic happenings in a dream. But the outlines of the figure had been clear and distinct in the moonlight, and she soon realized that it was Helen's! The next instant she was out upon the gallery and flying toward the rear end of it, where there was a strong trellis supporting a mammoth honeysuckle. She let herself down to the ground by means of this trellis (a feat she had often accomplished as a child) and was soon speeding breathlessly down the avenue. But it was not until she emerged from it that she again caught sight of the apparition, still far in advance of her and moving rapidly toward the *coulée.* She ran on and on. Presently the white figure·was again eclipsed in shadow, — the shadow of the gigantic cypresses and hanging-moss that sentinelled and screened the banks of the *coulée.* She herself soon stood within this weird shadow, alert, foreboding, and sent her swift glance through the open space before her. Helen's intention was as clear to her as if it had been voiced in words, or writ in blazing characters before her eyes; she had divined it in the moment of recognizing her, and then and there had come a luminous and overpowering sense of her own moral responsibility toward this weak soul!

The *coulée* at this point was a deep and sullen stream, as currentless and silent as a mill-pond. The moonlight lay upon it in silvery patches, here and there, and intensified the surrounding gloom. Just above where Beatrice stood, the whole breadth of the surface was covered with lily-pads, and beyond this treacherous carpet a fallen tree stretched from bank to bank; its long limbs upheld it some three or four feet above the water. Midway upon its slippery trunk stood the object of her pursuit, gazing downward with the look of one drawn by a terrible fascination.

Beatrice sped across the little intervening space, calling out, "Helen! Helen! stop! I will —"

Helen turned her head, and with a fearful shriek flung up her arms and threw herself face downward into the dark water.

Beatrice echoed her shriek, "Oh, my God!" She knew where the overseer's bateau was usually moored, and ran wildly to the spot. It was not there, nor anywhere in sight, — and there were no other means of rescue.

Helen's body did not rise. It was held down by the entanglement of her thin clothing in the jagged limbs of the tree. Thus they found her.

CHAPTER XXVII.

ABOUT six months after Evalina's wedding, a Dutch ship passed through the Straits of Sunda and swung out into the golden splendor of the Java Sea. On the deck, in a little group by themselves, stood Mr. Thompson and Mrs. Thompson and Beatrice; for Mr. Thompson had at last fulfilled his promise to his wife. They had been travelling in the Orient for many weeks, and were now approaching what he declared to be the most wonderful and interesting spot of all, the beautiful Island of Java. It was evening. The sun was setting gloriously, the moon was mounting upward triumphantly, — eagerly, as though she could not wait for her cue, but must spring upon the scene before the curtain dropped; the stars were boldly reconnoitering in a field of deepest sapphire. The two women were speechless with delight. Mr. Thompson was excitedly pointing out this and that, and talking with great volubility as if to enforce with his own eloquence the eloquence of beauty that lay all about. Mrs. Thompson turned to him with a laugh.

"Oh, Harold, don't! It is like pouring water into an overflowing bowl."

"Well, I don't want you to miss anything," he replied unresentfully. "Here, now, we are round-ing Point St. Nicholas, and on ahead yonder are the Thousand Isles, — you can smell their spicy perfume."

"'The Thousand Isles,'—that sounds like home ! "

"Did you ever see stars as big and bright as those, Beatrice?" Mr. Thompson inquired, and immediately added, "Come, now, I want you to see the kind of track we are leaving behind us on the water."

They followed him round to the stern of the boat, with that little bustle of hurry which his manner always seemed to demand, and were duly impressed by the curious fiery trail in their wake ; and then their eyes wandered back to the stupendous monument of Krakatoa, standing stanchly in the middle of the straits from which they had just emerged, and rearing itself grandly against the splendid sky.

When the Golden Day surrendered utterly to the Silvery Night, and the birds that shun the sun came forth to hover round the masts with their strange cries, and the shimmering fishes leapt out of the water and dropped back again in sheer delight, and the air grew dewy and heavy with incense from the spice-groves along the shore, the reclining chairs were brought up and conveniently placed, and the little party settled themselves for the night ; and even Mr. Thompson was presently beguiled into silence by the tropical languor, and dreamily watched the phosphorescent waves breaking against the innumerable little green islands until he fell asleep.

Mrs. Thompson too sank gently into the Land of Nod, and Beatrice was alone with the beautiful, strange, mystical world, the familiar heavens and her

own deep, yearning tendernesses of feeling. Always
and always her thoughts were loyally linking her past
with her present, and bringing the spirits of those she
loved close about her. Her inner ear hearkened to
their voices, her inner eye beheld their dear forms and
faces, — not as pictures or as memories merely, but
as real and gracious presences pervading her life and
feeding the glowing fires of human love in her soul.
The awful tragedy which had occurred on the eve of her
departure from the plantation had left its mark upon
her, had shown her — as nothing else ever had — her
moral equality with all mankind, high and low, bond
and free, and taught her the finer rights of every
individual, and his personal and relative accountabil-
ity before the throne of Justice. Before this throne,
Helen — with all external advantages on her side
— seemed to stand as her accuser, and to up-
braid her for the abuse of an overmatched power.
The final contest, she felt, was after all between
souls !

At dawn the steamer dropped anchor in the Batavia
Roads, and an officer from the guard-ship alongside
stepped aboard in pursuance of his perfunctory duties.
A fleet of little boats, sent out to carry the passengers ashore, hovered on the water like a flock of
ducks.

The Thompsons had accepted an urgent invitation
from Jack Vandever's sister Annie — whose husband,
Mr. Paul Brakenburg, was now a government official
in Batavia — to visit at her house ; and Mr. Brakenburg was at the landing waiting to receive them, —
rather blindly, he said, because there was some un-
certainty about the date of their arrival. As soon as

the ceremony of introduction was over, — a ceremony full of cordiality on the part of the host, and reciprocal courtesy on the part of the guests, — Mr. Brakenburg hurried them into the carriage out of the burning sun ; and a tawny coachman, protected by a bamboo hat as big as a parasol, sent the nimble little Macassar ponies flying up the Molenvliet.

Mr. Thompson took up his accustomed rôle, calling the attention of all to the singular street sights, — the shops and little thatched cottages ; the Javanese women sitting in the shade of spreading tamarind-trees and offering cooked rice to the passers-by ; buffaloes — little under-sized buffaloes — harnessed to odd-looking carts ; peddlers hawking their curious wares ; naked children sprawling about, and throngs of picturesque Arabs, Bugis, Malays, Chinamen, and Javanese. But Mrs. Thompson was more interested in hearing about pretty Annie Vandever, whom she remembered as a most charming girl, and who, Annie's husband assured her, was transported with joy at the prospect of meeting her. Was she well ; was she happy here in Batavia?

"She is happy anywhere, everywhere," said Mr. Brakenburg, proudly ; " she is like a bird, singing all the day ! But she is delicate, she has always been delicate, — that is why we are here. I think the climate is beneficial to her."

The Brakenburg residence faced the Königsplein, in whose royal neighborhood all families of pretension were ambitious to locate themselves. The house was sunk into a nest of dense foliage. Its deep, cool verandas, supported by numerous stanch white pillars, reminded Beatrice of the hospitable galleries of old plantation houses in Louisiana. Mrs. Brakenburg, who had evidently heard the crunching of the carriage-wheels, ran out through the arching trees to meet them, with a childish and winsome abandon. She was a slim, ethereal creature, a sweet and joyous spirit most delicately and exquisitely embodied. Her smiles of welcome, which seemed to spring from the liquid blue eyes, radiated over her whole lovely countenance. Beatrice remembered Miss Avery's description of her, and recalled the exceedingly tender tone and manner with which Jack Vandever had always spoken of this "little sister," and wondered that neither of them had been able to convey a more adequate conception of her singularly beautiful and charming personality.

Mrs. Brakenburg's meeting with Beatrice was touched with a peculiar interest and curiosity. Jack had frankly written her about his crushing disappointment, but in a way to disarm even sisterly resentment; and the gentle Annie had said to herself, "Poor old Jack! perhaps when I meet this extraordinary girl who refuses to love him, I may be able to do something in his behalf." But with the meeting this thought vanished, and she said again, "Poor Jack!"

The guests were allowed to refresh themselves with a bath, and then breakfast was served in the wide, breezy hall extending through the middle of the house. Before going out to breakfast, Mrs. Brakenburg explained to Mrs. Thompson and Beatrice, with much impressiveness, that she had a friend in the house whom she was sure they would be glad to meet, — Madame Rabino, an Italian patriot, a friend of Mazzini, and of Garibaldi ; a woman proscribed, banished, — a refugee !

Madame Rabino quite justified, in her personal appearance, this interesting definition. She was a woman of the stateliest build, with a dark, handsome face, no longer young, on which lay the pale ashes of a once fiery enthusiasm not yet wholly quenched. Her eyes were of an opaque blackness, somber and introspective ; but when she was aroused her glance was swift and keen, and burned its way to one's secret thought. She took a lively interest in the three Americans, approaching them with a remarkable directness of speech and manner, and speedily possessing herself of what she held to be the important facts about any and all persons, — facts pertaining not to their worldly possessions or social rank, but to their intelligence and their political and religious sympathies. She herself was a woman of wealth and culture and extraordinary intellectual brilliancy. Her mind was constantly occupied with great questions, her heart with great passions. All her life she had been the most enthusiastic of patriots, lending not only her purse, but the indefatigable labor of her hands and brain to the work of infusing something of the old Roman spirit into the dulled souls of her oppressed, discouraged countrymen. She had entered with all her great energies and capabilities into the operations of the secret societies ; had written almost as many pamphlets as Mazzini himself, and quite as spirited. With her noble beauty, her genius, her fine womanly intuitions, and a peculiar gift of holding others, especially the young, to their highest level, she had been in a measure the inspiration of Young Italy in its gigantic struggle for independence. Her husband and her adored only son had both fallen in the siege of Rome. After the surrender of the city she had left Rome, never to return until Italy should be free! Italy was her idol, but her sympathies were world-wide. She was enthusiastic in her advocacy of the political and social equality of all men.

"You in America," she said to Mr. Thompson at the breakfast table, "are entering upon a great revolution; not such an one as Italy has just experienced, but still, one fraught with tremendous interests."

Mr. Thompson smiled, as all Union men smiled in those days, and shook his head. "A mere scratch," he replied; "our Southern fire-eaters will bluster a little, and that will be the end of it."

"I think not — I hope not!" she answered quickly; "there are other and more important issues than the much-talked-of question of States' Rights. There are your three millions of enslaved beings, — they must be liberated, they *will* be liberated; the nineteenth century blushes at the idea of slavery!"

She looked across the table, and let her glance rest upon Beatrice's face with a peculiar intentness, — a thing she had done once or twice before, — and smiled a soft, magical smile which gave to her pale, dark, sorrow-marked countenance a singular touch of beauty. "Ah, my dear young lady! why do *you* blush?" she demanded.

"Perhaps because she is a part of the nineteenth century," replied Mrs. Thompson, with a laugh, to divert attention.

"I would rather Madame Rabino should know the

true reason," said Beatrice ; but under cover of some remark of her husband's, Mrs. Thompson returned, —

" Let us defer that a little while, dear ! "

When the explanation came, Madame Rabino did not appear greatly surprised. " I knew, the moment my eyes first fell upon her, that she was unusual, altogether out of the common order," she said to Mrs. Thompson, " I have never seen a more attractive, a more compelling face. A woman like that ought to do something great. She seems to me to be one of the children of Destiny ! "

" So she has always seemed to me," replied Mrs. Thompson ; " but she is terribly handicapped — in her own country ! "

" That does not matter ; the circumstances hedged about a great soul are nothing but straw ! " declared Madame Rabino.

During the few days they spent together under the hospitable Brakenburg roof, an ardent, almost romantic, friendship sprang up between the woman of fifty and the young girl of twenty. Madame Rabino loved to talk — in the right time and place, and to the right audience — of her stormy and thrilling past, of her noble dead, of her country's devoted defenders. Her pale cheeks flushed, her eyes brightened, she grew young again, as she described the heroic struggle of Italy for independence, above all as she pictured the siege of Rome ! " Oh, may you never know the agony of being shut up within your native city, with the guns of an ambitious, relentless foe booming at its gates, the hospitals fast filling with the dead and wounded, your own best beloved brought to you bleeding, dying ! Ah, never shall I forget that

thirtieth of April, that fatal thirtieth of April, when
my boy — scarce eighteen years of age — was given
back to me for just one moment, just one immortal
look, one triumphant cry, ' *Viva la Republica Romana!* '
And the faint little smile of sarcasm because he spoke
the words {n French, — oh, that was heart-breaking !
I felt myself killed.   He was always so joyous, so
gay, — my Aurelio !   And yet, and yet, there was
glory on that day, though all too brief.   It was your
country-woman, your own Margaret Fuller, at work in
the hospitals like one of us, who came running to me
with the glad message, as I lay on my bed, stupefied,
' The French are falling back !   General Oudinot is
retreating ! '   And my soul lived again."

Beatrice was a fascinated listener.   All this heroism,
this Spartan self-sacrifice, this fervency of affection
and devotion to principle, found an echo in her.
The glory of action appealed to her.   One day the
two were sitting alone in the shaded veranda ; the
gentlemen had driven down town, and Mrs. Brakenburg was showing Mrs. Thompson through her pretty
house, and exhibiting her various possessions and
belongings.

"Beatrice, why should you return to America ? "
Madame Rabino asked abruptly.   "Be cosmopolitan,
— make the world your home, or any spot in it where
you can find peace ! "   She looked at Beatrice for a
moment or two, and then added, shaking her head
slowly, "But at your age it is not *peace* that the soul
hungers for, but strife, excitement, action, the roar of
the world's battles ; and you are beautiful and gifted,
— I know, I see genius in your eyes !   If there is a
revolution in your country, which has for its secret

meaning the liberation of your people, you should be in the midst of it; you should lend your spirit to the cause. Women can do so much, so much!" Her face grew rapt and her eyes sparkled with the recollection of her own youthful career, when her heart beat high with hope and enthusiasm. But these stirring words were the cruelest she could have uttered.

Beatrice looked at her in anguish. "You forget, Madame Rabino," she said, "I have no country and no people. You — *you*, with your honorable name and splendid old Roman lineage, do not know what it is to have been born a slave, of mixed blood, — with the sensibilities of a proud, superior race struggling in your soul with the awful curse of a degraded and inferior one! I know, I *feel* that I possess those same moral forces which have been the motive of your life, Madame Rabino, — loyalty, patriotism, love of kindred, of liberty, of art; but wherefore, since I have no country, no kindred, no field of action, and since liberty itself is a mockery to me?" Never since her tragic experience at Madame Derouen's School had Beatrice spoken with such an abandon of frankness.

Madame Rabino was greatly moved. "My dear, stay with me!" she entreated. "I shall love you as if you were my daughter. I have a little place of my own at Buitenzorg, and I have some pets and some pictures and a good many books. I believe you can be happy there. Do not answer me now, think of it a little." She stepped down from the veranda and walked about under the trees. "I am an old woman," she mused; "I have lost my husband, my son, and my country; and yet how much greater cause have I

24

for gratitude, for happiness even, than this young and most beautiful girl! I can at least thank God for my past, for having given me something worth sacrificing for my country, — for having given me a country worthy of the sacrifice!"

CHAPTER XXVIII.

AFTER a few days the Thompson party, in company with Madame Rabino and the Brakenburgs, escaped from the oppressive heat of Batavia to the pleasant heights of Buitenzorg, making the journey in a rocking, swinging, well-padded, delightfully old-fashioned diligence, as high and commodious, and which afforded as fine a view of the passing scenery, as a modern tally-ho.

"Oh, you will like Buitenzorg!" Mrs. Brakenburg had repeatedly declared, and her confident manner and beaming countenance carried conviction to the hearts of her hearers. "Our place there and Madame Rabino's beautiful palace reconcile me to this Island!" And when they reached Buitenzorg, and she ran gleefully ahead up the winding path half hidden by broad-leaved palms and feathery bamboo, and turned about, laughing and radiant, to welcome her guests to her beloved bungalow, they understood her enthusiasm. It was a spacious one-story cottage, with a tiled roof and immense, inviting verandas, built on a shelving rock and overlooking a prospect as lovely as Eden. All about were sweet-scented groves and vine-clad arbors, with hammocks and rustic seats filling every convenient nook; and birds were singing, and there was the continuous sound of water rushing and foaming through a deep gorge below.   Here and there, everywhere amid the emerald foliage, were seen the picturesque forms of natives leisurely busying themselves with their small labors, — picking up débris, fetching water, carrying baskets of fruit.

A little farther up the slope, and reached by another path winding through dense greenery, stood Madame Rabino's palace, of almost royal magnificence, and still more commanding in its location than the bungalow.   At one corner rose a substantial octagon tower, from whose upper windows one might look abroad in every direction, upon almost every variety of landscape.   A narrow gallery ran round the tower, roofed with a gay awning and furnished with bamboo chairs ; and here, every evening a little before sunset, the party congregated to enjoy the scene.   The tower contained a fine telescope, which was to Beatrice a source of infinite delight, — a circumstance most gratifying to Madame Rabino, who was a constant and intelligent student of the stars, and in correspondence with noted astronomers all over the world.   Often, after all the others had gone down and retired for the night, these two remained, exploring the heavens until the dawn eclipsed the stars.

Beatrice had to confess that her star-lore was chiefly legendary ; and Madame Rabino replied : " My interest began in the same way ; and these precious old fables have never lost their fascination for me, because of the faith of those who once religiously believed in them."

Beatrice related the incident which had occurred on board the " Baltic," adding that since that night she had never looked upon the constellation of the

Virgin without the feeling that M. La Scalla's spirit was there !

"And who shall say that it is not there?" returned Madame. "He was a just man, and beautiful Spica may be the heaven of those who love justice, — who knows?"

The idea was not extravagant, at mid-night, under such a sky, when Earth was diminished to a mere point of support in the illimitable circumference of space, and the soul laid its grasp upon infinity !

Another night Madame Rabino said: "Do you realize, Beatrice, that we are in excellent company here? I know that at this moment scores of souls in our world are traversing these same blue fields as diligently as ourselves: I have a sense of their companionship! You will, too, by and by, when you come to know them — as you shall ! They are a grand company ! Ah, my dear, people who live among the stars can have few petty thoughts ! The charming Marchioness in Fontenelle's Entretiens sur la Pluralité des Mondes, declares, after listening to the astronomer's bewildering discourses about the 'vortexes,' that henceforth she shall hardly consider any earthly object worthy of eager pursuit ! This is too sweeping, but one can understand the feeling. People whose minds are occupied with great thoughts must always feel that a large part of civilized life is foolish and trivial."

It was these conversations, and the fascination of these nightly journeyings through the heavens, which finally decided Beatrice to remain, for a time at least, with her new friend. It seemed to her, moreover, that this remote Island, where many races mingled, and where the taint of ignoble blood was washed out in a generation, was the place of all places where she should not be continually reminded that she was a "mistake of Nature," as she had often bitterly described herself.

Mr. Thompson demurred loudly against her "desertion;" but Mrs. Thompson, to whom the sense of personal loss was greater, offered not a word of objection; and one morning, at Batavia, there was a tearful leave-taking, and the Thompsons sailed away, and Beatrice was left behind. In a way, her life became again much as it had been in her little court in the Old French Quarter,— a life of close intimacy with Nature, the world far away!

Madame Rabino had spoken of her pets. They were animals of almost every species known on the Island. The natives caught them and brought them to her in their tender infancy. On the slope back of the house was a grove with a mountain stream trickling through it, and this had been made into a stockade with the cages ranged round in it; and here Beatrice made the friendly acquaintance of stags, roebucks, panthers, royal tigers, and the elegant little mountain deer, and a great variety of lesser creatures, including whole families of monkeys, and birds innumerable,— from the magnificent peacocks, the fierce, wise falcons and gorgeous paroquets, down to the gentle ringdoves and gay, green-plumaged pigeons. There were very few of the creatures that might not be taken from their cages with perfect safety; and she soon had them posing as models for pictures. "It is my post-graduate course in zoölogy!" she said laughingly. She had opportunities also to study

direct from Nature; for the jungles and bamboo
thickets and mountain recesses abounded in curious
animal life. With a singular fearlessness she stole
into the haunts of these unfamiliar creatures, to get an
intimate knowledge of their habits and manners and
their unconscious moods and poses. Her eye was so
true and her memory so perfect that a few hasty
strokes of the pencil sufficed for her purpose. Once
she sketched a large tigress which had just been
entrapped in a pit, and whose mighty roar terrified
the whole neighborhood. She made a masterpiece
from this sketch,— a wonderful picture, which Madame
Rabino tried to persuade her to send to Rome or
Paris, for exhibition, but without avail.

"But what are you going to do with all your pictures?" Madame asked.

"Pictures do not lose in value," Beatrice replied;
"and if mine are worth anything the world may have
them after I am gone, as a reward for its hospitality
to me!"

The smile which accompanied these words took
away their bitterness. Beatrice, in fact, felt little
bitterness now; her buoyant spirit was beginning to
assert itself again. Never was there a young creature
more willing, more *eager*, to be happy than she!

Madame Rabino had turned her picture gallery —
rich in old Italian paintings, statuary, priceless Renais-
sance tapestries, and antiques of all sorts — into a
studio for Beatrice; and here, most of the time, she
lived and worked, and found that deep abiding joy
unknown to all save those who have the key to the
treasure-houses of Art or Science or Religion. For
many months she painted only animals; and then

her mood changed. She got out a worn portfolio she had brought with her, containing sketches and outlines of the scenes and faces most deeply stamped upon her recollection; and with these to guide or suggest, she began a series of pictures which she called "Memories." They constituted a panorama of the old plantation, with now and then a figure in high relief.

There was one which Madame Rabino especially admired, — the head of a youth, nobly poised. The black hair waved back from the forehead; the eyes — looking not at the beholder but beyond him — were both bold and sweet, the curved lips full and firm. "Oh, that is a wonderful face!" she exclaimed, the first time she saw it. "There is that same hint of the knowledge of unseen things which one detects in all your pictures. It is the ring of the true metal of experience. That is the face of my Aurelio as he waved his last kiss to me and went forth to battle, though there is no resemblance in feature. It is the *spirit* of things you paint: it is *universal truth!*"

Beatrice was still at work upon these pictures when, one morning, the mail was brought to her, — two letters (one from Mrs. Thompson and one from Evalina) and a bundle of American papers, all bearing upon one theme, the Civil War. Mrs. Thompson, writing from her city home, said nothing was talked of in New York except war measures and news of battles; that Jack Vandever (captain of a picked company of New York volunteers) was a more picturesque figure than ever in social circles, having been severely wounded in the battle of Bull Run, and sent home to recuperate; and that it was all she could do

to hold Mr. Thompson back from enlisting, in spite
of his fifty years !

Evalina's letter had a more anxious tone.   Burgoyne
had been among the first to respond to Louisiana's call
to arms.   Madame La Scalla had accompanied him
to New Orleans, and, at his earnest solicitation, had
sailed for Scotland, to stay " till the storm blew over."
The war might not prove to be a very serious affair,
but still there had already been some hard fighting ;
and Burgoyne had received a scratch or two, — nothing serious, just enough to " fire his blood a little,"
he wrote them.   Evalina wound up her letter by
philosophizing gravely, but without showing a very
lucid comprehension of the subject, on the chances of
war.   She said that if Burgoyne should be killed, —
which surely was the remotest of possibilities, for he
was an officer, and officers had advantages over private soldiers, — Mama would never be able to return
to the plantation !   Mama herself was, somehow, very
apprehensive and despondent, notwithstanding that
every mail brought the most encouraging and hopeful
letters from Burgoyne.

Evalina's next letter showed even a greater tension
of excitement and dread.   The North was pouring an
overwhelming flood of troops into the border States.
Oh, war was an awful, horrible thing !   They heard
only briefly from Burgoyne now; he was absorbed,
heart and mind, in the mighty contest.   The Southern
forces were concentrating in Kentucky and Tennes-
see, determined at all hazards to hold the Mississippi
River; otherwise New Orleans itself would be in
danger !

After the receipt of this letter Beatrice left her

paint-pots and brushes untouched for weeks, and spent the time chiefly in walking about, or sitting under the trees, or floating in a canoe on the river. There was a restless fire in her eyes, and a feverish flush on her cheeks, as though she slept little ; and an intense excitement trembled through her whole body. But she said nothing, and Madame Rabino — with a delicacy which characterized all Beatrice's chosen friends — only watched her in silence.

Another letter came, but not from Evalina. It was in Hugh's handwriting, and before opening it Beatrice went to her own room and shut herself in. A deathly faintness overpowered her, and she sank into a chair and sat for some seconds unable to break the seal.

The letter was brief and concise, and told its cruel story without aggravating preliminaries. It said, —

" We have just received the news of Burgoyne's death. Evalina is too greatly prostrated to write, but begs me to do so. She wishes you to know when, where, and how he fell, — which particulars we have from one of his comrades. It was in the battle of Shiloh, Sunday, April the 6th. Burgoyne, as you perhaps know, was a member of the Fourth Louisiana Regiment, Gibson's Brigade. This valiant corps was in the very thickest of the fight. Four times in succession it advanced up the slope of a deep ravine in the face of a terrible storm of musketry and artillery, and the brave men were mowed down by the hundreds. Then came the cruel command for the fifth and last desperate, hopeless charge; and our dear Burgoyne was numbered with those who fell. ' With him,' writes his comrade, ' lay that night on the Field of Shiloh ten thousand comrades and ten thousand foes ! ' "

An hour passed, and Beatrice — with the letter re-folded and returned to its envelope — sat stone-still.

" Dead ! dead ! " she repeated over and over, and tried to fit the word to its awful meaning, — wondering the while that her eyes were dry ; that her heart did not throb an agonized protest ; that she could still note with so much calmness the peaceful loveliness of the sapphire sky, the waving foliage, the bird songs, the rush of the stream in the gorge below, and all the little innumerable details of the life and scenes around her ! But — as in former crises — she herself seemed to be swept away on a soundless shore, apart, alone ; the world, with its life and its death, rolled majestically by·and beckoned not to her. She withdrew her eyes from the window and let them wander over the walls of the room, which were covered with her paintings. She saw defects in these paintings now which she had never noted before. One of them so offended her that she would have risen and taken it down, but that something held her fast, — a stiffening of the muscles, a deadening weight upon her heart. She could not so much as lift a hand. Suddenly her gaze became transfixed ; the scene before her faded, and in its place appeared the battle-field of Shiloh, — of Shiloh, when darkness had hushed the din of war, and the living soldiers rested, and the dead slept peacefully. And Burgoyne was among the *dead !* She could see him stretched upon the hillside in his glorious young manhood, his noble face upturned to the night sky, blood-stained and ghastly ! Her eyes dilated with horror, but yet fed greedily upon the sight. She would not flee from it, she would not spare herself a single pang ; she must suffer, she must *feel !* " Dead ! dead ! " she repeated again, and the word — grown to its full and terrible significance — broke the spell that was upon her, and she sprang up with a cry and turned to the portrait she had but lately finished, and labeled *Youth*. Her heart melted at the sight of it, and she gave way to a passion of tears. This mood was followed by a strange exaltation. She stood before the picture, her eyes upraised to it, her hands crossed upon her bosom.

"And you are dead !" she said. "Earth no longer holds your matchless spirit, — and Earth is void and meaningless ! Oh, that I might crowd all the energy of my lifetime into one supreme impulse, and die like you ! For death means life, means *love !* O Time ! speed away ! O infinite God ! is there purpose in this little span of suffering life for *all* thy children ? "

She wrung her hands, and then with a swift movement turned and left the house and walked rapidly over the hills, aiming toward the highest accessible point. There was so much spending power in her, so much need of action tending to achievement of some kind, — achievement and climax; and at last she sank down exhausted upon a mossy ledge of rock. The first thought which burst forth from the mist of half-consciousness in which she lay, was, —

"The soldier solves the strange problem of destiny dying : that is sublime, and it is simple. To solve it living is a harder task. The one means swift, triumphant flight ; the other, long, laborious journeying, with impulse often flagging, with discouragements thick in the way ! "

CHAPTER XXIX.

IT was characteristic of Beatrice that she rallied quickly from this sorrow, which she might not confess even to her friend. Her faith in eternity and immortality buoyed her above the accidents of time. This faith had been much strengthened by the reading of Oriental books (of which Madame Rabino had a valuable collection) and by conversations with a very learned Buddhist priest in the neighborhood, with whom Madame, though a devout Catholic, was on the most friendly terms. After a few days, moved by an inexorable conscientiousness which would not permit her to neglect her obligations, — to herself, her friends, or any living creature, she resumed her old occupations and interests ; though not, indeed, with her old joyousness of spirit.

Beatrice's creed was a singular compound of many religions ; but her chief article of faith was the firm conviction that one's place in the *hereafter* depended upon the discharge of one's duty in the *here ;* and one's duties were in the same ratio with one's capabilities and opportunities. She believed that in each individual consciousness was a special and peculiar law upon which rested the burden of personal responsibility. This had come to her on that awful night of Helen's suicide, when she had felt herself to be, in a way, the

destroyer of Helen's life, — simply through the force
of her implacable hatred. There was enough of the
mystic in her to convince her of the actual, demon-
strable power of evil thought; and certainly all the
evil thought of her life had set in one strong current
toward Helen, — not, as she confessed, in utter humiliation, because of Helen's puny contempt of herself,
but because Helen had won Burgoyne's love! Her
sense of justice finally led her to say, " I trespassed
upon her rights, not she upon mine ! What right had
I to love Burgoyne?" It seemed to her that death
itself, in so speedily reuniting those two, rebuked her
presumption. In passionate renunciation she took
Burgoyne's picture from the wall and laid it upon the
fire, and watched it shrivel to nothingness in the flame
of its burning.

Madame Rabino had, for some time, been troubled
with failing sight. Beatrice devoted herself to her
with unfailing affection, — reading to her, singing for
her, attending to her correspondence, and at night
taking observations of the heavens under her careful
direction. She was wonderfully patient under her
great affliction. "As my outer vision grows dim, my
inner vision becomes clearer," she said. "And that
is as it should be ; at my age, the spirit ought to be
able to dispense with some of the physical helps ! "

Often as they sat together Madame Rabino threw
out an intimation that, when she was gone, her house
and all that it contained — her books, her manuscripts,
the telescope, everything — would belong to Beatrice ;
and that it was her dearest wish that Beatrice should
take up the work which she laid down, — or, rather
continue it, since she had already taken it up, — but

all this delicately and with a lightsome inadvertence, to save Beatrice pain. She felt that there was no need of urging her wishes upon one with so fine and loyal a quality of friendship.

One morning Mrs. Brakenburg came hurrying up through the winding path with a bundle of letters. She knew where to find Madame Rabino and Beatrice, — in a little palm-grove, back of the house, set round with bamboo chairs, the bare ground covered with the skins of beasts. Some musical instruments were lying about, — a guitar, a banjo, a mandolin ; a bamboo table in the center of the space was strewn with books and writing materials. It was a charming place, with the cool air rustling the great leaves, the birds piping their *matinées*, the water murmuring musically in the gorge below, and flowers — orchids and other curious and gorgeous tropical things — blooming everywhere.

"I did not even wait to read my letter," she said ; "I knew you two would be so anxious to get yours !"

"Dear heart ! how should we have known we had any letters?" answered Madame Rabino.

Mrs. Brakenburg dropped into a chair, tore open her own single missive, and in a moment exclaimed, "Oh ! oh ! Jack is married ! Married to a Miss Convers, — shall I read it aloud?"

The substance of the letter was that Jack had come home on a brief furlough, and he and Grace were quietly married at the residence of Mrs. Thompson.

Beatrice had a letter from Evalina, conveying the intelligence that a Northern army had overrun the Têche country, and the old plantation house was a barrack for Union troops. The word came through

Cosette, who — together with a few loyal old slaves — was valiantly maintaining the dignity of the La Scalla name! She read this letter first, and then took up another, which to her great surprise was superscribed in Madame La Scalla's delicate chirography. It was the first she had received from her. She read barely a dozen lines, and then put the letter back in its wrapper, to wait until she should be alone.

Mrs. Brakenburg went away presently, and Madame Rabino strolled with her down the path; and then Beatrice, with unsteady fingers, reopened the letter.

Madame La Scalla wrote with a special purpose, which she set forth without circumlocution: —

"MY DEAR BEATRICE, — For years I have borne a secret on my heart, which I now think you have a right to know, and which only a consideration for the rights of others — the defenceless dead — withheld me from telling you long ago. Perhaps you will remember that at the time of Helen's death you accused yourself — in some wild, incoherent words — of being the cause of it; and that I kept you in my room all that day, fearing the impression might get abroad, among the servants at least, that you had actually *killed* Helen. *I* understood — pardon me, my dear child! — I think I understood *everything!* And it is because I fancy that I still see, in your letters to Evalina, traces of the awful experience you then passed through, that I now tell you this secret. Our first duty is, after all, to the living, who have human minds to think and human hearts to feel.

"After Helen's return from abroad, Burgoyne asked to be released from his engagement to her. I need not tell you through what stress of mental suffering and debate he finally reached the conclusion that this was the only true and honorable course, cruel as it was! You knew him, and can understand. Helen refused, with a weakness, and moreover a hardness, which I had never suspected in her. She upbraided him bitterly, and accused him of loving another — which he never denied. This only, of all she said to him, brought the flash of anger to his eye. He yielded to her in everything except the right to sit in the secret council-chamber of his soul. He was gentle toward her always, — as gentle as his father was to me! But the marriage was a mockery, and it was inevitable that it should end in a tragedy. For this, my dear, you were in nowise to blame, since God made you what you were, and since Fate, which takes no notice of the *arbitrage* of men, brought your life and Burgoyne's together! Burgoyne, it is true, made a grievous mistake in his boyish engagement; but he committed no crime. With Helen lay the blame; but her terrible death disarms censure. Otherwise, might not I, his mother, as well as you — but no matter, the past is beyond recall! I write this with the sole purpose of bringing peace to your soul, — you who have had such scant justice in this world!"

The letter brought not peace only, but an unspeakable joy, — such a joy, it seemed to Beatrice, as she had never felt before! an ecstasy of happiness and pain! In it she felt again the full tide of life surge through her being. The fact of Burgoyne's love — an eternal fact — re-created the whole universe for her. She walked forth again with a springing step; she listened with a new consciousness to the singing of the birds, and stooped and kissed the flowers as she passed; the heavens were a new revelation to her, and work was a delight! With this sacred memory which she now possessed, she knew that it would nevermore be in the power of any mortal to wound her self-respect: she was truly a soul emancipated from the bondage of petty things.

Mrs. Thompson wrote, begging to know whether

she was ever coming "home" again; and she answered, without any feeling of hesitancy, "Yes — some time! But my life-work is here, on this island, with Madame Rabino, — with the telescope, my paint-brush, and these poor, gentle natives."

THE END.